Scattered Pieces

A Novel By
Nanette M. Buchanan

Type of Work: Fiction
Published Date: February 2013
ISBN-978-0-9793883-7-8
ISBN-0-9793883-7-6
Cover Design: I Pen Books/Fideli Publishing

I Pen Books Division of I Pen Designs
ipendesigns@gmail.com
www.NanetteMBuchanan.com

Acknowledgements

To my family;
We are blessed as a family, in our love for each other, in our support for each other, and in our unity with each other.
Thank you for all you do, without you these pages would be blank as would be my heart.

To my readers;
Your emotional and spiritual support has been the reward while I continue to travel this incredible journey.
I thank you all.
Join me in spreading the words as I continue to pen.

A special thanks to Dr. Mechele Morris. Your input brought life to this fictional piece.

Read, Relax, and Enjoy.

1

*T*he alarm rang promptly at six and Janet Robinson woke up dreading the unavoidable business of the day. She stretched slowly delaying her morning rituals. No matter how she handled herself, she was convinced the day would prove to be her most embarrassing. She sat on the edge of her bed tapping the floor with her bare feet searching for her slippers. The alarm's buzz ceased; she hadn't set the snooze, and the radio announced the time and temperature for the day. The morning hosts on WPLJ were full of spirit shouting wake-up calls to their morning listeners. Janet was in no mood for their antics. She turned the volume down looking beyond the radio.

As she peered out of the window, she looked along the branches of the large tree that often held her morning inspiration. She began her morning prayer as she searched for the bird she called her displaced angel. Occasionally, it would sing as she prepared herself for what seemed to be daily disappointments. Some days it would remain silent turning its colorful crown as though it understood the day would be another test of her faith. She whispered "amen" as the bird moved back and forth on the branch as a response to the early-morning breeze passing through its wings. The warmth from the summer air told her the heat wouldn't wait until after twelve to make most seek the comfort of an air conditioner.

Janet wished she could return to her only comfort, sleep. With her eyes shut, and her body relaxed from the P.M. labeled medication she took night after night, she didn't have to face the realities of the day. She prayed each night that the next day would bring her a promise of employment; no bill collectors; no calls from her children's school; or, her siblings wanting to share the news of the condition of their ailing mother. Lately, she had a hard time taking care of herself or even being concerned with anything or anyone other than her children. Janet couldn't believe that everything in her life went into a spiral decline after the callous separation from her husband. She wasn't sure how long she could pretend to hold her world together. Especially since the world she envisioned no longer existed.

She ignored what her girlfriends called the warning signs. Now she would openly agree that Marcus had been cheating for quite some time. Their past would creep into her thoughts often, now that they were separated. She no longer needed to add the clues to her suspicions. Marcus gladly boasted about his feelings, the two-year relationship, and the woman who waited patiently in his Navigator for him to gather his belongings. It had been a year since he left. Janet tried, the first three months of their separation, to convince him to stay. After the arguments and calls from him and his newfound love, Janet decided she wouldn't wear the name, "Desperate". It was another two months before reality set in. She cried, didn't eat, didn't sleep, and when it was all said and done she needed stability.

Employment was first on the list. She was certain after a few weeks she would secure a job. Janet made several attempts but since the birth of their youngest, Erica, she had been disconnected from corporate America. They were the parents of three children. Marcus Jr., nine, Joy, seven and Erica, who turned five two months after her father decided to move from their apartment in Montclair, New Jersey to a condo in Plainfield.

Marcus took care of everything while they were married. The finances, family planning, shopping, the maintenance of the home, and their friends were all under his control. Janet was a stay at home wife and mother. Now a year later, she agreed with her family and the only friends that admitted seeing his game; she had been played. When her loving husband found a new romance with the woman he swore he had only a business interest in, he left Janet in the dark about her own way of life.

She opened her closet searching for an outfit that would speak confidence and experience even if her resume said she hadn't worked for the past five years. She quit college when she was told she was pregnant with her second child and the thought of returning was a fading dream. Marcus was employed by New Jersey Transit working out of the corporate offices and he traveled quite frequently. Continuing her education would depend on the on-going support of anyone other than Marcus to watch her young children. They talked often about it being a goal she would pursue in the future.

"Look how things have changed." Janet's words were the only sound in the closet until Erica's giggle startled her. Her child, who resembled Janet's older sister Faye, looked at her smiling with her thumb in her mouth.

"Good morning sweetie. Is your brother and sister up?"

"No." Erica answered, without removing her thumb.

"Can I taste that thumb this morning?" Her mother asked teasingly.

"Nope and neither can M.J." M.J. was the nickname the girls gave their older brother.

Erica left the room, her bare feet slapping on the polished wooden floor. Janet pulled a dress out holding it up for a full view but decided it wasn't appropriate for the interview. She paused to reassure herself that she heard the phone. The personalized music tone announced the caller, and she could hear Erica giggling and talking loudly on the line.

"Erica, what did I tell you about answering the phone?"

"It's Auntie Faye; she's coming over."

Janet picked up the cordless phone on her nightstand.

"Hey girl, how are you?"

"I'm good. What time do you have to be there?"

"The interview or welfare?"

"Welfare?"

"Erica, hang up the phone baby."

Janet walked through the apartment to check the open line. Her daughter put the phone on the arm of the couch and was now watching the television, which was audible through the receiver. Janet put the phone in its cradle and used the remote to turn down the television's volume as the Sesame Street characters sang and danced across the screen. Erica was curled up comfortably between the couch pillows and a throw cover, watching the show that her family knew was one of her favorites.

Janet stopped in the kitchen and pulled out a pan to start the bacon for breakfast. She promised M.J. bacon and eggs with cheese if he would help his Aunt Faye watch his sisters.

"Girl, are you really cooking that boy a full breakfast."

"Yes, I promised him. Besides, I don't know how much longer he'll have a full breakfast."

"What does that mean?"

"I don't have much savings left; it may be enough for one more month's rent. They won't take subsidies, and it takes too long to apply elsewhere. I don't know what welfare will do so let's just say I'm at the end of the rope."

"So what made you think you would need welfare? What about the interview?"

"I've been on interviews for six months now. No one is hiring, at least not someone like me who hasn't worked in five years or more. When I tell them how long I've been out of work, I get the stare first then the 'I see' comment. I go on to explain about the children, me being a mother and wife, and I get the same response. It's like being black I couldn't have stayed home to raise my children. When they ask about childcare, I don't know what to say. I don't have childcare; I was childcare."

"I'm on my way. Think positive, you'll get a job and everything will be fine. You may even find a man to take your stress away." Her sister replied making light of Janet's complaints.

"Who would want a stressed, unemployed woman with three children?"

"Don't be so hard on yourself? Your life is not over. Look at it as a new beginning."

"I'd be glad to start over."

"It will be alright girl. You'll see. I'm on my way."

Janet's appointment was at ten, and she began filling out the employment application at nine thirty. The navy blue dress, shoes and purse gave her a sophisticated look. She wore her hair penned up in the sweep Faye always teased her about. She was nervous about her appearance. The job was for a receptionist, and it didn't require experience. The salary was negotiable and Janet understood the position wasn't guaranteed even with the lack of background or skills. She was more than certain her next stop would be the welfare office. She filled out the two-page application and sighed.

The receptionist glanced over her glasses anticipating Janet's completion of the application she had given her fifteen minutes prior. She made it obvious that Janet was taking longer than most applicants. Her welcome faded when she passed an ink pen to Janet for her use. The nameplate on her desk read Ellen Flanders. Janet thought her appearance was more appropriate for a High School Principal. While thinking about who she would use for references she wondered about the woman's age. Her face showed no signs of aging, and her hands appeared to be soft lacking housework. Ellen Flanders was simply the gatekeeper. Her voice broke Janet's thoughts, and she quickly signed the application.

"Ms. Robinson, if you're finished with your application, Mr. Burnett will see you now."

Janet stood hoping she didn't look thrown together, too anxious or nervous. She followed the receptionist who was now waiting, stoned faced, at the door where the logo read Burnett and Reed LLC. The plush office of the accounting firm, though small, appeared to hold some comforts. The walls weren't as mundane as the other offices she had been in. The natural colored walls were decorated with scones and African-American art. Certificates and licenses were hung over pictures of what seemed to be conventions and seminars. Ms. Flanders left her waiting in a seat in the hall that led to other offices. Janet thanked her and sat reading a few of the achievements of Mr. Richard Burnett and Mr. Walter Reed. She was browsing through the company's brochure when one of the doors opened.

"Good morning, Ms...."

"Robinson, Janet Robinson."

"Yes, do come in and have a seat."

Richard Burnett replied using what Janet assumed was her application to direct her through the door. He took his seat behind the large executive desk as she sat in the chair facing him on the opposite side. He leaned back getting comfortable in his high back leather seat, which matched the office décor perfectly. Janet looked around in awe. The thought of working in the offices of Burnett and Reed were quickly slipping away. The office was not what she expected reading the address in the classified ads. She needed a small business to work for, one that would work with her inexperience. She was curious about the clients Mr. Burnett and his partner serviced. Janet began to feel uneasy. Her prospective boss noticed her nervousness.

"The offices have been renovated so everyone would have plenty of space, although it's just two of us. Mr. Reed and I are looking for someone to work the entire office for us. As you see Ellen is out in the front. She's not too personable. Are you Ms....?"

"Robinson, Janet Robinson." Janet wanted to scream. He couldn't remember her name. She needed him to remember the interview or notice she was different. She had become desperate. She needed the job or her whole world would collapse.

"Yes, can I just call you Janet? I'm really bad with names."

Janet's temper was building. She remembered getting out of her bed that morning; that was where her day went bad. She should have gone to the welfare office and skipped the embarrassment of another interview. Janet thought of how she would accept her fate and just go home. She decided to make one last attempt at selling herself.

"Yes, you can Mr. Burnett. I know that this may sound strange, but I've been on interviews for the last six months, and I really don't want to waste your time if you don't see the qualities you're looking for in me. I've been out of work for five years. I was married and chose to stay home and manage a family. My husband decided to have someone else manage his needs and left me with our three children and the small nest egg I saved for emergencies."

The polished executive sat attentively listening while she finished her statement without interruption. Janet became uncomfortable in her seat realizing her monologue might have buried her. She sighed, and feeling hopeless she continued.

"I don't want to burden you with my situation or influence your decision about the interviews you're holding today, but I need this job. I've never been in a situation where my choices were little to none. Even when my husband left me, I had a choice to give up what my kids and I were used to and live with family or make a fool of myself. I made the wrong choice. Today, well, I've got you or welfare Mr. Burnett. It was a chance I had to take."

"Ms. Robinson, do you work with computers?"

"Yes, I know how to use a computer, Microsoft, and a few other applications. I can't say I'm fast with it, but I know my way around the keyboard. I'm a quick learner. What type of work would I be doing, I mean if I got the job?"

Janet waited for the answer, again her self-esteem deflated. Mr. Burnett spoke about the minute duties, which seemed to be more than the average clerical requirements. She watched him as he spoke. His demeanor wasn't demanding, and she wished she could relax. She actually talked longer with him than any of the other employers during their interviews.

Mr. Burnett was open minded, nodding his head at her responses. Janet smiled quite a bit, more than she felt she should, but he told her it added to her appearance. She hoped it wasn't an attraction. The last thing she needed was a boss who hired her with the thought that she would be his playmate. His questions weren't invasive but Janet didn't want to fool herself into thinking she had a chance. He held her fate in her hand and it seemed he was too deep in thought for the outcome to be in her favor. Janet pretended to look around the office; he continued reviewing the information on her application.

There were pictures of him and an older couple on the shelves behind him; nothing displayed indicated he had a wife or children. Janet began to view him as a man and not an employer. She thought his age to be more than forty-five and she had to admit he was well kept. His eyes were hypnotizing, and she avoided looking at him too long. He wore a black suit with a white shirt. The gray and black tie added a touch of richness to his look. If Janet had to describe him to any of her friends, Tiffany would say he was a "fine" man, but too refined for her. Carol would have stripped him mentally and just smiled. She couldn't imagine him outside of the walls of Burnett and Reed, LLC.

"Well, Ms. Robinson, I see your dilemma, and I want you to know I'm an understanding man but...."

Janet rose to her feet. She couldn't stand to hear another rejection. The tears were beginning to build in her eyes. Mr. Burnett rose to his feet as well.

"Are you alright?" He could tell she was apparently upset.

"I'm fine. I won't waste your time. I'm so sorry."

Janet turned and left the office and didn't look back. Mr. Burnett called her name twice following her into the hall. He returned to his desk and used the intercom to inform Ellen to send in the next appointment.

2

The line at the welfare office was shorter after two hours of waiting. The caseworkers were actually handling the appointments quicker than Janet expected. There were two people ahead of her on the list, and she estimated it would be at least another hour before she was explaining her needs to anyone. Outside, the summer heat had reached its peak, and the air conditioners were doing the best to keep the waiting area cool. Those who were waiting for most of the morning were agitated that they were still there after one in the afternoon.

"How long have you been waiting?"

Janet wasn't ready to hold a conversation but thought it rude not to answer the woman who sat in silence next to her for more than an hour.

"I got here at eleven thirty."

"You waited for them to go to lunch?"

"Yea, I guess so." Janet didn't see anyone leave, but she imagined that the employees had taken their lunch breaks. It was then she realized that she hadn't eaten but a few pieces of bacon earlier that morning.

"Well, I ain't that desperate."

The woman stood up and starting cursing. She got louder and louder directing her words to the workers, clients, children and security. They escorted her out, but her words incited others and the lobby had to be cleared by both security and police. Janet remained in her seat pretending to ignore the commotion.

"Ms. I'm sorry we're closing the offices due to the disturbance here."

"I've been waiting for hours."

"I'm sorry. You'll have to come back." Janet didn't move and hoped she wouldn't be arrested.

"I can't come back. I won't have a home for myself or my children. Why would I come back after I've been thrown out? I need to..." She paused fighting back her tears. "Do you understand what it means to be homeless?"

"I can't say that I do but Ms...."

"Well if you can't say that you do, then you don't know what I would do if I don't see someone; I need help today. Please can I talk to them while they're leaving to go home?"

The guard was at a loss for words. He turned his back looking over the area for assistance. "Mike, I'll see her."

A caseworker whose nametag read Philip Shepherd came over to Janet and sat next to her.

"Hard day huh?"

"Hard year, hard six months, hard to get up in the morning, hard to go looking for a job every day, hard to go home and face my kids, hard to talk to my friends and family, and you know what Mr. Shepherd it's even getting hard to pray. You may think I've lost it, but I think for the first time I'm facing reality. I am at the lowest point in my life, and my kids deserve more than this from me. I need to start over or maybe just let go. I'm tired. I just want someone to tell me where to go so I can get back on the right track. Is this welfare office where I need to be Mr. Shepherd or are you gonna tell me about your programs and how they don't quite fit my needs? Tell me how I don't have the right needs; that my needs are not needy enough; how you know that the money I have is enough because I don't have the right family size. Mr. Shepherd what are you gonna tell me?"

The caseworker was stunned. After listening to all the excuses he usually gave clients on their first reviews, he didn't know what to say.

"I don't know we have to fill out papers and see what we can do for you and your kids? How many children do you have?"

Janet looked at him as she dissected his words. Her head was beginning to spin. *"What was he thinking? Would he try to take her children?"* Janet stood to her feet.

"You're right, you don't know and neither do I. Thanks Mr. Shepherd."

Janet returned to her apartment mentally fatigued. Though her efforts were gallant, the circumstances hadn't changed. She was tired. Marcus wouldn't take her calls. She longed to talk to him. He had a way of helping her sort out problems. He had a way of telling her she was worth the air she breathed. She sat at her kitchen table longing to close her eyes and just get away from it all.

Faye left a note stating she would bring the children home later. Janet smiled thanking God her children wouldn't see how upset she was. In the bathroom she kept her medication for pain and although nothing hurt other than her pride, she needed the tension eased. She took two pills and headed for her bedroom.

She could feel her fears mounting. She returned the bathroom and looked into the mirror. She needed to rest. She stopped gagging after swallowing four of her prescribed pain pills. Thirty minutes later she took four more. The silence in the apartment began to ease her. Her reflection was distorted and her bed was calling her name. She curled into a fetal position on her bed. The pain of failure would soon fad. Janet felt herself drifting. The ringing of the phone seemed to be distant. She reached for the receiver; knocking it onto the bed she could hear her answering machine picking up. The beep to record was followed by a voice that prompted the tears that flowed from her eyes as she tried to press the talk button to speak. She could hear Mr. Burnett as she fell deeper into what she prayed wouldn't become permanent slumber. She fought to gain consciousness, but she realized the exceeded dosage might have accomplished her original intention.

"Ms. Robinson, you shouldn't count yourself out. I'd be pleased to welcome you on Monday morning at 9:00 a.m. I hope it's not too late for you to find a permanent sitter."

3

*F*aye turned the key to the apartment door for her niece, frustrated that they had to come back for her to change her blouse. M.J. and Erica had the same feeling as their Aunt. They slowed their steps reluctant to pause for Joy, whose sloppy eating disrupted their day of leisure.

"C'mon y'all, hurry up, if you want to go to the movies. Joy, go in your room and get another top out of your drawer. Bring that blouse to me, so I can run cold water on that ketchup stain. I don't know why your mother insisted you wear that good blouse"

Joy obeyed her aunt leaving them at the door. M.J. and Erica proceeded sluggishly into the living room and found a seat on the couch. Faye went into the bathroom and filled the sink with cold water.

"Auntie Faye, Mommy is home. Her shoes are here."

Faye came to the living room where she noticed her sister's shoes and purse. It was unusual. Janet hated anything out of place. She became a cleaning fanatic. A habit she developed being that stay at home wife and mother. Faye stopped and listened. It was strange there was no sound of a television or radio. She walked into the bedroom and saw Janet lying in the middle of her bed. The operator was giving instructions for the caller to hang up if they wanted to make a call. Then the pulsating sound began, a reminder that the phone was off the hook, followed.

"Janet, girl you knocked the phone over. We stopped back to change Joy's blouse. Janet, Janet. Janet, Janet, wake up."

Faye began to shake her sister softly and kept shaking her progressively harder. She didn't want to upset the children but the fear of her sister being dead caused her to scream.

"Janet! Janet! Damn girl what did you do?!"

Faye closed the door, ignoring the knocks and cries of the children begging to enter the room. She grabbed the phone, pushed what she thought was the talk button and dialed. When a man's voice answered she made hysterical pleas for an ambulance giving him no time to identify himself.

"The address is five fifteen Claremont Avenue. I don't know what is wrong, but my sister appears to have taken too many of her pain pills. They're here on her nightstand next to her bed. Please hurry. I don't know how long she's been out like this."

"Ms. this is not 911, can I help you? I'll call them if you like."

"Who is this? Get off the damn line, my sister tried to O.D. I think. Who the hell are you?"

"Richard Burnett, you dialed my number."

Richard looked at the number and recognized it as Janet Robinson's. It was the last number he called from his cell phone.

"You call for the ambulance again. Will they take her to Mountainside? I'll meet you there; if they choose another hospital, please call me."

"Yeah, bye." Faye hung up the line not giving him a second thought. She dialed 911 and sat, waiting for their arrival.

Janet was barely breathing, and Faye could feel a faint pulse. She left her only to tell the children their mother was sick, and an ambulance was on its way to get her. M.J. and Joy started crying, and Erica consoled them while sucking her thumb. Faye couldn't possibly keep them calm and monitor Janet while waiting for the EMTs. She became frantic hoping the ambulance would arrive before her sister slipped further into unconsciousness. She left the children again to check on their mother.

Ten minutes passed, but it seemed like thirty and the sound of the ambulance's siren caused the children to yell, "They're here! Auntie Faye they're here!"

Faye could hear the EMTs approaching the door. M.J. told them his mother and Aunt were in the back. Joy happily led the way. The two men nodded as Faye stepped back from the bed pushing Joy into the hall where her sister and brother stood trying to see past the gurney.

"Is she gonna be alright Auntie Faye." M.J.'s voice was barely above a whisper. The six eyes held tears as she stooped between them. "They're here to help her. Let's go in the living room and wait."

Faye led the children away from the bedroom and the men who had immediately begun to attend to Janet's needs. Voices came across their radio asking for her vitals and giving them instructions of how to stabilize her until their arrival at the hospital. It was then that Faye remembered her conversation with the man she mistakenly called earlier. She would call him before they left for the hospital. She had no idea who he was or his connection to Janet. He seemed concerned. Maybe he knew something about Janet's apparent overdose.

Erica began to cry loudly. "Shhh Erica, Mommy will worry if you cry so loud. Right, Auntie Faye?" Joy wanted to cry too but waited for Faye to agree that it wasn't best for their mother.

Faye pulled the girls closer to her on the couch giving them comfort in her embrace. The girls sobbed quietly listening to the EMTs preparing for her transport.

M.J. stood and walked to the hall when he heard the gurney rolling toward the living room. "Is she alright," he asked. The men looked pass M.J. for Faye. "She's gonna spend the night with us at the hospital she'll be better in the morning."

Faye understood he meant days, but she knew the reason for the man's tactful statement, and she mouthed "thank you." They followed the EMTs out of the complex and to the street. Janet's family watched from the curb as they put her into the ambulance.

One of the EMTs walked over to Faye. He shook M.J.'s small hand and smiled at Erica and Joy. "You look like your mother."

"She's my aunt; you took my mommy." Erica said correcting the man. He squatted down as not to tower over the girls.

"Oh, I'm sorry. You look like your aunt, Ms. Robinson?" He looked up at Faye. She tried to smile but didn't want to delay him from transporting Janet to the hospital.

"No my name is Williamson, Faye Williamson. I'm Janet's sister, and these are her children. Joy, you and Erica get M.J. and get into the truck. We're following the ambulance."

The girls ran to the truck where their brother stood looking blankly into the back of the ambulance. Faye couldn't imagine what was on his mind. She would have to call Marcus to pick up his children while she dealt with the hospital and treatment for Janet. She sighed and looked at the EMT who now standing seemed to be waiting for her to collect her thoughts.

"Is she gonna be alright?"

"Yes, it may have been deliberate, or she could have made a mistake. The hospital will take test and depending on the level of medication they'll determine if she tried..."

"Janet wouldn't try to kill herself; she's got three children."

"I don't know and you weren't there were you?"

"No I wasn't. I don't know; you're right, but she's gonna be alright?"

"She'll be sore and she'll be sleeping a lot off and on. Maybe then she'll be able to tell you why. We're taking her to Mountainside Hospital. You can follow us but obey the lights. People will stop for us, but I can't guarantee they'll stop for you. Are you and the children okay?"

"The kids, well, we'll see. They'll be glad to stay with me for a few days. I don't know what they're father will say though. No matter, are we ready to go?"

"Waiting for her vitals to stabilize she's almost there; we gave her something to help her."

"I'll get the children situated. Thank you." Faye walked away noticing she was holding her breath. She told herself to breathe. She didn't know whether it was the circumstance or if the brother was just that fine. His eyes were beautiful matching perfectly to his skin tone. She couldn't wait to tell Janet about the fine man that attended to her. Faye hoped she would get the chance to tell her. Tears began to roll down her face.

"You're welcome." The EMT remained outside the ambulance until he saw Faye get into her truck. He returned to the rig and shook his head as he gazed upon Janet's face. "Girl, you don't know how blessed you are."

4

"Hello, Marcus?" Faye decided to make the call while driving to the hospital. It would take him some time to get to Montclair, and she didn't want the children to be alone in the waiting room. A female voice answered, apparently annoyed.

"Marcus, telephone," She said, "...no I don't know who she is. I know I shouldn't be answering the phone, and a female is on the other end for you. Are you gonna answer this call or should I tell her you got the message?"

Faye thought about hanging up. The drama was uncalled for. Marcus wasn't the best catch in the sea unless you loved crabs. Janet had her bout with them before she believed her husband was cheating. Faye could hear her brother-n-law debating with Karyn, his jealous lover.

"Yeah, who's this?" Marcus glared at Karyn. He realized she knew who it was. He would remind her later that he wasn't for her games.

"It's Faye. I need you to meet me at Mountainside Hospital, here in Montclair. The children are with me, but I can't keep an eye on them and exchange information with the doctors."

"Information about who? What happened?"

Faye and Marcus had a civil relationship but telling him that Janet might have tried to kill herself wasn't what she wanted to say. She'd wait to see him.

"Janet's being admitted in the hospital, I'll keep the kids with me, but I need you to watch them for a few hours."

"What's wrong with Janet?"

Faye could vaguely hear Karyn's questions in the background. The scene at the hospital wouldn't be good for the children if she followed Marcus there.

"I'm following the ambulance now. We really don't know what happened yet. Marcus, come as soon as you can and uh, don't bring Karyn."

"I'm on my way. You said the kids were okay right?"

"A little scared, we all are, but they'll be alright. Like I said, hurry."

Faye hung up the phone to avoid any other questions. Erica had fallen asleep in her car seat while her sister and brother stared out the window of the vehicle. They would arrive at the hospital in few minutes. Faye remembered she wanted to call Mr. Burnett. She took a deep breath realizing the number was on Janet's phone.

5

"*I* really don't understand. Maybe you need to explain it to me. Some hooker calls here, and you rush to her side? No, I don't understand it, and obviously, you don't have a valid reason for rushing out the door."

"I told you I'm going to get my kids. And the hooker is Faye, you know her!" Marcus was getting angry.

"And I told you I don't believe that shit. Two days out of the week you claim you visit your kids. Janet hasn't called here in months. When you were really visiting them, your ass couldn't get to her apartment on time. I'm supposed to believe you get there twice a week on time? Now some broad has the nerve to call, and you use those damn kids again as the excuse. You forget Marcus; I was the excuse a year ago. I know the game and your lies."

Marcus buttoned his shirt and walked toward the door.

"You're right Karyn. You know the game. You also know that I don't follow no rules. Yours or Janet's, I'll be back."

Marcus left without hearing Karyn's response. She was right about one thing he hadn't been leaving the house to visit his children. He wasn't happy with the choice he made, and he went out twice a week seeking new options. Karyn was an exciting fling that he thought would satisfy his desire for a challenge. Janet was too easy she agreed with any and everything he did to her and for her. Karyn added the spunk he needed in a relationship, or so he thought. After

21

the first six months the spunk lost its spark but his pride wouldn't allow him to walk back into the home he left. If Janet asked one more time he would have packed his bags. Marcus made up his mind that the length of their separation was because Janet was too stubborn to admit she needed him.

Janet hadn't called since Karyn called her and said, "Give up." Marcus expected her to fight for their love and when she didn't the game turned ugly. She threw the kids in his face as often as she could. She complained about the weekends, holidays, birthdays, play days, whenever; Karyn wasn't having it. She put her foot down and told him to make a choice. He told Janet his job was requiring him to travel more, and he would have to cut the children's visits. That was so long ago he was embarrassed to think his children no longer cried to talk to him. Janet never bothered to ask for any support, and he didn't offer. Karyn told him Janet had someone else, but Marcus knew he was the only one who would totally take care of her. If anyone asked, those who wouldn't call him a fool, he would say he wanted his family back.

Faye and Marcus had a good relationship until she met Karyn. She told Marcus the bronze bimbo wouldn't remain poised after they lived together. She was right. Karyn spent more time primping and preparing her wardrobe and showed no desire to take care of a man or home full time. She kept a job solely providing money for travel and leisure, her top priorities. Marcus would be perfect to fulfill her needs if he didn't have the baggage of a wife and three children. He had been paying for her affection since they met.

His fears of what would bring Janet or his children to the hospital caused him to go faster than the speed limit. As he took the exit off the Garden State Parkway, he hoped Bloomfield Avenue wasn't backed up with traffic. The thought of Janet's mother crossed his mind. Jocelyn Black had been sick, off and on. *Could they be at the hospital because of their mother?* She was diagnosed with an abnormal rhythm in her heart or blocked arteries. Marcus wasn't sure which and never bothered to ask Janet if her mother's condition had improved. He turned the radio volume up to drown his thoughts that continued to ask "What if?"

6

*F*aye waited, rocking nervously for anyone to give her information on Janet's condition. Her husband, Sherod picked up the children promising them pizza and the movie they missed. He agreed the hospital was no place for the children to be. Faye was grateful she would be able to send Marcus back to his home with a feeling of guilt. She was beginning to blame her sister's condition on the predicament he put her in leaving her to raise their children alone. She had been waiting fifteen minutes or more before a well-dressed man sat in the seat next to her and introduced himself.

He had to be about six four and between forty to forty-five years of age. His perfect white teeth and manicured nails told her he either spent a lot of time in the spas, or he was a businessman. He wore a pair of jeans and a white collared shirt. He was indeed handsome, and his eyes were almost hypnotizing.

"Ms. Williamson, hello, I'm Richard Burnett."

"Do I know you?"

"We spoke briefly about your sister, Janet. You dialed my number trying..."

Faye smiled, but she didn't know why. She didn't know the man but felt like they had been friends.

"Yes, please forgive me, I was nervous and..."

"No need to apologize, I can only imagine what you went through. How is she?"

"She's gonna make it. They're trying to pump the pills out of her stomach. I don't know what made her take so many."

"Has she tried this before?"

"Tried what? How do you know my sister anyway?"

Faye's tone changed thinking he had pushed Janet to the edge. She didn't know anything about their relationship, but if he was willing to come to the hospital, he must have felt guilty.

"Janet came to my office this morning for an interview. I had interviews throughout the day, and I left a message for her on her phone. I didn't speak with her after she left my office."

"I see. Well, I don't know much either. I was watching her children and returned to her apartment to change my niece's blouse and I...."

Faye began to cry. She couldn't repeat the way she found Janet. "The pills were on the nightstand next to her bed. I don't know if this was an accident, or I just don't know."

"Where are the children now?"

"My husband rushed here and took them out. I'm glad, that they don't need to be here, you know." Faye took a tissue from the box on the table near them and wiped her eyes. Richard was at a loss for words, hoping his presence was helpful.

"Have they updated you lately?"

"They said they would be back to let me know if anything changed or when they would be ready to admit her. I just couldn't stay back there with her. Her husband is on his way. Maybe he'll go back there and talk to them."

Richard thought about the interview and the emotions Janet exposed when she spoke of the husband who left her with their three children. He didn't know if he was speaking out of turn, but he needed Faye to know what was said.

"Ms. Williamson."

"Faye, call me Faye."

"Faye, your sister spoke about the problems she had. Her husband leaving her with their children, the problems she had trying to get a job and a few other fears she was faced with. I guess after leaving my office, she went to welfare and then went home. As a result of what she thought wouldn't be a day with any blessings, she's now in the emergency room. I think the worse thing for her would be for her husband to take charge of her life again. She led me to believe she wanted to be in control, so she wouldn't be depending on him. I may have the wrong idea. I mean, you know your sister better than me. However, I know for sure she wouldn't want him to take the children for any amount of time. I just don't think that would be best for her recovery."

Faye listened; she didn't know what Mr. Burnett's intentions were. He sounded concerned, but she wondered again if he was guilty of saying the wrong thing. Janet was fragile, and he admitted she told him just how fragile she was over the last year. She stood before replying to his comment seeing Marcus approaching the waiting room.

"Where's the kids? Where's Janet? What's going on Faye?"

Richard stood ready to introduce himself or be introduced.

"Who are you?" Marcus asked. His accusation was apparent in his tone and stare.

"Sherod picked up the children and took them to eat. They'll be fine. They'll stay with me for a few days."

"Stay with you? Where's Janet?"

Faye hesitated. The conversation between her and Richard was repeating in the back of her mind as Marcus continued with his questions.

"Is it your mother? What the hell is going on? And who are you?"

"Richard, Richard Burnett."

Marcus looked at Richard wondering how he fit into the picture.

"Okay, so Faye you ain't telling me what I want to know. Who's this dude and where's my wife?"

"Janet had a bad reaction to her medication, and Richard is..."

"I'm her employer. She works for me."

Both Faye and Marcus gave him a confused look. Faye's reaction changed to a smirk as she noticed how shocked Marcus was hearing Janet had a job. He stood and walked off frustrated. Richard hadn't backed down to who claimed to be Janet's husband. She knew Marcus would bombard Janet with questions once she recovered.

"Faye, I'm going for coffee. Would you like something? I don't know how long it will be before she's admitted, but I'd like to talk with her if they allowed me to."

Faye walked with Richard away from the waiting area leaving Marcus asking the triage nurse about Janet's condition.

"You don't have to stay. I appreciate what you've done and to be quite frank with you, I don't know why you're doing it. It's obvious you didn't hire my sister during the interview, so why now? She really doesn't need pity Mr. Burnett."

"I thought we were at beyond using formal names. No I didn't hire her during the interview. I had three other people to see, which I did. I called your sister this afternoon to let her know I was hiring her. She was to start Monday. As I told you, I based my decision on what I thought would be a commitment. She of all the applicants had a reason to want to work and be reliable, something that's hard to find in employees. When you called asking for an ambulance I thought what she said may have been true."

"What did she say?"

"She said I was the wrong choice. It was me or the welfare office. I hadn't given her any indication that she shouldn't seek welfare. I don't know what happened at that office, but it's obvious she thought this was another choice. I feel I could have helped her avoid this if I had handled the interview another way. So, I'm here. She doesn't deserve any more negatives, and I'm here to clean up the mess I created."

"Richard it's not your mess." Marcus was walking toward the two of them and stopped. He paced back and forth hinting he only wanted to talk to Faye. Faye continued, "As you can see it's been a mess for a while."

"Like I said I was her choice. I want her to know she made the right choice. Can I get you coffee or anything?"

"No coffee, thanks. Can you bring me a Coke?"

"Be right back."

Faye didn't know what to think. She felt Marcus staring at her as she avoided the waiting area and went to check the status of her sister. The nurse informed her as she had informed Marcus that Janet was being admitted and would be in a room shortly. She would notify them when she knew the floor and room number. Faye thanked her and turned to face the questions from her jealous brother-n-law.

7

"What happened Faye? I feel like I'm being left out of the loop here. Janet's been taking the same meds for years. What is she on something new now?"

"I don't know that's why we're here but whatever it is or was it didn't agree with her. What did the nurse tell you?"

"That I'd have to talk with the doctor, that's bull. I'm her husband. Since when don't they tell the spouse what's going on?"

Faye sat down next to him wanting to change his mood.

"To be honest Marcus, they don't tell them when they're no longer together. She didn't come in here as Mrs. Marcus Robinson."

"What the hell does that mean?"

"Just what I said, if Janet wants you to know what's going on with her health, she'll have to tell you. I called you for the children."

"And you let your husband take them with him. You obviously wanted me here I guess until her man showed up." Marcus looked in the direction Richard walked. His face showed his displeasure for the man who may have an interest in Janet. "What? You didn't know if he would show? Who is he anyway?"

Faye thought about Marcus and his arrogance. He threw Karyn in Janet's face and didn't care about her feelings. The game could be played both ways.

"I knew he would be here. I guess they've been taking it slow, you know." Faye looked for Marcus to react. He hung his head between his hands staring at the floor. He responded almost mumbling.

29

"It ain't happening. Janet wouldn't do that, and I won't allow it. They've got a father, me, and she's got a husband."

"Marcus, you don't like when the shoe is on the other foot, huh?" His complexion was changing. Being a fair shade of brown it wasn't easy to hide his emotions. Faye could see the veins in his temples pulsating. Although he wasn't a violent man, he tended to argue when he knew he was at fault. She didn't want to create a scene.

"Who are you trying to convince me or you? Karyn wouldn't like you spreading her love so thin." She tried to add levity to the situation.

"You know what I'm saying Faye. This thing between me and your sister is uh, a misunderstanding. You should know that. I mean I wouldn't be with Karyn if I thought Janet still wanted our marriage."

Faye started to answer, but she could see Richard was returning. She ignored Marcus as he continued to mumble about how things would be different if Janet just changed. She turned her attention to sizing Richard up as he got closer to where she and Marcus sat. He was a good-looking man; that thought crossed her mind again. He obviously felt he owed Janet for not hiring her. Marcus wanted to come back home. Her sister's life changed drastically in the matter of a day.

"Coke, excuse my manners man did you want anything?"

"No. Uh, yeah, I have a question. You said you were my wife's employer right?"

"Yes, I am." Richard sat in the seat opposite Faye and Marcus, putting his soda and two bags of chips on the table. Faye noticed the difference in Richard's manner. It was as though he shed the business mode. He was indeed man enough for both Janet and Marcus.

"Since when does the employer come to see about an employee when they're being admitted into a hospital?"

"What difference does it make Marcus?"

"It's alright Faye; he has a right to ask. When Janet left the office, I was worried about how she was feeling, I called her later and Faye was trying to reach an ambulance. The medical insurance hasn't kicked in yet, and I wanted to make sure the billing went to my firm."

"And what firm might that be?"

Richard took out his wallet and handed Marcus his business card that read, *"Burnett and Reed LLC"*.

"What does Janet do at an accounting firm?"

"Personal Secretary."

"Personal."

"Yes, some call the position an Office Assistant. We prefer Secretary."

"We?"

"Yes, she works for Mr. Reed as well."

"One pay, two jobs; that's slick."

"It's very good pay for a job well done."

Marcus couldn't put his finger on what it was about Richard he didn't like, but he knew he had to step up his game if this was Janet's new love interest. The nurse called the family for Janet Robinson to her window. Marcus was happy the interruption would change the air that had become thick. Faye and Richard followed as he led the way to the elevator. The three went to the fourth floor where they arrived to see Janet's bed being pushed into room four twenty. The intravenous medication hung over the side of the bed with the tubing attached to her arm. Faye stopped at the door as tears welled in her eyes. Marcus continued into the room not noticing her hesitation. Richard stopped with her and put his arm around her shoulder.

"She's going to be fine."

"I don't know Richard, why would she do this?"

"We'll find out. Just hold on."

Marcus came out of the room. His face told of his shock seeing the mother of his children feebly holding on.

"Faye, I want to know what happened. That's no reaction to medication, and if it is who prescribed it. What's the truth?"

"The truth is I don't know, stop asking me. I wasn't there. I found her and thank God, I did."

"Well I want to know something. Who saw her downstairs? Did you speak with a doctor?"

"The results won't be back until tomorrow. She'll be in and out of it until then. I doubt if we get any answers today."

"Somebody's got to tell us something. Did she try to kill herself?"

"What would make you think that man?" Richard interjected not allowing Faye to stammer her way through an explanation.

"You don't know what's she's been through. Oh, I'm sorry thought you and the secretary were getting a new start? Sorry she's got problems as you can see, real issues."

"Marcus, just leave. I shouldn't have called you. As usual, if you can't get what you want, or things can't go your way you'd rather destroy what is. This is partially your fault. Just leave! Go the hell home to your happy hooker."

"Somebody better have an answer for my questions tomorrow. I'll be back, get the story together. And uh brother put an ad in the paper. Janet won't be working for what did you say Burnett and Reed? She didn't work for me; that's why I left."

Marcus walked away hoping he had given Richard a reason to leave Faye and her sister to deal with the crisis alone. He was sure he would receive a call explaining the truth. He would then blame his behavior at the hospital on the fear of losing his wife and children forever. He would tell Faye that it was obvious Janet had some sort of breakdown. He would have to convince her that for the sake of the children she would have to let him move back home.

8

The timely beep of the monitor over her roommate's headboard woke Janet out of her drug-induced slumber. She didn't recognize her surroundings but knew the smell was that of a hospital. She had visited her mother enough to conclude she was a patient at Mountainside. Janet closed her eyes allowing reality to set in. She turned her head slowly hoping she wasn't plugged into any machines. The drugs hadn't worn off. She felt like she was afloat as she began to move her legs and arms. She was glad she wasn't stiff.

Janet had no concept of the time, but she was sure it was a new day. She listened for the nurses in the hall and heard nothing other than the beep of what she thought may be a heart monitor. The woman who wore the necessary wires that led to the pole hosting the monitor was resting. Janet wondered if she was in pain. Her eyes were closed, and the only confirmation that she was alive was the annoying beep.

Janet said a prayer for the woman hoping she would win her battle over whatever the condition was that held her captive and attached to man-made support. She found herself dosing again and wondered how long she had been fighting her own battle. She gave in for moments at a time angry that she found satisfaction in being overly relaxed. She couldn't remember her ride to the hospital, but she was certain the eight Oxycontins had a lot to with it. She nodded again pleased that the pain of failure was gone.

"Ms. Robinson, come on dear, let's get started here, come my dear."

The soft voice and hands of a woman brought Janet back to her hospital bed. She couldn't remember falling off to sleep, but she had lost the sound of the beeping monitor, which now sounded louder than ever. She turned to the melodic voice of a small Spanish woman in a white uniform who smiled as she removed the intravenous needle from Janet's arm.

"Yes, yes. You are beautiful my dear. You must eat now. I have your lunch for you."

"I..." Janet couldn't speak. Her voice was cracking from the dryness in her throat. The nurse whose nametag read C. Ramirez handed her a plastic cup filled with ice chips.

"Here you are my dear. I will bring your food. I wouldn't let them take it back again. You will eat for me today. Mrs. White, are you needing your medication?"

The woman in the bed next to Janet lifted her hand from the railing and let it fall slowly onto her bed. Nurse Ramirez nodded her head in the woman's direction and went out the door.

"Let me take your vitals." Ramirez rolled the pole with the blood pressure monitor close to the bed and instructed Janet to lift her tongue. She inserted the thermometer and looked at her watch as she pumped the bulb allowing the machine to take the reading.

"Yes, yes. You are doing well my dear. Let me feed you now. You must be hungry."

Not waiting for Janet to respond she removed the thermometer from her mouth and the blood pressure cuff from her arm. She exited the room and returned with a tray.

"Do you think you can use the rest room now or do you want to wait?"

Janet didn't think about the bathroom. She rolled her eyes realizing what the tube was along her leg. She slowly shook her head and sighed. "I'll go now."

The nurse moved the food tray away from the bed and drew the curtains. "We did this for your safety. You be careful when you stand you may not be so good to walk. If not you sit and wait for someone to help you, understand?"

"Yes ma'am." Janet stood. The nurse was right she was wobbly, but she didn't want the tube again. "I can make it if you'll walk with me."

The bathroom was directly across the room, and Janet was glad she didn't have to walk the length of the room to get there even if it was only twenty more steps. She felt weak, but she took her time and returned to her bed happy she got up. Nurse Ramirez adjusted her pillow and the bed, so she could eat.

Janet wasn't sure of the time, but she could tell from the meal it was early afternoon. The tuna salad and crackers filled her stomach, which gave a gurgling 'thank you' as she swallowed each mouthful. She couldn't remember when she ate her last meal. The small cup of peaches teased her sweet tooth. She wondered if seconds could be ordered. *Erica loved peaches.* Her children, Janet hadn't thought about her children since she was in the hospital. She couldn't remember when she arrived in the hospital. Questions began to flood her mind and tears rolled from her eyes. *Are my babies safe? Where's Faye?*

9

Faye looked at the clock; it read two thirty. She and Sherod had spent four days being parents to Janet's children a task they had done many times before, but the circumstances made it difficult. The hospital hadn't called to say Janet was allowed visitors. After her initial admission, visits were prohibited until she was evaluated. Dr. Lashauna Norris, a staff psychologist was evaluating the woman who was admitted near death due to the dangerous amount of Oxycontin in her system. The evaluation was to determine if it was an accidental overdose or if the patient was suicidal. Faye called the hospital each morning and was told the same story; the doctor left no notes indicating Janet Robinson could have visitors. Sherod assured her she would be sitting and talking with her sister by the end of the day.

The couple taught in the Bloomfield Public School system, and the summer days were open for all sorts of activities. The children usually enjoyed the outings with their aunt and uncle, but it wasn't the same without their mother. Sherod had entertained them since Janet was admitted. By Monday, without detailed activities planned, Auntie Faye and Uncle Sherod were boring. They were complaining about missing their mother, friends, day camp and home. Sherod volunteered to take them by the day camp and their apartment, leaving Faye waiting for the call from the doctor.

At three o'clock Faye decided a visit to the hospital would calm her nerves. Her husband hadn't called since before lunch, and he wouldn't be returning with the children until after four. She'd call him on her way. She hadn't heard from Marcus, and Richard called once a day for an update. She wanted to be able to answer questions before either of them called.

She slipped on her sandals and grabbed her purse, checking to make sure she had her cell phone and the business card Richard gave her when they left the hospital. Locking the front door, she remembered the overnight bag she packed for Janet was still sitting in her living room. Faye sighed telling herself to calm down as she went back inside. The phone rang and she quickly dropped the bag and her purse rushing to answer the call.

"Hello, Mrs. Williamson?" The voice at the other end was not familiar. The professional tone brought relief to Faye as she took a seat in the chair near the window. She listened while gazing outside as the woman introduced herself as Dr. Lashauna Norris.

"I'll be working with your sister over the next few weeks, if she allows me to."

"Janet is refusing treatment?"

"No, she hasn't. However, she's not responding as well as I hoped she would. Is it possible that before you visit with her, you stop at my office here in the hospital? I would like for us to get acquainted, and I believe we can have Janet home by the end of the week."

"You said you would be working with her for a few weeks. Are you saying she will be under your care after she comes home?"

"Yes, but we'll talk when you stop in. I've been to see her each day since she was admitted. Today is the first day that she was aware of my presence. You are interested in visiting today aren't you?"

The woman sounded as if she doubted Faye's concern. She wanted to know the diagnosis, but she was scared to ask. The pause on the phone between them let the other know there was more conversation needed.

"Why don't you take your time Mrs. Williamson? I'll be here whenever you come. Can I give you my number? If you decide to come another time, just call me."

"That won't be necessary doctor. I'm on my way."

Faye hoped the call from the hospital would calm her. Instead, Dr. Norris made her feel uneasy about Janet's recovery. Questions in her mind delayed her leaving her home for another hour. At three forty five, Faye reasoned with herself that talking to the doctor would be the only way to obtain answers. She repeated her movements she made prior to the phone call. She talked herself into calming down as she looked for her Bluetooth making sure her cell phone was connected.

"Rod, hey baby. How are the kids?"

"Playing, I'm worn out. We'll be there shortly. Erica is taking a nap while M.J. and Joy are playing something on their television. I'm watching a movie."

"Such a sweet Uncle Rod."

"Yeah, whatever, did the hospital call?"

"I'm on my way to talk with a Dr. Norris now; that's what I was calling for. I think there's enough chicken left for them to eat if they're hungry."

"Babe, are you kiddin? Uncle Rod did what he usually does."

"You didn't buy Mickey D's again?"

"Hey whatever works, they're fine. Like I said, I'm worn."

"Thank you. I hope Janet will be home by the weekend. That's what the doctor said anyway."

"Faye, she may not be up to the routine of the kids, home, or well, you know what I mean." Sherod hesitated as though he thought twice about what he was going to say. "We'll see there's no rush. We'll work with her, whatever she needs. Hey, did you check on your mother?"

"Our brother stepped up to the plate and took her out."

"Sam took her where?"

"I don't know, to lunch. I was glad he did. I'm dealing with Janet. He can deal with Mama."

"Yeah you're right he can deal with her better than dealing with his nephew and nieces or Janet."

"Listen, I'll call you when I get to Janet's room maybe she'll want to speak to the kids or you."

"Be safe, love you."

"Love you too."

Faye hadn't thought about Janet not being able to take over her motherly duties when she was released from the hospital. Sherod was right. She wouldn't be herself for what could be weeks. Faye understood Dr. Norris' statement about being under her care now that she spoke with her husband. She dialed her brother's number. They would have to share the responsibility of caring for their mother and sister.

10

"*Faye*, are you serious? Janet couldn't have meant to kill herself."

"I don't know Sam, but I'm on my way to talk to the doctor now. She did say she'd be working with her over the next few weeks. How's mama today?"

Jocelyn Black always worked and cared for herself until she was diagnosed with a bad heart. Even with her bout of diabetes she took her medicine as prescribed. She seemed to forget to take her medication more often since the minor heart attack she suffered after Christmas. Samuel and Faye alternated stopping by and taking her shopping while Janet spent time with her visiting and bringing the children to see her. Sam was single; the baby of the family and being the only boy was his mother's pride and joy. He loved taking care of his mother but since Janet had withdrawn from everything, including the family other than Faye, he spent more time with their mother than usual. He didn't complain, but Faye knew it was putting a damper on his free time.

"She's good. I wanted to take her to the movies, but as usual, she didn't want to sit in the theatre. I'll drop her off, and I guess check on her later by phone."

"You're talking like she's nowhere around, where are you?"

"She's in the grocery store. She wanted to stop, but you know mama that means she's shopping. I stepped outside to smoke a cigarette then you called. Mama's fine you take care of Janet. Hey, did you tell mama she was in the hospital?"

"No, I told her she was sick though. I guess we have to tell her."

"No, let's just wait. I don't need her to freak out. I'll tell her bits and pieces. Does she know Janet went to the hospital?"

"Yeah, I think I told her that the doctor still had to check on her."

"Cool, we'll go with that. Faye, tell me the truth though, do you think Janet is gonna be alright?"

"Sam, I hope so. Thanks for stepping in with mama."

"You got the hard part. I can deal with Jocelyn Black."

"Yeah, I think Joy was asking for her Uncle Sam."

"Everybody wants her Uncle Sam."

"Love you boy."

"Call me after you leave the hospital."

Faye hung up the phone feeling relieved. The hospital was closer than she thought or her conversations were longer than she expected; she thought about calling Richard before she spoke with the doctor. She turned off the ignition and dialed the first four digits of his office number. She stopped as she noticed the time. She didn't have any updated information and Mr. Burnett wasn't really a personal friend. She got out of her truck and entered the hospital looking for the office of Dr. Norris.

The corridor sounded with the echo of her sandal's small heels touching the floor with each step she took. She passed two nurses stations, went through the large doors and turned right as she had been instructed after getting off the elevator on the third floor. She wondered if Janet was still on the floor above her, or if she was strapped in a padded room in the back of the hospital. Faye shook her head promising herself not to watch any other movies that were remotely similar to "Psycho" or "One Flew over the Coo Coo's Nest." They were two movies she feared even before she could make a connection.

The sign read Psychology letting her know the directions she was beginning to doubt were precise. Two doors after entering the unit, the next door held a gold plate with Dr. Norris' name in bold black print. Faye tapped on the closed door and waited for a response.

"I'm over here. Mrs. Williamson?"

Faye turned to the sound of the voice, which came from an alcove on the opposite side of the offices.

"Would you like a cup of coffee or tea?"

"No thank you."

"I don't have a coffee pot in my office. I need one though. I spend more time out in this hall than I should. Thank you for coming. I really need to begin working with your sister right away."

Faye didn't know how her response would be viewed. Suddenly talking to a psychologist wasn't what she wanted to be subjected to. She waited in silence as the doctor poured her crème and sugar into her Garfield coffee mug. Faye took the opportunity to judge Dr. Norris' personality as it related to her appearance. She seemed to be more down to earth than her professional voice indicated on the phone. She was taller, and younger than Faye had imagined she would be. If she had seen her without her white lab coat and scrubs, she would have never thought of her as a doctor. Her nails and hair were conservatively done, though she was sure by the length of her hair, she wore it pinned up. It was the end of the day so it wasn't odd that she allowed it to drop over her shoulders.

Faye couldn't imagine the doctor wearing much makeup, if any; her face was without the blemishes that makeup would hide. She was definitely a "sister," and her office spoke loudly about her stance in her achievements and her culture. Frames on the walls were filled with diplomas, certificates of appreciation and accomplishments. There were a few pictures of Dr. Norris, the public speaker.

Her windowsill was filled with plants and black figurines most holding stethoscopes and prescription pads. Her radio was playing smooth jazz, which she turned off as she took her seat behind the mahogany desk. She offered Faye the choice of one of the two chairs that faced her.

Pictures of those Faye assumed were her family, were proudly displayed across the top of a bookcase which held medical reference books and guides. If her assumption was correct Dr. Norris was the mother of two young children, a boy and girl, who looked to be no older than four and two. The man in the picture was what Faye would call the all too happy husband. His smile said he was proud to have married a doctor.

"As I said I've been asked over the past few days to turn in my evaluation of your sister and I've been holding them at bay waiting to talk to Janet, you and the rest of the family."

"You've been holding who at bay? I'm sorry I don't understand."

The doctor opened a folder that she turned for Faye's viewing. She scanned over the papers not sure what the doctor would say her findings were.

"This is the report that was taken on your sister when she was admitted. Here is what Social Services and the hospital wants my signature on. I'm showing you this so you'll know what our fight is."

Faye's expression changed, and the doctor touched her hand reassuring her; she would be explaining everything as the conversation went along.

"Janet had more than enough Oxycontin and other medication in her system to cause death. The question is, was it accidental or purposely done. That's where I come in. I talk with her, you, other family members and make a determination based on what we discuss. Mrs. Williamson, Janet should have been willing to respond a day ago. She's dragging. I have to find out why. I've had many women, as you can imagine, that come to me wanting to...well you know. I don't think the worse. I work to find out what's going on, where their heart and mind is, etc. Social Services seek to protect the children, and the hospital seeks to get paid. Now that's the facts. I could sign off on this paperwork and Janet's children. She has three, right?"

"Yes."

"They wouldn't automatically be placed with family. That's what a lot of women think. They kill themselves thinking they'll leave their children with competent family members. Social Services take the children and place them, if they can, until the court determines what is to be done. It's a hassle, one that I try to avoid at all cost. I don't have time to spend in court because her heart is heavy and her mind temporarily shut off."

Faye listened and felt her tension easing. She liked Dr. Norris' way of putting everything on the table. She understood what Janet was up against before the explanation of the odds was completed.

"The cards are stacked against her because according to this, the Oxycontin that she took is from an old prescription. Her doctor gave her the medication months ago for pain. I don't know how long she's been keeping it or why she's still using it. It's obvious it wasn't used as directed but the refills are not limited she still can use them until October of this year. However, Mrs. Williamson, understand that the prescription was for pain, and of course, we don't need to talk about the dosage. It's up to you and your sister, and I say you because she chose you..."

Richard said the same thing. Janet chose him. Whatever Janet was thinking he was right she didn't want her sister to think she made the wrong choice either. She would work with Dr. Norris in whatever she needed her to do.

"So I guess what I'm saying is we've got some work to do and a short time to get it completed."

"How long will it be before Social Services demands the paperwork?"

"I can put a stipulation on her release. That's where I will need your help for now. Janet has to understand that this is up to her. Your sister tried to escape a situation; this was no accident. I need to know that the situation wasn't her life in total. I need to know what part of her life is causing her to want to let go. Was she deliberately trying to get rid of her life or her problems? I can tell them she was indeed in pain, and I don't doubt that she was. I can tell them that she is willing to get other help, be under my care and work through these problems and return to what she knows best. Being a competent responsible mother, which is all they care about. She will need you and the family to be behind her. But as I have talked to you I will have to talk with them to find out just what her problems may be."

"When you say talk to them, just who are you talking about?"

"Your brother, your mother, her husband, I wouldn't have to talk with them if Janet would speak with me. So far she hasn't and I can't make a report without knowing what to report. I need to know for myself that she is not suicidal. You do understand my point don't you?"

"Yes, Janet has to want to live."

"I knew you would understand. I signed the papers allowing her visits hoping that may cause her to talk to me tomorrow. Today is Tuesday; let's say we shoot for her being released Friday. I'm sure I can work it out with Social Services. You and I will talk between now and then. It probably would be better if you wait until she asks to see the children or I get a chance to speak with her before you just bring them here. Sometimes seeing the children will cause an emotional breakdown, we'll have to watch for those times carefully."

"Doctor, will Janet have to be drugged while under your care."

"I hope not. I'll know better after I speak with her. You go visit with her. See if she'll talk with you. If she does Mrs. Williamson, please let her know I am on her side. I want her to go home and be at peace with herself and her family."

Faye stood and waited for Dr. Norris to take a drink from her mug. She was glad she talked with her and got a clear understanding of what she would be facing. Janet had to face new fears, being able to keep her children. Faye didn't know what would be worse, Social Services or Marcus Robinson.

11

"Janet Robinson, please."

Faye waited as the woman typed the name into the computer and handed her a pass. She looked at the card for the floor and room number, and as she suspected it had changed. She proceeded to the elevator and waved it on when the doors opened showing two elderly passengers who were already aboard. She turned around looking for the gift shop. She noticed a piano in the waiting area and had no understanding why one would be there. The lobby was huge and after almost returning to her starting point, she finally spotted the shop. She wasn't disappointed. It sold candy, get-well cards, stuffed animals, and in the back of the store were the plants and balloons. Janet always loved plants. Faye would see if they had a small Aglaonema her sister could nurture.

The plant was perfect with signs of new leaves. She smiled to herself, pleased it showed plenty of life and promise. Faye paid at the register as she proudly placed the plant on the counter. She headed for the elevator while silently saying prayers for both the plant's growth as well as Janet's recovery, she didn't notice Richard Burnett.

"Hello Mrs. Williamson."

"Richard hello and its Faye."

He smiled and pointed to the plant. "Looks like new beginnings."

"I sure hope so. I was going to call you, but I just finished talking to the doctor."

"Dr. Norris, yes she's a fine woman and doctor. I spoke with her earlier."

Faye was taken aback. The elevator door opened, and Richard extended his hand allowing her to step into the elevator first. There were no other passengers so Faye took the opportunity to question the man she now thought may be a pervert or stalker.

"You know Dr. Norris?"

"She's a member of my church. She's on the sick and shut in Ministry as well. I asked her look in on a friend, Janet, and she just happened to have her as a patient."

"You didn't know that?"

"No, how would I know? I was waiting for your call. Lashauna, I mean Dr. Norris, called when she discovered it and told me she would be allowed visitors today."

"Did she say anything else?"

"No, I don't think she would tell me anything more, just that I could visit. I told her I had hired her though."

"You're sticking to that story huh?"

"It's the truth. Why else would I call her?"

Faye thought about it. There had to be another reason. She would keep her thoughts to herself as she replied hoping he didn't see her smirk.

"I'm being as honest as I can be. I'm concerned about her health because I feel somewhat responsible. I'm determined to see her through this, and if she wants the job when it's all said and done it's hers."

"Okay, I'm warning you though."

Her comment brought a smile on both their faces. Richard didn't mind the tease, and he understood what she meant.

"If I change my mind you'll be the first to know."

"Either way?"

"Either way, what does that mean?"

The elevator door opened and again, Richard was courteous. Faye stepped off the elevator and looked at the card to get her bearings. She pointed in the direction they needed to go.

"If you change your mind and want to admit you're a stalker." She continued walking with Richard in tow. He saw her smiling and let his fears fade.

"Best stalker she's ever had."

Faye heard his response and again kept her thoughts to herself. *"I know that's right."*

Janet's visitors tapped on the partially closed door; they hesitated before entering. Faye didn't see another name or bed number, which usually indicated there was only one patient in the room. She pushed the door open after she heard a muffled "yes."

The open arm embrace was met with Janet's face streaked with the tears that were flowing freely from her eyes. The sight of her sister brought a pain of reality. She sat up in the bed hoping her children were following. Faye embraced her sister bringing her face closer and rocked her gently. Richard stood at the end of the bed waiting for Janet's acknowledgment. Still holding Faye, Janet talked through her tears.

"Faye I am so sorry. I don't know what happened to me. Where did I go, why did I leave? Am I crazy? Faye, do they think I'm crazy?" She sobbed louder, a cry that was needed and not interrupted.

"What was I thinking? I know you know. I thought about us, you, Sam and Mama; I even thought about Daddy. Why did daddy leave us so young? We were kids Faye, why him and not me? It should have been me." Faye listened, and she began to cry as well. Richard turned and left the room, neither of them noticed.

Reginald Black, their father, was in a fatal car accident when his children were teenagers. He had been drinking with friends at his son's football game. They snuck in the beer and a little more putting it into igloo coolers and enjoyed the games recognizing there had to be future NFL players on the field. It was a weekly ritual for the fathers during the football season, and Reggie only needed a reason to get plastered. He had no concept of social drinking.

Janet and her father left the game with her begging him to allow her to drive. Faye, who was on the cheering squad traveled with the school on the bus after the games. Janet had her drivers permit and was confident she could get them home safely. In his state, she explained, they could be pulled over by the police or worse be in an accident. She blamed herself for his death because she lived through the white Toyota cutting them off. Unscathed she didn't receive a scratch.

"Will I be alright? Faye, I'm sick. Really, who does this to themselves?"

"Calm down Janet. Let's talk."

Faye took a seat in the chair next to the bed, and it was then that she noticed Richard left them to their privacy. She was sure he understood this was time they needed alone.

Janet went over the past few years disclosing details of a broken marriage, and a broken heart. Faye had heard most of the stories before, but she was sympathetic to her sister's need to vent.

"I've been holding on to Marcus like a cripple would a crutch. He let me fall knowing I needed him Faye. I couldn't stand up, and I gave up."

"Girl, I understand but it's not about that; not now. Your relationship with Marcus may never be what it was, but you've got children who need you. Janet you haven't given up on them, have you?"

Janet didn't answer, and Faye didn't want to push her closer to the edge. She now knew what Dr. Norris was talking about. She showed Janet the plant, which brought a smile to her face breaking through her mode of depression. She was just as happy to see her overnight bag and her items from home.

"You musta read my mind. There's nothing like your own toothbrush and stuff. Faye, do the kids know I snapped?"

"Stop Janet, everyone goes through rough times. They just know you were sick. That's all they need to know. You can't get yourself together concentrating on what others think and say. Your preservation is what's important to your children and our family right now. Did you talk to the doctor?"

Faye watched for Janet's reaction to her question. There was none. She gave Janet a minute to think before she asked another question.

"No, I didn't know whether to trust her or not. She's like the rest, filling in the blanks and getting paid. Does she know how the answers will affect my life, the lives of my children? I don't think so. If I don't give her any answers, she can't judge me."

"Janet, if you don't give her any answers Social Services will be the judge and jury, and you'll lose the children to the system. We'll have to fight to get them back. I can't fight the system, watch Sam, keep up with Mama's health, care for you, and keep my marriage. Maybe I'll just get a bed next to you."

"Faye, you don't understand what I'm..."

"Listen, I may not understand what you've been through, you're right. I didn't live your past or go through some of the things you've gone through. We all have issues. Yours may very well be heavier than mine but does that mean you can't carry some of your load until you can handle it?"

"So you're saying I'm dumping on you?"

"Janet, you did try to bail out right? You expected me to take in your children, explain it all to Marcus, our family and then what? I would I live after that, happy to do you that favor? You didn't leave me any reasons or excuses. What's wrong Janet? You don't want to talk to someone who studies the mind, but you want me to read yours. Last time I checked my profession was an educator. Dr. Norris is who can help you, let her."

"I just need time to..."

Faye was getting angry. Janet was making excuses to give up, and she was determined if her sister wanted to give up she wouldn't give in.

"You don't have time. You've got a job waiting; a doctor who needs to give you a positive evaluation and people who want to snatch your kids from you. Oh, and let me not leave out that ass hole Marcus, who doesn't know what he wants. I have needs too. I need you to get it together for you and for your kids. Fight back Janet, your life is worth a lot to me."

Faye stood and leaned over the bed giving Janet a kiss on her forehead. She didn't allow Janet to dispute her words, and she left her sitting in the middle of the bed with tears in her eyes. Richard was sitting outside the room in the lounge across the hall. The two left the hospital together.

12

*R*attled, Faye sat in her car trying not to cry. She declined Richard's offer of conversation over a cup of coffee. He watched from his Mercedes waiting for her to pull off, when she didn't, he drove his car to the empty spot near hers. He said a prayer hoping she hadn't given up on a situation that was getting more difficult than it may have been worth. He tapped on the driver's window causing her to look out at him with her now puffy eyes. She let down the window and tried to smile.

"I told you, you were a stalker," she said laughing through her tears.

"I only stalk pretty women who spend most of their time crying, open the door."

Faye obeyed mentally fatigued and too tried to think of an excuse not to.

"Richard, are you a God send, or a tormentor? You're a constant reminder of what my sister thought was another failure. I don't know that she'd be happy that you're so persistent."

"I haven't asked her for anything. Nor do I expect her to understand any of my motives. I am doing this for selfish reasons. I need a secretary, and I need to be able to live at peace knowing I didn't push her over the edge. Everything that has happened since then is connected to the fact that I didn't tell her she was being considered for the job. Something that simple could have stopped her from thinking of herself as a failure."

"I can't say that you are wrong, but I know nothing about this is simple. It's not easy for someone to want to take their own life and leave those that love them behind. I don't think that's an easy task. So, I think it's deeper than the interview or whatever you said or didn't say."

Richard knew she had a valid point, but he was determined to understand Janet Robinson. Faye's phone rang, and she searched her purse looking to answer it before the music stopped. She let the voice mail pick up when she saw it was Marcus trying to contact her. She listened to the message and rolled her eyes. She closed the flip top on the phone and looked at Richard.

"Richard, do you mind returning to the hospital with me? I don't want you to be in the middle of this, but my brother-n-law can make this ugly for Janet. I led him to believe that you might, well I let him believe that the two of you..."

"Where is he?

"On his way here, I need to call home. Can you stay around for another thirty minutes?"

Richard smiled, "Anything to stalk you and your sister again."

"You know; you're entirely different than your appearance projects you to be."

"Good, then your brother-n-law won't be the wiser."

Richard knocked on Janet's door and waited for her to answer. He agreed with Faye; it would look believable if he was already visiting when Marcus arrived. He hoped Janet would understand their attempt at keeping Marcus in the dark about the real reason Richard had befriended Janet and Faye. He knocked a little louder and opened the door, so he could see if Janet was sleeping.

"Yes."

"Janet? It's Richard Burnett, are you up for company?"

He didn't know how long it would take Marcus to arrive, but the time was limited for small chat. He had what he thought was a short time to explain the plans, he and Faye discussed. Faye went home and left it up to Richard to deal with Marcus, the jealous, cheating husband.

Janet grabbed her robe glad Faye brought her new one from home. She remembered Richard's voice fading on the phone, although she couldn't understand his message. Her memory of the interview was a lot more vivid. Richard Burnett, the man with the hypnotizing eyes came to visit her. Maybe Faye was right she still had a job waiting and a boss who had more than an employer's interest in her. She smiled as he reached to help her adjust the sleeve of her robe.

"I guess your thoughts about me have changed. First, I give you my story of misery and pain and then this. Did you come here to have me fill out my mental release papers?"

Richard flashed the smile of a man who liked what he saw but wouldn't touch until given permission. Janet was attracted to his subtle personality, but she remembered her judgment of men wasn't the best. After all she thought she would be celebrating her anniversaries with Marcus for years to come.

"I'm here to make sure you know you're okay. Do you remember my message I left on the phone?"

Janet hung her head too embarrassed to want to return to what memory she had of that day. The shame would only bring her tears, and she had cried enough over the past few days.

"No, no much of it."

"It doesn't matter. I do have papers for you to sign. But more importantly I need to know what your intentions are. Are you still seeking the job and will you accept the help from Faye, Dr. Norris, and me? Your sister said she talked to you this afternoon. I was with her but decided to leave the two of you alone; I'm back for your answer. Maybe if you answer me Faye will stop thinking I'm just a stalker."

Richard and Janet laughed and talked as though they had known each other for more than five days. Their conversation included discussing the care of the children once she could return to work to what her likes and dislikes were in family recipes. Richard almost forgot about the plans to keep Marcus at bay until Janet mentioned her children by name.

"Marcus Jr., hmm strong name and the only male, does he talk about missing his father?"

"Not as much as the girls do, but they're younger. He has his activities and friends. Their father has lied so much to them that I believe M.J. ignores him totally, another issue."

"And do you miss Marcus, your husband?"

"What is that, your question, or your doctor friend's?"

"No, it's mine. Faye told me Marcus was on his way here, and I want to make sure my presence is not standing in the way of your relationship. I want us to be friends Janet. I don't want to cause any problems for you or pretend not to be concerned when I am. Maybe I'll explain it better at another time."

"No, explain it to us now Mr. Burnett." Marcus didn't bother to knock on the partially closed door. He heard only the last two sentences.

"Marcus, this is Richard..."

"We met. Again, I ask; why are you here?"

Richard pulled out his card. "Janet, I don't know if you have the office phone number with you."

He was surprised when Janet read between the lines and answered with what one would expect if she and Richard had an intimate relationship brewing.

"I think Faye has my cell. All your numbers are in it. If you speak to her again tonight can you tell her to give it to you to drop off here when you visit tomorrow? She said she'd be with the kids and my mother most of the day."

Marcus sat in the seat that Richard left open. Although he was standing when Marcus walked in the room, he imagined Richard had a spot on Janet's bed. He watched the conversation between his wife and this man he didn't trust hoping he didn't have to ask him out of the room.

"No problem, anything else. I'll go by the apartment in the morning do you need anything?"

Janet was slow on her response and a little confused. She was pleased to play the game that Marcus and Karyn played with her early in their relationship. She smiled trying to remember how Karyn did while saying, "We're just friends." She wanted to laugh in spite of herself. Karyn would pretend she didn't understand Janet's anger. Marcus would learn a lesson, and Richard would be the teacher.

"Look in that overnight bag, no hand it to me let me check. You wouldn't know what I was talking about."

Richard handed her the bag while Marcus held his tongue. Richard knew the awkward position would elevate her husband's anger.

"I'm sorry man. I'll be out in a minute, soon as the little lady sends me on my way."

"How 'bout we cut the shit. I'm sending you on your way. This is still my wife, and I call the fucking shots."

Richard stepped toward the bed with his back deliberately facing Marcus. "What else did you need?" He continued to move around the bed closer to where Marcus was now standing.

"You're not leaving, are you? You just got here." Janet had reservations about being alone with Marcus.

"I'm gonna step out and give the two of you time to talk. It's six now. How about seven?"

Richard faced Marcus for a nod of approval. When he didn't get anything but a glare of betterment, he turned again and winked at Janet. "I'll be back sweetie."

He leaned and kissed her on her forehead. When he turned to step away from the bed, Marcus swung only to get his chin checked by Richard's right fist. Marcus staggered toward him as Janet screamed.

"Marcus, what the hell is wrong with you?"

Richard sat a slumped Marcus in his seat. "I'll be back."

13

S herod was relieved to hear the front door open, and his wife call the children by name. She passed his favorite chaise lounge chair in the den and paused to greet him with an affectionate kiss.

"Call your brother, something about your mom. She's okay, but she's upset with all of us. I guess she knew something was up when the kids told her they had been here since Friday."

"I didn't even think about her talking to them before we got a chance to talk with her."

"Well he said to call him when you get in. He didn't want to call you since he knew you were at the hospital. How'd it go?"

"Dr. Norris is really down to earth and willing to get Janet on her feet. I didn't realize how much she's lost over the years. It's strange, that walking in the other person's shoes thing."

Sherod didn't have any idea what Faye meant, but he rarely did when it came to her sister and her acceptance of "life according to Marcus." He didn't care much for Marcus and tried not to look at Janet as gullible. Sherod considered himself to be a player before he and Faye became serious, but he never wanted to dominate the relationship. Marcus went overboard, and he saw it coming before his wife told him about the problems Janet, and her abusive husband were having.

"Well, maybe she'll get the help she needs to heal and start new. Did he come to the hospital?"

"Who?"

"Marcus, who else?"

"I thought you were ... oh that's right I didn't tell you. She was really hired. Remember I told you about the guy that was on her phone when I was trying to call 9-1-1? Well, he showed up at the hospital. He and Dr. Norris know each other I think he said from the church. But anyway, he said she could have the job if she still wanted it."

"Just what she needs another man putting pressure on her. Does this guy realize she may not be able to handle the current situation? I hope you told him she needed time to heal. Faye, my sister was in that kind of marriage. Now look at her. Every man she deals with has to deal with her past. It never works on the rebound."

"What are you talking about?"

"That guy, what's his name?"

"Richard Burnett. I didn't say he wanted her to be in a relationship with him. He's giving her a job."

"That's what it will lead to. She gets the job, and if she wants to keep the job...."

"I don't think he's that way. I called him her stalker, but I was just teasing."

"That's some serious shit. You don't know this guy. She can't half ass remember him, and you don't think something's strange about that?"

"You're pretty good with choosing one's character. Save your judgment until you meet him okay?"

"Alright, not a problem but a man doesn't feel bad enough to do what this guy has done. What did Janet say when she saw him?"

"I don't know. Marcus was supposed to visit, and Richard volunteered to be the reception committee."

"Damn." Sherod looked around to see if the children heard him. "They're quiet. I think they're as tired as I am."

"I'll take over now. Thanks, I know they can be trying."

Sherod smiled and picked up the remote. He watched television for an hour before his eyelids were too heavy to keep open. Faye called her mother and explained Janet's problems. She used the same reasoning as Dr. Norris stated she would give Social Services. Janet had issues that needed to be sorted out with her help, and then she would be fine.

The children had been watching the Disney channel, but the table had turned and the characters were now watching them. Faye smiled at the sight of her nieces, and nephew curled together in the middle of the full-size bed. M.J. asked about his mother earlier. Faye hoped Janet would be ready to see her children soon.

As she walked through her quiet home, she couldn't fight the urge to shower and lay down next to her husband. She dosed off and on shortly after eight waiting for the phone to ring. Sam, Marcus, or Richard would have been her guess of those who would call, but the night brought her sleep shortly after she said a prayer for strength and guidance. The phone never rang.

14

Richard didn't return to Janet's room at seven and Marcus was now pacing back and forth, the length of the room. Janet was becoming more nervous by the minute. She had never seen him act that way and wondered was he really as scared about losing their marriage entirely as he had professed during the last hour. She wanted to talk about him taking the children until she got better, but Faye's talk about Social Services scared her.

"So where do we go from here Marcus?"

"Where do we go? I'm coming home. I said that. I'll admit my mistakes, now you admit yours."

"What was my mistake? You had a woman working with you in the office and in the bed. You denied your affair with her for over a year. What mistake did I make?"

"I can name two." Marcus turned and faced her. She could see the goose egg sized knot on his chin. Richard hit him just enough; he didn't really want to put him out. "You taking all those damn pills, and that so-called boss of yours."

"One mistake Marcus, just one. The pills; that was the only mistake."

"What about your knight in shining armor. And one more thing, if that punk puts his hands on me again, I'll beat his ass like I wanted to. This is a fucking hospital and he wants to square off in here?"

Janet replayed the scene in her mind. Marcus was trying to make himself look good. A tactic he used when comparing his faults to others. His faults never outweighed anyone else's. She thought about the

61

questions Richard asked. He and Faye were right. Marcus talked for more than ten minutes about incidents in their marriage where she could have stopped him from being the cheating, lying, undeserving husband he was.

"Marcus, I'm tired. Can we talk about this after I begin my therapy?"

"That's what I'm saying. You gonna be here a minute. I mean crazy people don't heal overnight. Not even with help; you may need more than just the therapy. Time with family, the children, and your two girl friends; Tiff and what's that other one's name?"

"Marcus, can you talk about this tomorrow?"

He knew or thought he knew Richard was coming back.

"I'm moving back home. I'll tell Karyn what's up, and I'll be there for you. I mean nothing between us or anything. Let me do this for you."

"No. You've done enough, and I thank you; now good night."

"Alright, I'll talk with Karyn anyway. I mean you never know you may need your life back. I mean your old routine when I was home would add the balance you're missing in your life."

Janet wanted to cry. Marcus thinking their marriage was balanced was about enough to make her black out. He was the root of her problems. The thought of him raising her children came to her mind. She smiled and clenched her teeth as she spoke.

"How dare you sit here and tell me you're gonna talk with the bitch you left me for to say what? That the dummy you married needs you. I don't Marcus, really. I need time to get you the fuck out of my system. I'm not doing as good about our so-called separation as our children. They don't even ask about your dumb ass, and here I am praying for you each day. I got a new prayer for you, "God helps those that help themselves." No thank you Mr. Robinson, stay with Karyn. I'll wait on God. He saved me Friday and my faith says if needed, he'll do it again."

Marcus looked toward the door as the intercom announced the end of the day's visits. The nurses began to check rooms bidding goodnight to all. Janet was glad the visit was being terminated; she wasn't ready for Marcus' reaction.

15

*R*ichard decided he had given Marcus enough of a challenge for one night; he would visit Janet again later in the week. Leading her on was not his intention; she needed a good friend. He drove home thinking of Dr. Norris and the times they spent getting to know each other over the past year. She too had been a friend who wanted to take the relationship to another level.

Lashauna was well educated, beautiful and all a man could ask for but her accomplishments gave her an air of arrogance that Richard couldn't ignore. She shunned off people who hadn't followed a path of education and self-development. Richard was surprised; she was a success with her patients, most of whom were the opposites of those she preferred to surround herself with.

They dated, wined and dined but Richard cut it short before the bedroom got heated. Lashauna ignored him for months after an all-night argument about sex, the physical and mental connections needed in a relationship. Richard couldn't explain why he wasn't attracted to her beyond friendship, but Lashauna felt it was just an excuse for his not wanting to be committed or deeply involved with anyone. She wouldn't allow him to convince her there was chemistry missing between them.

Richard agreed with her for the sake their friendship but Lashauna watched him closely when attending church and various community functions. She wanted to see who the woman was that would conquer Mr. Burnett.

Walter Reed, his partner had found Richard's love bouts humorous, especially now that he was dating Lashauna. He teased Richard often telling him she just needed a little more milk in her coffee. As a Caucasian that could hold a deep tan, he explained he had the best of both worlds. Walter and Richard graduated from Farleigh Dickerson University and after spending four years together and another ten in business no woman would come between them. Richard wished him the best and said a prayer of thanks.

Janet Robinson would fit into a unique category. He wanted her as a friend, but he had to admit there was an attraction. He knew to keep his thoughts to himself in light of her marriage. It would have to be friendship only, but with a controlling husband, he agreed with Faye, Marcus needed to know that Janet was special to someone else.

Janet caught his attention during the interview. She was vulnerable to an extent, but she had a good head on her shoulders. Richard reviewed her application at the close of the day and debated about the call. Elaine usually made the calls but after Janet's reaction, he wanted to speak with her.

He pulled into his driveway at his home in Verona, New Jersey hoping his sister hadn't cooked. The lunch he had with a client at two o'clock was still sitting in his stomach. He regretted suggesting Spain's a restaurant in Newark, which was known for their large entrées. The client loved the restaurant and ordered enough for them to have leftovers. Richard picked up the bag and carried it into the house.

Elaine Flanders greeted her younger brother with an inquisitive look when she smelled the food through the bag.

It was normal for him to bring a meal home during the week, but he never forgot to tell her. Sometimes where he ate lunch or dinner with a client was discussed when she made his appointments at the office. Very few clients knew, Ms. Flanders the stern receptionist at Burnett and Reed LLC was the sister of Richard Burnett.

Elaine's husband died after a battle with lung cancer. His death at the age of forty left her devastated. Richard moved her into his home and offered her a job at the office to keep an eye on her. She had her bouts with depression and reduced her interaction with friends tired of the "I'm so sorry for you" outings. Five years passed. She and her brother lived together and agreed they wouldn't impose on the other's lifestyle other than the cooking and cleaning. Elaine refused to let him clean or cook. He pitched in to help often, but it was usually too late.

The aroma reminded him he hadn't called. He could smell the gravy and onions that he knew would be the topping for a well-seasoned meatloaf. He slid past her standing at the entrance of the kitchen and raised his eyebrows hoping to avoid a scolding.

"So how was she?"

"Uh, she's up and responding. I didn't get to visit her, as early as, I thought. Mr. Little wanted to have a late lunch, and well, you know."

"Richard, you can't get out of it. You know you're wrong. You left the office at eleven. Didn't say you were having lunch with a client. I didn't have to cook all of this. It's okay. You'll be eating leftovers the rest of the week, between that bag and this stove."

"Okay, I'm guilty and the punishment is justly deserved. Leftovers cooked by one of my favorite restaurants and my loving sister. Please punish me more often."

"Seriously is that girl gonna be alright. I thought something was troubling her that day. I should have alerted you before she came into your office. That's something, how the mind has you thinking you've come to the end. You know, when you think like that you need something or someone to shake you loose. Really, been there, and it ain't a good place to be. What did Lashauna say?"

"You know she can't tell me about her patients?"

"I know she won't tell you about this one."

"What does that mean?"

"C'mon now; I'm your sister. There's more to it than you hiring her, and I know it, so does Lashauna."

"I felt guilty, I told you that. I wouldn't have been able to rest knowing I might have pushed her over the edge."

"How much baggage is she carrying? I read her application, no work for more than five years; two years of college, a husband she's separated from; there was something else that caught my eye. Oh yes, not much experience or training. So how did she out rank the other applicants? Walter wanted to know that too. I told him she was your choice."

Richard continued to lean on the counter as Elaine took the cover from the simmering gravy. She turned off the flame and the oven. He shook his head realizing she was right. Janet was the least qualified of all the applicants over the three-day hiring process. He couldn't explain why he chose her other than he wanted someone who would be committed to coming to work.

"She'll be a good employee."

"Oh, I don't doubt that, but now that she's got this struggle with self-worth..."

"Did Lashauna tell you that?"

"Who said Lashauna told me anything?"

"You're talking like you got an inside evaluation or something. I mean, how do you know about her self-worth or her struggles?"

"Don't get touchy. See that's what I'm saying." Elaine ran the faucet in the sink cleaning up the utensils she used for cooking. "You aren't acting like an employer. I brought those papers home you wanted her to fill out too. It's okay to admit it Richard."

"Admit what? I want her to be insured while she's in the hospital. I told you about her issue with her husband. He's as I thought, controlling, and I think he may very well be the cause of some of her problems. This will give her a little support. So what am I admitting to?"

"Burnett and Reed LLC is going to pay the bill of a woman who obviously has an existing condition of depression or psycho something. She tried to kill herself, and you're still willing to employ her. I don't understand you Richard, and I ain't dumb. You tell me what's the attraction? She's the type of woman you want in your personal life?"

Richard needed to think about that answer for himself. Hearing the question aloud sounded different than his conscious reviewing his past romantic encounters. No, she was married and probably would go back to her husband. Women like her always did. Elaine was right. He was attracted to women who had troubled marriages. Walter called them romantic dead ends.

"I don't know. There's something special about her Elaine. I've got my eyes open this time though. I know she's married, the mother of three, got some issues but what woman doesn't. I just feel the need to be a friend to her. A friend that's all."

"It's never all. You worry about them, get too close and get the boot as a friend or potential lover. You pushed Lashauna away and look at her and Walter, damn near happily ever after."

"And I'll dance at their wedding. We definitely wouldn't have made it. I understand you sis and thanks. I'll be careful of the falling in love this time. But I do feel that if I had even mentioned to her, she was being considered for the job she wouldn't be in that hospital bed. Walter didn't have a problem with it, and it won't hurt us at all with the insurance company once the papers are done. I'll talk to the representative myself."

"You may need to. Listen, since you're on your own for dinner, I'm going to shower and get ready for the television to watch me."

"Yeah, I don't think I want to dig in. I'll put the food up and call it a night too. Thanks for the talk, I needed it."

"Anytime, I bet Janet will fall out when she finds out I'm your sister."

"Why, did the two of you have words before the interview?"

"No just eye contact."

16

Marcus didn't respond to Janet's comments. He told her he would see her later. He didn't want her to be as prepared for his visit as she obviously was this time. The ride to his condo gave him time to think. Karyn would never allow the children to stay with them, even temporarily. He needed the upper hand, and the children would give him an advantage. Faye told him enough information. It would insure his transition home would be without any arguments. He would live with Karyn and regain his reign in Montclair with his wife. Janet needed him, and she'd just have to admit it.

Karyn was reading with her legs folded under her on the couch when he entered their home. The magazines were strewn across the coffee table, as though she was bored with reading any of the articles or browsing. She didn't look up to acknowledge Marcus, but she spoke harshly just as he took a seat in the recliner.

"I guess you saw no need to return my call."

"So much went on I didn't check the phone. I've been thinking about this mini crisis since I left the hospital."

Karyn knew Marcus had game but so did she. She could smell his bull before he threw it at her. Janet and his family were used as flimsy excuses in the past and held no validity since. She looked up from one of her gossip entertainment magazines and instantly frowned.

"Damn, who hit you?"

Marcus forgot about the walnut sized knot that formed just below the left side of his chin. The throbbing subsided. He touched it and the pain returned as a reminder. He hadn't ducked the blow.

"Listen, we really need to talk. Janet is in the hospital; she may be there for the next few days, maybe another week. Faye and Sherod have the children, but I can't expect them to keep them the entire time without my help. We need to split their stay, or I need to go home..."

"Home? This is your home or what is this just a temporary stay here?"

"Well, you know what I mean. The kids would be more comfortable at home, and I know how you feel about them running around."

"No, I don't know what you mean. Why don't you say exactly what you mean?" Karyn unfolded her legs and sat in an upright position as if it would help her understand him better. Marcus watched her deliberate movement and knew it was the prelude to an argument. Karyn's willingness to fight, her spunk, was an attraction, and now he despised it. After living with her for the past year she too had her pros and cons. He missed Janet's willingness to be submissive. Karyn was a freak in the bedroom and demanded his attention. They balanced his life, and he was determined they could learn to deal with it. Janet's mental illness would be the excuse to live between both households.

"What do you expect me to do? They're my children too. I can't ask her sister and husband to take care of them through this."

"So you ask me to either take them in or let you play daddy throughout the week? And just where is Janet while you're at the apartment playing your role?"

"We don't really know yet," he lied, "they haven't said if she would be allowed to stay at home or remain in the hospital. Either way she would be under doctor's care, and I would imagine medication."

"They're gonna give her meds after she tried to O.D?" huffed Karyn. She grabbed another magazine and took her original position on the couch.

"C'mon now. We're talking about this, aren't we?"

"Marcus, when you find out where Janet will be laying her head I'll decide where you'll be laying yours. The kids can stay here if she'll be coming home. I'm not okay with you being there every night with her. She's sick in the head, ain't nothing wrong with her ass."

"So, the truth is you don't trust me."

"You call it what you want, but if you think I'm giving you a free pass to walk in and out of here and there; you must think I'm crazy. NOT! Listen; think about it from this point of view. I want to spend a few nights a week with Malik. You know my ex..... How does that go over with you?"

"You and Malik don't have kids, and you weren't married. It's not the same."

"Yes it is. Faye and Rod have your kids, and you've been separated over a year. They didn't ask you to take the kids. They told you they would be watching them if you wanted to see them for a few days. How do I know you got the kids? You could be alone with her for those days. I ain't down with it. Bring your kids here there's enough room for a few days."

The exaggerated pronunciation of the words told him she didn't believe his story. He didn't respond and let her words simmer as she pretended to be more interested in her reading than continuing their conversation.

"I think she's got someone, so there's no need for you to be jealous."

"He's the one chipped you up?"

"Ain't nobody chip nobody up. I'm just saying that if that's what you're worried about don't be. I just know that you always agree that the children can come by or stay and then change your mind. This may be a minute, and I can't shuffle them around when you get tired of them."

"Yeah, you've shuffled them enough. Let them stay with Faye, or what about your mother?"

"Karyn these are my kids not baggage you just leave."

"You haven't been a father to them since when?" She paused for his answer. "Exactly, my point, you don't know the last time you spent the day or the afternoon with them. Why we playing this game Marcus? What is it that you want?"

"I want you to understand that I may have to stay with them for a few days out of the week depending on her treatments and therapy."

"Why don't you wait and see? I mean the kids go to sleep around what nine or ten? You do your fatherly thing then you can bring your ass home, why stay, for what?"

"I guess you're right. I mean if she tried it again, I could be there afterward, again and look like I really don't give a fuck, again."

"If she tries it again, the court will give you your kids and you'd have them here with you. I'd have to make other choices then, rather to stay with you and deal with them or whatever. But that's not the choice right now. You do you but you won't be sleeping with me and her in the same week. Shit, not and I know it. Forget it."

Karyn got up and pushed the books into one pile on the edge of the table. Marcus had to come from a different angle. She didn't want children, and she tried not to deal with his. She'd make other plans deliberately to avoid their visits or outings. Marcus put her wants first, and now he regretted it. He was hooked on her bedside manner, and it became an addiction. He could leave her attitude, but he needed her personal treasures. He didn't love her or Janet. He was addicted to their ways.

17

*L*ashauna poured her second cup of coffee while reviewing her completed evaluations for the week. Janet Robinson's wasn't in the pile. She wanted to give a complete evaluation within the days she promised Faye but Janet hadn't said anything to her. She answered her questions with "yes" or "no" and didn't elaborate about any issues or problems. All her weekly evaluations were to be submitted Friday morning. Today would be her final attempt before telling Faye her sister may be suicidal. She just didn't know.

She had a brief interview more of a discussion with Faye and Sherod. They seemed to be a well-balanced loving couple and perfect role models for Janet's children. As a professional, Dr. Norris felt comfortable with the children remaining in their care. If Social Services deemed Janet to be temporarily unfit, them living with her sister and brother-n-law wouldn't rattle her condition. However, she had expressed both fear and concern whenever the doctor mentioned her children's relationship with their father. Today she requested Marcus to visit with her, and she would see Janet in the afternoon. She hoped to gain another perspective talking with her husband.

Faye gave a short description of her sister's husband. It wasn't quite worded in a way that she could translate for her evaluation but being a "sistah" she understood the description of a man with a "playa" mentality. The appointment was at ten. She had a little over an hour to prepare herself. Richard would love to see her work her magic with a true "brotha" since he felt she thought herself above that sort of behavior.

It wasn't really about the behavior. She worked hard to get where she was in life and didn't feel she needed to be reminded that she was raised in the projects. It had been years since she lived in Newark. Her parents still lived in the Weequahic section, or the southward, but they didn't move there until the late eighties. They thought they had moved from the violence and criminal activity of the inner city. Lashauna knew it would only be a matter of years when it touched their neighborhood. After college, she moved to Glenwood and hoped to move into her own home soon. It was personal progress, something that Richard felt she loved smearing in other's faces.

Walter told her about Richard's feelings shortly after he romanced his way into her heart. He wasn't the typical "white boy," and he too had worked his way up the ladder of success. He and Richard owned their successful accounting firm for a little over ten years. Before dating Richard, she checked their clientele and progress. The firm was solid and well respected. She dated Walter only to make Richard jealous; it didn't work and the rest was history. She loved Walter but she hoped Richard would have tested her waters just once.

Dating a white man wasn't her plans but the attraction had always been there. It was more than mere curiosity. Walter fit the need one night after too many drinks. Dr. Norris crossed over, and her world became comfortable. She didn't have to announce her status, it was immediately recognized. Walter loved showing her off and telling his colleagues about her accomplishments. He was aware of what she and Richard could have had, and it was for that reason he told her Richard had an interest in Janet Robinson. Lashauna, Dr. Norris, needed to know why.

Calling her old beau seemed within reason considering he asked her to visit Janet as a part of her Sick and Shut In Ministry at the church. The church was where she found herself on Sunday mornings shortly after she and Richard were no longer an item. He and Elaine were members of Mt. Calvary Baptist Church and seeing him on Sunday while praying gave her peace. She didn't want to terminate their friendship; one he insisted should remain intact. Her immediate intentions were to subtlety stalk him. His pleasantries became sickening.

"Hey Rich, when you get this call, please return it..."

"Shauna, Shauna."

"I was leaving you a message. Good morning, how are you?"

"I've had better starts but now that I've had a cup of coffee; I'm coming to life."

"Well you know I have a standing relationship with coffee so I understand. I was calling to let you know that I had spoken with Valerie Hendricks about visiting with Janet. I didn't want it to be a conflict of interest being her doctor if all she needed was a prayer partner. Valerie can visit and pray with her. I don't want her to confuse the relationship. I'm in her corner, but I don't want someone else to cause a problem for me or her."

Lashauna was sure Richard would question what she meant, but he seemed to be preoccupied. She listened as he changed the station on his radio; it was then she knew he was in his car.

"Are you working this morning?"

"I work every morning. I was listening to you; I'm trying to adjust this ... hang on a minute. Okay, now my phone didn't charge last night and the...never mind. So Valerie was okay with seeing Janet?"

"That's our job in the ministry. I explained that she was a patient, and she told me she would see her tomorrow."

"I thought she'd be going home tomorrow. What's wrong with her being treated as an outpatient?"

"To be honest with you, I'm not sure she should be out. But, before we go into that any further tell me, why her?"

"Why her what?"

"You don't hire and take care of sick people every day. Walter agreed with you, but you know he has his reservations too."

"He's done some things that I had reservations about. Listen, she's a good person having a rough time. I may have pushed it and made it unbearable. I feel guilty so I'm helping her. That's it."

"Hmm, the rescuer, you feel the need to save her from who or what?"

"You said save, I said help. Listen I've got to go I'm late for an appointment as it is. Your man is holding it down and I know he's sweating looking for me to come through the door."

"Well if he knows like I know, sweat doesn't excite you at all."

"Shauna, let it go baby. I've never seen you sweat."

"You didn't look in the right places."

"Well, I'll let Walter know you need a romantic night out. I'll tell him it's on me, a gift to you for taking care of Ms. Robinson for me. How's that?"

"Later Rich." Shauna hung up the phone needing a stiffer drink than coffee.

18

Marcus spent the morning making excuses for keeping the appointment with Dr. Norris. Karyn didn't understand the need for an ex-husband's input in his wife's mental evaluation. Marcus left the bedroom after Karyn made the statement that Janet was no crazier than any other woman he dealt with including her.

"It's a game Marcus; she just went a little too far. She won't try it again that's a guarantee," Karen insisted following him through the house.

"That's my point. I don't want my kids to think that she might. She's taking them through some mental shit. If I don't talk to this doctor some bad decisions can be made that will affect my children."

"Where are they staying, with her or her family? Let them give the doctor that so-called information. You aren't in her life like that. You're only their father. Let them settle things and you keep them, just as they are. I mean, you will probably need to visit them more often, but that's it. What are you trying to be Mr. Salvation now?"

Marcus grabbed his car keys off the kitchen counter. Karyn kept her back to him, loading the dishwasher with the breakfast dishes. He sighed and shook his head. She didn't know she was making it harder for him to stay with her. Her fighting him tooth and nail about his decisions was making him uncomfortable.

"I'm out."

"Alright Superman don't let her kryptonite knock your ass for a loop."

"Yeah right."

He kept walking knowing that Karyn expected more of a response. As he got into the car, he thought about his decision to leave home and move in with Karyn. It wasn't the same as dating and returning home to his family. He could avoid most of their arguments by staying away from her for days. The distance always gave her time to think about the loving she was missing, and they would resume with the pleasures, they both welcomed. Now she had restrictions; the children's staying with them was one and his staying out all night was the other. He hadn't tried either, and was looking for a beneficial solution, one that would benefit his needs. He was certain Dr. Norris would have the answer.

Dr. Norris greeted him with a smile and politely offered him a cup of coffee. Marcus watched her closely as she left the office to get him a cup while talking to him from the alcove she called her haven.

"I've promised myself a coffee maker this month. I'm addicted and I need to stop pretending I drink less with it in this hall. Crème and sugar?"

"Yes," Marcus answered admiring the doctor's wall of accomplishments. He smiled thinking of the challenge she would be as a mate. The mental game alone would be worth his efforts. She didn't sound like a "sistah" with an air.

"I didn't want to give you too much or too less. Here make it to your liking." She handed him the packets of sugar and the creamer.

"Thank you. How long have you worked here at the hospital?"

"A little over three years, I actually work for a few hospitals as an on call. I'm on-site here."

"I see. So you deal with crazy folks."

"I wouldn't say that. There are some that are clinically beyond the norm, but for the most part, I deal with those who can be treated and just fell off their game."

Lashauna waited for his response. She could tell he wasn't ready for her to talk on a level where he could understand her. He was challenging her mentally. She was ready and expected his next move.

"Unlike Janet, people who don't have the support of their families often find themselves slipping away from reality."

"So suicide is not considered slipping away from reality?"

"Not when you're pushed. Sometimes facing reality with no way to vent, find a solution, or escape can back them into a corner. I really think that most people who contemplate suicide are in that corner. They think they're alone, and they give up."

"Well I guess you know better than I do but Janet has never been alone. She has her family, the kids..."

"What about you Marcus, you're her husband, are you in that corner with her?"

"No, I never thought about killing myself."

"What makes you think she did?"

Suddenly, Marcus felt he was being examined. Dr. Norris turned the table. He immediately became defensive.

"Doc, she took the pills not me. She didn't announce it so how would we know she felt alone?"

"That's why I'm working with her. I'm sure she gave signs of depression. I don't know if you saw it, and that's why you're here. That's what needs to be discussed."

"I don't know how I would be able to help you. I'm sure she told you we're not together."

"No, why don't you tell me about that. It's a good place to start."

"Faye must have mentioned it."

"No, why don't you tell me. Listen, we can't get anywhere if you're trying to avoid telling me what you know. Janet is not crazy if that's what you came to hear. She's of sound mind, though she's been hurt. I need to know how, when and by whom; that's the start of her healing and being able to cope."

Marcus heard the doctor's words but misinterpreted the meaning. He decided he, and the doctor would have to have a few sessions to cure his wife. He needed to be home where his support and love would benefit Janet.

"Janet is and has always been somewhat secretive about personal matters. I guess our marriage and our problems fit into some of the things that, like you said would push her to the edge. Alright, how can I help?"

"Being honest with your answers, try not to be evasive. If you think something that she has said or done in the past may be important, tell me. Janet hasn't really said much and that concerns me. I want to release her, but I need to be able to know she's safe."

"I guess no one has told you that I am willing to move home to help her through this. We have three children, and I don't want them to be tossed through the family like they don't have a father or a home."

Lashauna looked at Marcus and almost rolled her eyes. She remembered their meeting was professional, and she held her "attitude" for the moment.

"And just what would your current lady friend say about you playing house again with your wife?"

"Uh, she'll have to understand. I mean, it's for the sake of my family. My kids need their mother."

"Hmm..., I agree, but they need to know that the family is stable. How often do you visit with them now?"

"Like I said, we're separated. Janet didn't take it too well in the beginning, but the kids are okay. I don't get to see them as much as I should and that's another reason why I agreed to be a part of this, what is it, therapy?"

"No, not quite, this is simply a discussion for me to get to know some of the issues your wife has had to face over the past few months.

It is not therapeutic at all. As a matter of a fact she may not need therapy."

"Dr. Norris, Janet obviously needs something. A doctor, a suicide prevention program..."

"A stable marriage, supportive husband; yes, you're right."

"So you're saying it's my fault?"

"No, I'm looking forward to eliminating any faults or problems that have affected your wife, so she can get on with her life."

"So I am the fault?"

"Do you think you contributed to her wanting to escape some of her problems?"

"No. It was clear that our marriage was going sour. Apparently she didn't adjust to it well."

"So why are you here? Certainly not to help her readjust, you could have done that before this happened. I'm sure you talked about reconciliation over the past year."

"I told you. I'm here to help my children get their mother back. Tell me what I need to do."

"Your wife and children will be fine with you living where you live." Lashauna had enough of Janet's self-centered husband. "Thank you for stopping in, I'm sure I can work with your wife based on the information I've gotten from you and her family."

"So that's it? What's the diagnosis? Will she be able to come home without medication?"

"I'll be seeing her this afternoon. She may be released tomorrow at the earliest. I'll be in touch with Ms. Williamson."

"I'm her husband. Why would you call her sister?"

"That's who she has listed as the next of kin. I'm not obligated to discuss anything with you."

Marcus stood realizing the doctor had no intention on seeing things his way.

"Doctor, did she say it was our marriage that caused her to break down."

"Like I told you Mr. Robinson, she hasn't said anything."

"Maybe she'll talk to me today. I'm sure she'll be glad to know I'm willing to come home and help her get back on her feet."

"It's been a pleasure."

The doctor stood to her feet extending her hand and a forced smile. She kept her response to herself.

19

"I didn't think I would see you until I started working for you."

"I had to bring you the papers, remember? Elaine highlighted quite a few lines that you have to fill out."

"I know she wasn't happy about your hiring me. Has she worked for you long?"

Richard passed Janet the pen as she adjusted herself in the bed. He rolled the hospital tray positioning it across her lap and adjusted its height. She smiled and thanked him as he took a seat.

"You didn't answer the question Mr. Burnett."

"What was that, oh Elaine. She's my sister. She's been with us since her husband passed away. She's good people; you've just got to get to know her."

"I don't think we'll be doing lunch together; your sister? I wouldn't have guessed that. So, she knows about me being in the hospital?"

"Yes, it's okay Janet. So does Walter; neither of them knows why, but they know you're in the hospital." Richard lied realizing Janet would be uncomfortable with them knowing the reason for her hospital stay.

"So now I look like a charity case?"

"No, no, not at all. I told them why I hired you on Friday, before I called you. I told them you were rushed to the hospital, and that's all they know."

Richard thought about what Walter would find out later from Lashauna. He was convinced. She was professional. She wouldn't discuss her clients with him. Janet's secrets would be safe.

"I wouldn't hire you as an act of charity."

Janet continued to complete the medical and tax forms. Whatever Richard Burnett's reason she was glad she would have a job. It would be the first step toward being independent. She signed the last form and handed the packet to him. He put them in the manila envelope and moved the table.

"How are you feeling?"

"Better. I don't know, maybe this was the rest I needed. I seem to be thinking clearer, and I feel a lot better about things, relieved. The same relief I was looking for that afternoon."

"So remember that when you get stressed. Take a few days and rest. One day at a time Janet, one day at a time."

There was a knock at the door, and both Richard and Janet looked waiting for it to open. Marcus stepped into the door and upon seeing Richard paused.

"What the hell is this Janet?"

"Hello to you too."

"Janet, listen, I'll speak to you..." Richard stood to give them privacy.

"No, you cut your visit short the last time. Marcus, you should call before you come. I know you didn't come to see me. The children are with Faye at my mother's "

Janet knew his visit would bring unwanted drama. Marcus went out the door without looking back at her. The door opened again, and panic took over Janet's expression. Richard reached for her hand to comfort her. They both assumed Marcus was returning. It was Dr. Norris. Richard stood and smiled nervously. Janet noticed his reaction and questioned herself about the relationship he had with the good doctor.

"Afternoon people, Janet, Richard; I just saw Marcus leaving, seems like one happy family."

Her sarcasm broke smiles and the shaking of their heads.

"Well listen, I'm going to go. Thanks for filling out the forms I needed. I'll get them to Elaine so everything will be done when you come to the office."

"Dr. Norris, will I be able to work soon?"

Lashauna noticed Janet was lively with Richard in the room. It was the first time since she visited her that she got her to speak above a whisper. She made a mental note of their exchange of words as Richard told them both goodbye. He didn't think the doctor would give her a definite date for her to begin working. Richard was sure she would be questioning him about her employment. The doctor already had one question. What did he see in her?

20

"Janet, I'm glad to see you feel better today. It is because of your visitors or the thought of going home?"

"You said I should be honest with you; can we be honest with each other?"

"Of course, we can." The doctor took the seat near the window and pulled out her steno pad and pen.

"I don't think there's a need for notes. You'll be able to remember this. I'm not sick. Not in the least, I think you know that, as well as I do. I thought I was but after a few days of rest I've discovered I was tired. Tired, and fed-up. Some of the things that I was fed-up with I'll just have to get a grip and deal with them. The others I've got to separate myself from."

"I see so, what are the solutions? I'm sure you've also had second thoughts about death being the only way around these problems."

"Yes, and I don't know what to say about the pills. I really wanted a good rest, without the tossing, turning and dreaming. I wanted to wake up with a clear head and make some decisions about what to do next without anyone's interference. Now I've got you, my sister, my husband, Mr. Burnett and I still haven't heard from my mother, the children. Shit, I'm back at square one with more voices, more pressure, more demands and all eyes on me. But I'm not crazy. I'm not sick, and I don't want to die."

Janet was trembling and beginning to curl her body in the center of the bed. Dr. Norris made notes on her pad but never changed her facial expression so not to upset her patient. She needed her to be calm to finish their talk, but Janet had become fearful.

"What's scaring you? Is it the questions, the responsibilities, or the fear of returning to your home?"

"Why would I be scared of my home?"

"You said it best, your family, the questions. You don't want to be crowded. Am I right?"

"In a way, Marcus can't come back home. I can't trust him, and I need to be able to trust someone who claims they love me." Her voice lost its volume as she sunk deeply in her thoughts.

"What about your children?"

"What about them?" Janet sat up showing a new interest.

"Their relationship with their father."

"You said be honest? Well, to be honest they don't have a relationship with him because of his priorities. Right now, it's Karyn, his new-found love."

"They don't visit him."

Janet didn't answer. Dr. Norris thought she lost her connection with her again. Muffled and not much above a whisper, she responded, speaking into her knees, which were bent into her chest supporting her head.

"I won't make it depending on Marcus to come back; I just want to know why?"

"Why what?"

"I was the best mother and wife any man could want. I did for them before I did for me. That's why I'm here doctor. I lack self-love. See I can evaluate myself."

Janet's voice resumed to the perky person she was while Richard was in the room. Lashauna marked her pad and underlined the change.

"Look, don't get me wrong. I did allow some of this. I mean I never put my foot down or even tried to work or go to school. I mean really, I don't think he would have stopped me. I didn't try. I didn't try to do anything in our marriage but what he wanted. But then this thing with Karyn started, and I did put my foot down. I tried to work things out. I screamed, cussed, and shouted and shit…I'm here."

There was a silence. Dr. Norris waited for Janet to digest her words. She watched the distraught, mother of three reposition her legs again. It seemed like she was nervous about the situation she was in.

"Janet, I can sign papers to have you released tomorrow. But without you agreeing to come to my office for a few weeks I can't honestly say that I won't be seeing you here again."

"I won't be seeing you here again I can say that."

"Janet, honestly, you're lucky I saw you this time. You were blessed, and I want you to embrace the blessing and get yourself together. This is new support. You've got a job waiting, and someone whom you can talk to that won't look at you strangely."

"Well Faye is a good listener. I just know that she doesn't need my burdens and my mothers. Did she tell you my mom was sick? My brother does a lot with her now that, well, while I'm getting a grip on things..."

Her demeanor changed again, and the doctor made another notation. It was obvious there were rooted problems.

"Janet, we have to work some things through before I can give an okay for you to go to work. When can we make the first appointment?"

"Hmm, how long did you and Richard date?"

The question came across as though someone whispered "Gotcha" into the doctor's ear. She smiled trying to keep a professional appearance.

"What makes you think we dated?"

"Honesty, huh."

"We dated for a minute, about a year or more ago. Why?"

"You couldn't let go could you?"

"Janet, this is not about me."

"It is if I'm going to have therapy sessions with you and work with your ex, or don't you have any intentions on signing those papers for me to work?"

21

*J*anet was sure she would be on time. The traffic was heavier than usual, and the twenty-minute drive to the Montclair office would now be at least an hour. Richard would be calling, worried that she hadn't called. It seemed what started as a courtesy was now routine. Janet's start time was eight o'clock, but Richard didn't deduct her pay for her lateness. She was expected to call when she was running late. The drive from her sister's home in Bloomfield was a daily nightmare. Bloomfield Avenue was the easiest route to the office when there was no traffic. She turned up the volume on the radio and sighed reluctant to accept the delay when the light turned red for the third time. It seemed she had been trying to reach the Grove Street corner for more than ten minutes.

The new job started two weeks after her release from the hospital. Now after a month of therapy, Janet found her sessions with Dr. Norris helpful but she had a long way to go. Overcoming the problems wasn't as easy as she thought. Neither was admitting she had overlooked the problems for years. During her first session, she was introduced to another psychologist, Dr. Natalie Rhines. Janet smiled as she remembered the two-minute exchange they had.

"I'll be working with you during your therapy sessions. Dr. Norris thought there might be a conflict of interest between the two of you."

"There's a conflict alright; I don't handle them well, and she knows that. I need to speak to her honestly, I do. Do you think you could repeat our conversation to her? Word-for-word okay?"

The petite fifty-five-year-old woman was apparently shaken by Janet's request and snatched up her belongings leaving the conference room. She, being the senior psychologist, didn't take Janet's request well. She was insulted that the patient would request the very woman who didn't want to handle her case. Dr. Norris admitted to her colleague that she thought Janet shared an interest in the same man prior to her breakdown. Dr. Rhines understood her concern and volunteered her services. Janet didn't see anyone who would or could tell her she could leave. She didn't know exactly what she was expected to do, so she took a seat. Dr. Norris entered the room and closed the door shaking her head.

"You're determined to work with me, unbelievable."

"You say honesty is what our conversations would be based on, and you want to skip on me? I don't think that was honest."

"I was honest enough to tell you about Richard and me."

"Well, Richard should have nothing to do with your profession. I think that you and I connected and that connection will get me back on my feet. I need that more than anything else."

The horn blew a long annoying honk behind her, startling her into stepping on the gas and closing the gap between her and the car in front of hers. The cell phone rang, and she glanced at the clock; it read eight twenty.

"Janet, hi sweetie, it's Elaine." Janet could hear Richard and Walter talking in the background. She wondered if they all were huddled over the front desk, crowding in concern for her safety.

"Good morning Elaine, before you ask I'm on my way. There must have been an accident on Bloomfield Avenue."

"That's why I'm calling. Take your time traffic is backed up because of a big accident near High Street. It's got things backed up for miles."

"Oh, well I think I'm going to try to turn at the next corner and try another way."

"No, Richard said its Friday go get the kids and start your weekend"

Janet couldn't afford a day off, but she didn't want to sound like she didn't appreciate his thoughtfulness. He went above and beyond since her mishap.

"Elaine, can I speak with him please?"

"Richard, go to your office and pick up line one."

Two blocks later, she made it through the green light, and the traffic began to move at a progressive pace. Moving more than two blocks before stopping again she put on the signal light to make a right turn.

"Good morning."

"Well coming from Verona you could say that." Janet laughed trying not to show her annoyance.

"Take the day off. We don't have that much here, and I'll be leaving at one. Walter has meetings all day so I doubt if he'll need your assistance until Monday." Richard answered checking his calendar

"I could catch up on arranging the files." She said, causing him to pause.

"Listen, pressing hard put you in the hospital. No pressure, the traffic is enough. Don't go get the kids though. Join me for lunch."

"Lunch?"

"Yes, how about one thirty. I'll pick you up."

"Richard?"

"Yes, I know no surprises."

22

There was no doubt in Janet's mind that the ride home would be quicker if she continued to avoid Bloomfield Avenue. It was just nine o'clock and with nowhere to go other than home she decided to call Faye.

"Hey, do you feel like coffee or something?"

"Janet, where are you?"

"On my way home if you don't join me."

Faye readjusted herself on the couch where she was reading. Sherod decided to go back to sleep after the children left for camp. The morning routine was no more than the twenty minutes of small talk with them while waiting for the camp van. Sherod was catching up on rest he claimed he deserved being the sounding board for three lively children each morning. Faye could use the outing. She and Janet hadn't really spent any leisure time together since Janet was released from the hospital.

"Sure, what happened, why aren't you going to work?"

"Bloomfield Ave. is a mess and just as I was attempting to find another route Richard called. He told me to take off the day."

"Oh, okay. Well, are you coming here or do you want me to meet you?"

"I'll come get you. Better yet, I'll bring your coffee. Is Rod there?"

"Sleep girl, listen, I've got some running around to do pick me up with the coffee, and we'll ride together in my truck."

"No problem, I'm on my way."

The horn was blowing fifteen minutes later. Faye yelled "good-bye" to her half-conscious husband, grabbed her purse and locked the door. She watched Janet as she locked her car and approached her with what she thought was a peculiar look.

"You look like you've got a secret you want to tell."

"Does it really show?"

"Yes. What's the real reason you're not at work?"

"I told you. Richard told me to take the day. Well, not really the day."

"What does that mean?" The two got into Faye's Explorer and adjusted themselves. Janet continued the conversation bringing Faye up to date about her past month and what she had learned about herself. Faye waited impatiently for her to get to the reason she wasn't working.

"Janet, I'm really happy you're enjoying therapy and your relationship with Dr. Norris but what does that have to do with you not going to work."

"Can I tell my story? Where are we going?"

"I've got to make a stop in Union, and at that store in Millburn, you know the boutique you liked so much."

"Okay, listen. Richard wants to meet me for lunch. Faye I'm really nervous about it."

"Why? You're having lunch with your boss, maybe you're doing so well you're getting a raise."

"Raise for what? I don't do much, filing, some typing and reorganizing the desk at the end of the day."

"Maybe he'll give you more work. I don't think it's anything to be nervous about. Maybe he'll admit he likes you. It's been more than a month now."

"What's been more than a month?"

"That you worked there. You haven't snapped yet so everyone at your job should be more relaxed."

Janet frowned, but as she thought about Faye's comment, she understood. She was right; there were no longer questions about how she was feeling every two hours. Elaine couldn't find a reason to check on her. Janet thought they were all scared she would mess up the client's information or folders. Maybe they did think she was mentally unbalanced.

"What makes you think he's interested in me? Especially after knowing what I've been through, he doesn't need my drama."

"Maybe it will spice up his life. He doesn't seem like the type not to have a wife or someone special. He's not on the D.L. is he?"

"I doubt that. The doctor was dealing with him a little over a year ago."

Norris? She's not his type."

"They had something going on; that's for sure. I think she still wants whatever they had. That's part of the reason I'm so nervous. Suppose he does like me, what do I tell her?"

"Why tell her anything?"

"She's trying to help me deal with my life Faye. She has to know what's going on."

Faye disagreed but she wouldn't say she did. Janet had a lot to contend with. "So you told her about you and Marcus?"

"We talk about that ass. More than I want to, to tell you the truth. We've talked about daddy too, Faye. I know you all say that his death wasn't my fault, but it haunts me. I didn't know how much it affected me. Dr. Norris said that it even had an effect on my marriage, the way I allowed Marcus to do certain things. Faye, do you think that's true?"

The question hung in the air as Faye parked the truck. The two got out and entered the store where she had items to exchange. She was happy that her opinion wouldn't be discussed. She'd make sure the conversation would be entirely different when they returned to the truck.

23

"So you're really going through with this thing, huh?"

"Walter, this thing as you call it is important to me. I can't stop thinking about it. She's here. Every day, I see her, and I question myself. I'm tired of having to ask myself; is it the right time? You know; I believe that's why I called her back that day."

"Your call saved her life? You never told me that. I don't remember that at all. I recall you saying her sister answered the phone thinking she was calling 911."

"No, that's not what I'm saying. It's just fate, man. If I hadn't called her things would have been different. It was meant to be."

"Okay so fate threw her a bone. She ain't for you. She's seeing Lashauna. You don't want to get involved with a patient of hers do you?"

"I referred her to Lashauna. I knew about the issues. You're right I don't want to get involved with a patient. However, who's to say she's a patient because she's sick. Walter she's a patient because of her issues. I want to help her. I need to and to be honest with myself. I don't know why."

"Yeah, that's some ole' psychological shit. Lashauna would understand it, but man I don't know if that's good or bad. I mean you getting involved with her, and she's still married."

Richard couldn't get the conversation out of his mind as he drove to pick up Janet for lunch. He parked his car and approached Janet's unit feeling good. His afternoon plans were beginning to unfold and if it all went his way Janet would accept his friendship on the next level. He recognized her need to take her time and wouldn't disrespect the position she was in. He rang the bell and turned his back to the door, viewing the parking lot.

"Hey, Richard, please come in."

"I'm not too early am I?"

"No, I just wanted to check a few things before we leave."

Janet escorted him to the living room where he took a seat. She proceeded into the bathroom and continued to fix her hair and makeup. While shopping with Faye, she picked up a dress from the boutique that was perfect for a lunch with the "boss."

Faye teased her when she told her how the dress would speak when the conversation went into a lull. It was a mint green wrap. Her accessories were gold, and she hoped Richard wouldn't recognize her everyday black pumps and bag. She joined him in the living room with a confident smile.

"I'm sorry. I didn't keep you waiting long did I?"

"No, it's fine. You look good. It was worth the wait."

They left Janet's home discussing the foods that would satisfy their taste buds. They decided on Italian food. A restaurant in South Orange Richard frequented was the choice.

The restaurant was small, giving them the privacy needed to engage in serious conversation. The waiter poured the wine and promised them their salads would follow. Their order included seafood, pasta, salad, and desert. Janet felt a little nervous. She could feel the warmth around her head and neck. She hoped she wouldn't begin to perspire.

"Is the wine okay?"

"Yes, Sangria is never bad, or is it?"

They laughed together and as promised, the salads were placed before them.

"Are you enjoying working?"

"I don't know that I can call it that. It seems that I don't really do enough to consider it work."

"You will believe me. Copying papers and filing them is just the beginning. Walter and I will be talking to you about what we're expecting. We've really increased our clientele, and some of the contracts can be prepared by you."

"What does Elaine do; I mean ... I don't want to take her work?"

"She has more than enough work."

"Okay, so is this something I would have to be trained for?"

"Not at all, we can show you in less than an hour. You'll be fine. You work well with Elaine. We thought you'd have a problem sharing that office space in the front."

The small talk was killing Richard. He didn't know how to redirect the conversation. Janet ate the salad and hoped the wine would diminish the uneasiness she was feeling. She took a larger sip from her glass, and was grateful she wasn't driving.

"To be honest, I did too. Elaine is great though, she really is. A bit on the motherly side but we're getting to know each other. I'm comfortable there. You weren't thinking of moving me into one of those other offices were you?"

"Not at all, Elaine means well, and she gives a word of advice to us all. She speaks her mind, gives her opinion and says what needs to be said. I respect her for those qualities. A lot of people would ignore some of those things and create problems later."

Richard paused wiping his mouth with his napkin after taking a drink from his glass. Janet listened to him as he spoke more about Walter and Elaine being happy that she was there. He told her he hoped they hadn't made her too nervous the first few weeks of employment.

"Well it's good to know they don't think I'm a complete basket case. It's been hard trying to figure out whether people are dealing with me because they pity me. I don't want them to feel that way. I'm willing to work for my pay and harder to advance."

"That's good to know, and I can tell you that none of us are working with you out of pity. Enough about the job; how are you?" Janet looked at him without lowering her napkin from her mouth.

"I'm not trying to put you on the spot. Let me rephrase the question. You said that you and Dr. Norris were making progress, is it really working for you?"

"Yes, it really is. I will admit I still have things I have to face, my husband and my past, mostly, but for the most part, I'm more confident about my future."

Richard smiled. "And what about your future, I mean, where do you see yourself in say two to three years?"

"Well, I hope my financial worries will be at a minimum. M.J. will be getting ready for middle school and puberty; the girls will be growing quickly too. I want to be settled where they won't have to move around."

"Why would you have to move? Are you thinking about relocating?"

"It depends on Marcus. If I have to move to get away from him, I will. He told Dr. Norris, he wanted what's best for the children. He wanted to move back home for them. He never mentioned me. She's helped me to see that. I thought knowing it would be enough; you know, feeling unwanted. The problem is I get confused when he's around. I don't know why but I want his approval. I want him to be pleased with my choices, my actions and at times my thoughts. I can't live like that."

"So you said it depends on Marcus, what does that mean?"

"I'm not sure; that's all I can say right now. I haven't seen him since I've been out. No calls, no questions, no comments; he hasn't even called for the children. They've asked to call him, and I won't let them. I need to end the marriage and the relationship. I just don't want my children to suffer in all of this."

The waiter came with their lunch. Janet used the time to excuse herself. Prickly heat caused her hands to be clammy. She entered the bathroom seeking the stall furthest from the door. Closing the stall door behind her, she let the tears fall from her eyes. Just mentioning her relationship with Marcus rattled her emotions. It would be a while before her life would be stable without Marcus and lunch with her boss wouldn't change her feelings. Men like Richard wouldn't stick around knowing Marcus wasn't giving in. What she didn't tell him was that Marcus called every night. She didn't tell him that she couldn't trust being alone with him. A confrontation with Marcus would only have one of two conclusions; sex or an argument. She saw no need to argue, so she didn't answer his calls. The tears continued to flow as she remembered Marcus rejecting her advances in their bed.

She washed her hands and fixed her slightly ruined makeup. Putting Marcus to the back of her mind was best. Lashauna, Dr. Norris, gave her mental exercises to that would release the tension. She started her exercises and said a prayer while returning to her seat. Richard stood acknowledging her presence and smiled as she sat. She sighed deeply looking at the plate before her.

"So what are your plans for the weekend?"

Janet tapped her mouth with her napkin before answering. She didn't have any real plans. Her weekends were filled with cleaning the apartment and laundry.

"No plans as of yet. What about you?"

"Can I convince you to spend the afternoon at a movie or something? I wanted to include your children, but I didn't know if that was too much."

"Rich, I don't want you to think you owe this to me."

"Listen, you're an attractive woman. I love your conversation and wouldn't mind spending time with you. There, now it's out. I like you, with or without your issues. I want to get to know you. Is that possible?"

Janet was stunned, holding on to her thoughts; she smiled.

"I don't want to disappoint you Richard."

"How? Just say yes. Do you have somewhere you wanted to take the kids this summer? You think about it and call me later. I won't take no for an answer."

"You don't have children do you?"

"No, don't even have a niece or nephew. Life dealt me an empty deck."

"All the cards haven't been played. Your hand is surely better than mine."

"Do you play cards?"

"A little."

"Spades or Bid Wisk?"

"Some, I haven't played in years."

"I've been looking for a partner."

Janet wasn't sure what he meant, but his smile gave her comfort. She finished her meal allowing her imagination to tease her as they continued their conversation.

24

$\mathcal{M}$arcus couldn't stop Karyn. She began throwing his shirts on the bed off the hangers in the closet. She stopped listening when he told her it would just be for the weekend. Her silence told him the rage was soon to follow and throwing the dishes in the sink, breaking the glasses, was only the beginning.

"What the fuck is up with you?" Marcus yelled from their bedroom door. His shirts were sailing through the air from the walk-in closet.

"I'm helping your ass pack for the weekend."

"Ain't nobody asked you to help me pack."

"Shit, ain't nobody asked me could you come out to play either. But you decided regardless to what I said you were gonna play anyway. Well, damn it, you need clothes to play in, or were you gonna be the skins, and she'll be the shirts. Marcus, take your shit and get out of my place."

"It was for the weekend Karyn. I'll be back on Monday."

"Not here you won't. I told you how I felt. Bring the damn kids here for the weekend. I'll go to my sister's. But not at their house, you go there, and it's over."

She came out of the closet looking as though she had been tossed around. She pulled down her "Got an attitude, now what!" cut off tee shirt which revealed her hardened nipples. Her face was reddened from anger, and Marcus could tell from the throb in his pants she had won.

"So the deal is that they can stay overnight right? I won't go get them tonight, how about tomorrow night. I'll go over and explain the arrangement to them, and you won't have to go to your sister's. You can deal with them for a night right?"

"They go home Sunday morning?"

"Bright and early."

"Marcus, you don't need to do this. She's playing you."

Karyn came out of the closet where Marcus could get a full view of her body. Her sweats matched the tee shirt with the word "Attitude" across the seat of the pants. Marcus smiled when she bent over to pick up the clothes she threw from the closet. She didn't bother putting them back on the hangers. They found a place in the winged chair she had tossed them in.

"Now you're playing me."

"What..."

Karyn turned to find Marcus standing close enough to kiss her softly on her lips. He fondled her butt as he kissed her again teasing her with his tongue. He whispered in her ear.

"I love you Karyn, you need to know that."

"Marcus you can't have it both ways."

"I only want it one way."

Karyn tried to ignore the obvious. Marcus used sex to escape their more serous conversations. She knew she would weaken to his touch soon enough but the longer he tried to conquer her, the more pleasure she would receive.

She bent over again slowly knowing he was patiently waiting for the last shirt to be tossed. He positioned himself behind her and gently tugged at her sweat pants. Karyn took her hands and pulled the pants down for him giving him an eye full.

His response was immediate, and he dropped his pants allowing his erection to touch her inner thighs from the rear. He decided the position, though different, would be an added pleasure for them.

Rubbing her butt, he repositioned her, so she could rest still bent at the waist on the bed.

Marcus enjoyed watching her outer lips move back and forth over his two fingers. He could feel himself enlarging but he waited for her to ask for his love. She began to move quicker, feeling the need to release.

"Marcus, baby, give it to me baby, aww..."

His manhood responded. He loved their encounters, bareback and without restrictions. During his marriage, Karyn had been the third woman he was with other than Janet. They all insisted on condoms, and the pillow talk was limited. He put the tip of his penis to the edge of her vagina and teased them both before penetrating her fully. The warmth of her insides made him pump harder. Standing, he held on to her waist and lifted her hips off the edge of the bed. The position tightened her hold on him and they both trembled with pleasure.

"Karyn take it all baby, all of it."

He knew he was about to explode so he pulled out and watched her roll over and adjust herself on the bed. She opened her legs, an invitation he expected. He was beginning to ejaculate, but he wanted to feel her heat around his shaft. The touch of her body sent him into sexual tremors. She wrapped her legs around him and bucked back enjoying the ride.

"Cum again baby, cum again, yeaass." Karyn relaxed her legs feeling the rush between them. Marcus couldn't control himself. Sperm was still rushing, a sign of pleasure. Karyn fulfilled his desires again.

25

Faye didn't ask how Janet enjoyed lunch, but she made her promise to call when she got home with the kids. The children and Sherod were engaged in a debate about super heroes, which ended when Janet entered the house. She could tell from her sister's attitude her lunch with Mr. Burnett had little to do with work. Sherod was polite enough to wait until he heard Janet's car door close before he began questioning clues he too thought were obvious.

"How is Janet coming along with her job?"

"She said it's going well. I guess it is she had today off."

"Really? She looks good. Maybe she's finally getting it together."

"I don't know. Rod, let me ask you something. Does a man leave his wife just to see if she loves him?"

"Not unless he found out living wasn't easy without her."

"What does that mean?"

"We must be talking about your sister and her dead ass husband."

"Well, yeah, I mean I just think that Marcus is still in love with Janet. And you know what? I think she still loves him. That's why she can't move on."

"Seems like she's moving on now, she got a job, she's looking a lot better; how's her therapy coming along?"

"She says she's doing well, like you said, she's looking better. I think her boss likes her."

"I told you it was more than just a job, but if that's the case, why are you asking about Marcus?"

"You know Marcus he's always in the shadows. They've been doing this off and on thing for years."

"Baby that ends when you get married; he has to grow up. Kayrn or Janet; he has to choose. I never understood him. Why is that so difficult for him?" Sherod expressed feelings about Marcus often. He always said he lacked maturity.

"I just don't want Janet to make another mistake."

"If she takes his sorry ass back it would be a mistake."

"Rod, what about for better or worse; they're no different than any other married couple. Damn, they've got kids to think about."

"He didn't think about them or her. Janet forgot about them for a minute too."

Sherod left the kitchen where their conversation began knowing his words wouldn't sit well. Faye couldn't argue the point he made. Janet's attempted suicide was real. They were told by Dr. Norris it couldn't be ignored if she was to overcome her problems. No one knew better than Faye that Janet would still be with Marcus, not working, accepting only what he allowed or gave her, if it hadn't been for therapy.

She wished it was different. It was the love she saw early in her sister's marriage that she longed for. It was the relationship between Janet and Marcus that she wanted for herself. Faye was proud of Janet's accomplishments; how she moved on after their father's death, her marriage, her family but through it all, Janet was depressed.

Though she never attempted to kill herself before, she was slowly losing her vibrant spirit. Her attitude had been the same after the death of their father. Now Faye understood her sister's fear of being alone. The therapy sessions revealed her weaknesses, which included blaming herself for her father's death and her unsuccessful marriage.

Faye didn't want to take sides but hoped Marcus and Janet would stay together for the sake of the children.

The television could be heard from the living room. The six o'clock news was just beginning. Faye began to clean the chicken she was frying for dinner when the phone rang.

"Hello."

"Faye, we're home girl. Can you talk now?"

Faye wiped her hands on the dishtowel while looking for her glass filled with soda. She took a seat at the table. She was anxious to hear what Janet's lunch was like.

"Well, it's obvious you weren't fired. I noticed the dress fit you. What made you wear that to lunch?"

"I didn't know where we were eating. We went to an Italian Restaurant. Wine in the middle of the day and more food than I could possibly eat; I enjoyed it. I really didn't know what to expect."

"So what was the gist of the conversation?"

"He wanted to know my goals, you know, what I wanted."

"And you said?"

"I told him what I know I want. Stability for M.J. and his sisters, a home, a good job, Faye until he asked I hadn't thought about it."

"You didn't say anything about your marriage?"

Janet paused. She hadn't said she wanted to keep her marriage. She dropped her head in thought and slumped back into the chair in her room. She had changed into an oversized smock for comfort, but it felt like it was clinging around her. She decided to get up and keep moving. The anxiety would subside if she focused on something else.

"No, at this point I don't know where I stand in this so-called marriage."

"I see." Faye heard the anxiety in her response.

"Faye, don't give me that. You really don't see. Sherod is loving and attentive. But I don't know what goes on at your home. You smile, seem to be content, but do I really know you are? I've been trying to keep it together and pretend but behind these damn walls, girl I've been dealing with what Marcus calls love. Dr. Norris said that I need to face things head-on. So we talked about me. I began to really think about me. Most people know when they take charge of their wants and goals. You know, when what mama says doesn't quite fit what you want. For me, that was about the time dad died. You know we were close. A part of me died with him."

"Janet, I was there. I understand, but you forgave yourself and that was the best thing to do remember?"

"Did I Faye? No, I never really forgave myself; he was my Marcus. He told me what was best for me, what would be a danger, how my life would unfold as a young woman. When Marcus came along I allowed him to fill daddy's shoes."

Faye's tears were flowing. She let them fall as she held her head with one hand. She was caught in her own emotions. Janet's words brought clarity to her faded memories.

"He's been abusive Faye, and I've known it, well maybe I didn't. I thought it was love. I mean, don't we all want to stay home and raise our children? I was committed and devoted, and he used me because of it. But you know what? I love him. He's never hit me or anything, but I can understand the other forms of abuse now. I really don't want to upset myself, or you, so let's just say I need to keep moving on."

"So you're moving on without Marcus?"

"I don't know love is funny. It holds on when you want to let go, and sometimes it lets go when you want to hold on. I've been reading a lot of inspirational books and really being honest with myself and Dr. Norris. She's taught me meditation exercises and of course prayer. Together, it's all working for me. I don't want to go backwards now that I've got so much encouragement to move on."

"Dr. Norris and Richard are encouraging you to leave Marcus?"

"No they want me to get myself together. Faye, I need to be stronger than I have in the past. Then I can deal with Marcus and Karyn."

"I think you need to talk with Marcus. You both have so much to think about, the kids and your marriage have to be a priority."

"No Faye, I'm my priority. I can't manage the kids or a marriage if I'm not right."

"So why discuss your goals with the boss, are you thinking about dating him?"

Janet smiled. She knew where her sister's concerns were headed.

"He's really a good person. A friend, something else Marcus never allowed. I mean he didn't mind Tiffany and Carol, but I never went out with them where he became the parent for the evening. I was allowed friendship for on-line chats or over the phone. You were my only friend, and I guess he felt that he had to allow that. Marcus was a trip, when I think about it."

"Hmm, so what's next with your therapy?"

"I'm scheduled for Tuesday as usual. We talk about the days since my last session. Based on how I handled things we open new issues for me to deal with."

"Marcus is a new issue?"

"Faye, he hasn't really thought about the kids or me. He wants me to beg for his love or help. I won't. I'm done with that. Richard asked to make a date for all of us to go out. I think that's too much right now."

"You and the kids? You're right too soon."

"Well will you keep an eye on them when I do go out?"

"You just had lunch."

"Okay, your point."

"Janet, you are married. What will your kids think about your dealing with another man?"

"They can't think of me any different than they do now. I'm not leaving them and eventually he will meet them. Did you know that Karyn can't stand for them to even be around?"

"What?"

Faye didn't want to hear it. She was determined to put a bug in Marcus' ear about visiting his children. Janet just gave her the platform.

"That's my phone ringing. Girl, I got to answer that, it's my cell. I'll talk to you tomorrow." Janet sighed hoping the call wouldn't spoil her mood.

26

Marcus waited for Janet to answer. After hearing her voice mail, he put the receiver in the cradle leaving no message. It was close to eight o'clock. He knew she was looking at the LCD screen and purposely ignoring his call. The last time they talked she was in the hospital. Faye talked him out of visiting her at home. He saw the kids twice in the two months that followed without Janet's knowledge. Faye had been helpful in arranging the visits allowing them to skip camp while Janet was working. The children promised to keep the secret and not upset their mother. Sherod was against it but agreed the children needed to be able to see their father.

Marcus slowed down as he approached their house hoping Faye wouldn't mind his stopping by. Sherod usually ignored him but he really needed to talk to someone. Although he knew Sherod didn't care for his indiscretions, he wouldn't turn a deaf ear. He turned into the Williamson driveway and sat a few moments after turning off his ignition. The flood light on the garage came on instantly, and before he could get out of his car Sherod was looking out the front door.

"What's wrong man, you okay?"

"Yeah, I was wondering if you wanted to grab a beer."

"You drove from Plainfield to Bloomfield to get a beer?"

Sherod walked to the driver's side of the vehicle shaking his head grinning at The thought of the forty -minute drive.

"Is beer in Plainfield that different, you coming in, or we hitting The Spot?"

"Janet in there?"

"Nah, she went home about two hours ago. I know you didn't come here looking for her."

Marcus sighed. Sherod knew the conversation would be lengthy.

"Let me get my wallet man. We'll hit The Spot."

Marcus watched his brother-n-law jog back to the front door. Faye came to the door and waved not waiting for any sign that Marcus saw her. He didn't make any effort to wave back. While waiting, he thought about Richard and Janet in the hospital. If anyone had told him that she would be working and possibly dating her boss, he would have called them a liar. He asked Faye several times about the job and Mr. Burnett. She would only say that Janet seemed pleased with her job, and they didn't talk much about her boss. Sherod opened the passenger door bringing Marcus' attention to his question.

"Every man needs a forty-minute drive and a cold one, right?"

"Well, if it will help, why not?"

"Alright, so what's up? You were looking for Janet, and you forgot your way to the apartment?"

"Seriously Sherod, come on man; I don't know what to do."

"Don't miss your turn, take this left. Do about what?"

"Janet. She's working, and man she ain't the same."

"Start from where you got the idea that she changed. Maybe I'll understand you better. Make the right at the light."

"Where you going?"

"Just drive man. It's a bar off Grove Street. A little quieter than The Spot on a Friday night, I want to be able to hear you."

"I think I missed the change. At least, that's what Dr. Norris implied. She said Janet had to be going through some things to attempt suicide like she did. That's really been bothering me. You know the fact I wasn't there, and maybe even the fact that I didn't know she was that weak."

"What makes you think she was weak?"

"To kill yourself, you've got to be weak, are you kiddin'?"

"Or scared, or worried, or depressed, why would you consider that a weakness? Listen to yourself man. ... On your left, park in the back there."

Marcus parked as directed. The large neon sign flashed D.J's overhead as they walked into an entirely different crowd than The Spot catered to. Ole' school music was playing, and the atmosphere was better than Marcus expected from the appearance of the place on the outside. There were people on the dance floor, and a melodic blend of conversations and laughter was in the air. The two men walked through the couples, and Sharod shook hands saying hello to the friendly faces that greeted him. They paused at the bar that ran from the front to the rear of the establishment waiting to get the attention of the barmaid. The stools were filled with patrons who paid no attention to the people standing behind them waiting to order. Two barmaids and a bartender worked the length of the bar pouring drinks and taking money as the orders were shouted at them.

"Two Coors Draft, oh I'm sorry, did you want something stronger?" Sherod turned to Marcus as he ordered holding his hand in the air.

"That's cool, thanks."

The lighting gave them a dim view of the pool tables in the rear, and it was there that Sherod decided they would sit. Marcus followed him through the crowd holding his beer over his head.

"Okay listen Marcus." Sherod spoke a little louder to be heard over the music. The high back of the booth's seats gave the conversation a little privacy.

"There are people who are looked at as weak because they are. But there are others that are weakened by the conditions they choose to live in or with. Janet allowed a lot of things that I would say made her appear to be weak. It's like pushing someone in a corner. For a minute, they may want to give in, or give up. Even so, if you give them a chance to look up, see what the options really are, man they fight back."

"So this is her fight now."

"Yeah, she's fighting to survive. I'd say that."

"I see it as revenge."

"Revenge, revenge for what, and on who?"

"Me for leaving her and the kids; man she wants me to feel guilty about this shit."

"You? Marcus, I don't think this is about you anymore."

"What she's with old dude now, and that ain't about me?"

Sherod took a drink from his frosted bottle and grinned. Marcus began peeling the label from his bottle and raised his eyebrows waiting for an answer.

"Why you grinning man? I'm serious. She got this job and old dude scored, that ain't revenge?"

"I told you to back it up. When did you notice a change in Janet?"

"Yeah, I heard you. When old boy was at the hospital with her; she was talking shit and so was he. We got into it too. She didn't want to talk, and I didn't call her back. I called Faye and well, you know met the kids those times and man it's just messed up."

"What's the real deal Marcus? Are you mad 'cause, she's finally getting herself together or what?"

"That's not the real deal. Old dude is running things. He's got her working for him during the day and playing with him at night."

"So you're jealous."

"Hell no, but she's my wife."

"Marcus, you left her over a year ago. She was your wife then, what the hell is wrong with you?"

"I guess I always knew I was going back home."

"What, you just took a year off from your marriage? It don't work that way my man. You and Karyn still dealing right?"

"Yeah, but I told her that Janet needed me to help with the kids."

"Okay, so help. What's the problem? Look, stop playing with me. I can't down enough beers to be drunk enough to believe you really thought you could just walk back into that girl's life. What was she supposed to be doing in the meantime?"

"She was doing fine."

"Yeah and your definition of fine led her to want to kill herself. She had given up, on her marriage, on a career, on life."

"Her kids, family, me…"

"Hold up Marcus, you walked out brother. You had another woman help you move from your home with your wife and kids. I can remember her begging you to come home, and you ignored her. So I would say your marriage was done then. I agree with you that maybe she should have thought more about her kids, but you know what? She'll make amends with herself and God for that. You and I can't judge her for that."

"And what about this relationship with her boss?"

"What about it? You can't stop her from seeing someone else if that's what's going on, you're with Karyn."

"Man, this is some shit here."

"What do you want, your marriage or Karyn?"

The question hit him again. It beat his conscience more and more lately. He couldn't answer, and Sherod knew why.

"Both."

"What? Are you crazy?"

"Man, I had it like that for a while. Karyn insisted on helping me move, and she wanted to talk with Janet. Passion or maybe even lust told me this chick was what I wanted, and I stayed home as long as I could. I still want her, but I miss home. I miss the kids, and I even miss Janet. But Rod she's changed. I can't let her think she's free to date, and not be a mother to my children, or a wife to me."

Sherod frowned confused with Marcus' statement. He decided he would avoid getting angry. It was useless to argue with a controlling man's appetite. As the barmaid passed their booth, he ordered another round of beer. The crack of the opening break on the billiards table caused Marcus to turn and look at the players. He nodded his head toward the table and smiled. They joined the game challenging the players. Three games later they gave up the rack. The night continued with talk about sports and mingling with the people Sherod knew seated at the bar. Neither said anything more regarding Janet.

27

S aturday mornings became Janet's day for catching up. She did housework in the morning and left the afternoons free for Joy, Erica and M.J. Since her employment, she treated them on the weekend to simple outings, something they never did before. Dr. Norris told her it would create a lasting memory and permanent bond to the children. Now after eight weeks, she felt the outings benefited her more. Janet agreed that it was too soon in the relationship for the children to be on an outing with Richard. He understood and told her to bring the three over to his house for an afternoon cookout in his yard. They would never think of it as a date. He would invite a couple of their clients and their children. No one would suspect he and Janet were dating. Elaine and Walter would be told, but it wouldn't be broadcasted for obvious reasons. Janet was married with three children; that's all anyone else needed to know.

"M.J. let's go, why are you still in the bathroom?"

"Mama he's playing on the video games."

"M.J! I'm gonna be leaving with one child less if you don't get a move on."

"I went in the bathroom. I'm done; that's Erica being Ms. Busy telling on me. Joy is in the bathroom."

"I thought it was you, sorry. Erica are you ready for me to do your hair?"

"Uh huh."

"Joy, let's go baby."

M.J. entered his mother's bedroom and leaned on the frame of her door. He watched his mother combing and brushing his sister's hair. Joy walked pass him tripping over his foot he purposely put in her path.

"Mama! Boy you better quit."

"Okay, that's it. We're not going out if the three of you can't act right."

"Is Daddy gonna be there?"

"No stupid; why would he be at Mommies boss's house?"

"Don't call me stupid M.J. Momma is daddy gonna be there?"

"No Erica; M.J. go get me the burettes on her dresser."

"Daddy will come if you call him. He said you don't call him."

"Erica, Auntie Faye said don't tell."

Joy spoke and realized she was in serious trouble. Tears began to form in her eyes. M.J. entered the room with the Tupperware case filled with burettes. Erica was holding her mouth while Janet stood towering over her seven-year-old waiting for an explanation.

"Mama, she did. She told us not to tell you. M.J. knew too."

"Listen, your father doesn't live here. He's to see you at Auntie's house or at our home, nowhere else. Is that understood? Do you hear me? Nowhere else. If he can't pick you up from your Auntie's or here, he doesn't pick you up okay. I don't want to hear that your father came and got you from somewhere else."

M.J. lowered his head as he spoke slightly above a whisper.

"He picked us up at Auntie's."

Janet stopped putting the burettes in Erica's hair. She refrained from asking her children the particulars. She would talk to Faye. M.J. left the room knowing they would be walking a fine line the rest of the day. It was close to twelve before they were ready to leave.

The ride to Richard's Verona home allowed Janet to calm down. She couldn't understand why Faye didn't tell her Marcus had been there to see the children. There was no harm in his visits, and she would feel better knowing he cared enough to make arrangements with her sister. She put the thought to the back her mind concluding she would have to call Faye for the details. The children talked quietly during the ride still unsure if they were blamed for their father's actions. Janet didn't blame them, how could she? She turned onto Sherwood Drive and looked for the house numbered two-eighteen. The cars parked in the driveway told her that there were plenty of guests in the yard.

"Wow, Mom, look at those cars. Which one is Mr. Burnett's?"

"I don't see his M.J. There it is. It's parked in front of the house the silver Mercedes."

"Yeah, that's nice too."

M.J. had become a car fanatic after going to the New York car show with Sherod. His interest rolled over to the truck and boat show held at the Jacob Javitts Center as well. Sherod enjoyed taking him, and M.J. pointed out what he learned whenever he could.

"That car cost a lot of money Ma."

"I would think so, that's why he's a boss."

"Mommy you're a boss too. You're our boss."

Joy and M.J. laughed at Erica, who had no idea what was so funny. Janet parked behind Richard's car on the street not wanting to block anyone in the driveway. The children got out of the car and were given a visual inspection by their mother. Another family crossed the street and met them at the driveway.

"Hi, I'm Thomas McClain and this is my wife Ruby."

"Hello, I'm Janet. Janet Robinson and these are my children, M.J., Joy and Erica."

Tom as he was later referred to called over his daughter and son who ran ahead of the group and introduced them to Janet and her children.

"It's good to put a face with the name. I'm the CEO from McClain Ventures; I've talked with you on the phone often."

"Yes, I know the account well. Strange how you remember the company more than the name."

"Well Richard and Walter try to get rid of that feeling by having these outings. It's good for business, and it really gives us an outlet."

As they reached the huge yard, Janet's children stood in awe of the jungle gym, volleyball net and trampoline. Children were playing, in all three areas.

"Mommy I want to play."

"Erica let's find Mr. Burnett first, then you all can go and play with the other children."

Janet scanned the yard. She recognized Elaine, who was at the tables with an array of salads, breads, fruit and beverages.

"Hi Elaine."

"Janet, oh I am so glad you're here, and these must be the angels who you often talk about. They're beautiful. The little one looks just like your sister. Hi sweetie."

Erica smiled shyly and hid partially behind her mother's leg.

"Oh this is no place to be shy. There's so much to do here. Look there's a jungle gym, and we have smaller games for you to play. And sir, you must be Marcus Jr."

"Yes, I'm M.J. and this is my sister Joy."

"Well do you want anything right now? Juice, fruit, or the hot dogs are done."

"Mommy can we go play now?"

Joy became impatient watching two girls playing jump rope. Richard walked up behind them tempted to whisper softly in Janet's ear. He settled for tapping on her shoulder and was pleased when she turned and gave him a hug hello.

"Richard, thank you for the invitation, Elaine, I want to thank you both. This place is beautiful."

"It's yours to enjoy; kids make yourselves at home. If you need anything come and get your mom, me, or Ms. Elaine okay?"

Erica stepped out from behind her mother's leg with her thumb in her mouth.

"Can we go now?"

Janet looked at M.J. and Joy. They understood their mother's non-verbal warnings. The three children ran off to play.

"Let me show you the house. Elaine we'll be back in a minute."

Richard and Janet went pass the open-pit grill where Walter stood with a chef's hat and an apron.

"Hey Janet, what's up. I bet you never saw a white man smoke on the grill."

"You must do it well if they gave you an outfit."

"Best white-black barbeque in New Jersey. I even do chopped barbeque. It will make you slap somebody."

"I keep telling him he's more black than white."

"Is Dr. Norris coming?"

Walter smiled as though he didn't hear the question, she asked again.

"Is Dr. Norris here?"

"No, she's at a conference this weekend. She'll be back on Monday."

Richard and Janet entered his home from the decks sliding doors. The entrance was attached to the den where the furniture was upholstered in a multi-green motif. The pastel mint green carpet set if off perfectly. Janet couldn't imagine how they kept the carpet clean. The kitchen was off to the left while the living room and bedrooms were to the right. The house was beautiful. There were four bedrooms, the den, kitchen, dining room, and study to be shown and Richard let Janet take her time admiring each room. Although Janet knew the home belonged to Richard, Elaine's craftiness could be seen in each room. She couldn't imagine living in the luxury he could provide.

"So what do you think?"

"Need you ask? It's beautiful. I'm embarrassed to think that you came to my home."

"Why? I'm certain you've made it comfortable, and I know you have good taste. It's not about its materialistic value but the value you give it as a family."

"Well, I intend to keep the family values intact."

"You don't feel overwhelmed by the clients do you?"

"No, I met Thomas McClain coming into the yard. How many did you invite?"

"Ten maybe fifteen of those that I deal with often, who live locally; we all started out together in business. It's been a long struggle but worth it."

They stopped in the living room, and Janet looked down admiring the hardwood Prego floors.

"The house is beautiful. It looks smaller than what it is. The yard is huge."

"One of the reasons I bought it. I love Verona and didn't want to move if I ever got married. Now it doesn't matter. I'd move in a heartbeat if my wife wanted to."

"Yeah, marriage changes things. Introduce me to some of the clients. I don't want to be the stranger whom they begin whisper about."

Richard turned Janet to face him and looked into her eyes. She knew the kiss was coming, and she didn't want it to seem like she was anxious. She dropped her eyes and felt his finger lifting her chin. He gently positioned her, so he could kiss her as he wanted to. The kiss was soft and teased of passion. He kissed her deeper, a promise that it was meant and not just done because he could. Janet felt a warm feeling inside and hoped he didn't ignite a craving she hadn't felt in more than a year. The two separated when the sound of the screen door was heard.

"Mr. Burnett and this must be Janet. Hi, I'm Stephanie, Anthony's wife."

The two greeted her and Richard thanked her for coming. She was looking for the bathroom and followed Richard's directions to get there. He and Janet returned to the yard. Richard introduced her to the clients. Their greetings may have been genuine but Janet felt a bit uncomfortable about engaging in long conversations with any of them. Janet made her way back to the table where Elaine was sitting with her friends from church.

28

Walter called Lashauna as he was leaving Richard's home. She told him she wasn't feeling well. He told everyone she was out of town because he was tired of making excuses for her. Whenever there was an outing where she would come into contact with Richard, she was guaranteed to back out. The first few times she did it Walter made excuses for the both of them. Then he noticed it was the more intimate occasions that bothered her. She couldn't tolerate being around Richard for longer than an hour. They couldn't double date, go on weekend conferences, seminars, or even spend evenings at each other's homes. He needed to know why.

Walter wanted to confirm his suspicions. He loved Lashauna but always wondered had her feelings for Richard been buried. He and Richard talked extensively about his dating her. Walter wanted to make sure that his lifelong friend wouldn't be offended. He didn't give much thought to discussing her feelings about Richard. Lashauna flirted and teased him for months keeping him at bay. She mentioned Richard being upset with them about their relationship but allowed Walter's entry into her apartment, and he hoped her heart. He needed her to explain why she couldn't be a part of his social network when it included Richard.

The phone rang again and went to her voice mail. Walter put the key in his door and smelled her perfume. He concluded she didn't answer because she was at his apartment, what a pleasant surprise. He cut on the light in the foyer and took off his shoes. He knew if she didn't yell out his name, she was sleeping. It was just after midnight, an early night for Walter. If they had been together he would have still been at Richard's house. Her smell was faint though evident. He imagined her in the shower preparing for his arrival. He decided to spark up the night with a little wine.

Walter poured two glasses of Chardonnay over ice and proceeded to his bedroom. There was dim lighting in the living room, but he knew the path she prepared had a one direction. He opened the door slowly and noticed the covers were, as he suspected pulled back. He didn't see Lashauna lying in the bed. He sat the glasses on the nightstand and went to check the bathroom. There was no sign of her.

Baffled he stood at the end of the bed, and that's when he noticed a note on the pillow. Reading the note over again he decided not to follow the directions she left behind.

"I waited as long as I could. Not feeling well I showered, and rested. I thought you would have been considerate enough not to stay at Richard's all night. I guess your friendship with him is stronger than our relationship. I'm sure you're ready with the wine glasses and a stiff dick. Baby it ain't that easy. I think we ought to discuss our relationship and how I fit into your life. So when you get this message you can either; call me and hope I'll answer or come over and show me the man you really are."

Walter slowly took off his clothes and downed both glasses of wine before showering and going to bed.

29

*L*ashauna checked her schedule marking off the clients whose charts needed updating in the computer. Janet Robinson's chart was in the pile. Her appointment was at three. The doctor was pleased with Janet's progress but was beginning to be uncertain about her own stability. Listening to Janet over the past two months was becoming routine. Giving her encouragement and a direction to rebuild her self-esteem was easier than she thought. Janet openly expressed her desire to talk through her problems and experiences while participating in the therapeutic exercises Dr. Norris put before her.

If Janet had been any other patient, the exercises would not have been so intense. They both were hesitant to move on to the next level of treatment. As she looked through the evaluations, she prepared after each session, she read over the highlighted sections again. They would have to delve into Janet's personal relationships before she could finish the documents.

Lashauna looked at the clock. She was on her third cup of coffee and hadn't been at her desk two hours. Her eyes fell on a picture of Walter and Richard. She rubbed her fingers gently across the image of Richard's hair and face. He didn't come to church after his barbeque on Saturday. She looked for him to be seated in the fifth pew near his sister, his usual seat. After glancing through the congregation and not finding his face in the audience, she lost her need to hear the sermon. Excusing herself, she left the sanctuary and didn't stop although a few members of the Sick and Shut-In Ministry called her name.

The doctor sighed. Janet's therapy would have to take another direction. Lashauna didn't think she would be able to discuss her patient's relationship with Richard, if it went further than an employer to an employee. She picked up the phone and put it back in its cradle. She would have to think about how she'd proceed. Walter would have to be her unsuspected help.

The morning went by quickly as she busied herself with other tasks. She did her rounds watching her time as not to go beyond one o'clock. Walter promised to stop by and bring her lunch since she told him she was swamped.

The excuse was believable and Walter was predictable. The grilled chicken salad was more than enough, and their conversation was filled with tension. Lashauna chose to ignore what was obvious.

"Shauna, what's the problem?" She held her answer knowing he would continue to question her. "You and I both know there's a problem, what is it?"

"How was your night out?"

"What Saturday? Why is that always a tender spot with you? Anywhere I go with Richard or any time I spend with him is a problem. Why?"

The question opened the door. "How was it?"

"What do you mean? It was a barbeque. Clients, their families, food, and drinks what did you think it was?"

"Hmm, so were you the only one without a date?"

"No, there were other people there without a date as you put it. Shauna, I'm growing tired of this. I thought we discussed the fact that you and Richard didn't have any dealings or feelings for each other. I mean, I was the one against us being involved. You practically..."

"Seduced you? How many times are you going to remind me of that? I only asked who had dates Walt; it's not a big deal." Lashauna got up from her seat behind her desk and began bagging the condiments and leftovers. "Are you done with this?"

Walter handed her his tin dish and cover. She reached for his soda, and he stopped her hand with a gentle touch.

"Let's not argue about this. Tell me, do you still have feelings for Richard?"

"Who's asking him or you?"

"Shauna, Richard doesn't ask about you that way. I've told you that time and time again. As a matter of a fact since you're questioning dates, you'll be glad to know your patient has swooned Richard off his feet."

She heard his words and pretended they didn't penetrate her heart like a knife. It was what she needed to hear but didn't want to ask. She continued to clean the desk making more than the required trips from her office to the garbage receptacle in the hall. She often told him the salad dressing, the oil and vinegar, permeated the air and her clothing when left in the office trash can. It now served as an excuse to pull herself together. Walter didn't notice her change of attitude.

"So when did they begin dating."

"I don't think it's an official thing. He invited her to lunch and the cook out. They seem to get along well, and her children had a good time too."

"She brought her children there?"

"The cookout was for families, the clients had their children with them. Elaine enjoyed them the most."

"What time did they leave? I mean did you leave?"

"About midnight, with everyone else; I think Janet left around eleven."

Lashauna's thoughts were ahead of the conversation. She envisioned Janet and her children eating breakfast with Richard the next morning in the house that she walked through often in her dreams of the future.

"Sounds like everyone had a good time. Maybe I should have come, huh."

"That's what I've been trying to tell you."

"Walter it's just difficult to be in the company of Richard knowing he and I didn't work out. I don't want him upset with you because of what we have." Lashauna's quick response diverted his thinking.

"Yes, I hadn't thought of that. You're right. We've got one of those conferences coming up in a few weeks. Maybe the four of us could go. It could ease the tension between the two of you." Walter became excited about what he thought was the solution. "I think Richard plans to ask Janet to go with him."

"When is that baby?"

"Right after Labor Day, I think it's the following weekend. Do you think you can set aside a weekend for us?"

Lashauna looked at her calendar. Her eyes caught a glimpse of Walter and Richard again in the framed picture.

"Shauna, I've got to get back to the office. Think about it okay?" Walter stood realizing she had become distracted.

"Yeah, I'll mark the calendar. Will I see you later?" She stood hoping he hadn't noticed the attention she gave the candid image. Walter smiled and blew her a kiss from the door. She knew then; he noticed.

30

*J*anet rearranged the magazine rack in the waiting area and checked the incoming and outgoing boxes for the last time. Elaine called in to let her know she wouldn't be in the office, which gave her an added list of jobs that needed to be completed. After working all day balancing both positions she agreed Elaine had more than enough work to do. Walter and Richard met with her Monday afternoon with her new list of responsibilities. She hadn't tackled any of her work and leaving early would put off her scheduled assignments until her return in the morning.

Walter and Richard smiled passing her desk periodically during the course of the day. Neither questioned how she was managing the phones, the appointments that arrived early or late, the mail, or the correspondence that was to be sorted and checked.

She picked up the last of the letters that awaited Richard's signature. It was then she remembered her appointment with Dr. Norris was at three. It was close to two o'clock and with Elaine being off, there would be no one covering the front office if she left. She picked up the intercom and hung up quickly when she noticed the light turned red indicating her boss was on his private line.

"Lashauna, hold on please. Yes, Janet."

"Richard, I don't know if you remembered I have to leave at two."

"No problem. Just bring the letters; no leave them on the desk. I'll come out and sign them. Walter should be back soon. We'll be fine. I'll call you later on tonight, if that's okay."

"That will be fine. I'll see you in the morning."

Janet left the letters on Elaine's desk and looked around making sure she hadn't forgotten anything on her list undone. She walked out the office and hearing Richard laughing realized he must have taken a break from returning his clients calls.

"Sorry lady, so you were saying?"

"I was surprised you couldn't make it to church on Sunday. What's so funny about that?"

"It's funny you went to church looking for me. You were invited to my house and chose not to come."

"I was out of town."

"According to your man, you were due to return Monday. You got back early enough to get dressed for church and changed your mind before the sermon? That's amusing. C'mon girl I ain't Walter."

"What does that mean?" Lashauna's sheepish grin could be detected over the phone. She had adjusted herself in her chair, comfortably awaiting Janet's arrival.

"He would believe you actually went out of town, I know better."

"Well if you must know so does he." She began to twirl the end of her hair pleased he was willing to play along. Someone noticed her actions at the church and shared them with Elaine. His comment proved she had been a part of someone's discussion. "I didn't want to be overlooked by you because of clients and others."

"I don't think any of the guests could complain about being overlooked. It's obvious Walter has left your office, is your afternoon free?"

Lashauna sat up shocked that he didn't know Janet's appointment was in another half an hour. Her thoughts immediately went to him inviting her for an afternoon rendezvous, one she would have to refuse.

"Yes, but I'm free after four; I have another client to see and then I'm done."

Richard added suspense to the conversation. He didn't comment as though he was checking his availability. Lashauna's game was old and he had no intention on being her pawn. "Well my dear, some of us have to work for a living. Do you want Walt to call you?"

The doctor let out a sigh. Richard had a way of being annoying. "I called you remember? I know how to reach him."

"Oh, I'm sorry. Will you be at church Sunday?"

"I had planned on it why?"

"Look for me, I'll be there."

The phone went dead before she hung up.

31

*F*aye listened to her niece and nephew recounting their day at Mr. Burnett's house. She and Sherod talked extensively the night before expressing a difference of opinion regarding Janet's relationship with her boss. Sherod repeated parts of his conversation with Marcus telling Faye that no man who loves his family would think the way he did. Faye was determined to keep her hopes alive. She owed her sister that much. Marcus would have to tell her he didn't want his marriage. The guilt of knowing he was cheating before Janet was officially told always ate at her. If there was a chance, she could reignite their feelings; maybe she could rid herself of the guilt that she felt extended to Janet's attempted suicide.

Talking to Marcus would be too obvious. She didn't want him to think Janet asked her to speak to him. Karyn was relentless, and she hadn't spoken to her since finding out she went too far with "just teasing" her brother-n-law. Karyn and Faye's paths crossed at the gym where they both were in the same aerobics class. They had lunch and shopped together on occasion. Faye made the mistake of introducing Marcus, the cute man with the dimples, making sure to mention he was her sister's husband. It seemed that turned Karyn's curiosity on and the flirting became a three-day a week ritual.

Marcus used the week as a prelude to temptation. After picking up Faye as a favor to Janet and Sherod that Monday, Wednesday and Friday, he learned more about Karyn than Faye cared to admit. She would have done anything to relive the week and rent the car that the mechanic offered her. Three weeks later Karyn told her she wasn't interested in the aerobics class or the gym anymore. Marcus picked Karyn up the same afternoon.

Faye looked up her address in the member's catalogue and went to see her later that evening when she thought Marcus would have gone home. His car was parked outside of her unit and the guilt began to mount. She didn't want to be a part of their fling and hoped it wouldn't last. Karyn admitted to their sexual encounters leaving out what she called the embarrassing details.

The details kept Marcus attracted to her and Janet grew tired of his lies and late nights. Faye kept her mouth closed and now she wished she hadn't. She looked at the children playing again and picked up the phone. After two rings, she could hear music playing in the background.

"Hello."

"Hi, Karyn is Marcus there?"

"Faye, how are you?"

"Alright I guess, is he there?" She questioned, annoyed she had to speak with Karyn at all.

"What? You can't speak to me a minute. You can't still hold ill feelings toward me."

"No ill feelings. Come to think of it, no feelings. I just want to speak to Marcus please."

"Well he's not here. He's supposed to be talking with your sister today about the kids or something. So I guess he's with her."

Faye knew that wasn't true. Janet had been avoiding his calls as usual or at least that's what he said.

"Hmm... Well can you tell him to call me please?"

"Is there a message I can relay to him?"

"No, thanks that's okay."

"C'mon Faye, you act as though I wouldn't give him the message."

"Karyn, does it even bother you that he's married?"

"No. It doesn't bother him either."

"Later Karyn."

Karyn's response was inaudible. She pushed the end call button and waited for the dial tone. After dialing the seven digits she thought about the fool she was making of herself.

"I should have called his cell first, what the hell was I thinking." The phone rang twice, and then she heard his voice.

"Marcus, we need to talk."

"Faye? What's wrong with you?" Her voice sounded as though she was about to cry. He switched to his blue tooth thinking there was interference on the line. "Faye, can you hear me?"

"Are you on your way to Janet's?"

"Not right now. I was going there later."

"I want to talk to you, if I can, before you go to visit her. Are you just going there to see the kids?"

"Well, I had other intentions? Why? What's wrong?"

"Other intentions?" Faye closed her eyes in prayer.

"Well, I know you and Sherod are helping with her recovery and all. I want her to know I'm there for her."

"Marcus." Faye checked to see if Sherod or the children could hear her. She decided to whisper. "Don't go there with the thought you can live in both homes."

"What? Why are you whispering?"

"I don't want your kids or my husband to hear me. Did you understand what I said?"

"Yeah, I just don't know what you're talking about."

"Yes you do. You know full damn well what I'm talking about. She's not the same Marcus. Her life is changing daily. You better come with your 'A' game or forget coming. I shouldn't even give you a heads up, but I love your kids. You got somebody else and there's somebody looking forward to getting with Janet. If you keep playing she'll be out of your life for good. I told you when you got with Karyn it was a bad move. I tried to forget it, but I can't. I should have told

Janet what I knew, and maybe she would have been stronger about losing you. Well, she's got someone who's willing to give her strength. I can't keep telling her to wait on your sorry ass. Wake up Marcus."

"I got this Faye. I think I told you that before. I told your husband the same thing. Janet loves me and our family. I have decided to go home, you know a couple of days a week, to help her. She'll be glad to have me there, and things will eventually get back to normal."

"A few days a week; what are you supposed to be?"

"Her husband, Faye we haven't lived together in a year. It's gonna take a minute to get it back to where it was."

"That's just what I'm telling you fool. She doesn't want it back. She wants something entirely different."

32

*J*anet couldn't answer the question without pausing. "Can you rephrase the question?"

It was the last of the questions Dr. Norris was asking before they started their next session. Each session began with questions or a self-evaluation of how Janet was coping with sleeping, eating, work, family and pressures. Janet preferred the evaluations. It was easier for her to just tell the doctor what had gone on since their last session than answer questions that seemed to pierce her tattered defense.

"I'll try to rephrase it. You've been here for eight sessions, two months of counseling, if that's what you want to call it. Tell me what has been the most beneficial part of these sessions for you?"

"I guess being able to talk without the thought of conviction. You don't judge me. As you know, I've been judged by those I love most of my life. I know the difference now, and I don't think I want a relationship with anyone whose objective is to be judgmental."

"Okay, now let's move on. We've done the fundamentals. You've begun to recognize who you are and who you want to be. Most importantly, you've decided that you want to live. You have your home and family intact, for the most part. I know you want your husband to be a part of that..."

"I don't know about that anymore."

Lashauna began writing on the pad she picked up after answering the last questions on the evaluation form. "Can you tell me what you mean?" She watched as Janet sat back in the plush chair. She looked at her outfit which she was sure hadn't been worn more than twice. Lashauna wondered how much she had spent to fit in at Burnett and Reed LLC. Her manicure and makeup were beautiful, and every strand of her hair was neatly in place. Her look was impeccable. The doctor knew she worked hard at competing with the clients they dealt with daily.

"Sure, I don't want to wait on what he wants. I need to live. I don't sleep well wondering what he's doing with her, to her or for her. I don't eat well hoping he'll call or stop by and sometimes fearful that he'll do either. I pray that when I do see him; we don't argue or fight. I don't want him prying into what I'm doing now, who I go out with or where I go. Doctor, I think I've fallen out of love with my husband. It's been over a year, and I finally think I'm over him."

Lashauna cringed hoping she wouldn't mention Richard and love in the same sentence. She could see that Richard would love Janet's appearance, a mere façade of the woman he needed in his life. She couldn't possibly deal with the challenges loving a man of his caliber would present.

"What has brought you to that point? I mean, have you decided to be alone or has someone else stepped into the picture?"

Janet held her thoughts to herself. Richard had indeed stepped into the picture, but she didn't know if Lashauna had stepped out.

"No, I just think it's time. I need time to fall in love with myself again. After all I was trying to do myself in. This therapy has shown me that I didn't really know who I was or what I wanted. I have three children and me. I need to establish love in that circle first."

The writing on the pad began when she started her answer and went longer than what Janet thought was necessary. She smiled to herself thinking about the doctor's comments.

"So I guess that's where we should start, your relationships with others. Let's start with those that affect your personal life, such as your husband."

"There's not much to start with, our relationship is over."

"Is it really? You have three children together. I would like to think that your relationship will always be there is some way."

Janet was becoming uncomfortable. Dr. Norris brought up a point she hadn't explored. Of course, they would have to have some type of relationship. Why hadn't she thought of that? Marcus had become like the pimple she would get when it was that time of the month. She would pick at it; it would become an ugly blemish, and she would pray for it to go away. Now the doctor was telling her he or it, one in the same, would be returning. Yes, he was as frustrating as that menstrual pimple, a name, she and Faye gave it during their teenage years.

"I really hadn't thought of him or it in that way." Lashauna wrote "it" on the pad with Marcus' name in parentheses. Janet smirked at the pad and continued. "I can't continue to think of him as my husband. He lives with another woman. That was another thing I hadn't come to grips with. I wanted my marriage as any woman would. I wanted my husband, the father of my children in my home. Well, I guess after a year I had to stop kidding myself. Part of my problem, I think, came from me pretending he would be coming home after...."

"After what? Janet, you can't blame yourself for his straying from the marriage."

"You're right and that's why I said, I need to move on."

"On as in a relationship with another man?"

"No, on as in living without Marcus; there is life after your husband leaves you, right?"

"Right." The buzzer sounded softly indicating the hour had ended. Both turned looking at the clock as though the timer could possibly be wrong.

"There's our time. Janet I wanted to mention to you that I was going to put in your evaluation with the recommendation that your visits be cut to maybe twice a month. I don't think you're at risk of endangering yourself, and you certainly have recaptured your spirit and will to live. How do you feel about that?"

"I'd much rather that you tell them to kiss my you know what, but then that wouldn't be right. Dr. Norris, can I call you Lashauna? The session is over." Janet smiled teasingly. "Doctor, to be honest with you, I don't think I needed you as a doctor. I know you didn't want to have me as a patient because I work with Richard, but I needed an ear, one that would listen and not be bias. God sent me two. Richard was one, and you became the other. I guess I needed two friends."

"I'm glad the sessions have been of comfort, but I hope they've been useful for more than just a friendship hour."

"Take of the lab coat girl. I needed a sistah to talk to. Maybe you didn't choose me, but I chose you. Write your recommendation but if you really don't need me to come but what did you say, twice a month? Hell we can do lunch or something. Ask me what's up? How you doing? And check your pad if you like, but I'm really not beat for these formal sessions. I would like us to remain friends though. My sister is it for me, and sometimes I don't think she's really honest with me. Tiffany and Carol call every now and then, but I think they don't want to deal with someone who wanted to kill themselves."

Lashauna would have to think about it. She had never befriended a patient. Then the question was honesty; how honest could she be about her feelings for Richard?

33

Marcus wanted to talk to his wife. He knew Faye was hinting toward the relationship Janet had with her boss. Richard Burnett would have to be more than money to Janet. Money didn't impress her. Marcus wasn't impressed with him and couldn't see what, other than a job, he had to offer. It was close to four o'clock. Janet wouldn't be home, but he could wait for her. He was closer to her apartment than Faye's and Sherod wouldn't want to have another one-sided conversation with him.

Janet would have to leave Montclair and go to Bloomfield to pick up the children before returning home. Marcus could collect his thoughts while waiting in the parking lot. He turned at the corner of Bloomfield Avenue and High Street. The sight of his complex brought his first feeling of guilt. He slowly shook his head as he found a spot in the lot. He sat looking out his windshield at the door where he carried Janet across the threshold. Closing his eyes, he let the memory subside and got out of the car before another memory clouded his thoughts.

Sherod's comments rattled in his mind; the meaning was still unclear. Marcus wanted her to miss him; it was time he came home. He fumbled with his keys in his hands as he closed his car door. He walked to the unit as he had in the past not as a visitor but as a returning tenant. Finding the key for the front door, he turned the lock. He heard the tumbler disengage and smiled.

The Mountain Breeze air fresheners gave the house that clean smell that Janet seemed so pleased with. Marcus never noticed it when he lived there, but she was right; it was nice. The time of day gave just enough light in the apartment as Marcus made his way from room to room looking for nothing particular.

He went in the kitchen, checked the cabinets, the refrigerator, and under the sink. The tools he left were still in place, and again, he smiled. The closets looked just as he remembered everything was as it had been. There was nothing different. Janet hadn't made any changes, how could she not miss his presence? He went to the bathroom and again did a search and checked her inventory.

Behind the bathroom door hung her robe and a nightgown. The fragrance of her toiletries caused him to sit on the toilet lid pausing to take it all in. Marcus no longer held a spot in her heart. He needed to know did he still cross her mind. She changed the shower curtains they were now a soothing color. Marcus complained about a soft, powdery bathroom. He imagined that being one of her first tasks. That was minor; she could change them again.

The closet in the hall held most of their storage, seasonal decorations, extra linen and towels and room for items left by guest. He opened both sides of the sliding door. The closet went the length of the wall opposite the bathroom and the children's rooms. It looked roomy now without his golf clubs, and other belongings.

The thought of checking the children's room crossed his mind, but he looked at his watch. Today wouldn't be the day to talk with her. He needed to check the living room. Her room and the children's room would take more time. Curiosity boosted his adrenaline. He returned to the living room and didn't see anything that would make a visitor think Janet Robinson had been married. The pictures of the family, the wedding, even casual shots of Marcus and the children were no longer on the mantel. The photo albums weren't in the bookcase and he wondered if she burned them. Pictures of the children, her mother and brother, Sherod and Faye were in new frames and displayed throughout the room.

The room was clean, no spotless. Janet had always been a good housekeeper unlike Karyn, who waited until they couldn't walk through the rooms to clean. She never did any other cleaning until Marcus complained. They were so different, but the contrast is what turned him on. There were no obvious signs that Janet was dating anyone. He wondered if she wanted to; he needed to know. It was close to five; he would inspect the other rooms later. He sat back on the couch breathing deeply.

He wondered if she would know he had been there. He thought of leaving a clue, or just leaving a note to let her know he wasn't out of her life. Anger began to build as he remembered her making excuses for not returning his calls. She thought everything through. How their lives would be; how many children they would have; his career; her education; where the children would go to school and happily ever after. Janet had it all planned, then Karyn stepped into his life as an alternative. His fling ruined the plans.

Marcus scanned the room; he wasn't in the same home. He was going nowhere with his life, and Karyn wasn't filling the void. He looked at his watch. He'd be back.

34

The weeks that followed seemed like the beginning of a dream that Janet had early in her teenage years. Richard became her knight in shinny armor. The work at Burnett and Reed consumed her day, and the couple spent their evenings dining and dating. Richard respected her home and her children, careful not to take her away from being a mother. Janet wouldn't tell Richard but she wished he would disrespect her just once, and she wouldn't be mad if it happened twice.

Her schedule would be changing once the children began school in another week. She made arrangements with Faye and Sherod for the afternoon pickup. Sherod seemed pleased. He would still be able to see them daily, but Faye was hesitant. Janet wondered if the summer wore out their welcome. She hadn't mentioned anything to Faye about her allowing Marcus to visit, but she wondered if he was still pressuring her.

It was another Saturday of morning chores and laundry, but the afternoon would be different. M.J. was with his uncle, and the girls were having a tea party with their grandmother. Sam told Janet he would come and get M.J. the last two weekends of the summer, and the girls would spend the same weekends entertaining their mother. Janet and Faye protested, but their mother agreed with their younger brother it was only four days.

Jocelyn was doing a lot better and there were no doctor appointments to interfere with the weekends filled with dainty activities. Janet called them before the teapot went off, and they were setting the table. She could only imagine her mother and the small teacups pretending the crumpets were delicious and so much better than any other she ever had. Joy and Erica would be giggling and of course pouring more tea. The girls enjoyed their grandmother when she was healthy and full of spirit. Janet was glad she would make their weekends special.

Sam was concerned about M.J. Sherrod mentioned him not wanting to see Marcus, and the two men decided to be more than just uncles. M.J. seemed fine to Janet, but what would she know about his feelings. He didn't talk to his mother about his father. She called him after talking to the girls. He laughed when Sam told him his mother was checking on him. M.J. pretended he didn't want her to call when he ran out the door the night before, but he told her he missed her as the call ended. M.J. was growing up quickly, but he would always be her baby.

Janet didn't tell Richard she had two free weekends. She wanted to be without a schedule or time to be ready for anything. The Annual Marketing, Advertising and Promotional Conference was scheduled in two weeks, and she was pleased Richard asked her to attend. The Conference was being held in upstate New York. The four days promised to be fun filled and resourceful. Richard and Walter were introducing her to clients that needed a more personal touch. The small pool of clients included Wall Street executives and bankers. Janet was their personal liaison and was on call for them after hours. They handled international trade and stocks, and she loved the work, which included advertising and promotions.

It was a new facet for Burnett and Reed. The expansion of the company came as a surprise to her, but she welcomed the challenge. She was looking forward to traveling with them and learning more about the business. Walter thanked her for accepting the invitation. He hoped Lashauna would do the same.

Dr. Norris did as she said and recommended Janet's therapy sessions be reduced to twice a month for the balance of her prescribed treatment. She didn't mention Janet's invitation to friendship, but she did call her a few times between sessions. Janet thought about calling her to go shopping. She still had the bathroom to clean. Maybe she would call Faye to join them.

She picked up her phone and checked the last calls that came in. Marcus called her at nine; she must have been vacuuming the carpet, she didn't hear the phone ring. He didn't leave a message like he normally did. It didn't matter it would only say, call him. She was sure he knew the children weren't home. Faye would have told him. The thought crossed her mind again. Why would Faye tell him? Why did Faye tell him to visit the children there and not tell her about it? Faye loved to shop. She would let the doctor analyze her sister's intentions.

35

*I*t was close to one o'clock and Lashauna was having second thoughts about an outing with a patient and her sister. She only agreed, thinking she and Janet would be alone. It wasn't until the end of the conversation that she was told, "I hope you don't mind Faye joining us." She wanted to end the doctor-patient relationship two months ago, after the initial recommended sessions were done. After Walter told her Janet was definitely dating Richard, she lied and told her there would have to be at least another four sessions to complete the prescribed therapy. That would guarantee Janet's visits to her office for another two months regardless of what their personal relationship revealed. After all she did tell her in the beginning it was a conflict of interest, and Janet knew what the conflict was.

Although Walter confirmed they were seeing each other, she didn't notice a change in Janet's attitude. She didn't mention Richard or any other man as being special. If he was showering her with gifts, or taking her out, it didn't seem to change her responses about any of her relationships. Though Lashauna found it strange there was no mention of what she would suspect made Janet feel better, she held her questions for the right time.

Janet seemed to be more concerned about her relationship with her sister. There were feelings she wanted to share with Faye, but she was fearful of how it would be received. During the last two sessions that was the topic, Janet's fear of old and new relationships.

Lashauna needed to get closer so her new friend would reveal her innermost feelings.

She allowed Janet to talk freely without questions, as much as she liked. The freedom to speak without a peaked eyebrow response would help her overcome those fears. Lashauna was beginning to like her off topic conversations but not enough to cosign the relationship with her and Richard.

Janet let it be known that Marcus had been using Faye to keep an eye on her and the children. She no longer trusted her sister the way she had in the past. She went as far to say she was building a trusted bond with the almighty doctor who saved her wretched soul.

Lashauna heard the sound of Janet's horn outside her kitchen window. She looked on the counter for her keys. The horn sounded again. She waved her hand out the window for Janet to see she was on her way out. She'd keep her thoughts about being the chosen one; the one the patients could trust, the one who was still in love with her boyfriend's business partner, Dr. Lashauna Norris to herself. She knew she was the one who needed to be saved.

The day was beautiful and just from walking down her cobbled walk to Janet's car Lashauna regretted not getting out earlier. Janet unlocked the passenger door, and the doctor got in smiling.

"Girl, it's beautiful out. We started this day too late."

"Well I don't have a time clock to punch, no kids and no man. If my sister says she has to be back early we can still hang out if you want."

"I didn't know it was this nice out. I expected that damn heat from yesterday and the day before, this is really comforting. How are you? I haven't seen you since the what, fifth or sixth? When is your next appointment?"

"Thursday, I was tempted to cancel on your ass. Today will be a session if I'm right about Faye."

"So you still think she's filling Marcus in huh?"

"I just don't understand why. She never cared for him like that. I mean they get or got along well, even Sherod still talks to him but ... maybe, maybe, I'm paranoid." Janet threw her hand over the passenger's seat and looked out the back window as she backed into the street exiting the driveway.

"Maybe she thinks she's helping you and him get back together."

Lashauna was glad she agreed to shop with them. Faye might be helpful in keeping Janet out of Richard's grasp. Walter did say that he was still pursuing her.

"That's not up to her and besides she should talk to me about what I want first. I really don't want his tired ass back. I haven't had a stress headache or an argument since the hospital incident. I can do without his careless love. I haven't seen any signs of him trying to leave that tramp he's with." She pointed to Lashauna's seatbelt. After she was sure she was strapped in she put the car in drive and pulled off.

"Okay, what signs were you expecting?"

"C'mon now, take off that damn lab coat. You and I both know if he made a move to come home or see me; she would have made the tramp call."

"Tramp call?"

"Yeah, he may be your husband, but he's my man. If you were doing what he needs and not what you think he wants he wouldn't be here with me. I call it the call of desperation. They all do it. Why would I call someone's wife and tell them some mess like that? But that's what they do. Ms. Karyn Spalling has not called. Marcus hasn't made a serious attempt to leave her. Therefore, I'm not interested in him being secret squirrel trying to spy on me."

"Hmm, so are you saying that if she had called you would have considered taking him back?"

"Lashauna, did you hear me? I don't want his sorry ass back. I'm fine."

"Girl the winters coming, bed gets cold and lonely," replied the doctor with a contagious laugh. They both laughed as they envisioned a winter's night with Richard in their bed.

Janet answered breaking their sensual thoughts, "My nights won't get that lonely. I've done a winter without him. I think this winter will be better than the last."

Lashauna saw an opening. "Why will this one be so much better you got someone to fill that side of the bed?"

"Sure do. The two little ones that have filled it since he's been gone, Joy and Erica, even M.J. will have to find his room this year. He's getting too big to share a bed with us."

They continued to Faye's home with idle chat between them. Janet told Lashauna how much she appreciated her accepting the invitation to an afternoon out. She promised not to put her on the spot by shopping cheap, but she definitely couldn't afford not to look for sales. Lashauna didn't respond but made a mental note. It was obvious; Richard didn't give her money to shop for the conference.

They turned the corner and slowed down as they approached Faye's home. Again, Janet blew the horn. She moved a few items in the back seat while mumbling her children hadn't cleaned the back of the car as they were told. Lashauna's thoughts returned to her bedroom. She wondered if Richard was willing to wait for Janet to put her children out of the bed for him. She would have to ask him.

36

Richard worked most of the morning in his home preparing files and budget proposals for upcoming meetings. He sat motionless after Elaine announced Walter's car was pulling into the carport. He glanced at the grandfather clock in the corner of the room. Walter gave it to him as a birthday gift a few years prior saying the room needed a bit of character. Richard had to agree it added a special touch to his office space at home.

He relaxed easing into the high back winged chair and listened as Walter complimented Elaine about the aroma that filled the kitchen. He had become so accustomed to her cooking he could tell her the menu without opening a pot. Elaine laughed as he told her he would be back for Sunday dinner.

"You know I like to start my cooking on Saturdays."

"I'm not going to ask for any today. I'll be back."

The laughter continued. Richard could hear Walter's footsteps as he headed to speak with his friend.

"Hey guy, what's up?"

"That's my question. What brings you this way?"

"Oh, I can't just be in the neighborhood?"

Richard didn't answer. He gave Walter a snide glance as he returned to sorting the papers on his desk. Walter picked up a few of the printed sheets and talked without turning his attention from the reports.

"Are you still interested in Shauna?"

Richard froze. He turned his head as if he was adjusting his hearing. "What?"

"I need to know man. I think she's waiting for you to make a move."

"You are one weird dude. I think I told you that before. If I had intentions on making a move, as you say, why would I tell you?"

"I'm your friend."

"And that's why I wouldn't be making a move."

"If I wasn't dealing with her now, let's say it was someone else, would you?"

"No. She's not my type. I told you that too. Obviously, she's not your type either."

Walter put the papers down and sighed deeply. "I'm not her type, maybe your right. Richard she's shot out over you not me. This is really becoming a problem for us."

"Us? You're talking about you and her right?"

"Yeah, I can see right through her lies. I need your help."

"My help? Not a problem, I'll stay away from her crazy ass."

"She's not crazy man. I just need to know she's over you."

"Wait, she didn't say she was still into me did she?"

"No. I did. She won't admit it. That's what I mean. I really ought to leave her alone but I can't. You know, I think I'm... never mind."

"Yeah, she got you whipped. She didn't tell you she wanted to be with me but you think... What the hell is that about?"

"Okay so appease me. I'm inviting her to the Conference. She probably won't go but if you talk her into it I can really see her reaction when she sees you with Janet. She's still going right?"

"Hmm. She needs to see it to believe it huh?"

Richard suggested that Walter tell her before Janet mentioned it at any of the sessions.

"You knew that?"

Richard stopped again and looked at his friend. Walter was serious. Richard could read his feelings without asking. He was hurt, hoping not to lose a woman he fell in love with. A woman Richard warned him about.

"Yes, I knew it. She's stubborn and because she's a shrink, she thinks she can predict how others feel. I can't deal with her personality and to be honest I don't think you can either. You got up close and personal, and you know what they say about you white boys that taste a bit of brown sugar."

"Yeah, Domino just ain't the same no more."

The comment broke the tension and as if on cue Elaine brought them both a slice of apple pie.

"You're spoiled Richard Burnett."

"And you just come here to get spoiled, thanks sis."

"Enjoy. I'm going over to Mildred's, be back later. I cut the pots off. Don't worry about the kitchen. I'll deal with it when I come back." Walter waved with his mouth full and signaled the pie was delicious. He swallowed giving himself time to savor its taste before continuing the conversation.

"Richard why is Shauna so uncomfortable with you around? Did the two of you have some unfinished business?"

"I guess you could say that, but you'll have to talk to her about it. If she was someone else I would tell you, but my mouth is closed. She's your girl man, deal with it."

"You and her, I guess I was lucky to get her attention."

Richard refused to tell him what he really thought. Lashauna's plan backfired, and she didn't want to tell Walter he had been used. Any black man would have read between the lines. If Walter had been black, Richard might have told him. He didn't want his friend to be a patient, so he never let on that he was purposely picked up. He thought by now he would be enjoying the ride. Walter used his napkin to clean his mouth before speaking again.

"You ever had the feeling that you were in the way of someone's desires?"

"I don't know, why, you think you're blocking Shauna's desires?"

"That's what I want to find out. The only problem is if she desires you where does that leave me?"

"Walter, promise me you won't get mad when I say this."

Walter sat up ready to listen to any advice Richard could give him.

"Black women are different, especially those that have that prestigious job and a degree to back it. They want what they want when they want it. Let's just say I didn't agree with her plans for us. She's been trying to convince me since then that I lost an opportunity. What she doesn't understand is I don't mind missing out. I wished you well when you said you wanted to date her, be with her, love her. I still wish you well. But man, don't be surprised by her attitude when we're in the same room, she's upset because I backed out of what she thought was a relationship. Maybe she's embarrassed by it."

"How many people knew you were dating?"

"That's the funny thing. We went out maybe off and on for five months. I liked her company, but not for that type of relationship. She's a friend to me; that's it."

"I've got to know man. I assumed you did, but now..."

"No. I didn't even get close. We kissed, but I wasn't feeling her like that."

Richard wanted to end the conversation before Walter got him to say he got as far as the bedroom. He wouldn't believe nothing went on. Lashauna didn't believe it, and she was there.

"Well you know I was. I did. I mean we did. Whew, I think that's why I'm feeling like this. I love her man, but I love you too."

"Hey don't put it in the same sentence like that," Richard cleared his throat, "Go ahead man do you. It's not bothering me."

Walter fell back in his seat again. Richard could tell the situation was upsetting him. He couldn't explain his feelings any clearer. It was Shauna's feelings that were confusing him and needed to be exposed.

"Alright listen, invite her. Let me know you did, and I'll invite her too. But I won't tell her that I'm inviting Janet."

"She already knows Janet is going. I spoiled that plan. Damn."

"No, I'll still invite her or just ask her if she's accepting your invitation. That's it. I'll tell her I'm making dinner plans for the four of us; something outside of the conference activities."

"Shauna will see through it. She'll be prepared to cover her feelings. Richard, I don't know if she wants to be with me."

"Tell her you need to know, see what she says."

Walter let his head fall back, and his eyes close. Richard had a solution, but that would mean his friend would be alone and still in love.

37

*F*aye rode in the back seat enjoying the music medley being played on Kiss FM. She began to sing along, totally ignoring Janet and Lashauna's conversation.

"Get it girl, you're feeling Mary J. huh?"

"Was I loud?"

Janet laughed, and Lashauna responded by singing the chorus. She turned up the volume, and they chimed in. As 'Just Fine' faded to a commercial, they finished their rendition, rocking the vehicle to the very last beat.

"We'd be good at karaoke. The brothers would be throwing...."

"Throwing their beer bottles." Lashauna injected as she pretended to down a beer throwing it at an imaginary stage.

"I don't know what y'all talking about. They'd throw dollars. Have you seen some of those girls they give their money to? We could get paid for sure." Janet laughed at the thought of them being on stage.

"I don't know Janet. I agree with Faye. Don't laugh, as long as we don't sing we could really get paid."

"Doing what?"

"Let the imagination run free."

"Oh damn. I'm out of that. You both don't have to worry about going home and seeing your man's face when he sees you on the six o'clock news."

"Girl I know that's right. I didn't think about the gossip. Walter would be a bit embarrassed especially if I sang. And I know my patients would think I lost it."

Janet kept quiet, keeping her eyes on the road grinning because she could feel their eyes staring at her waiting for a comment.

"What? I wasn't singing remember? So I'd be with the news reporter telling them you both drank too much, and neither of you would remember a thing in the morning."

The parking lot at the mall was crowded, but it didn't spoil their mood for shopping. They walked through the Macy's entrance an immediately began looking at the tags on the apparel lying on the sales tables.

"These colors are really nice." Janet said, admiring the sleeveless shells. "I'd love to get this color in slacks."

"Maybe they have a few over here Janet."

She followed Lashauna and Faye as they passed a few of the racks. Janet didn't want to tell them that the prices were more than what she intended to pay although Richard told her to enjoy herself. She headed toward the pants where her sister was searching for her size.

"They aren't an exact match. The material is different. Let's keep looking. I can come back and get them if I don't find anything at another store."

Faye let the pants fall back in place. Lashauna fell behind the sisters and checked the tag. She wondered if this little spree was a gift from the boss. The shopping went from shoes to after five cocktail dresses.

Lashauna commented about the cost when Janet was trying on her selected items hoping she would mention Richard's generosity. She carried them to the cashier without giving the tags or Lashauna a second glance. Faye purchased a casual outfit after being persuaded to treat herself while Lashauna decided on shoes and a matching handbag.

The two hours gave them a chance to talk and get to know the others taste in clothing, jewelry and other accessories. The ladies put the bags in the car and decided to stop for lunch before walking the rest of the mall. They agreed Ruby Tuesdays would quench their taste buds and thirst.

Janet and Faye sat on the same side of the table across from Lashauna. Lashauna felt nervous for no apparent reason. She didn't know what Janet was up to, but her instinct told her the luncheon was the main part of her afternoon plans. She looked at the sisters over her menu and wondered if Janet was curious about Faye's intentions or hers. As a psychologist she could often read people quickly but after spending three months with Janet, she still wasn't sure about her mental state. She did realize she was a lot stronger than she or her family suspected. She concluded it was that same quality that intrigued Richard.

"It's my treat, so order the burger special."

"Janet, I don't want you to pay for my lunch." Faye looked at Lashauna for her to agree.

"And I don't want the burger special."

Janet laughed. "Order what you want really. I don't know if I'll be able to treat you guys after school starts. I've got to shop for the kid's school supplies and clothes. Today's kinda special for me and I wanted to share it with both of you."

Lashauna's thoughts gave her a twinge. The thought of Janet announcing that she and Richard were dating would ruin her lunch. The menus were given to the waitress as she took their orders, placing it on one tab as requested. "Can I get your salads now?"

"We'll take them now with our drinks please." Faye and Lashauna nodded in agreement. "Well, I want to thank you both for supporting me these past few months. I know that some would say it was fate that has us sitting here, but I don't want to believe that. I can't really trust what I believe, and that's why I brought the two of you together."

The arrival of their drinks and salads caused a pause in the conversation. Lashauna opened her napkin slowly, watching as Faye seemed taken aback by Janet's opening comments.

"I think a lot about the reasons I had that day to want to die. I really do. I think about my father's death and how I always felt my family blamed me for it. Faye, you remember everyone would say, 'Janet don't blame yourself, it was an accident'. I never blamed myself. It wasn't until I heard it for what must have been the fiftieth time each day after four weeks that I really felt it was my fault. You never said anything. Mama never thought about asking me how I felt afterwards, I really needed consoling from my mother. No one consoled me. Sam barely spoke to me. Eventually I, like all of you forgot about how I felt."

"Janet, I don't think Lashauna wants to hear this today. Maybe we could make an appointment or something."

Lashauna could see Faye's fears rising. She had something to hide and it was obvious. Faye took a drink from her glass and started eating her salad feverously avoiding Janet's stern look.

"It really doesn't bother me. We've discussed this in the office and if I'm right your sister wants to share what she's come to know with us. Am I right Janet?"

"Yes, I think this is a new beginning for me. It started that day when I took those pills. God saw fit for me to live and in order to do that I need to put the life I have ahead of me in order."

"Okay, I'm willing but Daddy died over ten years ago. You felt horrible and we all felt bad for you. I don't think anyone blamed you. You may have been blaming yourself, but no one blamed you."

"This is not a debate, there's no need for you to get mad about what I'm saying. After all it's me we're talking about not you, at least not yet."

Janet ate between her words and Lashauna took it all in.

"What the hell are you talking about Janet? I've stuck by you all of our lives."

"You're right and this is what today's about. I want to thank you for all you've done. I said that. But I need to clear my mind, like you said these are the things that I thought about over the years. I thought I was being blamed. You say I wasn't so, okay. But it crossed my mind as I swallowed each of those pills. There was more though. As you know I didn't date much and Marcus was my first love. I wasn't too promiscuous and emotionally I was still a wreck. I thought my family still loved me only because they had to and Marcus loved me because he wanted to. True love, huh?"

Faye could hear the questions in her mind. She knew about Marcus and Karyn and hadn't said a word. She spoke up quickly hoping Janet wouldn't ask her about their introduction.

"You and Marcus have a good marriage; every marriage has its rough spots."

"But why Faye? I swallowed those pills 'cause I thought I caused the rough spot. Because I thought Marcus didn't want me. I was leaning too hard on him. Damn, I couldn't even handle paying the bills, the shopping, nothing outside of keeping the home or the children. Shit, I couldn't even keep him in my bed!"

Faye sighed deeply. She said a silent prayer. Lashauna was amazed at Janet's demeanor. The woman who was timid during her observations of her at the hospital seemed to be in full control. The sessions were as she said a support, she definitely was not as weak as she imagined.

"Janet," the doctor interrupted, "I think you've gotten beyond this."

"No, no I haven't. I don't want this haunting me again. I've been sorry for my father's death since the accident. I won't be sorry for a lost marriage, especially when my sister is siding with my husband."

Faye's look of confusion made Janet giggle. "You look like you don't know what I'm talking about."

Faye didn't answer fearing she would tell on herself.

"Let's take a break. I really didn't want this to be so serious. It's just that I need to clear my mind." Janet leaned toward Lashauna and lowered her voice although Faye could definitely still hear her. "How am I doing Lashauna?"

"You're moving in the right direction I just don't know why you couldn't have discussed this with her another time. I think Faye would have felt more comfortable without me listening like this."

"No if she wants you to hear this it's okay. Maybe it's a way for you to get over this, like you said, and move on. I think what you're wondering is if I knew about Marcus and Karyn?"

Janet turned with the same confused expression Faye displayed. Lashauna wiped her mouth hoping the waitress would bring their meal before the two sisters were fighting. Her prayer was answered and Faye took the opportunity to quickly excuse herself from their table. The waitress moved the remains of the salad dishes and sat the lunch specials in their place.

"Doc, so tell me. Am I crazy or what do you call this? Am I wrong to want to have a clear mind about my past? So many people just get over it but I can't seem to get through my nights or my days without these haunting questions. I want the questions to stop. They buzz in my head daily. Did I marry Marcus looking to be loved totally, only to have him creep and finally leave me? And see, I told you, what did she mean 'if she knew about them'? I need that peace of mind."

38

Faye splashed the water on her face and patted it dry with the coarse hand towel. She pulled out her cell phone and dialed Sherod. She needed to hear his voice before returning to what she felt had become her trial. Lashauna was the only jury member, and she couldn't tell which way the verdict was going. Sherod would have to be her lawyer.

"Hey babe, what's up?"

"I ... I, Sherod I'm so sorry," Faye fought back her tears,

"I've betrayed Janet, and I think she knows it."

"What...?"

"I think she knows I know Karyn."

"Babe, you're not making sense. Calm down."

Faye leaned on the wall. She was beginning to feel sick. She wondered if Janet would keep the children away from her and Sherod. It would kill him, among other things. He loved them as if they were his own.

"Faye, where is Janet?"

"We're at a restaurant. I think she knows I introduced Karyn to Marcus. She was rehashing why she tried to kill herself. I can't sit and listen to her talk about how she lost her marriage knowing I introduced Marcus to Karyn."

"Where are you now?"

Two women walked by excusing themselves as they passed. Faye went into the last stall to finish her conversation. She lowered her voice realizing the echo in the bathroom made it seem as though she was on a speaker.

"In the bathroom, I needed your advice."

"Advice about what? You're still not responsible for Marcus' actions or their marriage. It's your chance to tell her the truth. Tell her why you didn't tell her."

"Sherod, I don't know why. Karyn flaunted until Marcus paid attention. Who gets with somebody the first week they meet?"

Janet entered the bathroom passing the women who were whispering about her sister's audible confession. She stood near the stall door and listened.

"Babe, tell her what you told me. You tried talking to Marcus right?"

"Sherod you were right. Marcus is and was an ass hole. I should have told Janet then. Now I'm sitting here today trying to defend myself because of his shit. I know she knows. I even let him be with the kids without her knowing, hoping he would go home. Now my relationship is on the line because of his ass. I love my sister and those kids. Marcus is fucked up."

"Tell the truth babe be honest with her."

"Yeah you're right. I guess I have to tell her. That's some shit though. What do I say, 'Janet, I introduced Marcus to Karyn'?"

"Call me back if you need me to pick you up."

Janet forgot about using the bathroom and returned to the table after hearing Faye tell Sherod she'd be home in a few. She didn't have time to fill Lashauna in. Her sister returned to the table and tried to force a convincing smile.

"Wow, my food must be cold. I'm sorry I thought I was getting sick. You were asking me about Marcus?"

"No you were telling me why it seems you side with Marcus."

"I guess I side with reason."

Janet could feel her anger building. Lashauna could see it as well. "Excuse me, Miss. Can I get another drink please?" She waved for the waitress hoping it would delay the inevitable.

"Make that another for all of us. You need another drink Faye, don't you?"

"Uh, yes, Janet don't get me wrong, I'm not saying that you were unreasonable when it came to Marcus. It's just that I thought the two of you would get back together. I didn't think he would move out."

"No, how would you know? I mean it wasn't like you knew what he was doing, or should I say who he was doing. But why not tell me about..."

"Janet, I couldn't. Karyn was just somebody I met at the gym. We weren't friends like that. The week my car was down and Marcus volunteered to pick me up they met, no, I introduced them. I've regretted it since. I tried to get his ass to connect with his kids thinking he would want to be with them, but Karyn's got his head so fucked up... Shit, I don't know what to say or what to do. I feel terrible."

"So you planned on telling me this today right?"

"Huh?"

"I mean shit Faye; it's been almost two years. You introduced him to that tramp, and I'm just finding out. You let him see the kids behind my back, and if I know your husband, he told you to tell me when it happened."

Faye couldn't eat. Janet was younger than her, but she was a lot wiser.

"I'm sorry. I know it may be too late for those words, but I mean it."

"Yeah, well I swallowed a few pills that day for you, Marcus, Sam and Mommy. I swallowed those pills 'cause I was a failure in your eyes. I swallowed those pills because I was a failure to my husband and children. But God sent someone who didn't see me as a failure."

Faye looked at Lashauna and felt jealousy creeping in the air replacing her guilt. She began to size up her sister's new "sistah-friend" as she wiped her tears listening to Janet's words.

"Richard Burnett, a stranger, had faith in me. Even with my issues he saw my pain. He referred me to Dr. Norris before she knew I would be her patient. There was only one problem."

The look of confusion went around the table full circle. Lashauna's expression of worry became noticeable.

"Are you okay?" Janet questioned knowing the doctor was put on the spot.

"I'm fine. At first, I was wondering, what problem? But then I remembered our little conflict of interest."

"No the problem was and is honesty. Miss, can I have the check please?" Janet said, summoning the waitress. "You see; you're like my family. Someone I've got to watch. The difference is I won't be swallowing pills over my relationship with you. I'll meet you guys at the register. I've got to pee."

Faye and Lashauna were left at the table. They left a tip hoping the conversation would be left there too. Their day of shopping ended abruptly. Faye didn't question Janet's last comment. She was sure watching how Lashauna reacted; she knew what her sister meant.

Janet took Lashauna home first. She and Faye waved a dry goodbye.

"I'll call you during the week. I don't think I'll make it on Thursday."

"Janet Thursday is five days away. Call me tonight, no, I'll call you."

"Now there's a thought."

Lashauna couldn't respond. She had been sucker-punched enough for one day. Janet pulled off thinking what she would say to Sherod and Faye about the children.

39

*J*anet hummed each song that played as though she was alone. Faye realized it would be useless to try explaining her attempts to talk to Marcus. She hoped Janet would listen to Sherod. He could tell her the introduction wasn't intended to spark an extra-marital relationship. Tears rolled down her face as she gazed out the window. She thought about Janet's words. The fact was that she took those pills thinking she wasn't loved.

"Is Sherod home?"

Janet's voice brought Faye's attention to what had become a long ride home. She wiped her eyes with her fingers trying not to cry as she answered.

"Yes, he's home. Sam is supposed to pick him up tomorrow morning I think they're taking M.J. to the Sportsplex." She responded hoping Janet would engage in a conversation for the remainder of the ride.

"That's fine. I want to talk to both of you before I go home." She continued humming the next song that played on the radio.

She drove a little further, and turned slowly onto Faye's street. Sherod was coming out of the house. She blew the horn bringing attention to their arrival. The ladies got out of the car, grabbing Faye's bags.

"Hey Rod, what's up?"

Sherod stepped out of the garage and looked at his wife for a sign that everything was as normal as Janet's greeting. When Faye continued to walk through the garage entrance to the dining room without saying a word, he knew trouble was still brewing.

"Hey yourself, you guys buy the stores out or what?"

"Hardly, but what I did get was priceless. I need to talk to you and Faye though, do you have a minute?"

"Sure. I'm looking for my screwdriver. Give me a minute."

Janet went into the house looking for her sister. She didn't see her in the dining room or the kitchen, but she heard her voice coming from the hall leading to the bedroom. She was on the phone giving details about her afternoon. By the inflection of her voice, Janet knew she was upset. She took a seat in the living room hoping her presence didn't disturb her conversation. Faye went into her bedroom and slammed the door. Janet smiled seeing Sherod waving the screwdriver as he came to join her.

"Where's your sister? Did she see you sitting here?"

"She knows I'm here. She'll be fine once she stops feeling guilty. I've learned to deal with what has happened; now she has to learn to deal with it."

"I probably know what you're talking about but fill me in so we're not talking on different levels."

"I've always admired you for that. You're real Sherod, and that means so much to people. You say what you feel regardless, but you also respect what others feel and that's important. I'm not gonna pretend with you. I was in the bathroom when she called you. I heard what she said. I didn't know about her introducing Karyn to Marcus. I did know about him visiting the kids here and then being told not to tell me. That's what I wanted to talk to her about, but she told on herself. Guilt is a bitch."

"Yeah, well you're right. She'll have to deal with it. But how do I fit into that? You know I don't get into family matters unless someone invites me in. Faye told me about Karyn and Marcus when she wasn't sure they were dealing with each other. I started talking to him about your marriage and what he thought were problems. It didn't matter, we both knew what was up when he said he was moving in with Karyn."

Sherod purposely left out the details. Faye filled him in every time Karyn called bragging about the "married man" and what she loved about him. He told Faye to tell her sister. His wife didn't think it was her place and encouraged him to talk to Marcus.

"What were the problems?"

"Baby girl, Marcus couldn't identify the problems. He was looking for an excuse. I told him what you did for him and your kids, was heaven sent. He couldn't see it. When a man can't see the value in his marriage, he could be with his wife for years, and he won't be satisfied. He'll always look for an excuse, the problems. You didn't end your marriage. Marcus walked away from it. Karyn just became a pit stop. He'll leave her too. Just do me a favor."

"What's that?"

"Don't let him run back to you. You don't deserve to be treated like that. Marcus has a lot of maturing to do. Now don't get me wrong, if you want him back it's all right with me. No one can tell you to end your marriage if you want to give it another chance. Janet, be careful. I love you girl like you were my sister, you know. I don't know what he's thinking, but it's not what he wants, it's what you want."

"I want you and Faye to know what I want. Well, I'll tell you. She's probably talking to Mommy or Sam. I'll deal with them later."

"She's not talking to Sam. He took M.J. to New York."

"It doesn't matter. Listen, I don't want Marcus seeing them here. This is not a stopover for visits. If he wants to visit them, he can see them at their home. I need to know when he's with them. I don't trust him. I don't want my children with him, when I don't know it."

"Fine with me, I agree, you should know."

"I've got to get things in order. Marcus is confused about what he wants and I don't need any confusion. Sherod, I'm thinking about dating other people and I don't need him running in and out of their life with his shit. Karyn doesn't want them in her house and that's fine with me. I don't want them where they're not wanted. But if he thinks he can sneak behind my back he's wrong. He's done enough sneaking. Everything needs to be up front and honest."

"You're right, let me get Faye. You guys need to talk."

40

arcus turned off the ignition and dialed the number again. He didn't see Janet's car, but he wanted to be sure she wasn't home. He decided Saturday would be the best time for him to see what she had in the bedrooms. Faye said she didn't want the same thing, the same marriage. He read between the lines and knew Richard was in the picture somewhere. Sherod denied knowing anything about her dating, but if she was doing fine without her husband, a man was around somewhere. He asked himself throughout the week, *"What woman could attempt suicide and three months later be getting along fine?"* Dr. Norris refused to meet with him and reminded him she didn't have to give him any information regarding Janet's therapy sessions. She ended the conversation with, *"talk to your wife."* He intended to talk to her, after he searched the apartment thoroughly.

He put the key in the lock confident that Janet didn't know he had been there, a week prior. The tumbler turned as it had before, and he entered the apartment and sighed. Part of him wanted to see evidence of her relationship with Richard Burnett. If she was in a relationship with anyone, Sherod was right, she had changed.

Marcus took a deep breath filling his nostrils with the smell of the Linen air freshener's aroma that circulated through the apartment. The kitchen was clean. She had done her Saturday cleaning and laundry before leaving. The dryer was still spinning. He put his hand on its window feeling the warmth. The dining room and living room had an added smell of lemon furniture polish. He sat on the couch and looked around. There was no difference in the room since his last visit.

After a brief pause, he continued to the bathroom. He looked in the medicine cabinet and under the sink. Places he hadn't searched before. Janet's medicine was on the top shelf aligned with the labels facing forward. There was no sign of anyone sharing her personal space. He didn't know what he was looking for; maybe shaving cream, razors, or after-shave. Whatever it was; it wasn't in the bathroom.

The children's rooms would be easier than the master bedroom. He continued pausing in the hall as though the unusual would leap out. Their rooms surprised him. Again, as in the rest of the apartment, nothing was out of place. That was unusual, they were children. He smirked as he remembered Faye saying they would be away the next two weekends. Janet had cleaned their rooms. M.J. had pictures of himself on the wall, pictures Marcus hadn't seen. He took his time looking at them and the people in the background. A few were from camp; the others were from sporting activities and school. He didn't realize how much he missed. M.J. was in a baseball uniform on the field making a play. He could tell the picture was a candid shot. He wondered if Sherod or Sam took the picture. Janet wasn't good with cameras.

The girls, being younger, didn't have reflections of themselves posted in their room. Janet was still their decorator, and it showed. Their closet door was open, and he was reminded he hadn't checked M.J.'s closet. He flipped through their notebooks in their backpacks and checked their dressers. The closet was huge and half filled; there was room for them to grow. He returned to M.J.'s room and opened the closet door. He noticed immediately Janet hadn't been in M.J.'s closet. Toys were scattered on the closet floor and thrown on the shelves. Marcus could hear Janet telling their son to clean his room and the closet told him M.J. still had his own interpretation of cleaning.

He went through the closet organizing the toys as he had when he lived there. Unlike the many times in the past, he wasn't angry. He was happy he could be a part of his family in a small way. He stacked the games, putting the pieces that were on the floor in their proper boxes and back on the shelf. He hung the clothes that were falling off hangers or had fallen on the floor. When he finished he sat on the bed crying silently. He missed his children. He would ask Karyn about his children being a part of their lives. He looked at his watch and estimated it would take him an hour or more to search the last bedroom.

The room was no different than the other rooms. He went into the bathroom first and pulled back the shower door. Janet had hung a curtain in front of the door, which heightened his curiosity. He asked himself why, but let the question go without feeding his mind with any answers. There was nothing strange in the bathroom. He checked the cabinet, and under the sink as he had in the other bathroom. He noticed her toothbrush and reminded himself to count the ones in the other bathroom.

The furniture glistened, signs Janet had polished the pieces longer than usual. Marcus imagined her in deep thought rubbing the smudges and fingerprints. He often watched her from the entrance of the room as she hummed through her routine cleaning. She had changed the color scheme from the burgundy and cream colors they selected to what seemed now to be peach or sand. Everything about the room was soft. The coral rug added the touch Janet said it would when he insisted it was too feminine. The king-sized bed was filled with assorted sized pillows adding a mixture of pastel colors to the bedding.

Marcus didn't agree with a lot of her decorating but seeing it now he realized the apartment was picture perfect and showed no signs of his opinions. He opened the large armoire, which had served as his dresser. The top half still hosted the 36-inch television. He pulled out the top drawer not knowing what to expect. It was filled with folded linen and pillowcases. The next two drawers held blankets, face cloths and towels. He lifted each of them carefully as he checked for any suspicious papers.

Janet kept her dresser as orderly as everything else. Marcus never invaded that area, and although he was curious about her having a man in her life, he couldn't bring himself to look in her dresser. He sat on the edge of the bed looking through the nightstand first.

As expected the Bible was the first thing he saw. The sight of it sent a chill down his back but didn't stop his snooping. There was a journal next to the Bible and a pen. Marcus picked up the journal and flipped through the pages. Skimming the words he could tell it was filled with Janet's thoughts about her sessions with Dr. Norris. He turned to the first page to check for dates. The sessions were numbered; no dates were indicated. There was a page where she inscribed, *"Dedicated to Marcus Jr., Joy and Erica."* Marcus was puzzled but read on. *"I hope you will never have to be where I am today. It is for you that I will complete this therapy, rebuild my life, and live a life so you all can be proud of me. I vow not to return to the mental state that drove me here. I cannot change what I cannot control, but I will no longer accept just anything or anyone controlling me. Remember you cannot live happily if you do not live totally. Don't let anyone or anything control you. Mommy."*

Marcus read the passage twice and put the book back into the nightstand. He asked himself, did she feel he drove her to commit suicide? The doctor said the same thing. A sick feeling came over him, and he put his head between his legs. He hoped he wouldn't puke. The feeling he had when Faye called him that afternoon returned. He couldn't lose the only woman he really loved or could he?

The night stands on the opposite side of the bed held a daily planner that had nothing noted. There was also a camp calendar and what appeared to be Janet's list of items to prepare the children for school. Janet's dresser was the only piece of furniture he hadn't searched. The clock on the nightstand read six thirty. He would save it for one final visit.

41

*L*ashauna waited impatiently for Janet's call. It was close to seven-thirty, and she was certain she would be home by now. She dialed her number and when the voice mail answered she decided she would call Faye. It wasn't that her patient included her in her search-and-destroy mission; she wanted an explanation for her comment. The Williamson's phone rang twice, and Sherod answered. There was music playing in the background, and he asked her to hold on as he turned it down.

"Sorry, hello?"

"Hello, this is Lashauna, Dr. Norris. Is Faye available?"

"Yeah, hang on." Sherod called Faye telling her the phone call was for her and who was calling. Lashauna heard two clicks on the other end. She thought she had been disconnected."

"Hello? Hello?"

"Yes, Shauna?"

"Oh, I thought I lost you. I was calling to see, first of all, if you were okay and secondly is Janet still there?"

"She left about ten minutes ago. I'm better than I was. We talked. Well, first let me apologize. I'm sure in your office you've seen worse sessions, but you shouldn't be subjected to that type of behavior during your down time."

"Listen, don't apologize to me. I analyze everything regardless." Lashauna laughed, and Faye understood without her giving details.

"Anyway, I was mad as hell, hurt, guilty, shit you name it. I called my mother and brother, and they did just what Janet claimed we did.

She was right; they pushed it off. It really hurt me to think we treated her that way. My mother said that through therapy the patient discovers who to blame. She kept repeating some mess about her blaming everyone but herself. When I asked her how she could blame Janet for the accident, you know, she told me that was not what she meant. That's exactly what she meant Shauna. My brother said Janet has been off since the accident. I was done, done. I didn't notice that about them, why?"

"Faye they didn't do it to you. You couldn't feel her pain. But is she okay now?"

"She talked to Sherod while I spoke with them. He came and got me, and we all talked. She didn't smear anything in my face about Karyn and Marcus or mention my mother or brother again. It's funny, if it had been me, we would have been fighting. I guess I understand her not being totally committed to dealing with my mother when she was sick. I would have accepted her yelling and screaming at me. Not Janet, her requests were simple. Marcus is to deal with her when it comes to their kids. I have to respect that. She's good doctor, better than me or you. How about you? What did she mean by that last statement? I couldn't figure it out."

"It's a long story, and she's probably told you. I dealt with Richard off and on for five or six months. I really thought we had something, but he moved on, but he didn't tell me." Shauna waited for Faye to respond.

"You thought you were still dating? I thought you and Walter were dating?"

"We are now, but that was one of those.... it just happened things."

"Richard didn't say anything to you?"

"He did, but I think he thought it was too late."

"So the brother blew his chances huh?"

"By the time I started paying attention, I was in Walter's bed seeing if white boys could jump."

"Well I guess he jumped enough."

They laughed while continuing the conversation as Shauna avoided the facts. Faye knew her sister was right. Lashauna was still in love with Richard.

"Shauna, will Janet be in therapy much longer? I know you don't have to tell me anything, but I wanted to know, is it working?"

"Your sister's a lot stronger than you think. I didn't think she was as strong as she is. Nevertheless, like most of the people I deal with who have attempted suicide she has a lot of issues she hasn't faced over the years. I think it's helped her a lot. She's willing to face her past. The death of your father, how family treated her afterward, and her relationship with you were the top of her list. I just hope that she doesn't confuse those who want to help her with those that want to hurt her."

Faye thought about Janet's last comment. Maybe she knew Shauna would try to hurt her.

42

*J*anet left her sister's home satisfied with what she felt was a personal accomplishment. It was as though a load had been lifted from her heart. She was sure her mother and Sam would call expecting her to blast them about their past behavior. She was done with it. Telling Faye how she felt was what was important to her. Their mother and Sam would go on pretending they hadn't hurt her. It wasn't debatable; her relationship with her sister was important. Faye knew now, and that was what mattered; their relationship would survive. She didn't want to pretend anymore. Janet felt they never accepted her apologies, her cries, her want or desire to be loved by them. The only one who stood by her was Faye. It was important to her not to lose the only family member she felt loved her.

The evening air blew through the driver's window and helped her relax. She turned the station seeking something slow and mellow. Her cell rang and she tapped her blue tooth hoping the call wouldn't ruin her peaceful mood.

"Hello."

"Good evening lady. How are you?"

"Richard, how are you? I'm fine."

"I guess the term 'shop 'til you drop' fits you now."

"If you mean did I shop all day, most of it. I spent the other part of the day clearing up a few things with my sister and Lashauna."

"Dr. Norris?"

"Uh huh, I thought it was time she knew that I wasn't blind to her extended therapy. I told you each session was about relationships.

After today, she shouldn't have any other questions about relationships, that is, unless she wants to discuss you."

"Me, why would she want to discuss me?"

"I don't know. If she takes the bait, she'll call me and tell on herself. I think she still has a thing for you."

"Okay, and what will she gain from taking the bait."

"According to you there's nothing between you two right?"

"Nothing other than a friendship, I told Walter that the other day. They're a strange couple. He's worried about me and so is she. There's nothing to worry about. Maybe I should talk to her."

"Well, I got my point across."

"Janet, do you have plans for tonight. Oh, where are the children, with Faye?"

"No Grandma and Uncle, I'd love to know your plans."

"I'll meet you at your house."

"I should be there in another ten minutes."

Janet ended the call happy her night was free. Richard had been the perfect gentleman over the past few months. She was tempted to seduce him, but that was where Lashauna made her mistake. She didn't want to make any mistakes, not when everything was going so well. She put her key in the door and for a moment, she thought she was being watched. She looked around the parking lot before entering the apartment. She shrugged and cut on the kitchen lights while kicking off her sandals. The clock read eight. The feeling came over her again. She decided to check each room for any signs of intrusion. All the windows were shut just as she had left them. She smiled and took a deep breath. She definitely was being paranoid. Hunger began to build, and she thought of frying a few chicken wings she had thawed in the refrigerator.

Changing her clothes became the first priority. She would be comfortable, something Richard teased her about. They had been seeing each other at his home and going out for most of their time together. Janet was always properly dressed. She opened her closet and grabbed her pink Phat Farm sweats from the shelf. M.J.'s pants fell on the floor. She wondered why they were still in her closet. She had separated the clothes she bought the children earlier in the month and hung them in their room.

She pulled up her pants and grabbed M.J.'s. She went into his room humming and opened his closet door. She froze. The closet was an ongoing daily argument between her and M.J. She told him she wouldn't be cleaning it for him. Friday, when they left the house for camp, she told him he would be cleaning it Sunday before going to bed. The closet was cleaned already. The games were stacked. The clothes were off the floor and hung properly on the hangers; the shoes were paired off and separated from his boots and sneakers. M.J. would have never done such a systematic job of cleaning. Her nerves immediately reacted. She knew someone had been in their home.

She looked through the other rooms for signs of the intruder. Nothing was broken or out of place. She went back to the door and checked the locks. There was no indication that someone came in. Janet stood in the middle of her kitchen thinking who would have access to her home and cared enough to clean M.J.'s closet.

She needed to speak to M.J. Sherod said Sam took him to New York. She didn't want to worry him over cleaning his closet, but she wouldn't be able to sleep if someone could enter her home when they wanted to. The doorbell rang, and Janet rushed to answer.

"Richard, I'm so glad you're here."

"Okay, what's up you seem ..." He touched her gently guiding her into the apartment.

"Scared as hell..." She cut him off mid-sentence. "Someone's been in my home..." Pausing again she tried to continue, unsure of herself. "My son's room..." She pointed down the hall. "They cleaned his closet."

She led him by the arm directing him to M.J.'s room. He listened as she explained her findings and the agreement she made with her son.

"Who has keys to your apartment?"

"Faye does, that would mean Sherod as well."

"Who else, your mother or brother?"

"They never had a key. The management does; I really don't think management would be cleaning the closet."

"You don't think anything else was touched. What about your jewelry, papers, or money?"

"I didn't check my dresser or anything else."

"You better check your room. I'll wait for you in the living room."

"No you're coming with me. Check with me. I might miss something. Richard why the hell would someone come in and clean my son's closet? That's freaky."

He followed her to her bedroom. He wasn't invited any further than the living room during the few visits in her home. His feelings stirred seeing the large bed and her in the soft pink sweat suit. He could tell from her shape in the outfit she didn't have on her bra or panties. He tried to change the vivid pictures that were entering his mind, but his desires had taken over. The phone rang; Janet pointed to it indicating he should answer it.

He frowned looking at her twice. She ignored his expression, and the phone rang again for the third time. A name appeared in the neon-lit screen, *"Dr. Lashauna Norris."* Richard was more than happy to say, "Hello."

There was no answer on the other end. He repeated himself knowing that she wouldn't answer. Janet gave him a bewildered look hoping the caller had nothing to do with the issue at hand.

"It was Shauna. She'll call back probably."

"I'm glad she heard your voice. Maybe now she'll tell the truth."

Janet closed the dresser drawer and pointed to the exit. Richard turned waiting for her to pass him and lead the way. She pretended not to notice his roaming eyes. He touched her softly on her waist as she passed him. She deliberately slowed her walk allowing him to hold her waist as he followed her into the kitchen.

"Alright, nothing is missing and I'm glad about that but it doesn't answer the question."

"We'll get your locks changed."

"I have to put in a request with maintenance. That's really why they weren't changed. Unless there's a break in, the tenant has to pay to have the change done. And it's not right away. It's a process. But I'll call them in the morning."

"Tell them you lost your keys."

"They would only give me a replacement key for the same lock and still go through the process. I think its two weeks. The guy isn't here during the week to change locks. The downfall of not being in my own house, they're really good about making emergency repairs though."

"You're sure you didn't leave a window open?" Richard asked as Janet mumbled the possibilities.

"M.J. may have cleaned up before they left for New York. My brother may have talked to him about it and brought him here to clean up. I'll talk to M.J. about it tomorrow. Whoever it was doesn't mean me any harm if they cleaned the closet."

"I don't know, talk to maintenance. Maybe they saw someone. I don't like the idea of someone being able to get into your place while you and the kids are here alone."

"So are you moving in or am I moving out."

"Girl, don't start something you can't handle." Richard said turning her to face him.

"I'm sure you'll help me along the way." She smiled as he gave her a tender kiss and a hug.

43

*L*ashauna checked the number. She was sure she dialed Janet's number. Richard was there and Janet knew that would touch a nerve. The patient was taking it a bit far. The doctor was a woman first. She wasn't willing to play Janet's game. She would have to surrender. Janet was more than she cared to deal with. She was tempted to dial Richard's cell phone. That would keep him on his toes. He would squirm more than Janet. He wouldn't understand the joke.

She told Walter she wouldn't be home until late and now she wanted company. He'd been acting different lately. His calls had decreased and when they did talk he listened more than before. They hadn't been intimate in over a week. She was glad for the break, but Walter was what she called a sex addict. He loved her body and was willing to please her in various ways.

Sex with a white man wasn't as bad as she thought it would be. She always thought that it was a matter of mind over matter. He was good looking and endowed. She let her imagination run wild as he explored her body. Whenever he got close to taking her to the point of no return she would move her hips causing him to lose control. He was not the typical white boy, not that she had dated many, but her clients talked.

Walter was good to her and she had to admit he was good for her. All her past relationships began with the smothering phase. Walter went a bit over board but it was subtle compared to the brothers who became leeches. He had his own money and his own goals, which allowed her to keep her individualism. He had no interest in persuading her to share in his career. The relationship was not a competition.

She turned on the television and used the remote to surf through the guide. Richard and Janet being together crossed her mind again. Janet was truly beautiful. She had never thought of her that way but after seeing her out of the office her personality shined. She admired her. Lashauna had never met any woman that she would honestly say that about. She picked up her cell phone and texted Richard.

"*Congratulations, she's a beautiful person. I learned a lot about her and myself over these past few months. I wish the two of you the best. Can you please tell her to call me, I owe her an apology.*" She closed her blackberry and let the tears fall. Lashauna understood Janet's statement she needed a friend, more than she needed therapy.

Her phone rang and she hoped Richard was returning her call to say she was wrong.
"Hello."

"Hey lady, how are you? I see you got in earlier than you expected."

Lashauna glanced at the clock on her wall. He was right eight o'clock was not what she would consider late.

"Let's just say I had enough excitement for the day and came home."

"Why didn't you call, I would have met you while you were out?"

"No, I don't think I would have made good company."

"What about now?" Walter waited anticipating she would say no. "If not, I'll call you tomorrow."

"Tomorrow, I thought you were asking about tonight?"

"I've got to be honest. I'm a little tired of begging for your attention."

"Walter, we need to talk. You're right. I've been avoiding the obvious for months. I need to clear up some issues in my life. Can you come by I'll make something to snack on. What do you want?"

"I told you. But I'm ..."
"You won't have to beg."

44

*T*he week went by quickly, and Janet was glad her brother agreed to pick her children up from camp. She turned the key to her apartment door and sighed realizing maintenance still hadn't changed the lock; Richard convinced her to call the police. The police filled out a report as she requested, searched the apartment, inspected the windows and door and indicated everything as intact on the report. Although the maintenance supervisor said he understood her concern, they had no proof that she had been a victim of a break in. It was obvious after a week that without any damages, her request for a new lock went to the bottom of the maintenance "to do" list. Sam and M.J. denied cleaning the closet confirming her belief; someone had visited her while she was out.

Janet didn't argue, and Richard suggested just changing the locks and replacing them when she moved. She thought about what he was saying. He talked as though he was sure she would be moving. Her life was definitely going in another direction, but moving wasn't in her immediate plans. She assured him maintenance would take care of it.

There was only one other issue she needed to handle. Marcus crossed her mind. They needed to discuss the children. She had gone to see a lawyer and was awaiting the delivery of her divorce papers. She agreed to hand deliver the papers to him. She was following Dr. Norris' prescription to "drama free" living. Since the outing with the doctor and Faye, she had to admit she felt better than she had in years.

She was determined to move on with her life without the drama from her past. She looked forward to it.

The conference would be her first time away since Joy was born. She thought about Marcus keeping his children for a change. Faye and Sherod would be away that weekend. It was their anniversary that Saturday and a well-deserved time for them. She wanted to ask her mother but decided against it. If she didn't get a sitter, she would have to tell Richard she wouldn't be attending. She wondered if Lashauna was still going.

Lashauna called daily leaving an inspirational quote on the machine. She didn't even act as though she expected to talk to Janet. Her voice held the tone of desperation, a tone that reminded Janet, of how she felt, three months prior. She didn't keep her Thursday appointment and Lashauna didn't mention it while leaving her words for the day. Janet's intention was to discontinue the therapy. While processing her divorce papers she asked the lawyer to draft a letter on her behalf to the court regarding her state of mind, employment and progress since her hospitalization. Lashauna would have to respond to her lawyer's correspondence within the next few weeks. Janet was preparing for the drama Marcus would throw her way.

The lawyer agreed she had met the required sessions. She would need to substantiate her ability to keep her children. She was sure her lawyer could expedite the proceedings since it was clear Marcus had abandoned her and the children. A letter proving she had her own means of supporting them and insurance would be beneficial. Richard was more than happy to submit the letter as her employer. They both were glad they hadn't made their dating known to any of the clients or her family. He showed her the text he received from Lashauna, but they knew she could only assume Richard didn't respond to her or confirm any of the statements Walter made about them. He told Janet he was sure Walter told her they were dating. Nevertheless, if questioned, she could only say that her patient was married and that she hadn't mentioned seeing anyone during her sessions. Janet wondered if the doctor took heed to her own advice. She needed to let go of her past as well. She could only hope the text message was the first step for her.

If questioned Janet's neighbors never saw Richard's car parked overnight. Now that the papers had been filed they both were honest about their feelings. He told her he couldn't guarantee he would be a gentleman if he stayed long while visiting. She was anxious, waiting to unwrap his package in more ways than one. They agreed it would be worth the wait. Without a sitter for the four days while they were away, the package would be like a gift under the Christmas tree, tempting. The conference would be good for both business and pleasure. She checked her messages, deleting Lashauna's and dialed Richard's cell.

"Mr. Burnett?"

"Ah, Ms. Robinson, how did the meeting go with the lawyer?"

"She accepted the letter and I should have papers to deliver to Marcus within a week. If he doesn't fight, it shouldn't be long at all. But it depends on if he'll fight back. I don't see what the fight would be about. We don't share any property other than the furniture here in the apartment, the car, and our children. What could he want?" Her questions were hypothetical but Richard answered keeping the conversation going.

"You baby, you. We'll put in a prayer. Faye and Sherod leave yet?"

"I needed to talk to you about that. I thought it was this week. They're weekend getaway is the same weekend as the conference. I may have to decline. I don't have anyone to keep the children for the weekend."

"Hmm. That's not acceptable Ms. Robinson."

"I don't have a choice. I can't tell Marcus here's the divorce papers and by the way, keep the kids while I go on a business trip with my boss," she laughed at the thought.

"No, that wouldn't go over well, let me talk with Elaine. We need you there. I wanted to surprise you, but I think its best you know what's coming our way with the expansion. That's the other phone. I've got to get it. Walter left early."

"Are we still on for church on Sunday?"

"Yes, service is at eleven. Elaine will be glad to see you there. I won't tell her you're coming. We'll talk with her on Sunday after church."

"I don't know Richard...."

"Listen, Erica and Joy love her, and M.J. is learning to play dominoes. They'll be fine for a weekend. They keep her company when they visit."

"Richard she's only dealt with them for a couple of hours here and there."

"They'll be fine. What's on your agenda this weekend since you're childless again?"

"I was thinking about talking things over with my brother and mother."

"Okay, may I ask why? I thought you decided to let that go?" He asked, pretending the persistent ringing of the other line didn't annoy him.

"It's like leaving a loose thread to a finished piece. I don't know it was just a thought. Besides, if Elaine watches the children next weekend the following week school starts. My getaway weekends with them will be over, so will the summer. I thought maybe the four of us could try to enjoy this last one together."

"Well sweetie, if you change your mind call. Let me know if you decide not to join us at church."

"We'll talk before then. I'm sure of that. I'll call Elaine later and ask her about the children staying."

"Janet."

The pause put her on alert. She hoped he wouldn't say that he loved her. She wanted to save the words for that romantic moment. The way he said her name from time to time was enough. Each time she thought he would confess to what she already knew.

"If you need me, call me. Don't get yourself worked up if your mother and brother upset you."

"Richard, are you worried I might still..."

"You've been working hard at regaining who you are. I believe you've found Janet Robinson, and I've fallen in love with her. Call me if you need me."

45

Talking with Walter didn't put Lashauna's mind at ease. They talked late into the night. The topic of the night was her text message to Richard. She expressed her concern for Janet more as a friend than a doctor. It wasn't until Janet missed her appointment and didn't return her calls that she realized her patient had become independent. She no longer felt the need for therapy but Lashauna needed her. Walter still wanted the relationship he longed for but Lashauna felt she had wronged him as much as she wronged Janet. Richard's words during their relationship came to mind. Her work didn't put her in a class above the clouds. Until now, she thought she deserved to be enwrapped with her clouds of success. The feelings she had over the past few days were more than gloomy, she couldn't see the clouds.

In her attempt to stir Richard's emotions, she disregarded Walter's and Janet's. The four of them were to leave for the conference Friday morning. She couldn't imagine the drive with the tension still present between her and Janet.

She wasn't quite sure where she and Walter stood. Telling Walter she couldn't attend the conference led to another argument about Richard. He told her to make a choice and when her emotions caught up with her tongue, he was walking out her door. She let him walk, that was Monday it was now Thursday. Janet's sessions and her assertiveness during their shopping spree proved her internal strengths. Lashauna needed her strength. She kept Janet's appointment time open hoping they could talk before the trip the next morning.

Anxiety was tapping on her shoulders causing prickly heat to rise on her neck as she poured another cup of coffee. She returned to her desk and decided she couldn't wait until the afternoon hours arrived. She dialed Burnett and Reed LLC, preparing herself to speak to Janet. While waiting for an answer she scribbled nervously Walter and Richard's name on her legal pad. She began to scratch out the letters that spelled Richard as the voice of a trained professional came across the line.

"Burnett and Reed, good morning, how may I direct your call?"

"Janet Robinson, please."

"Shauna?"

"Oh, hi Elaine, I didn't recognize your voice. You sound like you have a cold."

"Girl, that's this new-fangled headset. Richard said it would make things so much easier. He doesn't have to wear it, adjust it, get used to it, but it's annoying to me, not to mention it changes my voice. I didn't see you at church Sunday, how are you?"

"I'm fine. I needed a weekend of rest and overslept Sunday morning." She lied, and Elaine knew it.

"Well I missed you as did the Ministry. There were a few questions about some of the sick call visits, but you can deal with that later. Anyway let me get Janet for you."

The music began playing before Lashauna could answer. It wasn't long before the prerecorded medley repeated the first song. She was beginning to believe Janet wouldn't be answering.

"Hey Shauna."

"Richard? I was holding for Janet."

"She left for the day. Elaine didn't know she wasn't returning. Are you okay, excited about getting away for the weekend?"

The doctor could feel her stomach turning. It was as Walter said. Loving Richard was causing her to lose her essence. She couldn't describe it. The more he avoided her the more she wanted him. Hearing his voice brought a calming, sensual effect; one she found hard to describe. She wanted him totally. Richard was now an everlasting fantasy. Janet knew it. She knew how Lashauna felt about him when they met. Janet was a definitely a different type of woman.

"Richard, listen, I'm trying to clear the air with you and Janet. There're some loose ends we need to tie up, and I need to do it before this weekend getaway. I don't think I'll be going if we can't talk this through."

"I won't ask why. Don't you have an appointment with her today?"

Janet filled Richard in with her sessions, the progress, her doubts, and she even told him what she would be talking to Faye and Lashauna about during their lunch. It was all planned, and Richard respected her wish to allow her to handle things.

"She didn't show up last week. I haven't heard from her, so I wasn't sure she was keeping the appointment."

"You may be right. I didn't ask, call her cell."

"Can you tell me how to right this wrong?"

"What wrong?"

"You and I should talk first I guess. I need to know where we stand. I know for the past few months you've been trying to win your way with Janet, but you had your opportunity with me. I guess what I'm saying is why her or is she the fill-in because I began sleeping with your boy?"

Richard regretted he answered the line. He had always been straight with Lashauna, but he didn't need her to ruin things for Janet's divorce or their relationship.

"Let's talk about you. Janet and Walter have nothing to do with why you and I aren't together. You and I have a different chemistry. That's a combination for problems. We would clash as lovers, but we mesh well as friends."

"And Janet? Your excuse is flimsy to say the least."

He ignored her comment and answered her question.

"She's married. Until she decides what she wants, I'm a friend for her too. I will admit I do have an interest, but she's married." Richard hoped his answer would be convincing.

"Did you sleep with her?"

"No, and that's personal don't you think. Shauna this is not a therapy session unless you're getting something out of this."

"Maybe I am, hold on."

Richard waited fumbling the papers on his desk. He pushed the intercom for Walter.

"Yeah," the baritone voice came across the intercom. "What's up?"

"We're driving up tomorrow morning, what are you doing?"

"Shauna's hasn't said she's going so I'll meet you guys up there."

"What's up with that?"

"Man, she's in love, same shit. The problem is so am I. Nothing lost; I'll be a whore for the weekend, and I'll be fine."

"That ain't you and you know it."

"After a few shots of Hennessey, it won't matter. I don't know what she wants. She says she's over you, but she won't commit to me. She claims I'm who she wants to be with, but she's ... man I can't explain it. I told her to make a choice, me or you."

Richard didn't push the button again. He waited for Lashauna to answer. He'd have to back away from her completely, maybe then she'll understand. He disconnected the call. Elaine would have to take a message if she called again.

"Hello, hello Richard?" Lashauna looked at the receiver and hung up the phone. Her interest was redirected to the envelope that was certified and required her signature. The lawyer's name wasn't familiar. She checked her files thinking she had a pending testimony she had forgotten about.

"Damn." She read the papers through and was again impressed by the woman who attempted suicide no more than five months prior. The request was from Janet's lawyer. Lashauna was familiar with the paperwork. She was to fill out the forms for presentation in the divorce hearing for Mr. and Mrs. Robinson.

She and Janet had discussed her facing the demons who forced her into thinking taking her life was the solution. Marcus was her silent demon. She never said it, but she refused to talk about their relationship. She didn't say how she would be handling her husband, and the fact that he chose Karyn over his wife and children. The doctor read through the request again wondering when her fragile patient filed the divorce papers and if Richard helped her.

Lashauna sat back and sipped on her lukewarm coffee. Janet followed her advice. She told Faye how she felt about their family matters and her alliance to Marcus. She was sure there had been a similar discussion with her brother and mother. Janet also faced her, the doctor, from the beginning. She told her she wanted a friend, now Lashauna needed one.

She spent the next few hours trying to ignore the nagging thought that she was weaker than her patient, the woman who contemplated suicide. She looked around her office switching the position of the legal pad and file. She decided to compare herself, a childish gesture, with Janet Robinson.

After rapidly putting her attributes in one column, she began filling the opposite column with what she knew about Janet. Her education would not compare with Lashauna's, nor did her job experience. She moved on to personal characteristics. To her surprise, she had a lot of good things to say about Janet.

She pulled her file that defined her behavior, analyzed her conversations and spoke about her character. The same summaries she would be reviewing while answering the lawyer's questions. She sighed determined to win the characteristic challenge. She added the children, husband and marriage. She quickly crossed out marriage in light of the divorce papers that would be a negative. The points were close. Janet did have a relationship with her siblings, although she took a half point for the issues they had. Lashauna couldn't add any points to her column. She had little to no connection with any of her family members. They always wanted what she wasn't willing to give, money.

Having her own practice had to count, and she needed the points. She quickly added five to her column. Walter had to count for at least three points, but if she added him, whose column would Richard fall under. She scribbled across the entire pad. The tears welled in her eyes. Janet would be divorced, and Richard would be willing be her lover. It was time to let go.

46

Janet left the lawyer's office agitated. In preparing her papers for court she showed Janet the doctor reports from her hospitalization. It was recommended that she'd be evaluated by Dr. Lashauna Norris. The correspondence between the doctor and the hospital was vague, and it was recommended that a second doctor be consulted. Janet knew nothing about the request. She tried convincing herself that maybe the number of her sessions was increased only to obtain a report from Dr. Norris. She didn't really believe it, and the record showed there was no indication it was mandated or that Janet continued therapy for two months. Janet was determined to be early for her scheduled appointment and was certain it would be her last.

She got off the elevator and followed the corridor to Lashauna's office. She drank the last of her tea and lemon depositing the cup in the receptacle before approaching the office. She wouldn't need an hour to discuss her current discovery.

The office door was ajar. Janet tapped on the wooden frame not waiting for the doctor to acknowledge her. She pushed the door open and entered before Lashauna could pretend she was busy.

"Must be a light day when a doctor has no files spread across the desk."

"Janet, I'm glad you decided to keep your appointment."

Janet took a seat in the chair she had reluctantly occupied over the last two months. Now that she knew she wasn't required to be there, she thought about all the reasons Lashauna, her honest therapist, told her it was to her advantage.

"Lashauna, do you remember anything about our first meeting? Was there something that stood out about me when you met me?"

She looked at Janet remembering her state of mind when she walked into the hospital room. She was not the same woman. Lashauna noticed everything about her that day. She visually inspected her expressionless face, her twitches and nervous reactions to sound. She wondered why Richard had an interest in a woman who would attempt suicide. She sighed before answering, realizing her emotions were peaking. Emotions about Richard she couldn't control.

"I can't really say."

"Can't or won't. I meant what I said to you. I won't be taking pills because of you or anyone else, for that matter. You need to take heed to your own words. I'll admit I was frazzled, worn, and yes; suicidal. During our sessions, and yes they were as much yours as mine; I thought I could reveal myself to you. I wanted to change the image you had of me. Lashauna, I saw it in your eyes. You came to visit three days before I even spoke to you because of what I saw."

"What did you see? I didn't know anything about you to make any judgments or opinions." She hoped the lie wouldn't be obvious. "Like you said it took three days and Richard I guess, for you to talk to me."

"I had no idea that Richard summoned you to visit me. It's funny how God intervenes. He always gives guidance to his lost sheep. I really believe that. I was led to you for a reason. Lashauna, I saw me in you. My fears, my anxiety, my deflated self-esteem and my unwanted love, I saw it all in your face each day. Each day you looked at me, assuming I was out of touch with reality, and that love pushed me to the edge. Lashauna, you are only a step away from where I was. I didn't admit that loving Marcus was killing me and loving Richard is killing you."

Lashauna let her head fall slowly between her hands. She set her eyes on the papers on the desk avoiding Janet's glare. She let the words sink in as though she was a child being scolded. She closed her eyes feeling the wetness and warmth of her tears.

"I asked you to be my friend. We needed each other. I needed a professional ear, a listening ear, an analyzing ear. And you needed a sympathetic ear, and a shoulder to lean on. We're from two different backgrounds, sitting on different levels of accomplishments, and it's funny; we needed each other."

Lashauna wanted to respond, but the words were stuck in her throat. Janet paused, waiting for the doctor to look up. Their eyes met, and Lashauna noticed the tears in Janet's eyes.

"You love Richard. I don't know how to change the way he feels about you, but Lashauna you can't discredit who I am because he loves me."

"I never discredited you. If I did, I'm sorry, but I haven't talked about you to anyone, not even Walter."

"You need to talk to Walter about it. I've talked to Richard. What I'm telling you I've told him. You love him Walter knows it, and he's hurting. You and I talked about being honest. It starts within. Lashauna, can you be honest with yourself?"

"Honestly," she paused, "I guess not. I tried forgetting about getting with Richard. I tried to ignore him not returning my calls, avoiding seeing me at church and putting Walter up to dating me."

"What? If you knew he was setting you up with Walter why would you continue in the relationship leading him on? Does he know?"

"Hell no! He's a white boy who thinks he's got jungle fever." She wiped her face with a tissue and passed the box of Kleenex to Janet.

"Are you sure you don't have a bit of jungle fever too? Why stay with him almost a year if you thought it was just a set up?"

"It started out that way, or so I thought. Richard really didn't care one way or the other. You're right. I wanted it to be Richard's doing, so I pursued Walter after the first date, trying to make Richard jealous. Hell he's got more than a pleasant smile, and sultry voice. Anyway, I kept it going well beyond my intentions."

Janet watched as Lashauna went on describing the things Walter had done during the past year to gain her affection and attention. She laughed as she told about his questions of a lasting relationship and how she couldn't see the possibility of being with him much longer.

"You're right, you and Richard have brought me to the realization that you can't fake loving someone when you don't. I don't think I can love Walter."

"Lashauna you've been with him for almost a year, how could you lead him on like that?"

"Like what? It probably was a stupid bet between him and Richard anyway. I could see them high fiving after he shared my bed the first time. I went along with their game that's all. Now it's over. You're right I have to confront some issues. That's one of them; I don't know that Walter is the one for me. I've tried to tell him it's not working but he swears it's because I love Richard."

Janet was silent. She stood and walked to the window looking out onto the traffic below. Lashauna's eyes followed her not understanding her silence.

"Shauna, how could you hurt Walter like that knowing the pain you've suffered loving Richard? I would think you wouldn't want to have someone hanging on, hoping you would love them. You're deliberately hurting someone. You can't possibly be blind to his pain."

"He doesn't believe me. I have told him."

"When's the last time you slept with him?"

Lashauna thought about the last sheet toss the two of them had; it was Monday. They argued Tuesday and Wednesday. She planned on ending it before the weekend was over.

"I guess you're not answering the question 'cause you're still letting him find your soft spot. You're a therapist; you're a doctor of emotions, that ain't right doc."

"Janet..."

"I thought I saw me in you. I misunderstood my relationships with my family, and so-called friends. They created an emotional hell for me, and you create that hell for others. That's not where I'm coming from or going to."

"Janet ... you, you can't possibly understand."

"Why? Why can't I understand?" Janet walked around the room pointing to her various awards. "Dr. Lashauna Norris, what does that mean if you're sick Dr. Norris? How can you tell patients to be honest with you, and you're not honest with yourself or the people you say you care for? Did you ask me to be honest with you because of Richard's involvement? Never mind. Lashauna face the facts. You love Richard, and you can't control his emotions by hurting those he loves. I've talked beyond my time. Oh, you can mark this as my last visit. My lawyer told me these sessions were over two months ago according to the hospital records. I hope this visit doesn't sway your opinion about my progress. I really think I found myself in my sessions with you Dr. Norris. That was the point of the sessions, to bring me back to reality right?"

"Janet, we really need to talk, outside of this environment, as friends."

"I asked you to take off your lab coat some time ago. It really doesn't matter to me now."

"It matters to both of us Janet. I thought we established a friendship."

"That was my intention. But I can't see being friends with someone who causes the pain that drove me off the edge."

"I understand what you're saying but Janet, everyone is not suicidal."

Janet walked from the window as Lashauna stood to speak. She never stopped even when Lashauna asked what time they were leaving in the morning. Dr. Norris watched her friend as she walked down the hall and turned the corner leading to the elevator.

47

Walter left the office an hour after Richard. They agreed to talk later if Lashauna changed her mind about joining them on the trip. Walter hadn't heard from her all day and didn't expect her to change her mind. He locked the office and went to the parking garage to get his car. Looking down the rows of parked cars, he noticed a woman standing with her back to him near his car. She was the height and size of Lashauna but Walter couldn't imagine her meeting him in the parking garage. He quickened his pace curious to see who she was and why she was standing there waiting.

Lashauna heard the footsteps and turned watching Walter as he approached her. He stopped at the car parked next to hers, as though he was scared to get closer.

"Walter, I'm sorry. We really need to talk."

He didn't respond and went to his trunk for no reason. He opened it and slowly put in his briefcase. He tried to contain himself. His emotions were confused. He pulled himself together hoping Lashauna wanted to clear the air so they could move forward. Walter wanted her love, even if she loved Richard.

"Get in the car. I've got to pack so we can go to my place."

They rode for two blocks before he spoke again. "Shauna, I can't continue to do this. I know you love Richard. I've accepted that. I also know that Richard never loved you. I think it would be different if he did. You've got to face some facts. Like the fact that I love you. I loved you when you were trying to get with Richard. I've loved you a long time, but I'm not willing to be used. The game is over. You have to make a choice. I'm not severing my friendship or business with Richard. Being in a serious relationship with me would include you seeing him. You're not comfortable with that, and I don't know how you can become comfortable with it. So continuing our relationship is totally up to you. I'm not going to force it, but I'm not going to rehash this again."

Lashauna listened receiving her second dose of reality as tears fell from her eyes. She had no words that would explain her past actions.

"Walter, I don't know what to say. I'm sorry; I'm wrong; I shouldn't have; I could go down a list of things that I am at the moment. I'm not proud of any of them. You're right we shouldn't have to rehash this again. Love shouldn't cause pain. I know you love me, and I've allowed you to make love to me without really loving you in return. You deserve so much more. I do love you Walter, but I've ignored those feelings hoping Richard would be jealous and show it. No, show me that he at least cared that I was involved with you. He didn't care. He encouraged our relationship. It set me back Walter. I didn't want to stop loving him."

Walter pulled into his driveway and put the car in park.

"So have you?"

"I need to go with you this weekend Walter. Please accept me as you have in the past, as I am. I've got issues, but I've got you and friends who have put things into perspective for me. I'm sorry that I've treated you the way I have in the past, but I do love you."

"Well if you're going, you'll need to pack." He paused realizing where her car was parked. He grinned as he touched her hand.

"My bag is in my car." She smiled; pleased he accepted her apology.

"We'll swing by there in the morning when we leave."

"Are you willing to drive up in your car?"

"We're thinking alike. I want to know what changed your mind." Walter spoke hoping she would finally confide in him.

"I can tell you that tonight."

Walter cut off the ignition. "I've got other plans for tonight. Maybe we need to go get your bag."

"Okay but I've got to warn you. It's scary facing the truth."

"It would be scary if we didn't."

48

ichard and Janet left for the Pocono Mountain Resorts shortly after eight Friday morning. Sam was willing to pick up the children at camp and drop them off Saturday morning to Elaine. Although he and his mother agreed that it wouldn't be a problem for the children to stay with them, Janet insisted that he follow her request. Elaine was looking forward to their stay.

Checking into the hotel was a fiasco. There was a computer glitch, and the rooms were now scattered. Richard and Walter had secured rooms for themselves and the clients they represented. They hoped the rooms would be in the same proximity. Janet didn't have a room. Her reservation was lost in the system. She was frustrated and didn't think it would be appropriate for her to stay with Richard. She couldn't understand the reason the room wasn't included in the firm's total.

"I understand your point Janet but the hotel is full. It's not that big of a deal."

Janet stood close to Richard to be sure no one else would hear her response.

"Richard, I'm preparing myself for a divorce, and I want full custody of my children. I'm at a business conference with you as an employee not a lover. No one is supposed to know we're dating, remember?"

"And no one does; no one knows you're here with me. No one knows who you're married to. It will be fine."

Janet looked around the lobby. Richard told the hotel clerk he would be waiting for his partner before checking in. Walter would be there within the next hour.

"Richard, we've never slept together," she said coyly.

"Okay and if you don't want to we won't. Janet there's plenty of rooms with double beds. Baby, this is not about us getting together and no one is gonna ask where you sleep each night."

"Is Lashauna coming?"

"Walter said she was, why?"

"She's sending my evaluation to the lawyer."

"Her evaluation doesn't include anything you didn't tell her in the office."

"Suppose they ask her?"

Richard could hear the anxiety in her voice. He thought the weekend would be the catalyst they needed. With her divorce papers in place and her feeling secure and in control, he fantasized about passionately making love to her.

"Lashauna's not like that."

They walked over to the love seat in the lobby where they waited for Walter. Richard looked at his watch.

"Richard, if you and I sleep together that may cause the push she needs to go over the edge."

"What?"

"She still loves you. I don't want to flaunt our relationship in her face."

"So we're going to pretend to put on this boss employee relationship for her sake? No we're not. We're adults, and this is not high school. I love you and intend for us to be together with or without Lashauna's permission. I never told that woman I loved her, or led her to believe it. She needs to face that. She can stay in her room for all I care, but I'm not willing to pretend. I want you in the worse way. My only interest is to please you. Now if you don't want to sleep with me that's fine, but don't turn this around. It's not about Lashauna's feelings."

"Hey man, what's up Janet."

Walter's voice interrupted their conversation. Richard stood to shake his hand.

"Where's Shauna?"

"She went to the ladies' room. I told her I would be looking for you near the front desk. Did you check all of us in?"

Janet stood scanning the room. She didn't see Lashauna. Richard and Walter went to the desk to check in. She returned to her seat to wait. It didn't take long, and Richard returned with the two keys.

"This is your key my dear. You're in three fifteen."

"Where is your room?"

"They were right the rooms are scattered. We're on different floors. Walter and Lashauna are in the other tower. So we'll have to call them to get together."

"Where's your room?"

"I'm in a suite. You have one of the rooms we would have had to cancel. It worked out."

"Richard, I didn't mean for you to get another room for me." The thought of a suite gave her a rush. Richard was right no one knew her. Her thoughts were broken with his explanation.

"Listen I didn't know there would be a cancellation. So it's the same amount of rooms we would have gotten, nothing extra. C'mon I'll tell the bellhop where your bags are going. Can I interest you in seeing the suite?"

Janet stood smiling. She put the key to her room in her purse. She followed Richard through the lobby. He pointed out people he knew and greeted those within the distance of a handshake. The conference attendees were well over the amount of people Janet expected. Richard was right; they didn't care who he was with. There hadn't been many whispers about her and after the introductions she got less than a nod of recognition. No one spoke to her in any length.

There were no questions about how she met Richard, how long they knew each other or was she married.

They all seemed to be preoccupied with the purpose of the upcoming presentations or deals in the immediate future. Richard was recognized by his clients, introduced to their guests and those who wanted to be a part of Burnett and Reed. Janet had to admit she was impressed and even a little excited. Richard definitely made a lasting impression on a lot of people. She didn't really expect to fit in; she lacked the background experience. However, she was comfortable and understood most of the business terms they used.

"I should have asked you, do you want to stop at your room first."

"That would be fine. What time is the reception tonight?"

"It starts at seven. We're walking in at eight."

"Why eight?"

"Seven is the cocktail hour. They begin to serve dinner around eight. I will have drinks and special presentations in my suite at six. We will leave there about seven forty five."

"I see. Is that what the executives do?"

"That's what I'm doing this time. Usually I go about seven thirty."

Richard allowed Janet to enter the elevator. Her cell phone vibrated in her purse. She couldn't imagine who was sending her a text message. She'd wait to get to the room before checking it. Richard took the key from Janet and opened the door to what she knew would be heaven for the next few days of freedom. Her home gave her that now that she accepted single room service. A weekend of relaxation, she needed that. She smiled as Richard waved her into the room. It was larger than the average rooms. There was a king-sized bed, an area for entertaining, which held a table, couch and plasma television separated from the bedroom with two steps that were the length of the room. The couch was inviting. Janet couldn't resist the temptation of obvious comfort.

Richard closed the door watching Janet plunge onto the pillowed couch. He saw her relaxing for what he now thought was the first time since her release from the hospital. She finally let go of the shield she held for protection. Her giggles pleased him. He stepped down the stairs and looked into the stocked refrigerator that sat across the room.

"Something to drink?" He asked without really waiting for her answer.

"Yes, do they have soda? I don't want to drink this early."

"We can order lunch for the suite; it will be there when we get there."

"You never said what floor you were on."

"I'm at the end of the hall beyond the closed doors."

"The closed doors?"

"Suites are at the ends of the floors usually on both ends. I'm just a few doors away. No one from our group is on this floor so you can rest your mind about the gossip and the rumors."

Janet's phone vibrated again and she immediately checked it. It was another text message. She read it and deleted it. Richard passed her a ginger ale soda and waited for her to speak.

"It was Lashauna. She said she wants to talk before the reception this evening."

Janet filled Richard in with the details of her last session on the ride to the hotel.

"Well that's easy she can meet you here, and the two of you can join us in the suite."

"I'm not sure I'm gonna continue these free therapy sessions for her. I need to charge her." Janet laughed in spite of herself. She began texting a message. "I think I'll tell her that."

Richard shook his head and smiled while pouring his drink.

"Janet I want you to enjoy this trip. I did a lot of this deliberately for you so please enjoy yourself. If you don't want to deal with her issues don't."

She looked at Richard realizing she wouldn't be able to resist having him in her bed. She was scared to venture to the suite. The ambiance would create feelings she couldn't control. She completed the text while taking off her shoes. Richard watched hoping she wouldn't stop. There was a knock on the door, and Janet put her feet on the couch. Richard grinned knowing the gesture meant she was taking his advice.

The bellhop entered with her bags and thanked Richard for the tip. When asked had he placed the bags in the suite the young man said it was taken care of and everything was, just as he requested.

"Janet, I don't know about you, but I'm a little hungry. Let's order so we can eat lunch on the terrace."

"I'd love to. I just can't get off the couch right now."

Richard went to the couch and lifted her head placing it on his lap. She closed her eyes and gave him a sexy grin. He couldn't help but bend and kiss her forehead. She pulled him to her giving him the kiss she longed for. They both knew lunch would be delayed.

49

"What difference does it make Marcus? You pretend not to give a damn about my feelings. I don't want children. You knew that when we got together. I meant just what I said; I don't want children. If I don't want my own why would I want to raise anyone else's?"

"You wouldn't be raising my kids. I want them to be comfortable with visiting or staying overnight with me, where I live, that's all."

The argument started in the middle of the week when Marcus asked Karyn about the children spending more time with him on the weekends. It was now Saturday morning, and he posed the question to her again. She had ignored him and thought he understood her look. It was obvious she needed to make her point clearly understood when he brought it up for the third time.

"Marcus, your children are sweet, but I told you how I felt about children before we got together. If you need to have them in your life, get an apartment, and move back home. Do what you have to do. But you can't expect me to bend any further than occasional visits. Not a regular schedule, no, I don't want that."

"Do you hear yourself? Karyn they're kids."

"Kids make a mess; they cry and whine, and they talk to damn much. They'll take my business and yours to your wife. I don't want her in my life any more than necessary. Your youngest is what, three? I'm not the motherly type, and I won't be leaving my house just to satisfy your desire to be the loving father. You should have thought about that before you left your wife. That is what this is about right;

214

you trying to please Janet? I know that's what it is, you wanting her back."

"How is spending time with my kids pleasing her?"

"Marcus, we've been together for almost two years. Janet has this so-called break down, a miraculous recovery, and now she's got your attention. If this argument is the prelude to you wanting to go home save it, go the fuck home."

"This is my damn home. I pay bills here."

"And the lease is in my name. Go where you've got your name, and you can make the decisions. Your kids can visit. I never said they couldn't, but I can't deal with that every other week, every damn week, spending the night. No, I don't like kids like that."

"So I guess you'll never be a mother."

"No, don't have plans on it either. Isn't that what attracted you? Safe sweet cheeks you could fall between without the worry that I would trap you. I don't plan on having the so-called "family life." To be honest with you honey I don't think I want a marriage either."

Karyn left Marcus sitting at the kitchen table. He lost his appetite. The breakfast she prepared was cold, and he didn't care about putting it in the microwave. He understood her words but thought his children would fill the void of her early abortion and then miscarriage. When talking about a family Karyn explained her past and felt she had been punished.

She dated a professor while attending a community college in Boston. The affair as the Tribune reported caused a scandal in the small town, and the professor was fired leaving her to finish the semester embarrassed and pregnant. After telling her parents about her dilemma the only solution was to have an abortion before returning to New Jersey. It became the family's secret.

Karyn found herself in love and pregnant again two years later. She stayed with the father hoping to be married before the birth. He joined the military and Karyn found employment to help prepare for the birth of their child. After the first-trimester complications caused a miscarriage. The father came home long enough to see her regain her strength. The love she thought they shared became distant and soon her letters were returned, "address unknown."

Her relationships since then came with no long-term commitment. Karyn wasn't seeking the love of a lifetime. Marcus was the first man she shared her home with. He wasn't looking to marry her or have a family, but he did want his children in his life.

He dialed Sherod's phone and when the music for the answer machine played he hung up and dialed his cell.

"Hey man, are you with the kids today?"

"No, Faye and I are out of town. We won't get back until tomorrow."

"Oh, I was hoping to see them. I called Janet and didn't get an answer."

Sherod allowed the silence. He wasn't about to tell him where Janet was.

"You wouldn't know where they might be, huh?"

"We left on Thursday. I haven't talked to Janet, and neither has Faye. You're the first call I've gotten since we left."

"Well, have a good time man. When are you coming back?"

"Tomorrow, school starts Tuesday."

"Yeah, that's why I was trying to see them this weekend."

"You okay man?"

"Not really, but you enjoy your vacation. We'll talk when you get back. Thanks man."

"Alright, if you need to, call me back. You don't sound right."

"I'm good."

Marcus hung up the phone. He looked at the time. Ten thirty was early for Janet. She would have to dress Joy and get the others ready to be out before ten. That wasn't a norm for them. He decided to call Sam, a call he seldom made.

"Hello, Sam? What's up man?"

"Marcus?"

"Yeah, I know we haven't talked in a while. How are you?"

"Good, what's up?"

"I wanted to say thanks for helping Janet with the kids and all. M.J. said he spends a lot of time with you and Sherod. I really should be more involved with him, but I want to thank you."

"It's all good that's my nephew. So what's up with you? How have you been?"

"I'm good man. You know." Marcus knew from Sam's response the kids weren't with him. "Have you seen Janet?"

"She took the kids out of town for the weekend."

Sam smiled to himself thinking the lie would irritate the brother-n-law he couldn't stand. He warned Janet of his controlling ways. Now that she was rid of him, he'd help keep it that way.

"Wow, okay I guess everyone had the same idea. I was trying to get with them for the weekend."

"Funny you should say that. I asked about them being with me too; seems like Janet had other plans. Look man, I'd love to talk to you, but I gotta go."

"Yeah, man yeah. Thanks."

Marcus hung up the phone. For the first time since he left his wife and children he felt totally separated from them. Karyn was right he needed to go home.

50

The hours passed quickly. Janet found herself behind schedule. She organized her suitcase and accessories when she packed knowing she would be nervous and rushing. It didn't help she couldn't find one earring and was unable to clasp her necklace. She glanced at the time on the cable box. The neon LCD clock read seven twenty. She was sure Richard would be expecting her in his suite. His private reception began on time. She needed help desperately.

Her purple Adrianna Papell cocktail dress was a perfect match with her purse and silver sandals. Her South Sea Diamond Pendant earrings, with the matching diamond necklace and bracelet would be the highlight of her eye-catching ensemble. She looked through her luggage and carry on again for the other earring. If she couldn't find it she would be at a lost. Janet stood back looking at the room, which was now in total disarray. She took a deep breath and started to search again slowly. She didn't need to perspire and ruin her hair as well. She paused looking at the clock again. There was a knock at the door. Janet was startled. She became frantic hoping it wasn't Richard.

"Just a minute." She scurried around the room embarrassed that she had made a mess. Throwing items back into the suitcase she zipped it partially tucking in garments along the sides. She checked herself in the full-length mirror on the closet as she passed and then opened the door.

"Shauna, hey, uh come, on in." Lashauna stepped in as Janet quickly closed the door.

"We were wondering if anything was wrong. I volunteered to check on you."

"I guess Richard would have questions; I am late. I can't find my other earring. I couldn't clasp my necklace and to tell you the truth Shauna; I don't know if this outfit is right or if I will even fit in."

"Let me see the other earring and where's your necklace?"

Janet accepted her help. They searched for the earring, which sparkled under the towel on the bed. The earrings and necklace were perfect and Lashauna understood Janet's dismay when she thought she lost the final touches.

"Perfect choice Janet, I like it. I think it's a stunning outfit. Where's your purse?" The doctor walked to the door and waited. Janet grabbed the room key and put it in her purse. She smiled at Shauna, a silence indicating her thanks. Shauna responded, "You'll be fine."

Janet took a moment to look over the doctor's choice. Her silver Vera Wang cocktail dress spoke for itself. She wore diamond accessories. Janet was sure they would make a few of the guest jealous. "Your dress is beautiful, a Vera Wang?"

"Yes, I fell in love with it, and Walter nodded his approval. I decided why not. I don't splurge often."

"Well it's beautiful on you. To be honest with you, I only know the name because Richard insisted I try one on. Oh, I'm sorry. I promised myself that I wouldn't do that."

"Janet, I've done some thinking and..."

"Let's leave that in the past. We're here to have a good time. Shall we?"

The ladies walked into the suite filled with CEOs and other executives. The men were polite and courteous. The other women and wives whispered their opinions as they made their way through the large room. Richard and Walter were mixing and mingling with prospective clients and other guests.

"Let's get a drink. They've been roaming the room since six. I got tired of the fake smiles and introduction thirty minutes after I got here."

"Really, I would think being introduced as a doctor would be a plus."

"Not once you say you're a Psychologist. This just isn't the right setting. They want to know so much about the field and my clients. Then to repeat it over and over with each introduction, girl it's a pain."

"I don't really see the difference. A doctor is a doctor."

"Heart doctor, Surgeon, Dentist, the average person knows what they do from day to day. My days differ depending on the patient. It makes conversation for those who wonder about the field. Anyway, I don't want to talk about work. I really don't. I want to enjoy myself. Janet, are you sure you and I cleared up our misunderstanding? I really want you to be my friend. You were right; I need to face a lot of things."

Janet didn't respond seeing Richard and Walter approaching. She wondered what Shauna's reaction was seeing Richard in his black Giorgio Armani Tuxedo. He used his charming mannerism as he spoke to guest keeping his eye on Janet. Every strand on his head and beard was in place, he had the look of wealth. His walk of confidence held a taint of arrogance but she couldn't help but smile knowing he was her date for the evening. Walter's choice was a silver Ralph Lauren Tuxedo. Janet understood why he gave Shauna a nod of approval on her dress. They made a stunning couple. The two men walked toward the women parting the guests, as though they were walking a fashion runway. Janet saw the reaction of the women as Richard and Walter greeted them with soft kisses on their cheeks.

"So Shauna did find you. I thought I was being stood up for the evening." Richard smiled putting his arm around Janet's waist.

"She only needed a helping hand."

"Yes, and thank God, she came in when she did."

"Well, ladies will you join us for dinner." Walter extended his arm for Shauna to walk ahead of him. He leaned toward her as she passed him. He whispered. "You're beautiful."

Shauna felt beautiful. She was surprised that the sight of Richard and Janet together didn't send a shock to her emotions. She wanted Janet's friendship and Walter's love. She wouldn't lose them both for a fantasy that would never be filled.

The night went well. Richard and Walter made several acknowledgements of prospective clients, appreciations for others, investors and bankers. They spoke about their goals for Burnett and Reed LLC announcing the future office in Princeton, New Jersey. Dinner was served, and the floor opened for dancing and networking.

Janet had never been to a corporate function and wasn't sure about the dancing. She excused herself beckoning Shauna to join her in the ladies' room.

"Did you send back the packet to my lawyer?"

"No, but I will. It shouldn't be a problem. Do you think Marcus will protest?"

Janet talked from the stall hoping that she and Shauna were still the only ones in the bathroom. "I hope not, if he does it will get ugly. That's why Richard and I hadn't made our relationship public knowledge."

"And you think separate rooms will keep the talk down?"

"No, huh? I just don't want obvious problems. If they check the record, I've got my own room."

"Well, if you're worried about me, don't. I don't know much about Marcus and what I do know is enough. You deserve better."

The toilet flushed and Janet joined Shauna at the sink. "I'll be able to deal with him in court."

"What does that mean? You can't think that you won't have to deal with him later. You've got the kids."

"That's my next battle. I've got to deal with him without anyone being a liaison."

"Don't take this the wrong way or anything, but how does Richard fit in?"

Janet didn't want to answer the question she pushed the bathroom door open and smiled at Shauna.

"Janet I didn't ask that to pry, seriously. I didn't want you or Richard having problems."

"Problems? Marcus is a walking problem. So like I said he's my next battle."

51

Richard and Janet returned to his suite close to two o'clock in the morning. The party was winding down and there were only a few couples left on the dance floor. The settings at the tables were replaced with empty glasses and napkins a sign the seats had been vacated. Walter and Shauna left for their suite at midnight. Neither of them would remember leaving. Janet didn't know whether Shauna drank like that regularly, or she got bumped to numb her emotional pain. Richard showed everyone he had a serious interest in Ms. Janet Robinson. Shauna teased him by asking when the wedding was. His reply was soon. She drank more and talked less the rest of the night.

Walter didn't seem bothered as usual, but Janet caught him eyeing Shauna occasionally as she joked with Richard. She could only imagine the depth of his thoughts. Richard assured her his relationship with his partner was solid. She wondered how long Walter would be able to face him after he, and Shauna broke up permanently. She could see his anger mounting.

Richard asked Shauna to dance after Walter asked Janet. They both were tipsy minus the staggering. The DJ's mix was serious, and the floor filled with the guest who appreciated a bit of Rock and Ole' School R & B. The rhythm changed to "If this World were Mine" by Luther Vandross and Shauna leaned into Richard's chest. Careful not to let her fall, he held her up, and she immediately positioned herself for the dance.

"Do you want to return to your seat?"

"Are you saying you won't dance slow with me? That's fucked-up Richard."

"You're drunk."

"And you never danced with a drunk woman?"

Richard didn't answer. Walter and Janet left the dance floor returning to their table to watch what would be Shauna's last dance for the evening.

"Richard, I know you and I won't be together. Can you tell me what it is about her?" Shauna tried whispering in Richard's ear. "Have you at least tried her? Do her tonight and do me tomorrow. C'mon try us both before making up your mind."

He pushed her back stopping the dance. The couples dancing near them heard her attempted whisper. They looked at Richard, who was obviously embarrassed. One of his clients gave a questioning glance toward Walter and Janet. He mouthed 'good night' to Richard while quickly leading his wife off the dance floor. Their expression showed disgust. They knew Shauna was being more than flirtatious. He escorted her to the table.

"Walter take her to your room."

"What's wrong?"

"Take her outta here man. Good night."

Shauna didn't care one way or the other. She waited for Walter to stand and take her hand. "Richard, call if you change your mind."

Walter pushed her away from the table. He took his glass and downed the remainder of his drink before leaving.

"Call me in the morning man; night Janet."

Janet was stuck on Shauna's comment and how Richard ignored her. When he caught her gaze, he gestured for her to join him on the dance floor. The DJ mixed another slow jam before announcing the party would be coming to an end.

Richard didn't offer an explanation for asking Walter to escort Shauna from the reception. He asked if Janet would join him for a drink in his suite and she was pleased to accept.

"You're more than the average woman Ms. Robinson." Richard poured the wine over the ice cubes and handed her the glass. He poured himself a drink and joined her on the loveseat. Janet didn't know how to respond.

"You handled Shauna rather well. I guess I expected you to be upset with both of us."

"You didn't do anything and Shauna won't remember what she did. I don't think I could really be the jealous type. I never got upset about Karyn and Marcus. I think he brought her into our lives. Shauna is a friend by day and ..."

"A stalker by night, I'm going to talk to her and Walter tomorrow after the panel meeting. It's embarrassing, and I don't want you to be uncomfortable."

"Thank you."

Richard put down his drink and loosened his tie. Janet reached to help him with the button that was fastened close to his neck. Her hand touched his beard, and her fingers found the silky strands comforting as she stroked them slowly. Shaped and combed perfectly, the character it added to his features gave Janet an erotic rush. He closed his eyes relaxing as her hand roamed across his chest unbuttoning three more buttons on his shirt. He put his hand on hers and raised it to his mouth and kissed it gently.

"Janet I want so much in my life. I've accomplished most of it alone. Walter and Elaine have been my support over the years, but it's different. Everyone has someone special in their lives. There was a moment when I thought Shauna, and I would hit it off. I told Elaine how fine I thought she was on Sunday mornings. Shauna would only smile and nod hello; that was enough to touch something in me. Elaine made it her task to get to know the "doctor"."

Richard got up to refresh his drink. He filled his glass and offered to fill hers. Janet took off her shoes and wiggled her toes getting comfortable.

"It took about two months or more before I began dating her. We went to a few shows, dinner, the movies, nothing intimate or overnight. She was anticipating weekend trips, conferences I spoke of, and sex. Janet, over the time we dated it was something about her that didn't sit well with me. I enjoyed her company as a friend, but I couldn't see us as a couple. I knew having sex would complicate our relationship as friends. I backed off. She didn't understand why. I couldn't bring myself to tell her she wasn't my definition of the woman I wanted to spend my intimate moments with."

He took a drink from his glass and continued. "She used our friendship to stay in touch weeks after our last date. You know, calling to say hi, talk about church business, her patients, my clients, anything to keep me on the phone. I suggested she find a friend who wanted more, Walter became the friend. Now I feel that I've betrayed him. I knew the reason she dated him, but I encouraged it. The man loves her and she still loves me. Janet tonight Walter saw it. I know he heard what she said, and if he didn't someone who heard it will talk about it in our circle."

Janet put her glass on the end table. Richard leaned back into the arm of the love seat allowing her to lie on his chest.

"I don't know how to save him from the pain he's going through. I don't know what will make her understand we just don't fit. My life has changed so much over the past few years, and my future is rapidly changing to. God put you in my life for a reason. I want to know why, why you? She asked me that tonight. Why you, Ms. Robinson, why?"

"You were meant to be there for me when I was at a point of despair. Why? Richard, I never asked why. I just thanked God for you. Shauna is a woman who sets her mind one way. She set her mind on you."

"But I knew that and I introduced her to Walter. I told her what his friendship meant to me. It seems since she couldn't have me, she would destroy the feelings of those around me. Janet, Walter was the first, and I'm sure she'll try to harm you as well."

Janet thought about her court papers. Her fears were resurfacing. She pretended to be okay about Shauna's relationship with Richard. Even so, she had to ask herself, what if he was right?

"Your husband may find a friend in the 'doctor' when it comes to your divorce."

"I'll talk with the lawyer. I hope she's not that stupid."

Richard held her closer. "What do you mean?"

"If she writes me up as crazy, I'll have an excuse to act like it."

52

Marcus wasn't sure where his family spent the night, but he would be there when they returned. Janet never stayed out overnight unless she was with her family. It was eleven o'clock Saturday morning, and she still hadn't returned his call. She wouldn't ignore the message he left saying he had money for her and the children. He hadn't gone back to Karyn's. He was certain she would put him out, but she hadn't called either. When he left he took a few garments that would last until he could move his clothes back into his home with his family.

He made his second ride past the complex. There was still no sign of Janet's vehicle. He decided to pay Sam and his mother an unexpected visit. If the children were there he would use the excuse that he was there to pick them up. He dialed his mother-in-law's phone number and turned down his car radio.

"Good afternoon, Ms. Black?"

"Marcus, hey sugar."

"How are you? I was wondering…"

"Hold on," Jocelyn cut his words off in the middle of his sentence, "Sam, have you heard from Janet? No, okay. Marcus, I wanted to check before you get to asking. The kids ain't here, and Janet hasn't called me or Sam. How are you?"

Ms. Black knew Marcus better than he knew himself. She thought he was the best thing for Janet when they got married. After he left home, she joined her son in ignoring his presence. Their relationship would never be the same.

"I'm okay, trying to catch up with the kids before school starts."

"Well they're with Janet this weekend. I don't know where they went, but I think they left yesterday. Call her phone maybe she'll call you back."

"Thanks Ms. Black." Marcus smirked as he went through his phonebook hoping he could find the number for Carol or Tiffany. If Janet had a date, her friends may have the children.

"Hey Tiff, this is Marcus. Have you heard from Janet?"

"She's out of town. How are you? I haven't heard from you in a while."

"Out of town?"

"Some kind of conference, you know business. She'll be back to-morrow I think."

"You don't have the kids do you?" "No. I don't."

Marcus knew Tiffany wouldn't answer any more questions if she suspected he was just prying. He pretended to know about the conference.

"Listen, the conference is over early today right? I thought it was next week."

"Wow, we all were thinking that including her. She'll be in about five I guess."

"She should have told me to get the kids."

"They left with her."

"Okay, thanks Tiff. I'll talk to you later." Marcus disconnected the line. Tiffany left one question unanswered. *Who takes their kids to a business conference?*

53

Walter woke up later than he wanted to. His head was keeping beat to a rhythm he knew nothing about. Opening his eyes was a struggle. The movement of his eyelids caused pain across his forehead. He definitely drank too much. After leaving the welcome reception he couldn't remember anything else. Shauna had upset Richard, and they were asked to leave. He was glad the guests were scattered. No one heard Richard telling him to take her to his room. The panel conference would begin at one giving him two hours to get ready to discuss business.

He rolled over smiling at the sight of Shauna's caramel body. Her teddy, shoes and stockings were on the floor near the chair. Their garments told the story, of how they fell into the bed. He still had the condom on his limp penis. Walter couldn't remember the erotic episode they shared the night before.

The light on the phone was blinking. Walter got up and decided to shower before returning any calls. The water was therapeutic, and as he stood in the shower he tried to recall the evening's activities. The phone rang again waking Shauna. She reached for the receiver fumbling before saying hello.

"Hello," she answered in a raspy voice.

"Shauna is Walter around?"

"Humph," was her immediate response, "Good morning to your ass too! Walter; it's Richard."

"Shauna, just tell him the meeting is going to be held right after lunch. So I'll see him at one in my suite, and the panel discussion will be at two."

"Apparently you think I'm Janet. My title is doctor, not secretary. However, I will tell him to call you."

The phone went dead before he could respond. Shauna rolled over to close her eyes again, but the sound of the shower grabbed her attention. She got up wrapping the sheet around her naked body. Walter could be seen through the frosted shower door covered in soapsuds. She would have to make up for her drunken blunder. He and Richard would be sorry if she didn't have one of them permanently. If Richard wanted Janet, she would settle for Walter. She would keep her distance from the lovebirds, and the misunderstanding last night would stand as a concrete reason.

Walter cut off the water and opened the door to Shauna standing waiting for him to embrace her. She let the sheet fall to her feet and gave him a silent invitation.

"Hey, I'm glad you're up. I've got a one o'clock panel discussion and meetings throughout the afternoon. I won't return until later. You might want to go home and I'll catch you when I get back."

"Why? What's up with that?"

"Listen, I don't want this day to be a repeat of last night. There's another dance, mixing and networking, you might just feel out of place. I don't know what you said, and as I told you, I don't want to know. Maybe you were right. You and Richard can't be in the same room together."

Walter left her standing in the bathroom. He grabbed a towel from the rack and began drying himself as he walked into the bedroom. The blinking light reminded him the phone rang.

"Who was on the phone?"

"Walter, is this it? I mean you beg me to come here with you, and you send me home after you get your shit off?"

"Be real Shauna; I can get my shit off, as you put it, at home. I made love to you because I love you no matter how much of a fool you make of yourself for Richard."

"A fool! What makes you think I made a fool of myself?"

Walter walked by her again continuing to get dressed between both rooms. He stood at the sink in his briefs brushing his teeth. Shauna watched his tight thighs as he walked by and tried to deny she wanted to be touched by him before he left the room.

"Let's just say that it won't happen again. I don't want to be in the company of you and Richard together. You can't hide your feelings, although you claim there are none. So I accept it. You love Richard and me or am I wrong? You do love me don't you?"

He went to the closet where he got his pants and shirt.

"Walter you know I do. Richard is an ass, and he's trying to cause a problem for us."

"Really, who was on the phone?"

"It was Richard you have to meet him at one in the suite. The meeting is at two."

Walter looked at her watching him with her arms folded. Her pear shape and perfectly portion breasts took his mind off what he wanted to say. He slid his feet into his shoes.

"Thanks. Look, if you don't want to leave, just promise me you'll watch your mouth for the rest of the weekend."

"Walter, you can't ban me from talking."

"I haven't asked you for much, but I'm asking you to respect the relationship I have with Richard. If you can't do that here go home."

With those words, Walter grabbed his brief case. He gave her a kiss on her cheek.

"I'll understand it's over if you don't answer my calls."

"I'll be here when you get back."

54

*J*anet was happier than she had been in years. The call to her lawyer put her mind at ease. Marcus would have to prove her unfit for the courts to give him custody of the children. She hoped there would be no need for a drawn-out proceeding, but Richard was right anything was possible. She left Richard's suite after they had breakfast together. They wouldn't see each other again until the panel discussions at two o'clock.

She needed to relax. Her appointment at the spa was at eleven thirty. Richard teased her offering her a full-body massage. When she smiled waiting for him to prove his skills, he handed her the appointment card for a massage and facial. Mentally, she accepted the gift but her hormones were still awaiting satisfaction. The shower was no help. The warmth of the water eased her muscles and thoughts of Richard's bare chest crossed her mind.

He removed his shirt to avoid getting it stained. Richard put on his silk robe to replace it. His manners were more than Janet expected. Returning to the love seat and their conversation, they continued to talk about Marcus and Shauna. They kissed; a kiss of understanding, and Janet relaxed in his arms until she fell asleep.

The smell of his body brought her out of her slumber, and her need for a man's touch had reached its peak. Richard was already dressed and breakfast arrived. She woke up in his bed angry that she missed a perfect opportunity to surrender unto him.

She turned slowly under the showerhead as her nipples began to harden from the water pellets touch. She turned off the water convincing herself that if opportunity knocked again she would gladly answer the call. She got dressed and called Elaine to check on the children. The call to her mother and brother brought back the tension she lost in the shower.

"Why would Marcus call you?"

"He was talking to Sam before he spoke to me. He said he was looking forward to taking the children out over the weekend. I told him you were away."

Janet was glad she didn't tell her mother where the children were. Sam wouldn't tell, but she couldn't trust her mother. Marcus had a way of sweet talking her mother the same as he could sweet talked her years ago.

"I told him I thought the children were with you. Maybe he called Faye or your girlfriends looking for them."

"Who told him the children would be with them?"

"No one, I didn't; but you know if he called us, he might have called them."

Janet thought about it. Whatever questions Marcus had he wouldn't stop until someone answered them.

"When is Faye and Sherod due home?"

"Tomorrow, just like you, probably in the afternoon. What time are you coming in?"

She thought of her answer, "I don't know. I've got some meetings to attend. Mama I'll call you when I get in."

Janet put on her Baby Phat jogging suit, her water sandals and grabbed her notes for the panel. She had fifteen minutes to make it to her appointment.

The masseuse was more than what she imagined. Her fantasy massage was conducted by a man who had the look of a professional football player most of the time. There were other dreams where the masseuse was taller and worked on Wall Street. She now could add Juan to her dreams.

He touched her hand gently while speaking softly. He excused himself for interrupting her reading, but he politely explained it was time to relax. His accent was pleasant, and his smile was contagious.

"Miss would you like headphones and music? You close your eyes a moment and allow me to release your tension."

Janet smiled and accepted his offer. Closing her notes, she followed him through the reception area filled with women waiting for their appointments. They passed the sauna, weight room, and exercise room. Juan opened the curtain and handed Janet a terry-cloth robe with the hotel's insignia on the pockets. She could smell the white linen fragrance in the air as she disrobed. Returning to the table, she prepared herself for what she heard would set her hormones on fire.

Janet chose a male masseuse hoping Tiffany hadn't been wrong about the magic of foreign hands. Tiffany made a point of getting a full-body massage once a month; Janet told her it wasn't appropriate for her since she was married. The truth was that was what her husband said. Her friends would be green with envy if they knew Richard paid for her spa treatment.

She began to relax, and Juan began to whistle softly. He seemed to enjoy it as well. Janet removed the headphones. She was content to listen to the melodic sound he produced. His hands touched areas that hadn't been touched by a man in more than a year. She closed her eyes and let the fantasy begin.

Her muscles began to relax as she felt her nipples tingle. Chills began to run up and down her spine as Juan poured the warm oil down the middle of her back. The towel that was draped over her buttocks left the top of her thighs exposed. Juan touched them with his fingertips. Janet parted her legs. His fingers wrapped around them, and he massaged her muscles deeply.

Janet closed her eyes, and Juan's hands became Richard's. He spread the oil over her shoulder blades and around her neck. Using his thumbs, he massaged her shoulders. She could feel his breath as he whistled softly. The melody was calming, a melody she would remember in her dreams.

He gently lifted her hips massaging her sides. He took his time and did each leg, her toes, arms and fingers. Janet was limp. The mental orgasm was as her friend had promised, professionally done. Juan lifted his hands and Janet wanted to moan for more. Just as she was about to ask was her time up he returned with warm towels. She could feel her vagina throbbing.

"Ms. I leave you now. You relax; I'll be back with the stones."

She couldn't do anything but relax. She continued fantasizing. She was his prisoner, and it felt good to be held captive.

55

Richard waited for Walter to answer the question. He refused to let their talk turn into an argument. They needed to clear the air before the panel discussion began.

"Walter, don't get me wrong I understand you've fallen in love with her, but I don't want her around me at all. I've tolerated her, as long as I could."

"I'm not understanding, you or her. Is there something going on between the two of you?"

"No, and you know that."

"I can't tell. You tell me no, but her actions say yes."

"What do her actions really say? I want Richard to pay attention to me, and if he doesn't I'm gonna wreck his world? Walter, open your eyes man. This fling you got with the witch doctor is over."

"Over because you say so; who the hell are you to decide when any of my...?"

Walter couldn't finish the sentence. He didn't know what he had with Shauna. He couldn't call it a relationship. Richard allowed the silence to finish the question.

"Man, I need to apologize. I really thought the two of you would hit it off. Date a few times and decide what was best for you. I liked Shauna, but she's not giving up on the thought that I'll change my mind. Walter I don't want to hurt your feelings but I can't have her coming on to me in public. That's embarrassing for you and me. I don't want this to ruin our friendship, business or respect for each other."

"I told her she had to leave if she couldn't keep her mouth shut."

"I don't want her at any of the functions tonight. She can't be trusted. I hope you understand."

"Is Janet okay?"

"I don't know if she heard what she said. We talked about her in general last night. Janet feels the same way I do."

"How does a psychologist become so insecure?"

"She's human. We all have our insecurities. Her strengths give a false impression of who she really is though."

"Man." Walter stood and shook his partner's hand. "I'll see you in the conference center. I left the documents in my room."

"We good, or what?" Richard held Walter's hand awaiting his answer.

"We're good. I mean, if you and the witch doctor can't get along I'll respect your wishes. However, my brother, she's got me under her spell. I've got to deal with that but not right now. I'll see you in a few."

Richard knew Walter's response meant he wanted to continue his relationship with Shauna. He couldn't stop him, but he felt better now that he told him what he thought her intentions were. He saw his partner fall for women in the past without any disappointment later. Walter escaped their grasp and never gave them a second thought. Richard could tell from their conversation, he really didn't want to let Shauna go.

Richard left the suite and headed toward Janet's room. He hoped she returned from the spa refreshed. They would only have the evening together. He wanted it to be one she would remember. She hadn't called after her appointment, and he wondered if she had returned to her room.

He knocked on her door and waited patiently after hearing her voice telling him, "Just a minute." The door opened, and Richard could only smile.

Janet's hair was undone apparently giving her a reason to be frustrated. She didn't seem surprised that he stood in the door watching her go from the mirror on the dresser to the one in the bathroom. He closed the door and took a seat waiting for her to acknowledge his presence.

"I'm sorry; I'm trying to pin my hair. The moisture from the spa, sheesh ... Am I holding you up?"

"No take your time."

"What time is it?"

"Janet, don't worry, take your time."

Janet took his advice and took the pins out of her hair and started again.

"I talked with Walter. I think he's crazy, but he didn't sound like he believed my concerns about his relationship with Shauna. I really think he's whipped."

Janet came out of the room and stood in the middle of the floor modeling her hairdo for Richard.

"Personally I like the librarian bun," he teased.

"Gee thanks, I thought that was what I was going to have to resort to. Walter's in love huh? I hope she realizes he loves her."

"I don't care one way or the other. She's not worth the embarrassment."

"She didn't call, do you think she left."

"We won't know unless she calls. I told him tonight's event did not include an invitation for her. It would be easier if it was just the four of us. If she added more to her stunt last night, it might not sit well. I don't need the whispers."

"Understood, listen, enough of that. I want to thank you for such a lovely gift. I never had a morning like this. The spa was awesome. Do you go to spas often?"

Richard smiled; a devilish smile. "I do. We need to be going my dear. Can't keep the panel waiting; grab that Deluxe file. I think you have it. It wasn't with my reports."

Janet was focused, determined to keep her fantasy alive. "I have it." They walked toward the door where she paused. "What do you enjoy the most?"

"The thought that I pleased you." Richard teased.

"I was talking about the spa."

"So was I."

"Alright, get your mind on business."

"I'm making it my business." Richard allowed her to exit winking as she passed him in the doorway.

56

 aye's blackberry sang its tune twice while she was preparing for her last intimate night with Sherod. Their vacation proved to be the solution to a problem that was mounting between them. Her husband was ready to begin a family of their own, something she had put off for the past two years. They spent their time in upstate New York rekindling what had been missing for months, time for each other. The phone sounded off again, and Sherod reached across the bed and glanced at the LCD screen. The name blinked rhythmically with the music, "Karyn Spalling."

The water in the shower stopped. Sherod pushed the power button on the phone. The familiar beep sounded as Faye approached the bed.

"Why are you turning the phone off?"

"Why is it on? Are you expecting a call?"

"Honey, let's not ruin our vacation with this nonsense."

"You're right; that's why I cut off the phone."

"So, who called?"

"Faye, put the towel down. No, drop the towel. Let's get this last one on, away from home, some kind of different, you know, loving." He pleaded, licking his lips and grinning. His comment took her mind of the call.

"So, you think you can handle some kind of different loving?"

Sherod pulled his wife on the bed where he had been patiently waiting for the past hour. Faye let him lead her to his embrace. He was a passionate man, and she loved how he loved her. The problem over the years was he no longer knew how to prove it. Faye's family commitments were always her priority. Sherod thought once they were married, he would be at the top of that list.

The marriage was inevitable. Janet got married, Faye's sister who had insecurities since high school. Faye cried more at the wedding than anyone. She realized the sister she nurtured, after the death of their father found someone else to depend on, Marcus Robinson. Faye sought to fulfill the gap she felt after her sister left home to become a new bride. Sherod proposed, and they were married a year later.

Janet was pregnant with Marcus Jr. three months after her sister's wedding. Faye shared in the joy of the anticipated birth and was there. Then, there were Joy and Erica, the problems between Marcus and Janet began with Faye helping her sister cope. Through it all, Sherod loved his wife and accepted her love for her sister. It wasn't until his mother-n-law's sickness that he noticed he was nowhere near first on his wife's list of loving concerns.

Sherod thought of a separation, but he loved Faye. He loved Janet and her children too. He didn't doubt Faye loved him, but he wasn't on the top of her priority list. He needed the weekend alone to prove their love still existed.

He marveled at the sight of her thick thighs as she straddled him on the bed. She smiled as he whispered, "Drop the towel."

She obeyed. Slowly, the yellow terry cloth fell from around her breast. Once the towel fell, Sherod pulled it away exposing her totally. Her skin was damp with droplets of water still present around her navel. He held her hips bringing her body closer. He used his tongue to take off the water. As he kissed her navel, then her waist, he rolled her over slowly onto the bed.

He was determined to make her beg for his loving. Her whispers would turn him on; taking him to heights he hadn't been in months. Their lovemaking had become routine, but the weekend ignited fire within them that was undeniable. Faye could feel her body preparing for another romantic voyage. She closed her eyes allowing visions of her husband covered in sweat riding her as he had the night before. She felt his breath on her neck as his hands caressed her breast. He fondled each nipple until they hardened, aroused by his touch.

Faye's reaction caused him to moan. She opened her legs inviting him into her familiar. He accepted, moving down her body with his tongue. Sherod felt his nature beginning to rise to its peak as she rubbed his head gently leading him to where satisfaction would be guaranteed.

Sherod stopped, as he had many times before preparing to open the condom that sat on the nightstand. Faye stopped him but never uttered a word. He said a silent prayer of thanks. He entered his wife for the first time since Faye stopped taking birth control, unprotected; bare back, raw.

The heat, wetness and pulsating motion made him want to scream. He opened his mouth and could only close it as the sweat beaded on his forehead. The only sound that could be heard was the juices of their love. Sherod pulled back, hoping not to explode, he wanted more. Faye was willing to give him what he needed, the loving only a wife could provide. She turned over onto her knees.

She backed herself onto his penis, and instantly he began to find their rhythm again. He held on to her hips pulling her off and on his shaft. He was preparing to ejaculate when she used her vaginal muscles to squeeze him tighter. The sensation caused an instant eruption.

"Aw...damn...." They both released their passion. Sherod looked at himself as he pumped slowly back and forth. Looking at her cheeks as they opened and closed over his penis he began to shake. Her butt was filled with sperm and the sight of the wetness turned him on. He increased his pace and reached around her waist to finger her vagina and clitoris.

Faye began to whisper, "Rod, aww ... please. Deeper, give it to me, all of it."

"You want this. Aw ... damn ... aw ..." The sweat dropped from his face as he felt himself exploding as her clitoris hardened to his touch. Faye began to tremble as he came again. They both collapsed on the bed smiling and breathing deeply. Sherod kissed her cheek. She responded; their lips met, and the tune from her phone interrupted what would have been another round.

57

"*I* can't stay Janet. I've hurt Walt and thanks to Richard, I don't have any excuse for what I was accused of."

Janet and Shauna were talking in the lobby. The panel discussion was on the first scheduled break. They wouldn't be finished for another hour. Shauna asked one of the waiters to ask Janet to meet her near the concierge's desk. Janet was glad to step away from the confusing business talk.

"Shauna, you can't tell me you weren't aware of what you said to Richard while you were dancing. You said it loud enough for quite a few of us to hear you."

"I guess what they say about alcohol is true."

"What, the truth comes out when you're drunk, or people that are drunk don't care what they do or say?"

"So I guess our friendship is done, huh."

Janet wanted to snap. She couldn't believe that Shauna expected everyone to ignore her actions. She began to wonder if the doctor had her own mental problems.

"Shauna, I told you that day we had lunch I don't plan on you or anyone else causing me to return to the state of mind I was in. I didn't stop loving my sister. I just set up my parameters. You and I met, and I must admit, I longed for a relationship with someone who wasn't attached to my world. You were that someone; Richard is that someone. I can't choose between my friendship with you and my..."

"Well I didn't expect that," interrupted Shauna. "I just thought that you and I were above letting this come between us. You know like Walter and Richard. Walter hasn't let it faze his relationship with Richard, professionally or personally."

Janet could tell Shauna was breaking. She saw herself looking into her eyes that were red, apparently from crying. Shauna's beauty was beginning to fade. Janet wondered how long she had been secretly drinking.

"Shauna, don't leave just yet; here's my key. Go to my room please. I'll be there shortly. I have to attend the rest of this meeting. We need to talk, and I don't want you to..."

"Janet, I work with people like me. Remember? I'll be fine," she said refusing to take the key. "Call me about the papers for your lawyer. I'll hold your copy for you."

"Shauna, please be safe."

Janet stood holding her key watching Shauna walk out the lobby. She was tempted to run to the door in an effort to finish their conversation. She remembered it wouldn't matter. She had been in that state of mind often, many times, before taking the pills. She didn't hear anyone talking until it was almost too late. The voices, advice and long talks became muffled buried under guilt, frustration and depression. She returned to the conference room saying a prayer.

Richard and Walter were together talking near the refreshments. Janet approached them trying to hide her concerns, but her face told them there was a problem.

"Janet, are you okay?" Walter spoke first, assuming Shauna had given a message to the waiter who whispered in her ear.

"Shauna just left. She didn't sound right to me. Walter, I don't want to get into your personal affairs but have the two of you called your relationship off?"

"No, I uh...No I'm still seeing her, why?"

"She's gonna need someone. She's having a hard time dealing with things."

"What things?"

The Chairman of the panel tapped the gavel on the podium calling the meeting back to order. Janet and Richard walked ahead taking their seats at the table designated for Burnett and Reed, LLC. Walter went out the door into the lobby. He ignored the vibration from his phone twice. After Janet's comments, he knew the calls were from Shauna. He dialed her number and waited. The familiar ring tone by "Mary, Mary" began, he waited a few seconds before disconnecting the call, and then dialed again.

"Yes Walter, I left. What, did Janet run to you with our discussion?"

"No, listen how far away are you. I was angry, please. The meeting will be over in a half an hour or so. Meet me afterward."

"Meet me at home; that's where I'll be."

Walter wanted to reply but there was no sound on the other end. Shauna had hung up.

58

The panel discussion ended with investor's congratulating Richard and Walter on hosting a successful conference. Everyone agreed to be in touch over the next few months for updates and progress reports. Burnett and Reed's proposal for expansion was accepted with unanimous promises of support. The new office complex would be in Bergen County, northern New Jersey, not in Princeton as proposed. The site would be announced before the end of the year with the groundbreaking ceremony projected in early spring of the next year. Janet was surprised to find out she would be an intricate part of the planning for design, hiring and accepting bids for office space within the complex. It seemed everyone knew she was selected for the position. To her surprise, they congratulated her, as though she had been a part of the panel for years. She didn't know what to say and waited until the room thinned out to confront Richard and Walter.

"I want to thank you both for my new duties, when do I start?"

Walter laughed, looking at Richard, who stated, "You already started. You've been handling the reports and records since I hired you. Now if you don't want the challenge, I guess we can get someone else."

Janet nudged Walter, as he hugged her commenting, "We need Ms. Robinson for more reasons than one. Listen, I'm cutting out. Shauna is having a time with all of this, and I really want to be there for her."

"I didn't want to say anything but just what is the issue?"

"Richard, man, I guess it's a woman's thing. You told her not to show up. I told her go home."

"She feels rejected." Janet knew the feeling. "Loving someone who doesn't love you is hard."

Richard's expression let them know he was confused. "I didn't lead her on. I simply offered my friendship."

"Well I want her to accept my friendship. I really believe she would be over this if you and I weren't as close." Walter stated.

"So our relationship has to change now?"

"No, of course not, but I'm gonna take some time to be with her. I'm leaving early. I'll call you tomorrow to see how the ceremony goes tonight."

Janet listened as they talked of the last event planned for the weekend. Her thoughts drifted to calling Faye and Tiffany. She wanted to share the news of her new position and the marvelous weekend. The weekend had been a total enjoyment. She smiled thinking of the spa. Richard noticed her thoughts took her far away from the lobby where they stood.

"Can I interest you in a little music and wine before tonight's festivities?"

Janet laughed to herself. Her call to Tiffany would have to wait until the morning.

"I'd love to Mr. Burnett."

Walter turned the key, and the scent of Shauna's perfume led him in. He was pleased she decided to stay. He scanned the room, searching for her luggage. He continued into the bedroom, where he found Shauna lying across the bed. He approached the bed slowly, hoping not to awaken her. Walter leaned across her as he watched her breast rise and fall as she breathed comfortably. He kissed her cheek and thanked God that she was safe.

Shauna woke up an hour after Walter returned to the room. The sound of the television brought her out of the slumber she cried herself into. She realized she stayed longer than she intended. She rolled over remembering the note she was writing. The note she wrote wasn't on the nightstand.

"Oh God, did he read it?"

She got up and went to the bathroom certain he heard the water running. She used the cloth to wash her tear-stained face. Shauna sensed Walter standing behind her before seeing his face in the mirror.

"Do you feel any better?"

Shauna put the warm cloth on her face covering her eyes. She could feel the tears welling up. She knew Walter read her note.

"Baby, do you feel any better?"

"I guess so. I didn't mean for you..."

"I know. What do you want me to do with the love I have for you? I can't just forget I love you."

"But it's not fair Walter. I know that now. It's not right to have someone thinking you love them when you don't."

"Shauna, what you and I have is different from what you thought you, and Richard had. He never loved you that way. I always loved you, and I think in some ways you want to love me. If you just let go..."

"So we go on ignoring the fact that I loved your friend? How can you do that?"

"Let me ask you this, if you and Richard had a relationship, and then we met sometime after you broke up, would you consider dealing with me?"

"I guess I would."

"Okay, so what's the difference? I don't see one. I think if you had a serious relationship with Richard, I'd be a little upset."

Walter moved closer putting his arms around her waist. Shauna looked up into the mirror. Seeing Walter, with his head on her shoulder eased the tension. His brunette curly hair was moussed into place. He had an olive tone, which attracted Shauna when she met him. She looked into his eyes; he was right. She began to love him before she could tell him her reasons for allowing him into her bed. The note told it all, now he knew.

He kissed her on her neck and walked out of the room. She wondered whether or not she should mention the note. Walter returned to his seat in front of the television.

"Are you going tonight?"

"No. I told Richard I would talk to him tomorrow. If you're ready to leave we can. It's up to you."

"Did Janet say anything to you about me?"

"No, should she?"

"No. I guess not." If she was going to continue her relationship with Walter, she needed a relationship with Janet.

Walter looked at her as though waiting for a response. She needed to clear the air. The tension was mounting. If he didn't say anything, she knew she would.

Walter went to the closet and laid the Giovanni garment bag on the bed. He began with his suits carefully placing them in the bag. Shauna felt the tears as they rolled down her face. No matter what he said, she felt she was holding him in a relationship she knew was going nowhere. *"Why was he doing this? He read the note, didn't he?"*

She didn't want to make it look obvious. Looking around the nightstand and in the trashcan, she peeked back at Walter to be sure he wasn't watching. There was no sign of the pad, pen or note. She wanted to open the drawer.

"Walter I was missing one of my silver earrings. You didn't see it did you?"

"I put it in your jewelry bag last night. I'm sure you found it."

His answer was short. Shauna suspected he knew she was searching for the note.

"You know; honesty goes a long way. I was aware of you leading me on. I am Richard's best friend, he told me. I knew I was the bait to get him back. Can we put this behind us or hey, how about, we just remain friends? Let's say, friends with benefits."

Shauna wanted to comment, but she couldn't. He was only repeating what she wrote. The note was her way of making sure he wouldn't call her again.

"Walter, I was angry; not at you, but at myself. I looked at you as a friend with benefits, but you really mean so much more. I can't explain it. I guess I was..."

"Shauna, in that note you said you wanted a loving relationship; that you were looking for someone to love you and not your status. I didn't show you any of that? Why can't we start this thing over? I'm down. You want to be friends, with benefits, okay. I'm down."

Shauna heard her desire for Richard in his plea. "Walter, don't you see that's where I was emotionally with Richard. Right where you are, willing to accept him anyway, no matter how he really felt; that's not right."

He stopped filling the garment bag. "So what now, why did you stay to rub it in, to get me to beg you to stay? Well, I'm done. Go the fuck on!"

Shauna hadn't seen him angry, at least not at her. He turned and looked at her with new emotional pain. "Don't be here when I return."

Walter snatched the key cards off the dresser and exited the suite.

59

*M*arcus returned home after waiting the entire day for Janet's return. He stopped by her apartment off and on since leaving there early that morning. He was careful not to leave any reason for her to think he had been in her home.

He was certain that Karyn would want to argue about him staying out and not calling. He didn't care he was leaving her and going back to his wife and children.

He put the key in the door and noticed immediately the light in the living room was dim, a sign Karyn was still out. He looked at his watch, something he hadn't done all day. It was eight o'clock he couldn't imagine where she was.

After searching through the rooms, he returned to the kitchen to check the refrigerator. His stomach told him he hadn't eaten since the coffee and roll he had that morning. He looked in the refrigerator and was surprised there were no leftovers from Friday night's dinner. Friday's cuisine was usually fried chicken and there was always a piece left for breakfast with waffles or lunch. He began to wonder what she ate.

The thought crossed his mind that she probably ate out. *"With who?"* The door opened to the apartment and Marcus could hear her heels tapping on the foyer floor.

"Hey, where have you been?" His annoyance was obvious.

Karyn entered the kitchen. She was dressed in a jean pantsuit that was made only for her body. Her gold blouse added a glow to her face. Marcus was sidetracked by her beauty.

"I know you're not talking to me. You didn't come here or call last night. Why are you in my refrigerator?"

"What? You almost made me say something. I asked where have you been."

"Out, just like you, only I don't have an ex that I'm trying to get with."

"Karyn, please." Marcus closed the refrigerator door. "What did you cook last night?"

"Have you lost your mind? Whatever I cooked, whatever I ate; you weren't here for. By the way, your shit is in the room. I guess that's what you came for. I see you started by taking a few clothes with you. What was that shit about?"

Marcus remembered the clothes he had in his overnight bag. It was still in the car. He stood looking at her as she kicked off her heels and bent to pick them up. It was the teasing that usually led to the bedroom, but he was determined to ignore her.

"Karyn, we need to talk. I need something to put on my stomach though."

"The bitch didn't even feed you? Damn, she ain't crazy huh? Well, I ain't either. Get your stuff Marcus, go."

"You ain't putting me out Karyn."

"What? You feel better if you had control? Pack your shit, don't say nothing and ease your way out; okay do it your way. I'll be leaving in another hour or more so leave my keys. You know how we used to do. Only, Marcus don't call to tell me when you'll get with me again. We're done. I told you I wasn't found of you sleeping with your ex and then coming back here. I meant that."

"Janet ain't even home." Marcus wanted to pull the words back, but it was too late. Karyn gave him a look that said it all. She left him standing in the middle of the kitchen floor. He opened the refrigerator again, until he heard her voice from the bedroom.

"Get out of my fuckin' refrigerator. Go home Marcus, I got company coming."

"What the hell is that supposed to mean?" His ego wouldn't allow her to throw another man in his face. He made his way into the bedroom.

"I'm going out with some friends they're coming here to pick me up. I'd prefer you save me the embarrassment and leave with your shit before they come."

"You won't be embarrassed. I'll wait until they leave."

Kayrn continued to look in her closet. Marcus looked on the bed where his garment bags, shoeboxes, and other items were packed. He couldn't imagine her packing all of his things alone. She worked off her anger. He was sure she was still mad. She didn't look back at the bed to see him checking what she had meticulously arranged for him to inventory. He went to the far end of the room where the extended walk-in closet was now empty. He opened the chest drawers and checked the bathroom. There was no evidence that he occupied any space in the bedroom.

"So you didn't want to hear what I had to say?"

"No, you didn't listen to what I had to say. I made myself clear the night you moved in. I don't need you moving from here the way you moved from your wife. Take it all tonight and we're done, no explanations needed. It's easy to me, I told you our relationship had room for growth, but it also had some restrictions. Your past is yours. I don't want to be included in it. If you wanted me to be a side piece, you should have stayed home. You chose to leave home, leave what it offered and take what I offered. In some ways, I understand your wife. It hurts, but I'm not going to stop living because you've chosen to move on."

"You're blaming me for her attempt on her life?" Her words reminded him of what Dr. Norris said.

"Come on Marcus, she wanted her life back, and you were part of that. Now you're going to her, why? She's working. She's proven she's not as crazy as you thought, why Marcus? What is at the home you left that's attracting you? Janet was blessed. She didn't die. You missed the blessing. You feel guilty. You're going home to collect?"

"That's bullshit and you know it. I wanted my kids to be a part of my life."

"So you're still trying to kill her, take her kids. Show them that daddy can do it better than mommy. I can't be a part of that. I didn't wreck your home, and I don't want to be looked at like that. You wanted me; you left home, now you want them, so go home."

Karyn was making it hard for him to think. He felt guilty. She was right. He didn't know if Janet would take him back. He lost both his family and his fantasy. Karyn took her clothes in the bathroom and locked the door. The sound of the lock confirmed his fear. If his wife didn't accept him back, he didn't want to think about it, he would have to find a new home.

60

They decided to slip away from the festivities early. Janet was tired of the smiles, congratulations, and people. Richard saw the look on her face and agreed he too had had enough for one weekend. He excused himself from their table to say goodnight to a few of the corporate heads and give his card to a few new prospects. Walter had made his rounds without Shauna, but he assured them that there was nothing to worry about. Janet knew he still wasn't himself. She was sure Shauna was the reason he downed his share of shots before leaving, but she let Richard ask the questions. Walter was at the bar when Richard approached.

"I'm calling it a night. You okay?"

"I'm good. Thanks."

"Walter, I just..."

"Look, you and Janet have a good time. I'll see you guys Monday, new day new money."

Richard knew Walter. He was the closest friend he had; he was like a brother. He knew he was hurting. There was nothing he could say; he knew Shauna was the source of his pain.

"Call me tomorrow if you want to talk."

"I'm gonna call you tonight. I'll give you say, twenty minutes; just enough time to take your pants off. Before you get close to her, ring, it's gonna be me wanting to talk." He smiled at his friend. Richard appreciated his humor.

"No that's you wanting to cock block."

"Hey, I can't get none. Why not?"

"I'll see you Monday, forget calling tomorrow. Sleep off the hangover you're gonna have. Are you leaving early or late?" Richard's concern changed the tone of their conversation.

"Probably late." The men shook hands, and Walter waved to no one particular as he left the room.

Richard returned to Janet. There was a drink waiting for him. He looked at the glass and waited for Janet's explanation.

"I couldn't refuse the drink. One of your prospects; he left his card for you to call."

Richard took his seat and watched the dance floor as they took their time emptying their glasses. Ten minutes passed, and they were pleased to be on their way to Richard's suite. Janet took the time to check her phone only to find Faye had texted her after leaving a message. She decided to call her back before it got too late.

"Hey, it's me. You called and texted me? What's up?"

"Uh, oh yeah. What time is it?" Faye drifted off to sleep, not knowing the time.

"It's about eleven forty five. Are you in bed already?"

"Girl, I've spent the whole weekend in bed it seems."

"Faye I don't want to know about that now. What's up?"

"Hmm...no time, you must be about to get some relief yourself. Anyway where are the kids? I thought they were with Mama."

"Elaine has them with her, why?"

"Uncle Sherod wants to take them out tomorrow. Can we go and pick them up for you? We'll bring them to you, later in the evening. I think we made them a cousin."

"Really, oh Faye, I hope so. Sherod loves children. You guys must have put in some work if you think you're pregnant. I'll call Elaine in the morning. What time do you want to pick them up?"

"About ten, what time will you be home?"

"Call me, it depends on what time we leave here in the morning."

"Tell the truth. It depends on what time you let him loose to-night."

The sisters laughed and told each other "good night." Richard joined her on the sectional and handed her a glass of wine.

"Do you want anything else?"

Janet answered him with an irresistible look of pleasure. She laid her head back on the couch anticipating his kiss. Richard felt a rush come over him as he took the glass from her and placed it on the table next to his. The kiss led them to undressing each other. The clothes fell gently to the floor.

She couldn't remember the last time she made love to Marcus on the couch. As the thought of her past love making sessions attempted to creep into her mind, Richard's kisses began to explore her body. The thought of Marcus totally faded when Richard pulled the straps to her bra from her shoulders. His embrace included her taking the bra completely off. Her caramel skin was lighter, showing signs of summer tanning, her nipple's dark chocolate and erect. He used his tongue to tease her into total relaxation.

Janet felt heat rising between her thighs. The heat no vibrator had given her over the past year. She didn't want to rush his intentions, but she needed him below her waistline.

She reached for the rim of his briefs hoping to finally unwrap his package.

Richard was older, but the access weight brought on by age wasn't a discredit to his physique. His thighs were firm as was his butt, another turn-on for Janet. She fondled his rear slowly making her way to his front. She pulled down his briefs allowing his penis room to fall into her hand. She massaged him as he returned the favor removing her panties.

She parted her thighs, and they kissed before he chose the center of her body to travel down to her navel. He stopped at her breast fondling each in his hands and continued to kiss her softly. Once he reached her waist, he repositioned her body on the chaise lounge at the end of the sectional.

Janet gave in totally lifting her legs over his shoulders. She closed her eyes knowing she was on her way to sheer pleasure. Richard parted the lips of her vagina with his fingers. He gave her an oral teasing that made her cum twice. His penis throbbed waiting to enter. Janet was throbbing too. He took his time putting on a condom, and as he entered her; she could feel new juices flowing from her body.

Richard pushed gently almost making her beg for him. She couldn't stand his teasing any longer.

"Put it all in."

"Not yet," he whispered. He lowered her legs bringing his body close to hers. He took her into his embrace and began to move faster. He was going deeper as the pace quickened. Janet began to moan, holding him, hoping he wouldn't pull out or stop.

He lifted his chest to look into her face. She smiled seeing he was pleased and closed her eyes enjoying all of him. They could feel the other's muscles tightening and releasing to the rhythm of their juices. Richard didn't want to explode. He slowed down. Janet was there. She was tingling and unable to control herself. He wanted to taste her again.

His tongue found her clitoris, and she trembled as she released. Richard wanted to feel her entirely. He put his penis in again slowly and whispered in her ear.

"Janet, I need to feel you. Let me take off this condom."

"Richard, I..."

"Please baby, its okay."

She couldn't answer her body responded. His loving was all she needed. He pulled out and she stripped his penis of the protective rubber. She opened her legs wider and the man she loved filled her with his manhood.

Richard felt himself getting harder. He had never reached a point of no return. He always had control, but making love to Janet took over his thoughts. He felt himself beginning to sweat. He tried lifting himself up; he knew the warmth of her body, their juices and the movement was leading to the best ejaculation he ever had. Janet's legs were locked behind him as he pulled back to pull out, she rolled over. Richard was on the bottom, and Janet was pleased to ride him.

Sperm began to ooze onto his stomach. He had reached a climax and she did too. They both were twitching and moaning. Richard was speechless. Janet was moving slowly on the head of his penis and responded shaking as he released another load.

Janet rolled over on her back realizing they had gone further than they both expected. Richard didn't move and her fears began to take over. *"Maybe he thinks I'm trying to trap him."*

"Janet promise me something," he said in a soft voice.

"What's that?"

"I won't have to take you to a suite for this to happen again."

Janet smiled, pleased and relieved. "I promise."

61

Faye wanted to surprise Sherod. Thursday night was the first time in years that he expressed being disappointed with their relationship. She fell back into old habits. Habits of caring for Janet and her children, forgetting she had a marriage to nurture. The weekend put the sparkle back into their bedroom. Faye hoped the possibility of starting a family would solve the rest.

Janet proved she would be able to handle the separation and road to divorce. She was far from committing suicide since her employment with Burnett and Reed, therapy with Dr. Norris, and confronting her lifelong issues. Faye wanted their relationship to be based on more than the guilt she carried. Sherod came through the front door with the mail in his hand from the past few days.

"We've got one more day and then its kids again. Did you call Janet?"

"I told her we would pick up the children for her. She'll get them from us after she, and Richard come in. I figured we would see them for a few hours. Monday will be too hectic."

"Why didn't you ask me first? Faye, what is it with you? Your sister had someone caring for them, and you still stepped in."

"If you don't want them to come by I'll call her back."

"No, just let me know when you're making plans like that. Suppose I wanted to spend the day with you. We need to begin being together here a little."

"I'm sorry. I didn't think about it that way."

"You never think about it. Stop Faye, you can't save the world. You stuck your head in this before, with your father, with Karyn and now what? Let Janet handle her life babe. Talking to her and letting her vent is a lot less harmful. Stop trying to handle her life."

"You don't know the whole story Rod. I had to step in for her. My sister was devastated after my father passed. My brother and mother treated her like an outcast. She almost lost her mind. Then Marcus came along, and I thought he would be there for her. Someone she could depend on for love and support. Karyn wasn't his first affair. She was the one I knew personally and that made a difference since I introduced them. Janet was knocked to her knees again. Rod, do you know what the difference was, how I felt knowing I introduced her husband to the woman he left home for? I was part of the reason she attempted suicide. My gut aches thinking if she died, I would have been the outcast. My heart was aching because I helped cause her pain. I needed to stay close in her life for her to forgive me. That afternoon when we had lunch, she said she forgave me. All her feelings for me, momma, my brother and the doctor, were put on the table."

"The doctor?" Sherod turned to her in disbelief.

"Yes, something about not killing herself for people like her. She said Dr. Norris is in love with Richard, but he doesn't love her."

"So she's involved in another drama filled relationship?"

"Well, no. Richard never led her on. It's the thoughts of the doctor."

"Only your sister would get a doctor who is in love with a man interested in her. I'm sorry, go on."

"After hearing what she had to say that day, I thought about us. I'm glad we got away this week. I'm feeling good about myself, and that makes me feel better about you and me. Maybe we've been blessed to start a family of our own. I wanted the children to be here before school started and our schedules got loaded, hopefully Janet and I started on new paths."

Sherod wasn't sure about the paths his wife was referring to, but he liked the idea of her finally moving on. "The kids are welcome anytime. We'll pick them up tomorrow." He picked up the remote to surf the channels, and the doorbell rang. Both he and Faye looked at each other puzzled.

Sherod went to the door leaving Faye in the living room wondering who would be visiting them at ten thirty in the evening.

"Hey man, come on in. Babe it's Marcus. You just caught us. We got back a little over an hour ago."

The two walked toward the kitchen where Faye was now standing. The couple wondered what would bring Marcus to visit. Marcus looked around the kitchen hoping dinner was still out or at least there was something to munch on. Karyn left with her friends reminding him he was to leave before her return. In his anger, he forgot to grab something to eat.

"Can I get you anything Marcus, soda or water? I didn't cook we just..."

"Yeah Sherod was telling me, did you guys have a good time."

The men took a seat in the kitchen and continued the conversation.

"It was relaxing; that's for sure. Sherod spent a lot of time in the gym. I read a lot. Not much you can do over three days, but we decided to travel more, right Sherod?"

Her husband could tell she was rattling. It was as though she was avoiding a topic she knew would soon surface — the explanation for his late night visit.

"So what's up with you, man? You couldn't have been wandering in the neighborhood at this time of the night. Where you coming from?"

"Home, we had an argument about the kids visiting. Karyn doesn't understand the needs of a father. I left. I can't stay where my kids ain't welcomed to even visit."

"What? Karyn said they couldn't visit?"

Faye tried not to sound sarcastic. She knew how Karyn felt about the children. She told Janet that their relationship wouldn't last long because of it. Two years was longer than she expected.

"You already knew that though huh? She probably told you back in the beginning that she couldn't stand kids." Sherod said as he took the glass of water offered by Faye.

"Well we argued; I left, and that's what brought me this way. I was on my way to Janet's, but I didn't want to wake the kids, you know it being late and all. I'll go there in the morning. So I just stopped here on my way to get a room."

Both Sherod and Faye read between the lines. There was no invitation made for him to stay.

"We stopped and ate on the way home, or I would offer you something. Sherod you want to call for pizza and Buffalo wings?"

"No don't bother, you guys ate already, I'll grab something on my way to the hotel." Marcus lied as he swallowed tasting the thought of the pizza.

"You said you left? Where you plan on staying?" Sherod asked giving his brother-n-law a questioning glance.

"I just told you. I'm moving back home."

62

*J*anet and Richard left after breakfast. Walter called to say he didn't know how Shauna got home. He remembered they drove to the resort together. She hadn't answered her phone, but he left a message.

"Maybe she took a cab to the bus terminal or train station?" Janet didn't understand either of their actions. "Why would Walter tell her to leave if he knew she didn't have any transportation?"

"They both were drunk I guess, or hung over. Now he's upset. I don't want to over react because we both know where that will take us."

"Where?" Janet prepared herself for the answer.

"C'mon Janet; I start giving suggestions and showing concern, and they both twist it. Lashauna thinks I'm concerned because I love her and Walter, well he'll just be confused all over again. Let him deal with it. If there's a problem he needs to deal with it first."

"I hope she's okay. Maybe she'll answer a call from me."

"You can try. You don't have to though."

"I don't know Richard. I'm a little concerned. She's going through a few things. I've been there. It's not a comforting place to be."

Janet dialed the number. She got the familiar tune and waited for her voice to say, "Leave a message." She left a short message and dialed her home phone. The voice mail was full. Janet put her phone back in her purse and looked at Richard for an answer.

"Are you picking up the children early?"

"No, I think I'm gonna tell Faye and Sherod to drop them off. I'm going home and begin some ironing for next week. Richard I really enjoyed this weekend."

"I did too. I'm glad you could relax. This business venture should be good for all of us. I want you to consider handling a lot of the initial work on site."

"Really, that's a ride every morning."

"Janet, after your divorce what's keeping you where you are. Move on ... you the kids; move closer to the site. I promise you won't regret it."

"Where are you going with this Richard?"

"Nowhere, but I think a new start, a new environment, will do you well. Honey you deserve it."

Janet thought about her visions of Richard, the children and them being in a home together. His home was beautiful. She never thought of a home of her own. Her silence was the cause for Richard's explanation.

"It's not going to happen right away. You've got time to decide, but Janet, please think about it."

They rode for another forty-five minutes talking about personal goals and dreams for the company. Janet admitted she was in love totally, and it felt good to know he loved her too. They arrived at his home in time for Janet to run to the bathroom.

"Hey Elaine," Janet waved as she passed her running from the front door.

Elaine looked up from her magazine as Richard came through the front door smiling. "Hey Sis."

"Hey yourself; how was it? Did you win them over?"

"I got the business handled."

Elaine smiled, looking in the direction of the bathroom; her brother read her thoughts.

"We had a great time. How about you and the kids?"

"Please I had to make them leave with Faye and Sherod. They thought I had plans for today. Faye told them the plans were with them, and they threw me to the curb. They're really adorable, well-mannered and smart."

Janet returned to the room and gave Elaine a hug. "Thank you so much. I didn't know how much I needed that getaway. It wasn't all business, and it wasn't all pleasure. The balance served me well."

"I'm gonna check my calls. Janet let me know when you're ready to leave."

The two women got comfortable. Elaine wanted to hear more about the fabulous weekend. She was sure Janet would tell her how she got along with the real Dr. Norris.

Faye answered her phone thinking it was Janet. She and Sherod were on their way to New York with the children. An afternoon at the Bronx Zoo was on the agenda. It was close to twelve, and she couldn't imagine her mother or brother calling her during church hours.

"Hello?"

"You didn't look at your caller ID? I'm surprised. I've been calling you since yesterday."

It was Karyn. Faye wished she had looked at the caller ID.

"I just called to let you know your so-called brother-n-law will be looking for a place to stay. I threw his ass out."

Faye turned completely around hoping the children couldn't hear her response. "I can't talk about him right now."

Sherod frowned without looking at her wondering who his wife was talking to.

"Well I didn't call to talk about him. I just wanted to warn you. He stayed out all night Friday. I would assume he tried going home. Anyway, I told him before he moved in that staying out all night was a way out of this relationship. So he got his ticket to go home."

"Home? What would make you think he could just go home?"

"Oh, I'm clear; he thought that. Janet would be crazy to take his ass back. Oh, I'm sorry … I didn't mean your sister was still crazy or anything."

"What are you trying to find out? I mean if he went home or that's what you thought he was going to do, why are you calling me? I don't know where he is."

Sherod turned the music up in the rear of their vehicle trying to drown out her conversation that had increased in volume.

"I just knew he would come to talk to your husband."

Faye thought about Marcus' visit. "Like I said if he's home that's good I guess, either way it's not my concern. I told you I wasn't down with your relationship from the start. I'm still not."

"Well, your sister may want to know her loving husband is packed and coming home."

"Did you call me to gloat about putting him out? Cause if you did make this the last call about your relationship. I really don't want to be involved when it gets ugly."

"What you know something?"

"Just leave me out of it. Listen I've got to go."

"Well I guess we can go back to doing lunch after the aerobics class. I mean, after all our friendship suffered because of his ass too, right?"

"Whatever. … Later!"

Sherod didn't bother to ask. He read between the lines hoping his wife learned her lesson.

63

*M*arcus looked to park in what it seemed like the same spot he had parked in for the last two nights. He was wondering had Janet come home and left again. He didn't see her vehicle, and the mail was still in the box at the apartment door.

"Hey Mr. Robinson, how've you been?"

It was the maintenance man carrying his tools to the apartment across the courtyard. He waved letting him know he saw him.

"Hey man, I'm fine how 'bout you?"

"Good man, your boy is getting tall. He played on the same team as my son. I missed you at the games."

"Yeah, I missed a few. Take care now."

Marcus cut the small talk short. He didn't need to be reminded that he wasn't around most of the summer. The man hadn't paid much attention, but it was M.J.'s first year in the little league. Sherod or Sam usually went with him. Marcus got mad at the thought of how much he missed. Janet had to be coming home soon. He couldn't imagine where he should say his family spent the weekend. He parked his car after circling the parking lot twice. The spot wasn't far from the door to the apartment. He didn't want his car to be seen.

After parking, he took two of his overnight bags out of the trunk. He used his key to get into the apartment. Marcus walked into Janet's home and made himself comfortable waiting for her arrival after he put his bags in the bedroom. The thought crossed his mind to unpack all of his items while waiting, but he didn't want to seem too pushy. The move back home had to look as though he cared about her well-being. He didn't want the truth to surface, not for a few days. By then the children would convince her that "daddy" needed to stay home.

The doorbell rang, and Marcus didn't hesitate to answer. If she was dating his answering the door would put a damper on the new relationship.

"Mr. Robinson, I have a work order for the locks. I can fit you in now if you'd like."

"The locks? Oh, uh yes. How long will it take?"

"No more than fifteen minutes. I have everything here."

The man pulled his toolbox from behind him. Marcus didn't care one way or another. She'd just have to give him another key. He definitely would add that question to the list of other. What was she trying to prove? He retreated to the den leaving the man to change the lock.

The maintenance man yelled "Hello, Ms. Robinson" from what seemed like across the parking lot. The exchange of pleasantries didn't include any mention of the lock change or the presence of her husband. Marcus heard the voices as he was stirring from what started as a catnap. He got up to check the new lock. The lock was changed, and the two keys were on the counter. He took one and placed in on his key ring. Marcus imagined the look on Janet's face when she discovered her key no longer worked. He turned the lock, leaving it open for her entry. He returned to the living room waiting for her to walk through the door.

Janet had two hours or more before the children returned with their uncle and aunt. Her plans included putting up the few groceries she stopped and picked up, unpacking and a little alone time. She wanted to review the papers she was to give to Marcus. She thought about calling him. They could take the children out tomorrow and she would serve him the divorce papers. A smile crossed her face as she imagined the look he would have when he discovered he had been served.

She carried the groceries to the door with the intentions of returning to the car for her luggage. She put the bags down to get her keys, and she noticed the door was slightly ajar. Normally, she would have been upset, but seeing the maintenance worker with his tools crossing the parking lot had to mean he saw her as he completed the job. A new key was on the counter, and she placed her key ring next to it. She would have to question why she wasn't given two keys. Returning to the groceries, she grabbed two of the four bags and turned into Marcus, who stood at the opened door.

"Need help?"

"What the hell are you doing in my house?" Janet questioned as she stormed pass him.

Marcus didn't answer he grabbed the other two bags. He followed Janet into the kitchen. She took the bags from him and put them on the floor.

"What Marcus? Why are you here?"

"I guess you're wondering how I got in huh?"

"No, actually I'm wondering when you're leaving. What do you want? The children aren't here."

"They haven't been here all weekend."

Janet was shocked. *"Was he here in my place all weekend? He used his key."* She glanced at the key on the counter.

"Where's the other key that was left?"

"Oh I put mine on my ring." Marcus showed her his key ring with the shiny new addition.

The argument was mounting. Time was winding down. Faye would be at her house with the children shortly; Marcus needed to be on his way.

"So obviously you have something you want to say or do that I don't know about. What would make you think you get a key?"

"Just like you didn't change the lock until today, my name is still on the lease."

Janet thought about the detailed guide she followed. Shauna told her to put all her business in order before making drastic changes. She sighed; glad she had changed the bank accounts after her first few checks.

"Oh, so this is the place you can run too when you want."

"Actually I decided I'm coming home." Marcus replied with no reaction to her questioning stare.

"What makes you think you can just move back in here like we've been living together? Marcus, if you think I need you here; those days have passed."

"The children need me and you can say what you want, you do too."

Janet left him standing in the middle of the kitchen floor. She went into the bedroom to retrieve the divorce papers. The overnight bags caught her attention. She felt the heat rising; she was beyond angry. She grabbed the manila envelope from her dresser drawer and one of his overnight bags.

"What the hell is this Marcus? You moved your shit in without even asking? You just come back in our lives like that? Do you realize the effect your leaving had on all of us? You can't think we haven't moved on without you."

"Well, I don't like the way you're moving. Your life or the children, you need me. The head of a family is the man. This is where I belong, I realize that now."

"What, your ho' put you out? I wasn't waiting for you with open arms. Who do you think needed you? When we needed your ass, you kept walking. I begged your black ass to stay, and you walked. Fuck if I want you to stop walking now!"

She handed him the envelope and returned to her bedroom for his second bag. Marcus read the address on the envelope.

Recognizing the lawyer's name, he was sure the decision to file for the divorce wasn't Janet's. He would fight to get her back or fight to take the children. She had a choice.

"Here's the other bag. Did you bring anything else with you?"

"No."

"Did you unpack anything? As you can see this is a permanent thing. You can live anywhere you want but not with us."

"You served the papers; that means the ball is in my court. I'm calling time out. We can work through this. You still love me, I can tell. You know I still love you."

Janet couldn't believe she was hearing this again. For the two years, he had been with Karyn, he had been preaching from the same pew, the one in the back of the same church. She decided after the therapy, there would be no more room in her heart for his excuses or lies. That was the first step to her recovery. She wouldn't go backwards. Marcus continued to talk about what he saw in the near future. The time he wanted to make up for and how he planned on doing it.

As she opened her closet, the tears ran down her face. The choice was simple, but the task would be hard. She had to start somewhere. She threw the luggage on the bed and frantically began to pack odd items she would need. She was relieved. She made the decision to have a safety deposit box with her papers kept at the bank. She went to the children's rooms and packed for them as well. She stopped in the bathroom to get toiletries and touch up her appearance before confronting Marcus.

"Where are you going?"

"You're right Marcus your name is on the lease. Everything here you bought. You gave it to us. What I've taken, I bought. I've worked hard over the last few months trying to recapture what I lost of myself. I don't plan on giving you the survivor's speech. But this is what I want you to know; I will survive. The worst is over."

"So you think the worst is over. Where were you this weekend? Where were my kids? I'll build a case against your crazy ass, and you won't see me or them."

"Just what I thought."

"What?"

"Just what I thought, your love only lasted for a moment. A few minutes ago, you were professing your love. Now you're telling me how you'll hurt me. Deliberate hurt, that's what you've done to me over and over again. I'm tired of hurting. I'll be back with the police to get my other belongings."

"Police, what the fuck does that mean?"

"I need it documented. Have your lawyer contact my lawyer. Thanks Marcus, you've been a blessing as usual."

Janet left without looking back; Marcus didn't know what to say. He was sure she didn't leave any personal belongings or paperwork that would give him a clue where she was going.

64

*J*anet fumbled with her luggage trying to stack it in the back of her vehicle. She tried not to appear shaken. The thought of Marcus watching from the apartment window encouraged her to move her weekend bags around quickly, making room for the luggage and other necessities she brought with her. She left the new key on the counter, a mistake she made while rushing out the door. She couldn't go back to get it now. She threatened to bring the police with her to stir a comment. Now she would have to deal with management, ask her lawyer about the options or follow through on the threat. It was just about dusk. She wondered about the children and decided she would call Faye.

She cleared her throat as Faye answered, "What's up girl? Missing your children?"

The tears started falling from her eyes. She attempted to talk through them. "Can I meet you at your house?"

"Janet, what's wrong?"

"I'm okay. I'll be okay. You haven't started this way yet have you?"

"No, we're almost home though. Are you sure you're okay?"

"We'll talk when I get there."

"Janet, don't..."

"I'll meet you at your house Faye."

Janet pulled the car over. She had gone three blocks from the only place that had been her home for more than nine years. She had no idea where she would go or how she would afford to stay there.

Her job was secure, and she had prioritized the bills that had accumulated over the last year. Marcus stopped sending money for those bills knowing she couldn't pay them.

She sighed deeply seeing now how she had been manipulated. She got the packet of Kleenex from the glove compartment and wiped her tears. *"This is just what he wants."* She put the car in drive and pulled into the ongoing traffic. She dialed Richard's cell number.

"Hey, I was on my way in my truck."

Janet was stunned thinking he called, and Marcus answered her home phone.

"Why?"

"I asked you to call me; that was three hours ago. Where are you?"

Janet was silent. She needed to take a breath to keep the tears back.

"I'm on my way to Faye's. I had to leave my place."

"What? Someone broke in again?"

"Marcus was the burglar. He had a key. I forgot about him."

"So why are you leaving?"

"He claims he's moving back home; where his name is on the lease. Richard nothing there is mine, and he'll remind me of that daily. He claims he still loves me and wants me and the kids. When I told him how I felt about that and gave him the papers, well the wheels turned. He brought in his overnight luggage, and I'm sure he had all intentions of bringing more in regardless of what I wanted. I just got the kids settled. They don't ask about him as much and I don't need them upset."

"So you're going to stay with your sister for a while?"

"No, no, I don't want to do that either. I'll stay there tonight, but I have to find a place for us. I really don't want to go to a hotel, and really I can't afford the expense."

"I'll meet you at Faye's"

"Richard, no really, that's not why I called."

"I know why you called. I'm on my way."

Janet let the windows down and shut off the air conditioner. The summer breeze blew in her face calming her nerves as she drove slowly through the city traffic. The dilemma was beginning to choke her again as she turned onto Grove Street. She smiled thinking of how lost she had been earlier in the year traveling the same roads going to work at Burnett and Reed. It was now second nature, the route from home to Faye's and then to the office. She pulled into the driveway, and the evening spotlight brightened the walk to the front door. After turning off the ignition Janet froze. She had no idea what she would say to her children.

The sound of the screen door opening brought her attention to the stoned walk. Faye stood at the door waiting for her sister to get out of the vehicle and greet her. Richard's truck pulled into the driveway. Janet looked into her rearview mirror feeling an uncontrollable urge to scream. She took a deep breath and let her head fall back on the headrest. She couldn't move she was weakening.

Richard opened the driver's door while Faye entered on the passenger side. Janet's eyes were closed. As she opened them slowly she spoke.

"I don't know what to do. I've tried to be strong, but I can't do this."

"What's wrong?" Faye was scared her sister was slipping back into desperation. She looked across the seat for Richard to answer the question that Janet ignored.

"He's there Faye. Marcus was in the house when I got there. His luggage, his clothes, his fucked-up attitude, Faye he brought it back in my home. I left, but where the hell am I going with three children, no savings and..." Janet began to cry.

"C'mon babe, get out of the car. You can't sit here. The children will wonder what's wrong. Faye, do you think Sherod will watch them while the three of us talk."

Faye nodded, closed the door and looked at her sister through the opened window. "Janet, you've come too far to slip back. We won't let you."

65

*A*t the end of the week Marcus found himself thinking about the divorce papers he would be showing his lawyer on Monday morning. He needed to talk to someone on a personal level. Sherod was the closest person he had to talk to about it, but he didn't want a call to him to look as though he was chasing Janet. He was sure she was staying with her sister until she felt too crowded, and then she would come home. *What if she doesn't come home?* The thought kept nudging at his heart. He needed to talk to Richard Burnett and Dr. Norris. They had influenced Janet in a way he couldn't any longer. He would make the doctor understand his views as a husband and a father. She would help him bring his wife home. His appointment with her was scheduled for Monday afternoon.

Marcus had no doubt that Richard would be an obstacle. The doctor would be able to convince the court it was best for him to return to his home, his children and his wife. He wouldn't sign the papers. He would fight for his marriage in court.

The television volume increased during a Pepsi commercial, he searched for the remote. The phone began to ring. It rang twice, stopping before he could answer. The caller ID showed a familiar number, and he smiled as he returned the call.

"Hey man, I was just thinking about calling you. I didn't want Janet to think I was stalking her. She needs time to think."

"Listen, tell Karyn to stop calling here. She caused trouble between you and Janet, now she's trying to bond with Faye. Faye won't say it, but I will; it ain't happening."

"So why you in that female shit, that's not my business."

"No, as usual it's a spill over. I don't want to hurt Karyn's feelings and Faye won't. She's not gonna wreck our world with your shit. She hasn't been calling here and we like it that way. Tell her, that's the least you can do."

"I'm confused, do I owe you something?"

"No, but I would think you would think about your children, Janet or maybe Faye. After all we've never got between you and your wife."

"Did Faye tell you Karyn only thought about dating me after she talked it over with Faye?"

"Doesn't matter to me; just tell her don't call again."

"Sherod is Janet there?"

"I haven't seen her today." He knew the lie would bring other questions.

"Sherod, stop alright. I know she's there."

"Listen; call Karyn, so she'll know where to reach you. Later man."

"Wait a minute. Why are you angry with me? I did like you said, I'm home."

"Why? Because I said so, cut the bull man. Karyn threw your ass out, and you didn't have the balls to get a room somewhere. No you push your way back on the woman you know may be weak enough to take you in. Marcus that shit is low. Now, on the other hand, what the fuck do I get for being your brother-n-law? The kids and your wife, for how long, until your sorry ass realizes she's moved on just like you did two years ago. Take some responsibility, man. You fucked up your marriage. Now what, you come back into her life to finish her off?"

"Man, I don't get you. We've talked about this and all you've hinted at and said is what I should have done. Now I did it. I tried to stay away, but Karyn wouldn't allow the kids to be a part of our lives. I couldn't live with that, so I came home. Now you tell me to keep going? What the fuck is that about?"

"Marcus, you're too late. She's moved on man. She's happy. The kids are too. You don't put your family on the street just to say you're the man."

Marcus listened understanding fully what Sherod said and didn't say. It was what he didn't say that added a new level of anger.

"So she's moved on huh? Well, when she gets to your house tell her that's what she better do. That stuffed shirt bastard she's working for will have to pay for her and three kids if he wants to fill my shoes. I'll see them both in court. She's still married. I'll have her labeled unfit before this is over."

"Yeah man, listen. I've changed my mind."

"About what?"

"You and Karyn forget this number."

"Sherod man, look."

The dial tone sounded in his ear. He returned to the silence of the apartment except for the voices on the television. He walked through the apartment again, taking his time in each room. Janet hadn't changed much; only items that would remind her of a marriage had been removed. The pictures of the two of them, the entire family and individual shots of him were no longer on the buffet in the hall. She had replaced them with pictures of M.J. playing, Joy and Erica in a dance recital, and the picture he always loved of her and Faye.

He had become emotional after completing his walk through the apartment. Beer wouldn't calm his nerves and the thought of alcohol in the house was a joke. Janet allowed the beer and wine, occasionally, but the death of her father became her excuse to avoid alcohol totally. Marcus convinced himself sleep would have to intoxicate him for the night again. He sat on the bed unsure if he would be able to sleep comfortably in his home, alone.

66

S herod placed the call but failed to get the information Janet needed. He hung up mumbling to himself, *"Asshole."*

"How did it go Rod, what did he say?"

"Nothing, as usual he doesn't have a clue."

Janet and Faye entered the den. The children were in bed early. School had begun, and they still hadn't adjusted to the change of their morning schedule. They hadn't been any trouble as Sherod tried to make Marcus believe. He and Faye understood the arrangements were temporary.

Richard had a business associate who had property available. He tried to encourage Janet to look at a few of the moderately priced homes. She promised she would but didn't ask for any other information. She was looking forward to renting, something she could afford, but there weren't many choices in the area near her children's schools.

"Did he say what he was doing this week or where he was going?"

"Janet, I messed up. He made me angry and I never thought about asking him what his immediate plans were. I would imagine he'll be going to work, and maybe he'll see the lawyer. He has what, forty-five days to answer your papers?"

"How'd you know that?" Janet teased. "Faye I believe he's been married before."

"Or divorced, huh? Wow, I didn't know they gave anyone that long. That's over a month, what are you supposed to do until he decides to fight it or not?"

"One thing for sure I want the rest of my stuff. I'm going to talk to Richard again about his friend. Maybe there's a home for rent. If I attempt to buy Marcus will attempt to take it, I know he will. Once I get a place I can get my things and move."

"Why not get your things and put them in storage? At least, you'll have them. I mean, Marcus might have something up his sleeves. You don't want him getting rid of your stuff."

"Girl, if he throws out my things..."

"I think Faye is right. Maybe you should consider putting it all in storage until you can move it into your own place. Make the arrangements. My boy will escort you; the police uniform will keep Marcus back if he shows up."

"Okay, let me get some things set up first. How can I reach you?"

Sherod thought about his schedule. He wouldn't be free until lunch. Janet's call wouldn't be answered until later in the day.

"I'll call my man now. I'll give you his number, and you can make the arrangements with him. I think he's off on Monday's too, so this will work fine if you can get the truck for tomorrow."

"Faye, will you be available for a call?"

"I should be... but you know what? I'll let you know in the morning. I might be able to take off if you're sure you'll be moving your things tomorrow."

Sherod gave her a look of disappointment. Faye read the message on his face and shrugged her shoulders as she continued offering her services.

"That's if you need my help."

"I'll be okay. If I need you, I'll call. Thanks Sherod I don't think I'll need your friend either. I don't want anyone else involved in this. I'll deal with it myself."

Janet left the two of them and went to check on the children. She needed to get rid of the feeling that had overcome her. She knew they meant well, but she could tell their home was becoming uncomfortable. The last thing she wanted to do was to wear out her welcome. The two of them had done so much since she, and Marcus broke up.

The children were sleep. Joy was snoring with her legs entwined between her sisters. M.J. was nearing the edge of the queen sized guest bed. Janet smiled in spite of her anger, frustration, and disappointment. She adjusted the three children for comfort. She could hear Richard saying she would be moving on. She didn't want to believe that her move included more drama. Her memory continued to flash snapshots of episodes in her marriage, their separation, her lonely days and nights. Janet missed her past, before Karyn Spalling, before love walked out of her door, before Marcus stopped loving her.

The reality was creeping upon her. She pulled the bedroom door closed and stood facing it fighting her internal fears. She didn't notice Faye peeking into the room.

"Did you call Richard?" Faye whispered, she noticed Janet couldn't speak. She touched Janet's shoulders and turned her toward her. She embraced her as she had many times since the death of their father. Janet buried her head in her sister's bosom trying not to breakdown.

"I've got to stop this. I've prayed for the opportunity to be totally free of Marcus. Faye, now that I have the opportunity, I'm scared as hell. I've got a new job, a new man, and now I've got to get a new home. I prayed on my knees night after night while he was on his knees with that damn tramp...."

"Girl, she was the one on her knees."

Janet laughed in spite of herself and pushed Faye back gently. They smiled and hugged. "It's true you have to be careful what you pray for."

"I don't think you prayed for Ms. Fast Ass. If I hadn't been stupid, Janet, I feel so guilty."

"Don't, it wasn't the first time. I knew about the others, well I didn't want to admit I knew. But he had stepped out on me before. You, Sam and Mama were right. I didn't want to see it. Now, I just can't see me and the kids starting over. I really feel empty."

"You want some tea, coffee? I do. And you need to call Richard.

The sisters made their way to the kitchen. Sherod left them up talking. He listened to bits and pieces of their conversation, until he allowed sleep to take over. It was after twelve before Faye tapped him to join her in their bed.

67

The papers were spread across the lawyer's desk. Joshua Curry loosened his tie. Although the air-conditioned office was quite comfortable, he had become bothered by his client's excuses. He listened intently as Marcus explained again how he wanted to teach Janet a lesson. He didn't respond allowing his client to rant about his wife; the mother of his three young children, the woman who attempted suicide after he deserted her; the woman he felt was incompetent. Nothing he said showed her incompetence. Janet Robinson had been a woman who was dependent on a husband who felt his marriage. The certificate and ring held no bond on their relationship. It wasn't his job, as his lawyer, to convince him he was wrong.

Marcus would pay for his representation, and the judge would force feed him the rules of marriage. He looked over the papers filed by Janet's attorney. She chose a reputable firm; Joshua Curry knew them well. After being in the group of elite top divorce lawyers himself for more than ten years, he knew his client didn't have a leg to stand on. He was certain that by Marcus abandoning his family and having no proof of support for two years, it would give the judge the impression that he didn't care about her or their children.

"Marcus, I would forget this revenge thing man."

"Listen, forget we're friends. Be the lawyer okay. What can I do to get this over with and have my kids with me?"

Joshua wanted to forget they were friends. Marcus made the comment, as though they were weekend buddies. Joshua hadn't seen him since the couple got married. He always felt he should have shouted aloud when the question, *"If there's anyone here..."* arose during the ceremony. He knew about Marcus and a few of his discretions. The invitation to be a groomsman was payment for his silence.

"Alright, as your lawyer and not your friend, we could fight this. What do you want me to do? I mean she's working. She provided for the kids while you were playing under someone else's sheets, and she's not asking for alimony. I don't know why but she's left that up to the judge."

"She tried to kill herself; she's crazy."

"You don't believe that, if you did the kids would be with you."

"I was trying to get them, but I decided to move home."

"Did you look in the mirror and say that shit?"

"What?"

"If the judge heard that he'd have your ass nailed. You thought she was crazy, but you wait until she files the divorce to say so? C'mon man; I need a report. What about the doctor? You said she was evaluated and then had therapy. Do you know the doctor? Maybe a negative report would help?"

"What else?"

"That would do it. Where's she staying?"

"With her sister, she has a home not far from where we lived."

"Faye's married now right? Get a statement from her and her husband maybe. I mean, do they want her there? Maybe she's straining their home life. It's hard to say man she's done everything right and you, well..."

Marcus thought about Sherod's call. Maybe he would help him with a statement.

"Never mind all that. Well maybe, we'll see. I'll get the doctor to confirm she's off. What about her and her boss? That's got to count for something. I mean you and I both know when he stops banging her; she won't have a job."

"The mirror man, damn have you looked at yourself in the mirror. You married her. Janet is not the bitch on the street. You got to change this attitude. You sound like you're upset that she doesn't need you."

"Again, are you being the lawyer or the friend?"

"No that time I was being the judge."

Joshua put the papers back in the manila envelope. He wrote on a note pad and clipped the message on the envelope as a reminder.

"Alright then, when do you plan on seeing Dr. Norris? Soon I would hope. I'll need to contact Janet's lawyer about your intention. I can wait until you see if the doctor is on your side or at least agreeing with you in some way."

Marcus thought about the question. He made an appointment through the receptionist. She told him unless it was an urgent referral she wasn't available until the end of the month.

"How soon do I need her report?"

"We've got forty-five days to answer, but I wouldn't wait if you plan on fighting."

"I made an appointment."

"Marcus, man, you ain't a patient. This is business, call her and tell her you're stopping by. Better yet go there and catch her off guard. If Janet is crazy, she'll see you worrying that Janet will relapse. Yeah, go there. Go today."

"Alright. What else?"

"Don't' bother Janet. Call me after you've talked to Dr. Norris. Ask her to give you a copy of the report she's making. If she needs my request for it, call me."

68

I t was still early and Lashauna had downed three cups of coffee. The appointments from the prior week had her rattled. She hadn't written her reports or made any notes in the folders. Her mind wasn't on her patients or their problems. Walter was right she needed and deserved a break. He realized she needed time to herself. Their relationship was slowly changing. They spoke on the phone more since the conference and without his unannounced visits she felt the void between them.

A vacation would put things in order for her personally and professionally. She put her cup down, paying closer attention to the keyboard as she typed an e-mail addressed to the hospital administrators. She gave them the dates of her intended leave of absence. She flipped her calendar checking the dates and hit the send button. She'd leave after Marcus and Janet Robinson's divorce hearings.

Lashauna called Janet's lawyer a few days after filling out the courts requested forms. She told her lawyer she would be more than happy to make herself available if her testimony was needed during the proceedings. She reviewed the last sheets of the forwarded packet before putting it in the envelope. She would have to arrange for a courier to pick it up. Janet's lawyer was confident that there would be no need for a personal appearance. Lashauna heard that time and time again, she'd still keep her calendar open. Divorce proceedings and child support cases always had surprising turns. The two professionals talked about the cases they knew of that took that sudden turn. After the lawyer described Marcus just as Lashauna remembered him self-centered and arrogant, they agreed the possibilities of a judge hearing the case and having questions were inevitable.

She looked through her Rolodex remembering her appointment with her spiritual advisor. She didn't want to miss their session. She always felt so much better after their relaxing afternoons. They hadn't talked in a month or more but Janet was right; she needed a friend, someone to talk to. Lashauna was sure her relationship with Richard and Janet had to be reviewed honestly for her to heal. She was broken, and her advisor would pray with her and for her; an instant shot of spiritual reality. After making several attempts to call Janet, not knowing what to say if she answered, she decided she would send a letter to her while she was away. Then she would face Richard and Walter. There was another reality that crossed her mind; she would have to relocate.

Her thoughts were interrupted by the sound of a male's voice. She put her pen down and closed her journal, which definitely wasn't written for all eyes. She thought for sure her three o'clock appointment had been canceled. The voice got louder, an indication he was getting closer to her office door. She stood unaware who the visitor could be.

"Dr. Norris, I'm glad I caught you." Marcus closed his Blackberry putting it into his pocket. He stepped into her office without the doctor's response.

Lashauna's look of confusion changed to a look of irritation. "Why are you here Mr. Robinson?" She sat in her seat and watched Marcus as he made himself comfortable in the chair on the opposite side of her desk.

"You don't mind, do you? I mean I'm not interrupting anything am I?"

Lashauna smiled trying not to show her annoyance. She realized he had purposely "dropped in." "You're here now, what can I do for you?"

"I don't know if you're aware that I have attempted to move back home…"

The doctor didn't want to show an immediate interest. If Marcus was moving home was there a chance that Janet and Richard didn't hit it off during their weekend together? Reality kicked her reminding her she needed to let go of the past.

"What would make you think that would concern me? Your wife is no longer my patient."

"Yes, I was told that you might be the key to help me understand her problems."

"Problems? Who told you that?"

"Dr. Norris, or can I call you Lashauna?"

"Dr. Norris," she replied coldly.

"As you say, Dr. Norris, she came to you with suicide on her mind. Is there a clinical cure for someone wanting to kill themselves? I mean, the reason she wanted to do herself in came from the lack of self-esteem and support, right?"

Lashauna hesitated. She picked up her pen and rapidly tapped it on her desk. Marcus watched her as though it was her move on a chessboard. He knew the doctor was choosing her words carefully. She was fully aware of the position he wanted her to fall into.

"People that are suicidal have various reasons or shall I say situations that cause them to think that their death is the only solution. I've come to find that people that really want to kill themselves do."

"So Janet is a little off? She needs people to help her cope with those situations that had her thinking that way right?"

"Exactly what do you want? I can't discuss your wife's diagnosis or condition without her being here or giving me written permission."

"Doc, you've been informed that we are getting a divorce. I know you have. I just need a statement from you that says the best thing for her is her family, which includes me."

"I can't say that would be the best for her. She's made progress, and that's what I can say. I have my report, and notes prepared for both lawyers. I believe her lawyer will forward your lawyer a copy of my final evaluation."

She glanced at the envelope still awaiting the courier's arrival. Marcus appeared to be thinking. His blank stare gave the impression that he accepted what he heard.

"So, if there's nothing else Mr. Robinson..."

"I'll get my kids from her. I've already taken the apartment back. She's ill, and you know it. I'll get your damn license if you try to write it up any other way."

"Listen, you do you. You've been doing that for over two years. Let me tell you about you, since you're interested in evaluations. Your sorry ass led her to believe you would take care of her and your children for a lifetime. Somewhere along the way you smelled another and wanted to see if you would get better service outside of your home. Now you're back to repair what you destroyed. You can't fix what has been broken with promises, and a good lay. I'm sure your lady on the side will tell you the same."

"You don't know what you're talking about." Marcus heard enough. He stood to leave, and Lashauna stood to deliver her final verbal blow.

"I don't know who you wanted to replace your wife with, and I'm more than sure that your wife has replaced you too."

Marcus turned the knob of the closed door and turned to say good-bye. Lashauna caught his words in the air with words of her own.

"I'll see you in court. I can't wait for them to ask me why Ms. Robinson had given up on life with a husband and three children."

Marcus froze. He had no idea that the question would be one she may have to answer. The doctor opened the office door allowing him to step in the hall.

"Yes, every now and then my initial evaluation and any other encounters with family becomes part of divorce hearings. I'm looking forward to telling them how supportive you were. Good day Mr. Robinson."

Marcus opened his Blackberry and texted his lawyer. *"That didn't work. I'm on my way back to your office."*

69

*J*anet checked her watch. It was close to two and there was at least another trip to be made. After talking with Faye and Sherod the night before she knew her decision would be to call Tiffany. Tiffany offered her home many times to Janet and her children in the past. Marcus and Tiffany had a love-hate relationship, more hate than love. There were several occasions when she felt his condescending attitude needed to be checked.

Tiffany had her share of abusive relationships and chose to be single after losing a few teeth and her sight in one eye. After the dental work and repair to the bones around her eye, her beauty was restored. She had always been a very pretty girl and after God spared her life, she vowed no man would hold a warm spot in her heart; no man, except Sam. Tiffany and Janet's brother had their own again off again encounters. Janet told them both the sexual attraction kept them coming back for more. She was sure Sam was more than willing to help her because he would be in Tiffany's company for the day.

The two of them, Sam and Tiffany, met Janet at eight in the morning at what was Janet's old apartment. They waited ten minutes after Marcus pulled off before entering. Enough time, if he followed his daily routine, to be on the Garden State Parkway heading south. If Sherod was correct, the appointment with the lawyer wouldn't be until after ten.

She looked at her watch again. There were only a few things left. She wanted to take everything. Sam told her it would take too long to pack the kitchen. She had to choose between her dishes in the kitchen, the linen for the bedrooms and the towels for the bathroom. She was packing as much as she could while he and Tiffany took the next truckload over.

Sam had two of his friends helping him with the furniture, the loading and unloading. Tiffany directed where it would be best to put everything. She lived in Montclair, what most called "Upper Montclair." The homes and neighborhoods of the area were beautiful. Her father passed away leaving her his home, which was too large for one occupant. As an only child with both parents deceased, Tiffany hadn't tried to fill the rooms and never used the entire home. She welcomed the call from her longtime friend who needed to live where her husband wouldn't dare visit.

They returned to find Janet had packed her bath towels, face cloths, linen and most of her dishes. The truck would hold the balance of her belongings. Tiffany convinced her there would be no need for them to bring the dinette set or her bedroom furniture. They packed the children's rooms, and the rest of the furniture. After packing the truck, there was nothing left in the apartment.

"Girl, you're determined to take everything huh."

"Tiff, he hasn't lived here in two years. This stuff is mine, all of it. I took care of it. I listened to the bill collector's threats and when I got a job, I bought a few things to make me feel good. Why should he keep it?"

Janet was too angry to cry but mad enough to take it to another level.

"That tramp he was with didn't let him bring her shit! So he was gonna come home and suck up my luxury. Sam, this is it. I packed a set of dishes; I know you have some, but he ain't eating on the set with my initials. He can have the rest. I was going to replace it all."

Sam walked by with his friends behind him laughing as they continued to work. They grabbed the boxes and walked past the women smiling.

Tiffany understood Janet's frustration and her need to be in control.

"Whatever makes you feel at home; I want you to be comfortable. The kids will be glad to see their rooms after being at Faye's."

"I don't know girl, those rooms in your house could swallow these things they call a bedroom. My room is the only one that can come close, and that's to what your sitting room? Tiff, I want to thank you. I didn't want to be a burden to Faye and Rod, they would have let us stay but I could tell it was a strain. I fought with the thought of Richard coming to my rescue but I'd rather owe you the favor then to owe him. He's sweet but I don't want that over my head. I owe him enough already."

They stepped out of the way of Sam and his crew again. The men smiled and excused themselves.

"How much did you tell them you were paying?"

"Who, I asked Sam to show up. If they know like I know they're in it for the ride. I can barely slip Sam anything."

"I'll take care of him." Tiffany smiled watching the back of his jeans going out of the front door. "You're not dealing with Richard because you think you owe him, are you?"

They walked through the apartment checking for any items they overlooked. Janet closed all the closet and cabinet doors without giving her an answer. Tiffany gave her a questioning look. They went out the door and Janet beckoned the maintenance man over to the truck.

"Thank you so much. My husband should be home shortly. I'm sure he'll be in touch with management." She handed him the apartment key.

"Well, I for one hope you'll feel safer in your new home."

"I'm sure I will, even after you changed the lock it just wasn't the same."

70

Marcus dialed her number repeatedly, but he got no answer. Sherod assured him Janet's cell phone number had not been changed. He called his lawyer the minute he walked into the apartment and discovered she had taken the furniture and all of her belongings. It wasn't until he was asked that he checked his children's rooms.

"Everything is gone. Where the hell did she take all of that stuff? Who's paying the storage fee? Her dumb ass, man what is she trying to prove?"

Joshua spent the afternoon listening to Marcus complain about Dr. Norris and now the call about the empty apartment. He put the call on speaker as he packed his briefcase to leave his office for the day. He shook his head grinning as he imagined Marcus' expression when he noticed Janet was a step ahead of him again.

"Listen man, I'm about to leave here. We'll make all of this a part of the divorce hearing. Write down what's missing and we'll get it back."

"Where could she have gone with all that shit?"

"Marcus your concern should be; are they safe? That's all. You've accepted to fight about the rest in court. It will be over in a month or so."

"I guess you're right. Reality is a mother though. Josh man, what about the kids?"

"You said you wanted custody. We'll fight for it and see what happens. That's the best I can offer."

"Why not tell me my chances?"

"Look man, I've given you more than most of my day. To be honest with you, you'll probably get joint custody, if that. Janet is a good mother; she's a good woman, and man you fucked up a good marriage, but you know that. What do you want from this? You pushed that woman to the edge. That ain't a good thing. Listen, I'll be in touch. If you have any questions call me next week. I should have the evaluation and a date for court. I'll try to rush it."

"What's the rush?"

"The sooner the better for you and me."

"Hmm, alright later man, and thanks."

Marcus put the phone on the receiver. The silence in the partially emptied apartment seemed to be intensified. A feeling of loneliness bounced off the walls. He walked through the apartment as he had the night he cleaned M.J.'s closet. He missed his family. He found comfort in the recliner and let his thoughts carry him away.

Marcus was angry with himself and Janet. Her filing paperwork for a divorce showed she wasn't the woman he married. That woman knew the role he played in her life. The role of being the provider, being needed, gave him authority. His role of being both husband and father was taken away. Janet proved that by leaving the bed they made love in, but taking all evidence of the life they had together. He looked around the room wondering if her feelings were the same when he left her. She would ask for alimony, and child support while crying about abandonment and abuse. Joshua wouldn't challenge much. He didn't understand their marriage. Janet was his showpiece; he kept her polished for those special times, when expressing his love was more than the roll in the sheets. Karyn made him feel special. He was her prize. She told him that often. He never felt like much more than a need with Janet. He did what a husband and father was expected to do, no more.

He compared the women. Karyn set her expectations and when he didn't fill them, she told him. He couldn't name any of Janet's expectations. He knew no more about his wife then what he knew when they got married. He was sure; she changed, but if asked he couldn't tell anyone anything about her habits or views now. Janet had become a different woman over the years, especially after he became a different man. He picked up the phone again, dialing her number, hoping she would answer.

71

*T*he divorce hearing was scheduled for ten o'clock. Janet and Tiffany had breakfast and coffee on Halsey Street a few blocks from the courthouse. During the three-month wait, Janet changed the children's school, her contact numbers and her route from work to Faye's house. She had no contact with Marcus. He picked up his children on alternate weekends as he had over the past two years at his sister-n-law's home. Sherod made small talk when their paths crossed, but their friendship was scarred.

"So do you think today will be it?"

Janet was caught in thought hearing only part of her friend's question. "What happened?"

"Aw hell, you're not having second thoughts, are you?"

"It would be hell if I was. No, I should have done this when he walked out the door. I wonder if that would have been better. He's been too quiet. I know he knows where I work. He hasn't bothered my family about contacting me either. It's just not his "m.o." You know Marcus. It seems strange. I wanted him to see how far I've progressed, what I've accomplished. I want him to know what I do for a living, especially since I'm not just a secretary. I want him to know I'm in love with Richard. I want...."

"Hold on girlfriend, why does he need to know anything? He left you and didn't care how you made it. You took it hard, became depressed, and well, we know where that led. Did he help you through your depressive state? Janet it wasn't until he thought you were getting back on your feet; had a job and a man, and then he brought his ass home. I've always told you I respect your decisions and Lord knows I've got your back, but you don't need to rub it in his face. I know it feels good to be able to give him that dose of reality. Girl your blessings can't be recognized by nobody but you and those of us who prayed for you. Marcus was too busy trying to get his. Believe me, he knows what you've gone through, and if he doesn't know how, oh well."

"I guess you're right. Yeah, you're right."

"Is Richard coming to the court proceeding?"

"No, he said if I needed him, call. I told him you were with me. I'm glad you're here; I still need support."

"Please as many nights as you spent with me in the hospital? Where else would I be? Janet, I wanted to tell you, I'm proud of you."

"Thanks. I thought about divorce a thousand times Tiff. To be honest with you if it wasn't for Dr. Norris, and the process her therapy took me through, I don't know if I could have ever filed for a divorce."

"Mental abuse is just as bad as physical. I think it takes longer for everyone to see it."

"I almost snapped when I saw his bags in my bedroom. Girl it was like he brought a part of that chick he was with into my home. I don't know if we would be here today if he stayed with her."

"The time was approaching. I mean you and Richard make a great couple. Tell me you haven't thought about marriage."

"Just like every woman who is in a good relationship. Look Tiff, I'm not trying to rush things. One of the things Dr. Norris said was face each issue knowing what it is and what you want from it. Richard is a good man, a man who is interested in me, and I'm interested in him. We've gotten to know each other, and we're taking it slow. I'm not trying to make the same mistake twice. The "happily ever after" is at the end of fairy tales. Now it's time for me to live in the real world."

"I heard that. Well, you and the children can stay as long as you like, or as long as you need. Listen before we get all teary let's get out of here. We've got thirty minutes to park and get to the court."

The elevator was packed with employees and people referring to their court papers for directions. Tiffany pushed the number nine and stepped to the side. The bell rang indicating the closing of the doors. A woman yelling, "Hold the door, please," delayed their movement momentarily as the door reopened quickly. She stepped in breathing deeply smiling and nodding thank you to all who adjusted themselves making room for her and the briefcase she carried.

Janet smiled at Tiffany and nodded toward the woman. Tiffany read her friend's lips as she mouthed the woman was her lawyer. The elevator stopped on the ninth floor, and the three women excused themselves making their way out before the doors closed.

"Good morning lady." The lawyer smiled as she recognized her client was walking with her.

"Good morning. Tiffany this is Ms. Foxworthy my attorney. This is my girlfriend Tiffany. The friend I told you I moved in with."

The ladies shook hands as they walked to an available table in front of the courtroom marked Judge Evans. Janet put her folder with the papers Ms. Foxworthy requested on the table. The lawyer did the same with her briefcase.

"So are you ready for this? I guess you're saying 'finally' huh?"

Tiffany wasn't sure why Janet chose a young white woman for her attorney. She would definitely ask her why she didn't choose a black firm. She gave the lawyer another look. This time she was checking her persona as a woman not as a professional.

Katherine Foxworthy was what the card read that Tiffany flipped through her fingers as Janet talked candidly about the past few months. Her shoulder length straight hair told nothing about who she was. Her nails were manicured with clear polish, and she wore nothing to attract attention to her face or body. Tiffany thought, *"plain Jane,"* and tried to focus more on their conversation.

"I called Dr. Norris. She left a message on my phone that I thought was quite interesting. It appears that Marcus has been trying to talk to her. He's trying to convince her that she wouldn't want to testify, and she might consider changing her report. She's a little worried that he and his lawyer may have trumped-up something about her and your now lover, Richard. Minor snag but it could bring some questions about her testimony."

"Well if she testifies on his behalf, we could use the same reasons. She's scorned. What did she say she decided to do?" Janet suddenly felt a pang from the sudden frustration.

The door to the courtroom opened. An officer began to rattle off the names on the clipboard. A hush fell between the lawyer's and their clients as they listened for their case to be called. "Janet Robinson versus Marcus Robinson," the officer paused for a response.

"Attorney for the plaintiff," Katherine announced as she gathered the few papers, she and Janet were reviewing. Janet and Tiffany followed her lead into the courtroom.

The room was smaller than either of them imagined. The lawyers seemed to have their own seating, which left Tiffany and Janet in the audience with the other plaintiffs, defendants, and supporters.

"Where's Marcus?" Tiffany's voice was a little louder than she expected. She covered her mouth and smiled hoping no one was paying attention.

"Girl, I don't know and I hope he overslept. This is gonna be a mess Tiff. Suppose Dr. Norris is right. If Marcus puts a twist on things where does that leave me or my children?"

"Little Ms. Pure Bread didn't seem like she was worried."

Janet couldn't help but snicker. "Ms. Pure Bread?"

"C'mon she looks like she needs a good one. A few rounds, she is too ... something."

"She's one of the best according to Richard's sources."

"Great, even your lawyer is tied to him; the doctor, your job and your lawyer? Girl, I hope that fool for a husband of yours doesn't get wind of this."

Janet rolled her eyes and looked around the court for her soon to be ex-husband. She covered her mouth as she felt laughter building. The group of polished lawyers made Ms. Foxworthy look like a misfit. Her pinstriped suit and white blouse was shouting for a replacement. Janet liked Katherine. The few times they spoke, ate out, and talked strategy for the day's hearing, she found her to be in the mix of things. Tiffany had drawn her attention to the basics. She was plain, but she came highly recommended. Janet thought twice about hiring a female attorney as she listened to Richard rave about her. He concluded, if the top executives used her to save their finances from greedy wives Marcus didn't stand a chance.

The court clerk made another announcement for attorneys to report if they were not there for the first roll call. Tiffany tapped Janet's leg bringing her attention to the other attorneys as they walked to the front of the courtroom.

"There's Joshua, Marcus must be here."

"Wow, I haven't seen him since we got married. Did he ever get married?"

"No, I think they're still engaged. He's a good catch though. Hey, there's your ex sitting on the far side, next to the last row. Guess he doesn't want to be noticed."

The lawyers dispersed after meeting with the clerk returning to their special seating or their clients. Katherine approached Janet and Tiffany. They moved over making room for her to sit.

"I have to ask you this although we've discussed it before. Are you willing to talk with the court mediator before seeing the judge? This is just a procedure. Some couples get to the court and change their mind. If you want to we can use this as an opportunity to see what he wants or what his intentions are if we precede. If you don't want to see the mediator we can move forward as planned."

Janet looked over her lawyer's shoulder at Marcus, who was talking to his lawyer. She wondered what he was telling Joshua he wanted to do. She looked at Tiffany hoping to read an answer in her eyes.

"If we talk with the mediator, will that delay the divorce?"

"It depends on his lawyer and what is said during the meeting. There are times when clients leave the mediator, and they actually reconcile. I guess reality sets in. Anyway, the choice is yours, and I'm obligated to explain it again."

"Give me a minute."

Tiffany and Katherine gave her a questioning look.

"Not that I don't want the divorce, far from it. I'm just thinking about Marcus and the dirty games he plays. Talking with the mediator could benefit us. I want to know what he intends on doing or what he wants."

"Okay, I'll let Mr. Curry know."

72

*M*arcus listened as his lawyer explained the mediator wouldn't help his case. He glanced at his wife taking in the same information from her lawyer. Tiffany was listening intently, but didn't join the conversation.

"Marcus, what do you want me to say?"

"A mediator is fine. What harm could it do?"

"What is there to discuss is the question? You want your children, and Janet won't agree to that. Do you still want the furniture or the cash for what she took?"

"Listen, whatever it takes to force her into coming home is to be done. Did you talk to her shrink?"

"She's not budging. She's not even answering my calls. Listen I'm going to talk to your wife's lawyer. If she wants to go in front of the mediator, that's good with you?"

"Yea, yea, whatever."

The plum suit fit Janet perfect. The multicolor blouse brought out her color. He wondered what she thought about when she changed her hair. The new style enhanced her appearance. Although it was shorter than he had seen her wear it, the cropped cut aroused him. He wanted her to stand. He imagined her shapely figure unclothed. He allowed himself to continue his vision as he relaxed in his seat.

Marcus could feel the warmth of her skin as he imagined touching her once again. He glanced at her standing on the other side of the courtroom talking and smiling with Tiffany. Her make-up was more than the hints of color she wore when they were together, and her lips were painted in a hue of plum. He could feel his passion building as he imagined the love sessions they had. The thought of her body responding to their movement caused a rise in his pants. He quickly looked to his left and right to see if anyone was noticing his reactions. He became uncomfortable.

Joshua and Katherine were approaching the clerk. Marcus stood hoping to relieve the pressure of his manhood throbbing against his zipper. He would have to fulfill his need before the week was over. He had been yearning for Karyn as well. She agreed to have dinner with him on a few occasions, but those outings didn't lead to his bedroom. His body heat was rising at the thought of the two women. He proceeded to walk out of the court.

Joshua and Katherine separated themselves from the other attorneys to discuss the meeting with the mediator. Janet tapped Tiffany and nodded in their direction.

"I wonder if you would see the mediator today."

"I sure hope so. I don't want to delay this much longer. I've got butterflies in my stomach like I'm waiting to be sentenced."

Tiffany looked across the court where Marcus once sat. It was now empty.

"Hey, how about some air. They'll come and find you. Let's get some coffee or juice. A different view would do you some good."

Janet agreed. They grabbed their belongings and walked out the court. Ms. Foxworthy looked up, and Janet pointed to the door. Her lawyer smiled understanding her client would be out in the lobby.

"Tiff, do you think Marcus will be more cooperative during the meeting?"

"I don't think he cares, look."

"What the hell is he thinking?" Janet was stunned for a moment.

"He's looking for a way to win. She's here for show, I'm sure. Didn't you say she didn't want the kids to stay in her home?"

Janet sighed. She watched, trying not to stare. Karyn Spalling was there with her husband to support him; she assumed. Tiffany was there for her so why not have someone there to support him.

"Maybe she's changed her mind. Where's the vending machine?"

73

The small room held the two lawyers, their clients, the mediator, and the court transcriber. There was only room for their seats and two long tables. The tables were put together giving them extra width, and the parties were divided on two sides facing each other. The mediator and the transcriber sat with the microphone and folders facing the clients and the lawyers. After the introductions, the mediator explained the proceeding and began the questioning.

"I've gone over your papers with the attorneys, and they've indicated that you would like to try to come to an agreement before seeing a judge. That's why we're here."

Janet sat back in her chair. Her mind was on the scene she witnessed in the lobby. Marcus and Karyn stood at the elevator talking. Anyone could see they were in some kind of personal relationship. Karyn stood closer than a friend, whispering in his ear, smiling while holding his hand. The attention brought an instant smile to his face.

"Ms. Robinson, do you agree?"

"Uh, oh I'm sorry can you repeat that."

Katherine spoke softly, "We need to know if you're willing to take the outcome of this meeting before the judge as final. There would be no need for us to ask any other questions. The judge would review what we've agreed to, and make the divorce official."

"Is there a way to object if necessary during this meeting?"

Marcus frowned at Janet's question. "What would you object to? You called for this mediation."

Janet rolled her eyes and waited for Ms. Foxworthy to answer.

"If you don't want to continue we won't." The mediator saw the need to answer before the argument began. His experience paid off. It definitely taught him how to deal with most of the husbands and wives who came before him and had obvious differences. The lawyers opened their pads preparing for the first question disregarding their client's behavior.

"Ms. Robinson, you have been working for close to a year now, are you currently in a permanent position or is this a temp to hire job?" The mediator's coldness made it sound deplorable to work in a temporary position.

"No, it's a permanent position. I work for Burnett and Reed. There is no temp agency involved." Janet answered returning his attitude. She shot a glare over to Marcus.

The mediator continued without looking up. He flipped the pages of the papers before him.

"Yes, Richard Burnett is your employer according to your documents. When you were in the hospital you were already working for his company?"

Janet remembered the papers she filled out. Richard's insurance paid for her medical bills because he said she was employed there when she was hospitalized.

"Yes, I was still on probation then."

"I see. You filed for your divorce after you, and Mr. Robinson had been separated two years. What sparked your action?"

"I was ready to let go of the past. Marcus seemed to be happy living outside of our marriage and had no intentions on coming home."

Marcus repositioned himself in his seat causing the man to look over his glasses. The interruption caused a moment of silence before Janet continued.

"I asked Marcus time after time to reconsider and after my stay in the hospital and therapy, I decided it was better for me to move on."

"And the children?"

"What about my children?"

"Who takes care of them while you work?"

"They're school age. The youngest is in kindergarten. My sister and brother-n-law watch them from time to time."

"What is the reason for your husband picking your children up at your sister's house rather than your home?"

"I wasn't able to; rather I didn't want to have Marcus in my home whenever he wanted to be there. He tends to stop in when he wants. After I moved from my apartment, I told him that he would be able to pick them up and return them to my sister as he had before."

"I see. Why did you move?"

"My husband moved his things back into our apartment without calling or consulting me, as though he hadn't been gone. I couldn't stay there with him. We've been through a lot. I've gotten over it. I didn't want to return to the state of mind I was in a year ago."

Marcus began to smile. He nudged his lawyer drawing attention from the mediator.

"Mr. Robinson, these questions are directed to Ms. Robinson solely. Your lawyer will be able to ask questions that you may have shortly. Please refrain from making sideline remarks or distractions."

Marcus avoided the mediator's stare. He focused on the note, "Chill man" which was on the pad Joshua pushed before him.

"Ms. Robinson, are you still seeing Dr. Norris or taking any medication regularly for depression?"

"No."

"Are you scheduled for any further appointments with Dr. Norris or the hospital as a follow-up to your diagnosed depression?"

"No."

"Mr. Curry, you may ask any questions you may have."

Joshua sighed as he made check marks on the paper lying before him. He tapped his pen, as though he was nervous about asking his prepared questions. He took a sip of water from one of the glasses that had been filled and placed on the table.

"Ms. Robinson, as you know, this meeting is to agree or come to an agreement about the terms of your divorce. Do you feel that as of today, you're able to support your three children?"

"I've supported them for two years and ten months without any financial support from my husband. I guess that would prove my ability to support them."

"So you didn't move with the intention of seeking support?"

"No. I have the same job that I've had over the past ten months which pays more than welfare or any other means I would have to apply for."

"More than what you would benefit from a divorce?"

"I'm not asking for anything. I don't want his money. I want my freedom."

"She's crazy. Every woman wants something!" Marcus blurted loudly.

"Mr. Robinson, your lawyer will ask the questions and make the comments. Refrain from any outburst please."

Joshua looked from the mediator to Marcus, knowing it wouldn't be long before Marcus voiced his opinion.

"What about your children and their needs?"

"Mr. Curry, I take care of their needs. If their father wants to give them anything he can set up an account for them or bring them what they want."

"Bring it where? You live with that lesbian friend of yours. What about that Mr. Mediator? I have a say on where my kids live, right?"

"Mr. Robinson, I'm sure your lawyer will discuss your concerns."

"Ms. Robinson, I'll ask this since it came up. What are your living arrangements?"

"I share a home with a friend of mine. She owns a home in Montclair. The children have their own bedrooms and so do I. They actually have more room than they would if we lived in our old apartment."

Joshua looked at Ms. Foxworthy, who hadn't made any notes on her pad nor reacted to any of the comments made by Marcus. He didn't want to play dirty and Marcus did.

"What is your relationship with Richard Barnett?"

"He's my boss."

Janet could feel her hands sweating. She sighed saying a silent prayer for strength.

"My client's concern is the welfare of his children." Joshua interjected.

Janet started to answer, but her attorney touched her hand gently indicating she should remain silent.

"Maybe we should ask what those concerns are. Mr. Robinson, without details, do you have problems with your children living with their mother?" The mediator posed the question and waited with his pen on his notepad.

"Their stability is a concern, yes. Janet's stability is a concern. That's why I moved home. She was diagnosed with depression, what if...?"

"Without the details; so you have concerns with the stability of your wife and the children." The man began writing on the papers. His facial expression changed as though he was debating what needed to be done.

"Do you have property together?"

Janet responded, emphatically no, while her husband waited for the mediator to look his way. "Yes, she took all that we own."

The mediator looked over his Versace frames. He took the glasses off and leaned forward. "Mr. and Mrs. Robinson, there must be something you agree on. If not, we have no terms to give to the judge. She will have to hear your problems and decide based on how you answer her questions. I really need you to think about this and decide whether the two of you are willing to compromise. If a compromise can't be met you will be scheduled to see the judge."

The lawyers didn't say anything. It was as though Janet and Marcus answered on cue, "I want to see the judge."

74

Tiffany and Richard laughed as Janet described her frustrations and unspoken words during the mediation.

"I wanted to scream." Janet mocked Marcus, "*She took all we own.* His punk ass has no idea what I took. Half of the stuff he left I got rid of."

"What did the lawyers say?" Tiffany didn't ask the details as they drove home from the court. Janet called Richard and asked him to meet them at Tiffany's home. They sat listening intently as she explained the outcome of the meeting.

"After we stated we wanted to see the judge; Ms. Foxworthy began to pack her briefcase. I think she knew we were going before a judge all along. Joshua hesitated like there was more to be said. Marcus looked at the mediator for him to say something. Well, as Tiffany calls her, Ms. Pure Bread, told the mediator to contact her office with the date for the hearing. We walked out like we won a case at the Supreme Court."

"So, you've got to go back to court?"

"Richard, she didn't look back and neither did I. I guess they call that attorney confidence. You heard her Tiff; she said she'll call me later this evening. You guys want something from the kitchen?"

Janet got up from the couch where she and Tiffany sat. Richard followed her into the kitchen. He smiled when she turned into him accepting the kiss on her forehead.

"I'm glad the day went well. Did Lashauna show up?"

"No, as a matter of a fact I didn't even ask Katherine what the rest of their conversation was. She was telling me that Marcus was trying to force her into retracting her statement. I don't know that she can withhold my medical report if my mental health is questioned. I wouldn't think so."

She turned to the cabinet and pulled out three glasses.

"I'll be back later. I just stopped by to see how things went. I promised to drop some papers off to a client for Walter."

"Oh, okay. How is Walter?"

"Walter is Walter, dealing with the distance between him and Lashauna. I think he still loves her. They haven't talked for weeks now."

"Have you talked to her?"

Richard paused not knowing why Janet asked the question. She went to the refrigerator and pulled out the pitcher as though his hesitation didn't bother her.

"No why?"

"Well she's stressing about you and her being brought up in court, so I thought maybe she would call you."

"What?"

"Katherine said Marcus was threatening to bring up the relationship between you and her. I don't know the rest I have to ask when she calls me. I just know that Lashauna is worried about it. I was hoping that the mediation would be enough to end this today."

"Maybe I ought to call her. Elaine mentioned she hadn't seen her at church."

"Well Katherine spoke with her, so I don't think she needs you to check on her. Tell Walter to call her."

"It can't hurt to give her a call."

"Depends on whose side she's on."

They walked into the living room, and Richard said his goodbyes leaving the two women to chat more about the court proceedings. Tiffany watched as Richard's truck went past the window exiting her driveway.

"You know he's going to call her right?"

"I'm not worried about that, they are friends. Maybe she'll tell him what Marcus said. I'm sitting on pins and needles waiting for Katherine to call."

"What was up with Karyn showing up?"

"That didn't come up. I mentioned him leaving home and wanting to live elsewhere, but I didn't bring up her name."

"Girl, that's the difference between you and me. I think I would have told the whole story."

"If I had mentioned Karyn, he might have brought up Richard."

"So, you and Richard didn't break up your marriage. That's what the proceeding is about right? I mean, if you prove he left you and three kids for the golden fuzz..."

"Golden fuzz?" Janet looked at Tiffany and shook her head.

"You know all men think another woman's fuzz is new-found gold."

"Shit girl, she's got brown naps like the rest of us."

75

"*I* was surprised to get your call. My lawyer said you hadn't answered any of his calls."

Marcus stepped into Dr. Norris' home pleased she asked to meet with him. He left the courtroom angered by both his lawyer's inability to counter Janet's exit, and the fact that the proceeding would be held another day. They stood with blank facial expressions as the mediator told them they would be notified of a date to go before the judge. Joshua couldn't tell him what he thought would happen or what their immediate plans would be. They went their separate ways after reaching the parking lot. His cell phone rang, and the call was an invitation for him to come to the address given.

"Please, may I offer you a drink?"

"Yes, thank you." Marcus looked over at the liquor cart that sat near the end table. "I'll have Grey Goose on the rocks." He was pleased she had his brand of Vodka.

"Mr. Robinson, I called you because I wanted us to have a chance to clear up any issues you may want to present in court."

Marcus smiled glad he had the upper hand. He took a drink from his glass and carefully put it on the coaster she provided. He sat back on the couch, making himself comfortable. The doctor's home had a contemporary flair. She looked more relaxed than she had when he visited her office. Her outfit accented her toned body. Exercise gear did her justice. The definition of her hips and thighs drew his attention as she took a seat on the plush pillows that were arranged around the coffee table.

"And what issues might that be? I'm sure you understood the messages we left."

"Sure I did. I'm not understanding, why you would assume anything you had to say about my personal relationships would affect my evaluation? What do you think, you know about me?"

"We're alone right?" Marcus looked over his shoulder emphasizing his sarcasm. "You didn't invite anyone else to this meeting did you?"

"Why would I?"

"Well then, let your hair down Doc. Look you can fix this for me and you. My wife is dating your ex. Unless his punk ass isn't worth the fight, change your report. You don't have to make her insane, just one with issues, as you say."

"Just who is my ex? Walter Reed? We are still in somewhat of a relationship. We were in a relationship when I met your wife. Is that who you are referring to?"

"C'mon Lashauna, or is it still Dr. Norris?"

"Dr. Norris this is still business."

"You're a little underdressed for business. We're at your home, and it's after hours. Lashauna, I wasn't born yesterday. Did you think you could get me drunk and fuck your way into keeping your license? Are you that good?"

"Is that your usual line? I want you to understand Lashauna. I'm damn good at whatever I do. I don't take threats well. My livelihood means a lot to me, and I wouldn't jeopardize it for you or your wife. What that means Marcus is that I evaluated your wife, and my findings stand. As I said to you before, you're not much of a support system."

"You don't know what you're talking about. Janet is weak, always has been. I married her to give her stability, something no one else would have given her." Marcus moved closer to the end of the couch toward the doctor. "She's not as hot as you, or any of the others I had over the years. Maybe if we had you as a marriage counselor, you would have saved both of us. There wouldn't have been a reason for me leaving home if we had sessions with you. You do provide one on one sessions, with couples right?"

"You said she was weak. You gave her stability?" Lashauna's question made him sit back with his glass in his hand. He took another drink before answering.

"Do I need to put my feet on the fucking couch? All right, listen. Janet was a pretty girl, but she wasn't a street girl, you know what I mean? She hadn't been around. I might have been her first. Anyway, I knew that about her, and I wanted that type of woman for my wife. But Doc, you don't fuck with your wife. Every now and then, a man needs that freak in the bedroom, that excitement that women of knowledge give their man. So I stepped out."

"So this wasn't your first time stepping out. Did Janet know about the other times?"

"No, I don't know, maybe this one and the one before. I never left home until this last time though. I thought about Janet whenever I was with Karyn, that's the girl I was with. Anyway, thoughts about home, the children and Janet interrupted my day, my nights, my sleep, and my romantic pleasures. I knew I had fucked up my marriage but as a man, hell, I wasn't admitting that shit. So I stayed with Karyn. I started missing my kids, and that brought reality to the front. Karyn wasn't having the kids around. She just wanted us. I was whipped by then though. The things she did to me physically kept me bound."

"So why fight the divorce?"

"I need to be at home. That's where I belong. Now if she won't accept me than I want the kids. She tried to kill herself that's proof, she's crazy."

Lashauna reached for his empty glass and gave him a refill. She refreshed her wine with two ice cubes and repositioned herself on the pillows.

"You've said a lot and I really want you to explain it so I can understand. I think you understand me right?"

"What? I understand that Janet convinced you that she's okay. I don't believe she is."

"So you don't believe she's okay, but you think she'll be alright if you take her kids from her."

"I made those kids. Shit I made her."

"You broke her too. She was simply tired; tired of fighting the thought of you loving someone else. A lot of her "crazy" was you. She didn't try to kill herself, and my report says that. It was an accident. She tried to rest. Simply sleep; recoup; rest her body and mind. Those days in the hospital she got energized and came out prepared to take on the challenge that reality was giving her. Her fight is the fight of many women who go through depression, domestic violence, and you're right, they commit suicide. I thank God that Janet didn't."

"Listen, I would love to play this game with you, but I'm here only because you wanted something from me. I listened to you now you listen to me. Janet has a choice, come home or lose her kids. Your evaluation isn't from your personal point of view. Fix it or maybe..."

Marcus paused and licked his lips. "We can forget the thing between you and what's his name, Richard? You do best when the patient lies on their backs right?"

Lashauna gave him a devilish smile. "I don't think you could pay for my services. Listen I just need to know one more thing. Suppose she comes home, will you stop your play outside of your home?"

"C'mon Doc, She's not that crazy. She knows my needs. If it wasn't for others like you butting in she would be home, or dead."

Lashauna got up, and Marcus rose to his feet. She took his glass from the table and put it back on the cart. He knew it was an indication their conversation was over.

"When will I hear from you, or will you be contacting my lawyer?"

"I'm sure your lawyer will call you. I'm glad we had this opportunity to talk. You're right. I need to think about your children and Janet's welfare. I'll send an addendum to my statement."

"Thank you and listen whatever way this ends. I owe you. It could benefit both of us. I'm sure you won't regret an evening of pleasure with me."

Lashauna opened her front door and simply smiled saying, "I'll keep it in mind."

76

The phone call was shorter than expected. Ms. Foxworthy told Mr. Curry there was nothing more to be resolved by waiting any longer than the date they agreed upon for the hearing. Joshua placed the receiver in the cradle and sighed. He needed more time. After receiving no addendum from Dr. Norris, he would have to get another psychologist to dispute her findings. His call to other doctors led him to a few of her colleagues who stated they would stand by her decision. There were two reputable doctors who agreed to meet with him after hours. However, after discussing the case, they both stated that without a session with her, they couldn't say whether Janet was unfit as a mother or crazy. The other problem was Janet or the court agreeing to another evaluation was slim to none.

Ms. Foxworthy and Janet had the upper hand. He didn't want to call Marcus. He knew his client didn't have any proof for his claim of her being unfit, and that was where their case ended. He would have to change his attitude if he expected any judge to give him custody of the children he abandoned. Marcus still believed that the threat of losing the children would bring her home. Joshua used his pen to flip back the pages of his notes. It was almost six months. Janet made no attempt to return to her husband.

The hearing was scheduled for Monday. There was no need to pretend he would find helpful information in two days. Marcus was talking with Faye and Sherod. If they made a statement about Janet's continuous need for their support he agreed to submit their written statement. Joshua warned him they needed to say they went above and beyond the call of family support constantly. Marcus hadn't called since, that was a week ago.

The lawyer closed the file labeled Robinson. There were other cases to prepare. Marcus would have to understand his loss. He once accused Joshua of flirting with Janet. Thinking about their past, the wedding and now the divorce, she would have done better if he had tried flirting with her. She was shy in a sexy way, and he was sure after three children and Marcus she was more than ready for a mature man. If her dealing with Richard Burnett was true, he scored big. He promised Marcus he would look into their questionable relationship.

He and Katherine had met twice since the mediation. Ms. Foxworthy was more than professional, but she did break her stern demeanor during their last luncheon together. She assured him his client was blinded with misplaced jealousy. She told him that Janet and Richard began dating after she was employed there. Her statement was supported in Dr. Norris' evaluation. Janet was asked about relationships in therapy, and she never mentioned a man. She wasn't reluctant to talk about anything, although Dr. Norris did indicate she was hesitant to discuss Marcus. It took more than two months of therapy before she talked about her marriage.

He could only agree with her that Marcus was more than crude regarding his adulterous activities. As she put it, "He hung them on the wall in his home" leaving Janet little room to be the trusting wife. Katherine was certain that her client loved her husband on the morning of her accidental overdose. She would be proving that if the judge was to ask her. Joshua was sure she had more information than she was willing to share.

Delaying the call wouldn't help the situation. Joshua dialed the number and pushed the button waiting to hear the voice come through the speaker. "Hey, you must have a confirmed court date."

"Yes nine o'clock on Monday, the same court. Did you get anything from your in-laws?"

"No, I mean a lot of advice from Sherod, and Faye didn't say much. I thought she would slip and say something to Karyn though."

"Karyn? You got back with Karyn?"

"Brothers got needs. She's okay with the booty call thing. I am too."

"I thought you wanted your marriage."

"No, I want my family. Janet and old dude are fucking by now. He can keep that bed board."

"So the divorce is cool. I mean you're not trying to make her come home?"

"No, but I still want my kids. Faye and Sherod would still want to be in their lives. So her support is my support; the best of both worlds my friend. Karyn gets what she wants, no kids, I get what I want Karyn and the kids. I'm set as long as you do your thing. She has nothing on me accept my leaving her two years ago. She's moved on, so have I, the judge and everyone will agree. But the children have to be secure. Can they say that if she's off her rocker?"

"I don't have any proof of that." Joshua was becoming agitated.

"Dr. Norris will send the proof. I called her. She said you'll have it by the end of the week."

"She answered your call?"

"We're on good terms. I even went to her house, talked and shared a few drinks. It would have gone further, but I am a man with morals."

Joshua put the call on hold. Monday couldn't come soon enough.

77

*T*he minister stood in the foyer as he did each Sunday morning after service. Elaine and M.J. stood together waiting at the front door for his mother and sisters. The nine o'clock service was crowded. Elaine nodded to all who passed giving them a smile and a warm wish for a blessed week. Janet told them she would meet them after taking the girls to the restroom. Richard stopped to talk with someone from the Sick and Shut In Ministry hoping Lashauna had been seen or heard from over the past few weeks.

They all walked to the car waving to friends as they pulled out of the parking lot. The children, Janet and Elaine talked about the upcoming winter break while Richard seemed engrossed in thought. He parked the car after the fifteen-minute ride but didn't turn off the ignition.

"You guys go in. I've got a run to make."

Elaine got out of the car with no questions. The children followed. Janet waited for them to close the door and head toward the house. Joy and Erica led the way, running up the walk.

"You're going to look for her, aren't you?" Janet knew the answer.

"No one has seen her. Walter didn't reach her by phone. I've left messages and now I'm worried. No matter what her troubles she's connected to the ministry. They haven't heard from her either. There's something wrong. I'll just feel better knowing she's okay."

"Call me." Janet kissed him gently and got out of the car. Richard waited until he saw her wave from the front door, then he pulled off. He didn't want to alert Elaine or Janet to his fear for Lashauna. The doctor did not return any calls from the church members or her co-workers. They thought she was working but the submitted evaluations, reports, e-mails and phone calls could have been made from her home. No one thought of questioning her actions until they realized a month had gone since they actually saw her.

Richard turned into her driveway. The garage door was closed, but he could see the top of her Mercedes through the small paned windows. Walter told him he didn't think her car had been moved, but he couldn't get her to answer the door. Richard approached the front door mentally returning to the day Janet was found by Faye. He didn't think he was strong enough to be a witness to any form of suicide.

He sighed and rang the bell. Music could be heard, and Richard relaxed waiting for the door to open. Lashauna opened the door, and the aroma of her Sunday dinner rushed out into the air.

"Hey Richard, what brings you this way? My house is not in your neighborhood."

Lashauna sounded as though she had been dozing. She stepped to the side allowing her unexpected guest to enter her home. Richard looked around the large room, there were no apparent signs indicating her state of mind.

"How've you been? You don't return calls, so I've been sent to check in on you."

"By who? I've been in contact with those who I need to contact. Who else has been looking?"

"Walter, my sister, and the church members."

"I'm weaning relationships."

Richard walked to the kitchen with Lashauna in tow. She frowned as he continued to walk through the home as though he was searching for someone to be there.

"Who are you looking for?"

"Just checking you out, so you're weaning relationships huh?"

"I plan on leaving in a couple of weeks for a month or two and I don't want to be attached to any relationships."

Richard turned and faced her. The house was in order. Each room looked as though she had been in them over the past days. Lashauna looked tired. Her face was drawn and her eyes were distant. If he hadn't been told she wasn't at the job, he would have concluded that she was working long hours. He took her hand and led her to her couch in the living room.

"Sit here; tell me what you've been doing with yourself."

"Just like that? What's up with you, what have you been doing?"

"Smells like a big meal." Richard ignored her question. "Are you expecting company?"

"No. I just had a taste for a few things. Something different for a change, now answer me."

"Are you okay? I mean really okay? You don't look like you're getting much rest for someone who doesn't go in daily."

"Doesn't mean I'm not working." She gave the rehearsed answer.

"When's the last time you saw a client."

"I haven't. I'm finishing up a few things before I leave. I was really behind in clinical evaluations, panel analysis reports, board referrals, you know. I sent all my paperwork into the ministry for new members to get involved. I've been busy."

"Why?"

Lashauna frowned pulling her hand away from his. She feared he would detect her nervousness in her touch. It was time to take her medication, it kept her stable, but she didn't need to be pushed.

"I was swamped and I needed to catch up. I know it would break me, but I needed to get all of it done before I leave."

"So why not return the calls. Lashauna people are worried about you."

"People and you? Are you worried Richard? How does what others are worried about bring you to my doorstep? A few months ago if I had invited you, you would have refused. So why are you here?"

"You wouldn't answer their calls. Walter tried to visit you never answered the door. I was worried too."

"So you playing superman again?"

Richard wondered if her sudden disappearance was a ploy to get him to respond. "Call it what you want. You don't have any kryptonite do you?"

"Well, if I thought as I had months ago I would have said I was the kryptonite."

Richard smiled still uncomfortable about her intentions.

"Relax Mr. Burnett. My therapist said a sabbatical would be the best thing to help me with my problems. I'm taking her advice. You're safe."

"You go to a therapist?"

"Yeah, we have issues too."

The corners of his mouth turned. Lashauna got up and excused herself leaving Richard on the couch by himself. He wondered what brought on her need for therapy. He could hear her rattling pots as the smell caused his stomach to reply. Her recliner on the opposite side of the room held a set of headphones and a book. It was obvious she was listening to the music and reading. Perhaps that's why Walter saw the car but didn't get any answer at the door. It had been almost a year since he had free access to her home.

Richard was curious and went to read over some of the CD covers that were strewn on the floor. The music was some of what he heard through the front door. Her selections were definitely a plus. Jazz artist never seem to fade and she had some of the best. He stood looking at the back of a few of the cases. The title to the book in the chair grabbed his attention, *"How to walk away from painful relationships."* He was tempted to pick the book up and read the synopsis, but Lashauna's voice caused him to drop the book and respond to her question.

"Would you like something to drink?"

"Uh, no. I didn't know you were into jazz."

"I've been allowing it to work through me. It's soothing, and I can get a lot of reading done with it in the background. You've heard my music in the office." She returned with two glasses of soda. "I didn't know if you still drank soda, it's all I have."

"It's okay. So you've been doing a lot of reading?"

"Richard, I'm okay. I'm getting through some personal things, but I'm good." She flopped on the couch and invited her friend to join her.

"I've really got to get back. Elaine cooked and Janet..."

"Is probably waiting, listen, I'll call Elaine later. I'll contact the ministry and Walter as well. But I've got to do this my way. Thanks for stopping by."

The two walked to the door. Lashauna reached for his hand.

"You're a special man Richard. Janet is truly blessed to have you as a friend and so am I. I'm fine, but I'll be better. Don't worry about me. There are things I'll want to talk to you about after I come back so don't run off with Janet on me."

"Thank you."

"Thank you? Why are you thanking me?"

"I thought I was one of those relationships you were getting rid of."

"No, I'm just learning what kind of relationships are worth keeping."

78

The court clerk read the names of three cases on the court roster. She didn't pause for questions posed by people in the audience. After the roll call, she announced there would be a recess for lunch. Ms. Foxworthy asked Richard and Janet if they would mind if she handled some business during the break. It was twelve o'clock and for the hour and a half, she could get some problems out of the way. Janet wasn't sure if her case wasn't one of the problems but Katherine didn't seem disturbed about Marcus or the fact that Dr. Norris had not arrived.

Marcus nudged Joshua as the trio stood near the rear of the courtroom. Ms. Foxworthy put on her coat and collected her other items leaving Richard and Janet deciding on lunch. The men waited until she reached the elevator to approach her. Joshua handed her a copy of the papers that were filed for full custody of the children. Marcus shadowed his lawyer smiling as she gave the documents a quick glance. Her response surprised them.

"I was expecting these papers earlier this week. Have you given the clerk the court's copy?"

"I did. There should be no questions."

"Good well until this afternoon. Have a good lunch."

Joshua watched her get on the elevator. He wanted her to rant and rave about his late filing, and not giving her time to prepare Janet for this new request. Marcus waited for Joshua to say what was next.

"Well?"

"You tell me bro." Joshua wanted Marcus to drop the case.

"That lawyer is as smooth as your wife. Neither of them seems to be worried about this. Doesn't that say something to you?"

"Yeah, they want to fight until the end, you hungry or what?"

Joshua hung his head looking from the floor to the button for the elevator. The indicator lit up, and he chose to stand in silence waiting. The elevator doors opened, and the car began to fill with everyone heading for the first floor lobby. Richard and Janet were the last to get on before the doors closed.

Marcus watched Janet, who was glowing with confidence. Her transition over the past few months was amazing. She no longer looked like Mrs. Robinson the housewife. Her attire accentuated her shape. The view of her cleavage in her V-neck sweater added a touch of mystery to her sassy style. The camel colored wool skirt matched perfectly with her handbag and shoes. The outfit was simple, but it had a character of its own. She looked like she was ready for an executive meeting with the Board of Directors.

The elevator stopped, and Richard allowed Janet to step out before him. It wasn't until she turned to smile at him that her eyes met Marcus' stare. Richard followed her eyes and seeing her husband he gave him a respectful nod. Marcus nodded back reluctantly.

"Man, I can't believe she brought him here with her."

"Karyn was with you during the hearing. What's the difference?"

"You really don't understand do you?"

Joshua exited the elevator annoyed with his client's remarks. They walked out the front door of the court building realizing they didn't have any plans for lunch.

"No I don't, where to? It's a little brisk for walking. Where did you park?"

"In the lot." Marcus pulled out his keys.

"Nah, I'm right over there, come on we'll ride in my car. Explain this relationship you and Janet had again."

Richard drove through the downtown traffic to the diner. They beat the lunch hour rush getting a seat near a window. Janet let her thoughts drift catching herself when the waitress asked for her order for the second time.

"Why did you let me drift off like that?"

"I thought about your situation. You might need a moment to take it all in."

"Thanks, I just want this to be over. Katherine told me to prepare myself for the worse."

"What does she think would be the worse?"

"Marcus applying for full custody and the thought of me losing to him...."

Richard didn't let her finish her statement.

"Let it go, don't claim it. She's just telling you what he might do. The judge will see through his claims. You're a fine woman, and you're going far. Not to mention I love you."

Janet smiled, not wanting to get overwhelmed with emotions. They ate lunch talking about future plans and avoided making predictions about the divorce hearing. They returned to their seats in the court ten minutes before the court clerk called the roll.

Richard tapped her arm gently as Katherine walked in the court shortly after all the names were called. The smile on her face made it more than obvious that she had information that she wanted to share.

"What is it? Did Dr. Norris show up or send more papers?"

"No, her evaluation will stay as it is. The judge said she didn't need it. We'll be heard shortly."

Janet turned to see if Joshua and Marcus were talking. She read Marcus' face. There was something going on and not knowing, was eating at her nerves. Her soon to be ex was fiddling with his Blackberry, and Joshua seemed engrossed with the case before the judge.

"You spoke to the judge, why?" Janet whispered.

"She called me into her chambers. There were a few questions about Marcus's filing for full custody, nothing to worry about. We could postpone the hearing but there's no need to. Dr. Norris submitted a solid evaluation, if they want to dispute it, they can." She lowered her glasses and looked Janet in the face. "They won't though. They've played their trump card, but we have a full house."

Janet was confused. She knew the terms weren't legal, but she didn't play cards well and didn't have a clue about poker. She wanted to know exactly what card he played and what they had over him. She leaned to whisper in Richard's ear watching Marcus as she spoke.

"What's wrong?" Richard questioned her hesitation.

"Nothing I was going to tell you something, but I lost my train of thought."

Karyn Spalling took her seat next to Marcus. Janet didn't want to believe that Marcus would prove his stability using her.

"Janet Robinson versus Marcus Robinson; approach the bench please."

79

"You understand the reason for this hearing?" Judge Edith Evans looked over her black-framed Vintage glasses for a response from Janet and Marcus. The lawyers gave a nod agreeing with their clients as they answered, yes. The woman who looked as though she had served on the bench for more than thirty years read through the documents and closed both folders.

"Well, let's get started." The elder's face told a story that could be misinterpreted. Janet saw her sweetness through her stern grimace. There was softness in her demeanor. The black robe demanded respect, told who she was and her plight to her seat on the throne of justice. She was truly a matriarch in someone's family or any household that was connected to her. Janet was relieved knowing whatever her decision was, it would be fair.

"Mrs. Robinson we'll start with you." Judge Evans shot a glance to the table where Joshua and Marcus sat.

"Are there any objections with that Mr. Curry?" Joshua answered with his hands as if offering Ms. Foxworthy and Janet the floor.

"Mr. Curry, let me warn you. We can do without any of your courtroom antics today."

Marcus didn't want to seem nervous, but if she didn't care for Joshua, the playing field was uneven. He tried not to show he was unconcerned as she referred to the folder while Janet repeated her reason for wanting a divorce. The judge looked at him, as though she could see his thoughts. He pretended to write on the pad before him.

The judge raised her brow at his action and turned her attention to Janet.

"Mrs. Robinson, would you be looking to change your name."

"Changing my name?"

"Yes using your maiden name after the divorce. It's just a question that I must ask."

"No, I mean I didn't know I had a choice. But no, my children have that name. It would be better for their records and mine too. No, your honor, Robinson is fine."

"Now your children, you have three, right?" The judge continued not waiting for an answer. "Yes, have you secured their education near your new home?"

"Yes. They ride on the school bus and return on the bus."

"I see. When is it that your sister and brother-n-law care for them?"

"It's only during the summer your honor. School has started, and I live and work closer to the school."

"Hmm." The judge looked at the papers before her. "So they don't watch them daily?"

"No. They visit with them off and on and sometimes during the holidays. They helped me through a hard time. I was blessed to have their support."

Janet was becoming nervous. She didn't understand the questions about Faye and Sherod. The judge continued to look at the papers. Ms. Foxworthy tapped Janet on her hand and smiled. Her touch didn't calm her client's nerves.

"Your honor as you can see from all of my client's documents, she has secured a job, a new home, and a school for her children. She has paid the bills, both medical and personal, that were behind at the time of her depression and her husband's abandonment. She waited more than two years for her husband to come back home. Now that she has gotten over the hurt, pain and shame her husband is back to get more than he's ever given."

"Ms. Foxworthy I have every intention on finding out his reasons for returning home. I don't need your summation or speculation. I have all I need to make that determination before me. Now Ms. Robinson do you have any requests other than what I am reading?"

Janet looked at her lawyer not knowing what requests may have been made. She hadn't talked with her about anything other than visitations. She was still requesting Marcus to pick up the children at her sister's house.

"Your honor I think my client has the right to present his case before any consideration is given to Mrs. Robinson's request." Joshua stood hoping the judge would forgive his interruption.

"Yes just what I want to do. Ms. Foxworthy, for the record, will that be all. Mr. Curry is quite right. His client's disputes, requests and any other items on his behalf must be presented."

Joshua smiled and nudged Marcus as he sat down. He opened his folder pulling out papers to reference. Marcus leaned forward to see if Janet was paying attention to the commotion at their end of the table.

"There is a question about Mrs. Robinson's depression, her state of mind, and the capability of her providing a stable home for her children. Dr. Norris has been kind enough to send us her updated evaluation, and she's on standby if we need her. However, her entry will be done via video. Mr. Curry, Ms. Foxworthy will this be a problem for either of your clients?"

The lawyers whispered to their clients and responded "no" to the judge. Each team was anxious to get the hearing over. Joshua felt he had to give it his best effort. He hoped Marcus wouldn't ruin their chances. Judge Evans covered the microphone that was clipped to her robe and spoke to the court recorder. It was obvious that the woman, who was no more than twenty-five, knew what the judge wanted. She nodded her head and left the courtroom.

It took her no time to return. She loaded the computer with a disc, and everyone sat attentively waiting. Marcus wrote on the pad before him questioning his lawyer's actions. *"What's on the disc?"*

"We'll have to wait and see. The answer sparked another question. *"This is not your doing?"* The voice on the DVD began speaking. It was Dr. Norris, and she was introducing herself to the court. The clerk pushed the pause button.

"Mr. Robinson, your dispute or argument as written seems to be with Dr. Norris' final evaluation of your wife. She has been released in good health both mentally and physically. Mr. Curry, have you secured a psychologist to dispute the doctor's findings?"

"Your honor Dr. Norris has submitted two reports. At our request, she checked her notes and compared them to the hospital documentation. From this, she finalized her evaluation. I have not received the final report nor has Ms. Foxworthy indicated if she or her client received a copy."

"Mr. Curry the court has received the final report, and the copies provided by Dr. Norris for both parties. She did express concern that the court would not receive them as she submitted. It was given to the court this morning. After allowing your client the same opportunity as I have given Mrs. Robinson, I suggest both parties look at the video provided."

Marcus hung his head looking only at the table where he sat. Joshua couldn't imagine what the doctor turned in, but he knew from Marcus' reaction; it couldn't be in their favor.

Joshua asked the judge for a moment to speak with his client. Judge Evans smiled understanding the need for them to confer was in order. She nodded to Ms. Foxworthy, who didn't oppose a ten-minute break in the hearing. The court clerk called another name, and the persons stepped forward replacing the Robinsons at the table before the judge.

Janet returned to her seat next to Richard. They listened to Marcus quibbling with Joshua as they walked past them toward the back of the court. Ms. Foxworthy tapped Janet on her shoulder as she followed them.

"Mr. Curry, can I have a moment with you?"

Joshua was glad to escape Marcus' excuses for seeing the doctor prior to the hearing. He met Ms. Foxworthy in the lobby. His mind drifted as he noticed what drew him to his profession. The hall was lined with lawyers and their clients. The money that was made daily was well worth the clients like Mr. Robinson. Although he was a friend, Joshua decided he would be compensated for what was a waste of time.

Ms. Foxworthy found a seat on a bench near the window where no one was sitting. She smiled as Joshua made his way through the hall crowd.

"Crowded here today, Joshua this is ridiculous. I know you have a job to do for your client, but I don't think you want to go as far as viewing this DVD."

"So I take it that you know what this final evaluation entails."

"Yes, I was called into chambers this morning. It was requested by Dr. Norris that her final evaluation be released to the court and my client. Joshua if your client disputes her findings you do realize her final decision must be heard."

"I'm not understanding; other than saying your client is sane, and capable of keeping her children, what else would this DVD prove?

"Did you know your client went to see the doctor?"

"He told me he was invited there. There's no harm in that."

Katherine detected an attitude. "I'm looking at the interest of my client as you are yours. Joshua this is not a murder case. Your name won't go into the headlines. Marcus is selfish and your name as a lawyer need not be smeared trying to win this hearing. If he won, and that's unlikely, he wouldn't keep those children. They'd be with their aunt and uncle more than with their father. His life is unstable, and you know it. However, I won't get an opportunity to tell him or put it on record. If you dispute the doctors finding the DVD will tell it all, to him and my client. I don't think after all she's been through, she needs to see or hear what went on during his humble visit."

Ms. Foxworthy stood and putting her professional twist on her attitude she walked back into the court. Joshua was still sitting taking in what she said and imagining the worse. He looked at his watch he had three minutes to convince Marcus. It wasn't worth it.

80

Marcus listened as Joshua gave him bits and pieces of the conversation he had with Janet's lawyer. He added his own beliefs but was certain to explain there was no need for either of them to be embarrassed.

"If you know what's on that DVD you need to let me know now."

"What are you talking about? I went to her house. She offered me a drink, and after our conversation, she promised she would submit a change to the final evaluation. What is there for me to be embarrassed about?"

Joshua looked at the judge and the couple before her. It wouldn't be long before she submitted her summation of their case. He had to be blunt his suspicions needed to be answered.

"Did you and the doctor get busy?"

"What?"

"Did you fuck the doctor?" Joshua's whisper had an agitated tone.

"Hell no, I would have loved for that to be the case, but no. But I tell you what, if that damn report is in my favor, I'll reward her with a night of ecstasy."

"So, we won't see that on the DVD?"

"Man, you taking this too far. I told her how I felt about the situation, being a father and being concerned. It's not what you think, believe me."

"Alright, tell me something. We don't have anyone who will dispute her findings. I do have a doctor, who has given me a written document about depression and the effects. You want to go with that? It's all we've got."

"Janet and Marcus Robinson..." The clerk called their names bringing a silence to the muffled talk among the audience. The table was cleared for them to take their prospective seats once again. Joshua stood and looked at Marcus.

"Man, believe me. Go with whatever you have. The DVD can't show what I was really thinking."

The judge allowed Joshua to present the report from the disputing doctor. She glanced over the document and told him to proceed. After explaining that his client's concern was not only for the safety of his children but the welfare of his wife, the judge stopped him.

"Am I to believe that your client left his wife and three children with what he considered to be a stipend to live off, and now he has concerns?"

"Well your honor, yes. I agree with you. It looks entirely different, but he left in haste. They've argued over the years, but he's always kept his relationship with his children. He wants to right a wrong your honor by being a father to them because he believes it's hard for his wife, being unstable and a single parent. Your honor, it is documented, that Janet Robinson coped with those difficulties by attempting to kill herself."

"Not according to your doctor or Dr. Norris. They both agreed that the attempt was an accidental overdose. There are some points that you've brought up that I want you and your client to clarify for me. Mr. Robinson, you used a key to return to your home, correct?"

"Yes, ma'am." Marcus rose to his feet adjusting his suit jacket.

"Same key you had since you left your home?"

"Yes."

"So you've always had access to the home you left?"

"I guess you could say that."

"You waited close to a year after this, accident with your wife, to use that key. Why didn't you come home when she was sending your children to your sister-n- law's home? Why didn't you use that key when she didn't have a job, or upon her return from the hospital as she was going to therapy? Why wait until her life was in order to come back?"

"You honor; I realize I was wrong. I thought about it day after day, and the years passed. After she tried to kill herself, I figured the hospital would be putting her away, and the children wouldn't want to live where their mother almost died."

"I see." The judge's response caused the bailiff and the clerk to shake their heads slowly. Marcus took their non-verbal actions as a cue, he stepped the wrong way."

"Your honor here's the point I was trying to make. I know when Janet will accept what I say. Usually it's after she has no other choice or when someone else convinces her. She was looking for someone to rescue her. If she told me, she needed me to monitor her depressive state I would have been there. That's why I believe she got so close to her sister."

"My question was simple, if you knew she needed you, you knew the children needed you; why didn't you move back home sooner?"

Marcus didn't want to bring up Karyn or his desire to stay with her. He could feel his temperature changing. He wasn't winning the judge over. He took his seat. The judge knew there wasn't much more he could say. He had no plausible excuse. She gave the clerk to DVDs and gave the lawyers instructions.

"I'm not going to go over this entire DVD. Mr. Curry after viewing this, I will allow you to speak with your client, and then I will render my decision. Ms. Foxworthy you may not want your client to view this. If that is the case we can break ...you know what, why don't we do that?"

The lawyers and their clients watched as the judge gave her staff directions. They were sent to separate rooms similar to where they met for the mediation hearing. Each room was equipped with a DVD player, and each lawyer was given a DVD. Their instructions were simple; watch the final evaluation as presented by Dr. Norris, discuss it and wait.

Neither client wanted to view the entire DVD. It was purely coincidental that both views stopped at the same point.

After hearing, *"C'mon Doc, she's not that crazy. She knows my needs. If it wasn't for others like you butting in she would be home, or dead."* Both rooms went silent.

Janet wiped the tears from her eyes. Ms. Foxworthy closed her folder and waited for her client to speak.

"So now where do we stand?"

"Janet I would imagine Judge Evans is expecting Marcus to present his dispute. He has that right, although I doubt if she would care to hear what he has to say. I'm certain you've won the case, but we have to go through the motions. How about you? Are you okay? Dr. Norris was worried about you watching this video. She was determined to prove that he didn't love you so you could move on. Janet's thoughts froze; had she been the proof Lashauna needed to prove Richard didn't love her. The table had turned.

"Katherine did they say that the doctor brought this DVD to the judge purposely?"

"No, a courier did. I believe the doctor was on her way out of town."

81

*I*t had been three weeks since the hearing. Janet and Marcus were officially divorced. He had been granted visitations, and as she requested he would be picking the children up from her sister's home. Marcus didn't speak during the summation, and he left Joshua sitting at the table after the hearing was over. Janet thanked Ms. Foxworthy for all her efforts. Afterwards, she held a lengthy conversation with Joshua, who explained the position Marcus had put him in.

Lashauna hadn't returned any calls Janet made to her the week of the hearing. After calling the hospital and inquiring about her, Janet was informed she would return in two weeks. She wanted to thank her for being honest and not letting her emotions stop her from being a professional.

She arrived at the hospital around two and went to Lashauna's office where for months, she unleashed her fears. There was a note on the door for any visitors to see the receptionist who sat behind the door that read the Department of Psychology. Janet turned to exit disappointed that she wouldn't be able to reach the doctor again. The receptionist was smiling and talking on the phone. She placed the call on hold as Janet approached her workstation.

"Good afternoon, I'm looking for Dr. Norris. She left a note for visitors to see you."

"Yes, your name ma'am"

"Janet, Janet Robinson." Hearing her name sounded so different now that she wasn't attached to Marcus. A feeling she welcomed and wanted to share with the good doctor.

"Ms. Robinson, yes I was instructed to give you papers from Dr. Norris." She returned to her personal call, and said her goodbyes as she opened the file cabinet to retrieve a manila envelope. The receptionist handed Janet the envelope.

"Can you please sign this sheet? It's procedural; there are medical evaluations in there."

"Do you know when Dr. Norris will be back?" Janet posed the question as she looked in the folder. She couldn't tell without pulling the papers completely out whether they were the same documents she and Lashauna discussed during her last session. She hoped it held more information than the video. She wanted to know how and why Marcus went to her home. Janet held her questions and thoughts to herself for the past few weeks. She didn't feel the need to discuss what only Lashauna could answer.

"Dr. Norris is on a leave of absence. She left things here for..."

The receptionist paused catching herself before talking about the clients the doctor worked with. Janet raised her eyebrow. The woman understood all too well the expression on Janet's face.

"For? You've seemed to cut off your sentence. Did you mean people like me, her clients or crazy folks? I'm not the one. Do your job and remain professional before you lose your job."

Janet turned to leave, and the receptionist completed her sentence after the door closed.

"... her friends."

Janet headed for home where she could review the packet page by page. Richard was working, and the children were spending their day after school with her mother. She pushed the disc in and turned up the volume. She sang along with each Jill Scott tune hoping the music would relax her.

82

Marcus parked his car and walked slowly to his apartment with the letter marked confidential in his hand. He couldn't imagine why he received the call to meet Dr. Norris only to receive an envelope from a receptionist. She mentioned there were others who were there to pick up items left by the doctor, including Janet. He thought of calling Joshua, but he hadn't returned any of the lawyer's calls since the hearing. He wondered if he needed to call him now.

He tore open the envelope after throwing his keys on the kitchen counter. The house had begun to look bad. It had been three weeks since he lost it all. The visitations were the same but the family concept wasn't. The thought of bringing them to the apartment without Janet would kill him. Karyn didn't want the children there while she was visiting. After arguing with her over the matter, he made the choice, he couldn't stop seeing her. He called for dates, after work drinks, and her favorite, shopping. She finally gave in. He decided he wasn't losing her, and he would explain to his children as they got older.

Janet brought back the furniture she didn't need. It held his memories of the marriage. He asked for small items that had some sentimental value, and she assured him they had been discarded. Marcus was sure she was lying. He took his seat in the recliner that he lounged in with each of the children when they were younger. A remnant of the loving home they had.

The letter was printed on Dr. Lashauna Norris' letterhead. He sat back and smiled hoping he would have another face to face with the woman who caused him to lose it all. He read it methodically knowing she would never have sent a letter without a hidden message.

"Mr. Robinson, I'm sure by now the hearing is over, and you are back with your outside fling. I wrote this letter as exactly what I am, a psychologist, but don't forget I am a woman first. I would never deny that your wife had problems but that push over the edge was you; at least eighty percent of it was you. I'm not at liberty to discuss her case nor would I if I could discuss it. I wanted to let you know you, and your wife became a wake-up call for me. After learning my habits in love were quite similar to your wife's, I began tracking you, your habits and your pathetic lifestyle. There's a disorder that I have. You love having a woman who depends on your love to get them through each day.

You had that Marcus, and it went over the edge even though Janet caught herself. She recognized it before she almost took herself out. She, like many of my patients, was slipping. You had her believing you were the only man she could have possibly been with. Men like you seldom understand woman like Janet, nor do you care until it's too late. I guess what I'm saying is Janet is one of the fortunate ones. She actually got over you and moved on. Few women do and those that don't aren't the same.

My opinion, not that psychological bullshit, is that you all should rot in hell. Every last one of you, who string us on to the point of no return only to find you didn't give a shit from the start; you all should rot in hell. And you will Marcus believe me; you will."

There was no signature; no closing and the end of the letter left him puzzled. Was her last sentence a threat?

Janet reread the letter. She turned her music down wanting to hear her voice as she read the scribbled writing again. Lashauna wasn't herself. It showed in her writing. There was not signature and the last sentence could be taken many ways. She understood Lashauna's disappointment, but she sounded like she needed a good drink and a good friend who would allow her to talk things out.

Janet, I am so sorry I couldn't do this face to face. I know when my circuit is overloaded. Yes, I can admit it now. I loved and still love Richard. So for that reason alone my fuses are blowing. It's just something about those men who get you to love them and then move on.

So I guess it's only right that you were able to tell me what was wrong in my world. Me, the psychologist, didn't have it figured out. I'm taking a break from my job. If it's meant to be it will come back my way.

I know how you were able to evaluate me after meeting your arrogant ex-husband. You understood the type of men women don't long for but seem to always fall in love with. Richard, Walter, Marcus and so many others open their mouths, their wallets, their homes and the zipper but never their hearts. They all should rot in hell...believe me. They will.

As she peered out of the window, she looked along the branches of the large tree that held her new inspiration. She remembered when she felt the way Lashauna did. She was right. They all should rot in hell. But Richard wasn't that type of man. She thought about that morning it changed her life. She remembered her prayer that she recited each morning; praying for love to return, praying for a blessing. She understood the doctor's need to take a sabbatical.

Janet looked on the outer envelope again for a return address. The message was clear to Janet. She was covered, protected by a blanket of blessings, and she recognized it more and more each day. She smiled as a bird on the branch near the dining-room window turned its colorful crown as though it understood the days had passed when any man would test her faith. She whispered "amen" as the bird moved back and forth on the branch. It sang gaily, and the soft melodic tone eased her into an after work nod. She didn't fight it knowing she would be awake around dinner. Her children would be at the table talking about school and other activities. Tiff would keep them all laughing with her input and comments, and Richard would call to get a daily update. Janet felt surrounded by what she considered blessings. She was definitely in a different state of mind than she had been over a year ago.

Lashauna didn't understand her as a patient or a friend. A strange feeling came over her as she thought about leaving a letter for her at her job. There was no other way to contact her. Lashauna was hurt, scorned. Janet wanted to talk with her as they had done so many times before. She needed to hear the words she told Janet during many sessions. "Your belief and faith have to work together. You will recognize your blessings when you let go of your past ... you have to let go if you want to move on."

Other Novels by Nanette M. Buchanan

Family Secrets Lies and Alibi's

A Different Kind of Love

Bruised Love

Skeletons Beyond The Closed Door

Gossip Line

Bonded Betrayal

Stranger Within

The Perfect Side Piece

The Hustler's Touch

Duplicity

The Corner Pew

Purchase Your Copy Today

www.NanetteMBuchanan.com

Books are available in Kindle, Nook and other ebook formats